STEPHANIE
LAURENS
MARY
BALOGH

JACQUIE D'ALESSANDRO
CANDICE HERN

It Happened One Season

AVON
An Imprint of HarperCollinsPublishers

AVON BOOKS
An Imprint of HarperCollins*Publishers*
10 East 53rd Street
New York, New York 10022-5299

"The Seduction of Sebastian Trantor" copyright © 2011 by Savdek Management Proprietary Ltd.
"Only Love" copyright © 2011 by Mary Balogh
"Hope Springs Eternal" copyright © 2011 by Jacquie D'Alessandro
"Fate Strikes a Bargain" copyright © 2011 by Candice Hern
ISBN 978-0-06-199337-4
www.avonromance.com

First Avon Books mass market printing: April 2011

Avon Trademark Reg. U.S. Pat. Off. and in Other Countries, Marca Registrada, Hecho en U.S.A.
HarperCollins© is a registered trademark of HarperCollins Publishers.

Printed in the U.S.A.

10 9 8 7 6 5 4 3 2 1

Contents

The Seduction

of

Sebastian Trantor

STEPHANIE LAURENS

SEE

The Fall
of Rogue GERARD

"IT Happened one
Night"

Prologue

Sebastian Montgomery Trantor sank back in the wing chair angled before his library's hearth, and smiled rather smugly at the blaze roaring in the grate. There was something intensely satisfying in sitting snug in his own home while beyond his walls a tempest raged.

Outside, the wind moaned, rising to a bansheelike crescendo before dying away to a dismal drone. Rain swept in sheets across the lead-paned windows, punctuated by the staccato patter of hail. It was a very good night to be safe inside.

Brandy glinted in the cut-crystal tumbler on the table by his elbow. The weight of the leather-bound tome he was perusing felt comfortable where it rested across his thighs.

Gaze fixed on the leaping flames, he reached for the tumbler, sipped. Savored the complex flavors as the brandy slid down his throat, felt the warmth of the fire on his booted feet.

All were comforts he'd worked for, had envisaged, planned, and striven to achieve, and now he had them: the gothic monstrosity of Grimoldby Abbey that he'd purchased when it had been one step away from irredeemable ruin had been transformed into a modern home sporting every comfort. His investments had prospered further, enabling him to indulge his interest in ancient languages, scripts, and cryptography. His library would make any expert swoon.

He'd found and employed staff who, like him, appreciated a quiet, restful life, one undisturbed by unnecessary fuss.

These elements—a large, old, but comfortable home and the staff to go with it, money enough to do as he wished, an excellent library and the few other material comforts he enjoyed—had been the stuff of his dreams through the years of his army service. As a second son, he'd done his duty and, as was his nature, had enjoyed the endeavor while it lasted, especially as his knack for ciphers had ensured he was in frequent demand for special assignments, in turn ensuring he'd never been bored.

But the wars had been over for several years. On returning to England, he'd set about assembling his dreamed-of future life. And now it was his.

His to wallow in and enjoy.

Smiling again, he set down the tumbler, picked up his book, and focused on the page of Mesopotamian hieroglyphics he was slowly working his way through.

He'd barely completed a line when someone started hammering on the front door. Not just a knock, but a ceaseless battering.

He frowned, listened to his butler's footsteps as Finley crossed the tiles of the hall to the massive oak front doors. Faint sounds of an arrival reached him; the library door muffled the voices, yet apparently Finley had admitted whoever had sought aid. From the desperation of the hammering, aid had been the goal.

Imagining an overturned carriage or some similar mishap and having every confidence that Finley would deal with the matter quietly and expeditiously, Sebastian refocused on his page.

The library door flew open.

He raised his head but, recognizing the intruder's boot steps, didn't rise.

His brother Thomas strode directly to the fireplace, bringing a lingering scent of ozone and rain.

Without looking his way, Thomas bent and held his hands to the blaze.

Sebastian glanced back to see Finley standing in the open doorway, a question on his face. "Bring another glass." Sebastian looked at Thomas. "And prepare a room for his lordship."

Finley bowed and withdrew. Sebastian heard the door click shut.

Before he could ask what had brought his brother out on such a night, Thomas whirled.

Sebastian was shocked by the haggardness in his face. "What is it?"

Thomas stared at him, after a moment opened his mouth, then glanced at the door. "Wait. I don't want to be interrupted."

Sebastian obligingly possessed his soul in patience while Thomas fell to pacing agitatedly before the hearth.

Eventually Finley returned bearing a tray with another tumbler and the decanter of port Thomas favored.

Finley set down the tray, then glanced at Thomas. At his curt nod, Finley poured a generous dose of the port, restoppered the decanter, and handed the glass to Thomas.

"Thank you, Finley," Sebastian said. "That will be all."

Finley bowed and retreated.

Thomas swigged a sizeable gulp of the port.

Inwardly wincing—he'd rarely seen his brother so distraught—Sebastian murmured, "I'm surprised to see you. Isn't Estelle's time near?"

His sister-in-law was expecting her fifth child, one everyone held high expectations would be Thomas's long-hoped-for heir.

"The time is nigh—well, now." Thomas took another gulp, then lowered the glass. "She's had the baby."

Thomas's grim tone declared the news wasn't good, but he then fell into a brown study, staring at the half full glass in his hand.

"And?" Sebastian prompted.

"It's another girl!"

"Ah."

"Five girls! *Five!*" Thomas raised his head, set his jaw. "I've come to tell you—no more. Estelle says no more, and I agree with her. Aside from all else, having girl after girl does nothing to protect the estate—quite the opposite. Do you have any idea of the costs involved in dowering, then puffing off, five chits?"

Sebastian had no idea and didn't want to know, had lived in the fond hope that he would never have to know.

Thomas drained his glass, set it on the mantelpiece and fell to pacing again. "Estelle and I . . . the whole purpose was to have an heir to whom the estate can safely be passed, but after five daughters it's clear she and I are not going to bring about that so-desirable end."

"I . . . see." Sebastian had a dreadful premonition as to where this was leading.

"Precisely. And as it can't be me, it'll have to be you." Thomas halted and fixed his gaze on Sebastian. "For the sake of the estate and, heaven help us, the Trantor name, you'll have to bite the bullet, marry some chit, and get the family the heir it needs."

"Hmm." Sebastian flirted with the hope that he'd fallen asleep over his hieroglyphics and he'd wake up and discover this was all a nightmare. But no—Thomas kept talking, his gaze boring into him.

"You're the only one who can do it. You know what'll happen if you don't—after you, Mad Freddie will inherit the lot and promptly lose it at cards or on some flea-bitten nag. The notion doesn't bear thinking about. Even if you and I won't be around to see it, it still doesn't bear thinking about."

That was hard to argue. Mad Freddie was the family

nickname for their cousin Frederick, only offspring of their father's younger brother. Suffice it to say that not even his doting mother, Pamela, turned a hair at hearing her darling so described. There was no denying Freddie's propensity for foolish wagers and idiotic starts. Even his late father had recognized the problem and left his own estate in trust until Freddie reached the age of forty. However, as the primary estate of the Trantors was tied to the title of Viscount Coningsby that Thomas currently held, as matters stood, on Thomas's death the estate would pass first to Sebastian, nine years Thomas's junior. If Sebastian had no heirs—the point that had, with the birth of his latest niece, become critical—then on Sebastian's death the estate would pass to Freddie. As Freddie was a good thirteen years younger than Sebastian, there was an excellent chance that, barring Sebastian's marrying and begetting an heir, the estate would, in the fullness of time, fall into Freddie's hands.

Thomas raked a hand through his auburn hair. "Frankly, the family will be on your doorstep as soon as they hear, badgering you to marry without delay. Once they learn of our latest effort, they'll panic—at least all those who draw from the estate will, and with good reason."

Sebastian raised his brows. "Why? That's always puzzled me. It's not as if they stand to lose anything—the estate will continue to thrive in either your hands or mine, and they're all much older than us. Even your girls—all five of them—are likely to be married and safely supported by their husbands before you turn up your toes."

"True, but if you imagine that's going to keep our aunts and cousins from panicking at the prospect of Freddie ever inheriting, you'll need to think again." Thomas paused, then added, "I think it's the uncertainty—the prospect, however remote, that something unexpected could happen to both of us, and then they would indeed be faced with dealing with Freddie."

Sebastian grimaced. "They can't deal with Freddie—no one can."

"To be perfectly honest, I'm less concerned with our aunts and cousins than with all the others who, should the unexpected occur and both you and I die, will be left without a hope. Not just my girls, but all the people on the estate. Hell's bells, we—you and I—have known them all our lives. What odds that, should Freddie inherit, within a year the estate will be bankrupt and they'll be dismissed and turned out of their homes?"

Sebastian sighed. "I doubt you could find any bookmaker willing to take that bet."

"Exactly." Thomas dropped into the armchair on the opposite side of the hearth, his gaze on Sebastian's face. After a moment, he said, "I never thought I'd have to ask this of you—I know you've never seen yourself as the marrying kind—but for the sake of the family, the name, and the estate, can you see your way to taking a wife?"

Sebastian could almost hear the bugle, could feel the tug of loyalty, of familial devotion. He was accustomed to answering duty's call no matter how irksome . . . and really, how hard could it be? "Yes. All right. I will."

Thomas blinked. "You will? I mean, I hoped you would agree, but I wasn't sure . . ."

Sebastian picked up his glass, sipped, and started to plan. "It's February. The Season will start soon. I'll go up to London, look over the candidates and find one who'll suit." He glanced at the amber liquid in his glass. "And then I suppose I'll do what I can to get us our heir."

He glanced at Thomas, saw his brother sink back into the chair, saw some of the haggardness leave his features.

"Thank God." Thomas met his eyes, almost managed a smile. "There's hope for the Trantors yet."

Chapter One

$\mathcal{T}$hree months later, Sebastian sorely regretted his altruism. It wasn't the begetting of an heir that had him stumped, it was the detail that preceded that—the securing of a suitable wife. Although he'd scouted far and wide through the ballrooms, drawing rooms, and salons of the capital, thus far he'd found not a single likely candidate, not a single young lady whose company he could stomach for longer than five minutes.

For some, his tolerance could be measured in seconds.

Which was why, after taking one turn about Lady Rothbury's ballroom and confirming the absence of any chit he hadn't already struck off his list, he slipped away.

Walking quickly and silently down the corridors, he penetrated deeper into the unlit portion of the Rothbury mansion. He'd been there once before; if he recalled correctly, his lordship's library was at the opposite end of the house from the ballroom, which would make it the perfect bolt-hole. He would have left the house altogether, but his aunt, Lady Fothergill, had said she would attend; she'd expect to see him doing his familial duty and dancing with young ladies, but as she'd yet to arrive he saw no reason to prolong his exposure to the garrulous hordes.

Not only were most of the young ladies on the marriage mart certifiable twits—or if not that, then painfully shy—far too many of them giggled.

Some even simpered.

A sense of relief filled him—much as when he'd sighted English pickets after a quick trip behind enemy lines—when he reached the end of a dark corridor and the library door. Grasping the knob, he turned it, blessing Lord Rothbury when the door opened.

Not that a locked door would have kept him out.

There was no lamp left burning, but faint moonlight flooded through the uncurtained windows; a quick survey confirmed the room was empty. He stepped in, closed the door, then paused and looked at the lock. There was no key in it, but . . . it was the work of a minute to trip the lock with the small tool he still carried in his pocket. Old habits died hard.

Heaving a sigh of relief, feeling tension—and the sense of being constantly hunted—drain away, he glanced around the L-shaped room. A large mahogany desk stood facing the door, an admiral's chair behind it, with piles of correspondence neatly stacked on either side of a leather-framed blotter. A lamp stood on one corner of the desk, but lighting it would result in a weak glow showing beneath the library door. Turning to survey the shorter arm of the room, Sebastian saw a wing chair tucked in the corner, facing the distant window, yet remaining wreathed in shadow. A lamp stood on a small table alongside.

Crossing to the table, he lit the lamp. By its glow he scanned the nearby shelves. The last time he'd been there, he'd been searching for a particular volume of ancient texts; his lordship shared his interest in such things.

"Ah—this will do." Drawing out a hefty tome, he opened it, then sat in the armchair, settled comfortably, and gave himself over to Herodotus in the original Greek. Not Mesopotamian, but as a distraction, it would do.

Uncounted minutes later, the doorknob rattled, jerking him back from far away. Smugly smiling at his forethought in locking the door, he waited to hear footsteps retreat.

After a moment of silence, the sound of metal sliding and probing inside the lock reached his ears.

Inwardly swearing, he reached out and doused the lamp. Whoever was breaking into his lordship's library could pick locks, too.

It took them longer than it would have taken him, but eventually the bolt clicked back. A moment later, the knob turned and the door was cautiously opened.

His eyes were still adjusting to the moonlight. The large and heavy book held closed on his lap, he sank back in the armchair. Its wings would conceal him while he waited to see who entered the room. He couldn't see the door, but if they went to the desk, he'd be able to peer around the chair's side and see them. Unless the intruder looked specifically into the heavily shadowed corner, they were unlikely to notice him.

Tabitha Makepeace glanced quickly around the library, then whisked inside and shut the door. Pausing with her hand on the knob, she debated, but then reluctantly released it; locking the door would make her feel safer, but she might need to beat a hasty retreat.

Faint moonlight washed through the uncurtained windows, lighting her way as she crossed quickly to the desk. "With any luck, no one will come this way, but I'll need to return as soon as I can."

Muttering to herself was a bad habit, but as long as she was alone, why not? Especially when she had to focus on a task, the commentary was helpful.

She searched, found tinder, and lit the desk lamp. She adjusted the wick and shade so a pool of light fell on the desktop, then dumped her reticule on the desk's corner, drew up the admiral's chair, sat, and considered the front of Lord Rothbury's desk. "Where, exactly, would he keep such information? In a notebook kept specifically for the task would be my guess—my hope. A journal, perhaps, but as the intention would be to conceal the information forever, a notebook's more likely. So where? Here?" Eyes on the desk, she nodded. "Yes. I'm sure it would be here." She glanced at the door. "If he keeps the door locked, perhaps he might feel safe enough to just leave it in a drawer."

Leaning forward, she drew out the first drawer on the left.

Ten minutes later, after much muttering and rummaging, then putting everything back exactly as she'd found it, she sat back. Frowned. "I knew he was fastidious and pedantic—that's why he's certain to have written the information down and kept it all in one place, in one book. But who could have imagined he'd be so compulsively neat? There's not even one chewed pencil or half-used stub of sealing wax, let alone an errant piece of string." She gave a contemptuous snort. "So it'll be here, neat, safe and secure. Most likely in a hidden drawer or compartment."

She glanced around the library again; she'd been working in the light, so the shadows beyond the desk appeared denser. She returned her gaze to the desk. "I'd still wager it'll be somewhere in here rather than on the shelves."

Bending once more to her task—literally—she checked under the kneehole, then systematically checked each drawer for length, depth, and width. "There has to be some anomaly somewhere."

Five minutes later, with a huff of frustration, she sat back and regarded the disobliging piece of furniture. She narrowed her eyes. "I know you're hiding it, but where?"

Abruptly, she sat up. "Your desktop is remarkably thick—thick enough for a hidden compartment." She pulled out the top left drawer, put her hand in the gap and felt upward, but even reaching to the back of the space and feeling carefully with her fingertips, she detected no line or telltale gap. There was no give in the wood forming the upper surface of the space.

"All right. Not there." Replacing the drawer, she searched above the drawer to the right, with the same result. "The center drawer, then——" She broke off, sensing triumph. "Of course! That's it." Hurrying, she replaced the right upper drawer, drew out the center drawer and set it on the blotter. "Even though there's a lock on the center drawer, he doesn't lock it, but just keeps his pens, ink, pencils, and so on in there, so no one would suspect that that's where he hides his secret documents."

She felt around the upper surface of the space in which the center drawer fitted. "Yes! There it is. Now where's the catch? Perhaps if I push on the front center of the panel . . ."

A distinct click rewarded her. "Oh, yes—the panel hinges down, and yes, yes, yes! There's a notebook."

Triumphant, she grasped it, waved it as she straightened; pushing back the drawer, she set the notebook on the blotter. Pulling the chair closer, she sat straight, drew in a huge breath, then almost gingerly opened the front cover of the notebook.

It was a slim, black-cloth-covered volume, the sort many gentlemen used to keep appointments, addresses, or wagers. "Wagers of a different sort, this time," she murmured as, scanning the entry on the first page, she confirmed that she'd found what she'd come for.

"The payments are noted, obligingly neatly, and yes, they start just when Suzanne said the blackmailer first contacted them— in late March, just after her engagement was announced. And more payments followed." She flicked over a page, frowned. "But they get progressively further apart. Hmm . . ."

She flicked back and forth, page to page. "The time between the first payment and the second was a week, but then the period between became ten days, then sixteen. And— thank you, sir—Rothbury's noted the details for his next payment. Next week." She whistled. "Five ponies—that's five hundred pounds! To be paid . . ."

She stared at the words neatly inked on the page, then flicked back again, checked. "What are these words? Latin? I've heard them somewhere—lauds, terce, sext . . . aren't they the hours monks observe for their prayers? Something like that. Papa will know—I can inveigle it out of him."

Frowningly studying the notations, she mused, "So in all his entries Rothbury's noted the amount demanded and the date in plain English, then a time in Latin, and if that's the time he's to make the payment, then these words on the following lines must be the place . . ."

Frustration gripped her. She'd come so far; she wasn't in any mood to be denied. "There must be some trick to it." She tried to sound out the word she assumed was a location, but it was an impossible construction of consonants. "Certainly not phonetic." She looked back over the five previous payments noted. "Wherever there should be a place, there's a random collection of letters." She spelled another supposed place name aloud. "E. L. J. Z. E. L. D. M. U. F. T. P. C. L. T. R. F. What godforsaken language is that?"

"It's a code."

"*Wha*—*!*" She jerked upright and spun around so abruptly the chair nearly tipped over. She ended flung against the curved back, gripping the arms, staring at a man—a gentleman—as he unhurriedly rose from the depths of an armchair tucked in the shadows across the room.

The chair faced the windows; until he stood, she hadn't been able to see him.

He straightened to his full height and started toward the desk.

Her heart was thumping. He was still beyond the circle of light thrown by the desk lamp; she couldn't see him clearly—just his outline—yet she sensed masculine power, felt a titillating frisson of danger. His stride, long and languidly graceful, did nothing to dispel the effect. His body, long limbed, broad shouldered, solid yet lean, underscored it.

Ex-military, she guessed, and hoped that meant he'd be easily led.

Then the light found his face and she jettisoned the thought. Steel gray eyes locked on her face, his gaze level and far too acute. His lips were firm, his jaw squared, his cheeks long and hollowed beneath sharp cheekbones. Sable hair was fashionably yet conventionally cut; he was immaculately dressed, his style reserved and severe—Brummel would have approved.

Most striking of all was the aura of purpose that emanated from him.

As he neared she felt her heart speed up. Felt her lungs constrict.

Felt irrationally irritated that in order to hold his gaze she had to risk getting a crick in her neck.

"Who are you?" She assembled a frown and directed it upward. "And what the deuce are you doing here, skulking in the dark?"

Halting beside the desk, he considered her for a moment, then one dark brow arched. "Strange—I'd thought to ask you the same questions."

His voice was deep, resonant. Hypnotic.

She inwardly shook herself. She was hardly some impressionable miss to be beguiled by a handsome face, a melodic voice. She tipped her chin higher, endeavored to look superior. "I'm here on a mission. And you?" Attack would undoubtedly be her best defense.

He tugged one earlobe. His lips faintly curved. "I suppose you could say I came to the house on a mission, too, but I've decided to leave it in abeyance for the nonce." He glanced at the notebook she still held open in one hand. "But you were trying to decipher a code."

She frowned and looked down at the indecipherable writing. "How do you know it's a code?"

"Because I'm an expert in such things." Sebastian held out an imperious hand. "May I?"

The lady, not exactly young yet not that old either, hesitated, but then, albeit reluctantly, offered the book.

He took it, wondering why his instincts insisted he should

feel pleased she'd complied—that she'd trusted him that far. Why wouldn't she? Opening the notebook, he smoothed the page.

She watched him—he could feel her gaze on his face, beaming from bright, tawny-hazel eyes lushly fringed by red-brown lashes. She had the most amazing hair—a welter of tightly curling, flaming red locks. Even though someone had tried to restrain them in a conventional topknot, errant strands had escaped and wreathed about her forehead, cheeks, and nape.

Her skin was the rich creamy silk, not quite translucent, occasionally found in combination with such fiery hair. Now he was closer, he could detect a faint smattering of freckles across her nose.

She was fine boned, fine featured, yet the curves delectably encased by her tight bodice assured him his estimate of her age wasn't wrong. She was mature, heading toward ripe— which, he suddenly realized, was one of the things that had been wrong about all the candidates he'd thus far examined.

From the corner of his eye, he saw her eyes narrowing. Her face was heart-shaped, her chin decidedly pointy, but her lips were luscious and wide. Ruby red and tempting.

He flipped over the notebook's pages, noting that Rothbury had made one entry per page, on six pages.

She shifted, stretching up to look, then point. One delicate fingertip indicated the line of apparently random letters. "This is the part I can't make out."

"Indeed. The part in code." He glanced at her, caught her eyes. "But what's the rest?"

She sat back, frowned up at him. "Never mind about that—can you make out what the coded bits say?"

He considered the coded line again, then flipped back to the earlier entires. "Yes—certainly. In time."

She sat forward. "How much time?"

It wouldn't take long, but he wasn't going to lose his only connection to—only hold over—this strange and distracting lady, not until she'd satisfied his curiosity.

It had been a long time since he'd felt curious about anything involving a woman.

"In order to interpret code accurately, it's usually necessary to have the context."

Her eyes narrowed even more. She frowned. Direfully.

Entertained—she really did have a black frown and he couldn't recall the last time anyone had tried to frown him down—he was about to explain the meaning of "context" when her gaze left his face.

To boldly assess him. To measure him up, then down. Then she considered.

At last, lips tight, she looked up at him. "I assume the coded part is a place name, or directions to some place or spot. Some location."

He held her gaze. "The location the blackmailer stipulated for his payments."

Her expression momentarily blanked, then she scowled. Ferociously. At herself. "Damn it—I said all that out aloud, didn't I?"

When she glanced up at him, he nodded.

She huffed and glared at the desk. "It's a bad habit—don't ever get into it."

After a moment, he shut the notebook. Waved it. "Are you going to tell me what this is all about?"

She studied her hands, lightly gripping the desk's edge, then glanced up and met his gaze. "Can you really read codes?"

"I said I could, didn't I?"

"In my experience, gentlemen are rarely truthful."

Forthright. He raised his brows. "I am."

She didn't back down, just considered him some more, then asked, "How did you learn to read codes?"

"I've a natural talent and I was in the army. The commanders learned about my knack, and so I was forever being called in to decipher and decrypt enemy orders." And to intercept them. "I became, and still am, something of an expert."

"Hmm."

She fell silent. He gave her a moment, then tried another tack. "You haven't yet told me your name."

Coolly she replied, "You haven't volunteered yours, either."

"Trantor. Sebastian Trantor." He sketched a bow. "At your service, Miss . . . ?"

She seemed to come to some decision. "Makepeace." She shifted to face him and extended her hand. "Tabitha Makepeace."

He closed his hand about her delicate fingers, briefly shook them. Reluctantly releasing her, he held up the notebook. "And this?"

Tabitha didn't want to trust him, but she needed the information in that little black book and he seemed to be the key. Very possibly her only key. And he had fallen into her lap; looking a gift horse in the mouth was usually unwise. "I'll tell you, but you have to promise to hold what I reveal in the strictest confidence. It was revealed to me in confidence by others, and concerns them, not me, so I couldn't reveal their secrets if you don't promise—if you won't sincerely swear never to repeat what I tell you."

Without hesitation he held up one hand at shoulder height, his large square palm toward her. "I, Sebastian Trantor, solemnly swear never to reveal a single word of what you tell me—on pain of death."

He sounded like he meant it, even the last part. Impressed—by his impulsiveness if nothing else—but loath to show it, she nodded curtly. "That will do. Very well . . ." Where to start?

She drew breath and plunged in. "Since the beginning of the Season, several young ladies of my acquaintance have become engaged to be married. That in itself is nothing unusual. However, in four instances I noted that soon after the announcement appeared in the *Gazette*, the young ladies and their families retired to the country. That was . . . odd. Indeed, knowing the young ladies involved, it was distinctly strange. I suspected something was wrong." She'd suspected something else, but . . . "I visited one of the young ladies in the country and she told me the truth behind her retreat from town—she and her family were being blackmailed."

"Let me guess." The words held a certain menace. "There's something in the young lady's past that, should it become public knowledge, would scupper the match?"

"Exactly. I checked with the other three, and found the same tale. And while the . . . for want of a better word, transgressions involved are all different, and all ridiculously minor in the wider scheme of life, if those transgressions were broadcast throughout the *ton*, all four matches would be in jeopardy."

She drew breath and went on, "I spoke to two of the fathers involved—asking about the blackmailer and what was being done to bring him to justice."

"And were promptly told to mind your own business."

She looked up, met his eyes, saw understanding rather than condemnation in his gaze. She inclined her head. "Indeed. They were full of fear that any investigation of any sort would upset the apple cart and destroy the alliances they were otherwise so happy to have made. They—the two with whom I spoke—were convinced that the blackmailer's demands would cease once the weddings took place." She held his gaze. "But I can't see that happening. What I believe will happen is that the fathers involved will cease to receive demands. I think the demands will go to their then-married daughters."

He nodded. "Of course. If the secrets, whatever they are, are enough to endanger the wedding, then clearly they can later be used to threaten the marriage."

"Which brings me here." With one hand, she gestured at the room. "Lord Rothbury is one of the fathers involved. I haven't spoken directly to him, but his daughter, Suzanne, is one of the blackmailer's targets. That's why she's not here tonight, but in the country. Tonight's ball was already arranged, so the Rothburys couldn't cancel without raising questions, so they've put it about that Suzanne's recovering from overexcitement at the prospect of her wedding." Her disgust at such a slur being cast on her friend—by her own parents—rang in her tone.

Leaning against the desk, Sebastian considered the intriguing Miss Makepeace. "How is it that you know these four young ladies, all of whom are targets of a blackmailer?"

She tipped up her pointy chin. "We belong to the same association—a club of sorts."

"A ladies' club?" He raised his brows. "I didn't know there were such things."

He'd deliberately made his tone dismissive; as he'd hoped, she bristled.

"The Sisterhood was established six years ago. We have a very active membership."

"Indeed? And what does the Sisterhood do?"

She narrowed her eyes at him. "We discuss things."

"Such as?"

"Men."

"Ah." His eyes locked on hers, he managed not to grin. "Does that take much time?"

Her gaze grew flinty. "If you must know, understanding the ways of gentlemen is essential to the well-being and future happiness of young ladies expected by their families to wed. As they cannot easily avoid the altar, then best they front it with a sound understanding of how to interact with their husbands-to-be."

"A novel notion." One many of the young misses in Lady Rothbury's ballroom could greatly benefit from. "So all four ladies you've identified as targets are members of the Sisterhood. Is there any chance that the blackmailer learned of their secrets through the club?"

He was impressed that she didn't immediately discount the idea, but after frowning consideringly for several moments, she shook her head. "I doubt that could be—I didn't even know they had secrets of such a nature, so I can't see how anyone else might have learned of them." She met his gaze. "I'm the club's president, and besides, these secrets are not the sort of thing young ladies chatter about, not even with their closest friends. And"—she slumped back in the chair—"I asked, and they all swore they hadn't breathed a word to any acquaintance."

"Well, they've clearly told someone at some point, but as neither you nor they have any idea whom, let's leave that angle for the moment. Tell me—why is it that you, specifically, have taken on this mission? I gather exposing the blackmailer is the mission to which you earlier referred?"

She nodded. Again she considered him, then her lush lips twisted wryly. Her gaze remained steady on his. "Let's just say that I have a great deal of empathy for their predicament, and feel that it's incumbent on me—almost by way of paying a debt—to assist them and free them from the blackmailer's coils."

Looking into her hazel eyes, he was tempted to ask who had blackmailed her, and when, and what had happened to them . . . and who had saved her. But he sensed any further probing would be one push too many. At least, at that moment. Later. . .

She was intriguing, a puzzle in many ways, multifaceted and fascinating. She was rather like a piece of code herself; he was looking forward to discovering her key—the single fact that, once known, made the rest of her make sense. He hadn't felt so enthused about learning a lady's secrets for a very long time.

The consideration behind the steel-gray gaze trained on her face made Tabitha feel . . . odd. She couldn't place the strange sensation—a trepidatious thrill? He seemed an unusually observant man; being the concerted focus of an inquiring and intelligent mind . . . perhaps it was understandable she felt both wary and excited. She cleared her throat, focused her own gaze on the matter at hand. She nodded at the notebook he still held. "So can you decipher the locations stipulated for the payments?"

He looked at the notebook entries again, flipped back

through the pages. "Yes. It's a straightforward substitution code. See." He shifted to show her one entry, with a blunt fingertip underlined a section of the coded location. "The letters E L J Z E L—six letters, with the first two letters being repeated for the fifth and sixth. That six-letter string occurs either at the beginning of a putative location, or at the end."

Shifting closer, she looked as he flicked pages and showed her. "It's in every entry." She glanced up at him. "So what does it mean?"

"Church. I'm almost certain it means that—not many other words have that geometry. First two letters as last two letters with only two in between."

She felt her heart sink. "Do you have any idea how many churches there are in London?"

"Hundreds, I imagine, which is why we need the rest of the code. Sadly, I can tell from that one word that the substitution isn't just a matter of replacing one letter with the next in the alphabet, or anything like that. Rothbury knows something about codes—he's used a key."

"What sort of key?" She swung to glance at the desk. "He would have written it down—he writes everything down."

"I don't think so." Trantor stood, his gaze tracking the volumes in the shelves behind the desk. "I think he'll have used a page in a book."

"A book?" She swung to face the shelves, then scanned the library walls. "There are hundreds of books in here."

"Yes, but we only need one." Trantor's deep voice was calming. "And I've a feeling I know just which one." Stepping away from the desk, he glanced back at her. "We can't take the notebook—Rothbury'll panic, and I take it we want him to go to the next rendezvous and make the payment so we can keep watch and catch the blackmailer when they come to collect."

How had it turned into *we*? She decided to fight that battle later—after he'd supplied the location she needed. "I'll make a copy."

"Make sure you don't miss any letters—and I'll need all

the entries. I'll need the earlier ones to check the validity of any deciphering I do. While you copy, I'll follow my hunch and see if I can find the key."

"What if you can't?" She was already smoothing a fresh sheet of paper on the blotter.

"Don't fret—I'll still be able to decode the locations. It'll just take a great deal longer."

His tone suggested he was already absorbed; a glance over her shoulder revealed that he'd pulled one particular tome from the shelf and was swiftly scanning page after page.

She bit her tongue against the impulse to ask what he was doing, exactly what he was looking for, and why in that particular book. She could ask later. They needed to get whatever they had to do done and leave the library—or at least she had to, in order to return to the ballroom before too many of her connections realized she'd disappeared.

Selecting a pencil—perfectly sharpened, of course—from his lordship's neat stack, she opened the notebook to the last entry, and started transcribing the entries in reverse order.

She'd just finished a last check of all six entries to make sure she hadn't missed or jumbled any letters when her unexpected coconspirator gave a satisfied humph.

"Got it." He glanced up from the book in his hands. "Page one hundred and ninety-seven. Write that on your copy."

He shut the book as she turned to do so. "What title should I write?' She spun back around, pencil in hand. Met his gray eyes. "And shouldn't we, well, take it?"

"No need. I have a copy in my library. I'll just need the page number and I can work from there."

"Excellent." She spun back, set the pencil back in its assigned place, then folded the sheet of paper and reached for her reticule.

Trantor plucked the sheet from her fingers. "I'll take that."

Before she could protest, he'd tucked it into his inside coat pocket.

His gaze roved the desk. "We need to get everything back exactly the way it was."

"Precisely what I intended to do." She closed the notebook, and returned it to the hidden compartment, closed the hinged panel, then stood as Trantor obligingly lifted the center drawer and eased it back into place.

She surveyed the desk, found nothing amiss. "Good. Now—" She broke off.

They both looked at the door. Heard the footsteps approaching.

She swiped up her reticule, slid the cord over her wrist as she swung to face Trantor. "Where can we hide?"

She looked into his steel gray eyes—and realized she expected him to answer. Expected him to save them.

He didn't let her down.

She had a second's warning—a subtle shift in the clear gray—then he seized her arms and hauled her to him.

He bent his head, in a whisper repeated, "Where do we hide?" Answered as his lips lowered to hers. "In plain sight."

Then he kissed her.

Like a lover.

Like a man who had every right in the world to part her lips and drink her in. To claim her mouth, to slide his arms about her and lock her to him.

As the latch clicked and the door opened . . . as her senses spun . . .

"Oh! I say!"

Through the haze of sensations fogging her brain Tabitha recognized Lord Rothbury's stentorian tones.

Then came a titter.

She didn't care. She just wanted more of the firm lips moving so confidently over hers, more of the tantalizing taste of him, more of the wicked caress of his tongue. . . .

Trantor broke the kiss. His lips, hovering over hers, murmured, "Play along."

Slowly, giving every appearance of languid reluctance, Sebastian lifted his head and turned to survey their audience.

Inwardly swore as he recognized the ladies lurking behind Rothbury. His lordship he might have been able to inveigle with some slick tale, but Lady Castor and her sister, Mrs. Atkinson, had had him in their sights, hoping to snare him for one of their daughters. No mystery why Rothbury had chosen to visit his library in the middle of a ball. By the same token, the pair of gossiping harpies wouldn't be satisfied with any glib excuse.

His lordship was still in shock, his mouth opening and closing to no effect. Finally, he found his tongue. "Trantor? And . . . is that Miss Makepeace?" His tone suggested utter incredulity.

There really was no help for it, and if some part of him cynically noted that he felt no real qualm in taking the only solution that presented itself, he ignored it.

"Indeed, sir." Summoning what he hoped was a besotted smile, he looked down at Tabitha Makepeace, still securely held in his arms. She'd been trying to turn and face the threat, but he'd prevented it.

Not having to let her go seemed an excellent idea.

But for the moment . . . still smiling fondly, he released her, but caught her hand, raised it to his lips, and pressed a lingering kiss to her knuckles.

The horrified widening of her bright eyes suggested she guessed something of his intent.

Before she could say or do anything to endanger the smooth execution of his plan—one which, with any luck, would save them both—he glanced at Lord Rothbury, smiled at Lady Castor and Mrs. Atkinson. "You're the first to learn our news. Miss Makepeace has just done me the honor of agreeing to be my wife."

The shock on Tabitha Makepeace's face would have instantly given them away. Luckily, she was still facing him, and not their equally stunned audience.

"Have you lost your *mind*?"

They'd just parted from their host, Lady Castor, and Mrs. Atkinson in the ballroom's foyer. Sebastian had glibly excused them on the grounds of having much to discuss, then with Tabitha on his arm had turned determinedly toward the stairs.

Somewhat to his surprise he was feeling distinctly self-congratulatory as he escorted his recently acquired fiancée down the main stairs to the Rothbury's front hall.

Outwardly fetchingly distracted, but apparently inwardly aghast, at least she'd waited until they were out of sight of all others before protesting.

"No. That was the only way to get us both out of there without having to explain ourselves. If you think for a minute, you'll realize it was the only possible way forward. We need Rothbury to go ahead with his upcoming meeting, remember? We could hardly tell him what we'd really been doing in his library."

"Yes, *but* . . . you have no comprehension of what will come of this. What repercussions will ensue! I'm not sure most people will even believe it."

"Why?" He glanced at her. "Are you so unmarriageable?"

She looked ahead. Under her breath returned, "You could say that."

He was intrigued, but before he could decide how to further probe, she frowned.

After a moment, eyes narrowed, she turned her head and caught his gaze. "I just realized . . . I know why I was in the library, but why were you there?"

"It doesn't matter." And it truly didn't. He smiled pointedly, patted her hand where it lay on his sleeve. "Now buck up and smile for the nice butler."

Her lips curved in an expression of sweet docility that was patently false.

He didn't need to hide his appreciative grin. "Who did you arrive with?"

Her lips thinned and she looked ahead. "No one."

He blinked. As they continued steadily down the long staircase, he murmured, "Even I know that's not acceptable."

"Well, it is. When you're over twenty-five, people stop worrying."

He bit his tongue. *How could anyone stop worrying about you?* probably wasn't a wise thing to say. "How did you get here?"

"My father's carriage. And before you turn into a bore and start lecturing me about driving through London's streets alone at night, my coachman and groom have been with our family for years."

And doubtless would obey any instructions she gave, no matter how outrageous. Or potentially dangerous.

Clearly Miss Tabitha Makepeace needed taking in hand.

The notion sat remarkably well with him.

That kiss had mellowed him to an amazing degree.

Who would have thought he'd meet such a firebrand—a lady of such promising, alluring, and enticing passion—in Lord Rothbury's library? She even had a mission—a real mission, a dragon for him to slay. He'd missed that, the action, the excitement of pitting his wits and will against a foe.

"In that case," he said, as they neared the foot of the stairs and Lord Rothbury's butler came hurrying from an anteroom, "I suggest we depart forthwith." Stepping down to the tiles, he halted and glanced at her as she paused beside him. He arched a brow. "Unless you'd prefer to go back to the ballroom and face the music?"

She met his gaze, then shuddered. Eloquently. Turning to the butler, she said, "My carriage, please, Baxter."

Baxter shot him a suspicious glance, but bowed and replied, "At once, miss."

As Baxter retreated, Sebastian lowered his voice and asked, "Where do you live? I suspect, being your fiancé, I should know."

"Bloomsbury. My parents rent a house on Bedford Square."

"Excellent. I'm staying at my brother's house in Cavendish Square—I'll see you to your home, then walk from there."

"I could drop you off on the way to Bloomsbury."

"No, no." He needed to know which house to call at tomorrow morning. "I'll use the walk to think through the code."

Baxter returned with her cloak—a deep russet velvet a shade darker than the russet of her silk gown. Both shades complemented her complexion and her wonderful flaming hair. Sebastian took the cloak and draped the soft folds over her delicate shoulders, then escorted her onto the front steps. A black town carriage had just drawn up. A groom leapt down and opened the door.

He tightened his fingers about her elbow in warning, and heard her sigh.

She waved a hand his way. "This is Mr. Trantor, Trevor. He's insisting on seeing me home, so will be traveling with us to Bedford Square." She looked up at the ancient coachman peering over the side of the carriage. "So it's just home, Gifford."

Gifford cast Sebastian a measuring glance, but, if anything, viewed him with approval. "Aye, miss."

Feeling he'd managed the situation thus far reasonably well, Sebastian handed Tabitha up into the carriage, followed her in and sat beside her. Trevor shut the door; an instant later, the carriage rocked, then rattled off.

An instant after that, Tabitha swiveled to face him. "I can't believe you think this is a good idea. If any of the Rothburys' guests haven't yet heard the news, they will before they leave. Lady Castor and Mrs. Atkinson are two of the biggest gossipmongers in the *ton*—they'll make sure absolutely everyone hears the stunning news. So we've just left a ballroom-full of people believing that we're engaged. It'll be all over town come morning!"

He settled against the squabs. "So?" The carriage was comfortable, not spanking new but in excellent condition. He knew nothing about the Makepeaces' circumstances; he supposed he'd have to bestir himself and look into such matters.

Tabitha stared at him, unable to accept his utter imperviousness to the calamity that, courtesy of his ridiculous assertion—his wonderful plan to save them—was now hanging over their heads. "Engaged," she repeated, with greater emphasis. "*To be married.*"

"That is the general interpretation."

"But we're *not*!" She felt as if steam were issuing from her ears. "You can't just tell people we are, then walk away." Bad enough that they were lying to the entire *ton*, but for her—specifically her—to be the perpetrator of such a fraud was . . . "Aside from being all-but-unbelievable, and therefore certain to be talked of, me misleading the *ton* on such an issue, only to later deny it, is the sort of behavior for which people are socially exiled for life!"

He regarded her with calm curiosity. "Are you so enamored of the *ton*, then?"

"That's not the point! The point is I live with these people, go about among them, consort with them constantly—"

"Do you want to expose this blackmailer and rescue your friends from durance vile?"

His calm, but uncompromising tone pulled her up short. She drew breath. "Yes, b—"

"Then I suggest you play along for the nonce. Once we've solved the riddle and exposed the villain, then we can decide we won't suit after all." His lips curved. "I hereby give you permission to jilt me once my usefulness in your mission ends." He held her gaze. "What could be fairer—or more sensible—than that?"

Sebastian watched her chew on the question. Waited patiently until she'd reluctantly realized that there was no good answer, then he asked, "So, are we in agreement?"

The black look she cast him would have made the devil quail. "Oh, all right."

Chapter Two

I realize this is highly irregular but—sir, ma'am"—Sebastian embellished his plea with a courteous inclination of his head—"if you will indulge me, I'll endeavor to explain."

It was nine o'clock the next morning. He stood in the Makepeaces' townhouse in Bedford Square, on the carpet in the center of their drawing room, and, gaze fixed on the older couple seated on the sofa, waited for permission to proceed.

Over breakfast, he'd thought to ask his brother's butler, Wright, if he knew anything of the Makepeaces who resided in Bedford Square. After consideration, Wright had informed him that he believed the family were known as the eccentric branch of the Wiltshire Makepeaces, the gentleman being said to pay far more attention to books than to the world around him.

Sebastian could empathize; during his brisk walk to Bedford Square, he'd considered how to use the fact to his best advantage.

Mr. Makepeace, whose attire alone would have declared him a scholar quite aside from his tufted white hair and the heavy-lensed spectacles perched on his nose, blinked owlishly.

In contrast, Mrs. Makepeace, a comfortable-looking matron with what Sebastian hoped he was correctly reading as an unruffleable composure, looked decidedly intrigued. It was she who declared, "By all means, Mr. Trantor, do proceed. You perceive us agog."

A swift glance at Mr. Makepeace suggested that might well be true; behind the thick lenses, his blue eyes gleamed shrewdly.

Sebastian proceeded with all due caution. "I should preface my explanation by informing you of my situation. My brother, Viscount Coningsby, has been unable to provide the family with the heir needed to ensure the title and entailed estates remain in safe hands. Consequently, I've agreed to step forward and do my duty by the family by marrying and begetting the required heir. Prior to this year, I had not planned to wed. Since returning from the wars, I've been pursuing my long-held interest in ciphers, codes, and ancient texts, and have been restoring Grimoldby Abbey, in Lincolnshire, into a suitable house for myself and my library."

As he'd hoped, Mr. Makepeace now looked as intrigued as his wife. He went on, "As anyone in the *ton* will tell you, since the beginning of the Season I've been attending the usual balls and parties, attempting to identify a young lady suitable to take as a wife. All to no avail. Last night, I attended Lady Rothbury's ball. Despairing of finding any suitable parti there, but expecting to meet my aunt, Lady Fothergill, once she arrived, for the interim I took refuge in his lordship's library. I was reading when your daughter, Miss Tabitha Makepeace, entered the room."

"She was attending a ball?" Mrs. Makepeace cast a puzzled glance at her spouse.

Mr. Makepeace observed, "Trantor here saw her in the library, not the ballroom." He waved at Sebastian to continue.

"I daresay that was her goal—I can't imagine her willingly whirling down any floor."

Sebastian kept his lips straight, inclined his head. "Indeed. She was dressed for the event, but dancing wasn't her purpose. It transpired she was on a mission of sorts—one that, after I surprised her in the act of execution, so to speak, she consented to explain to me. In confidence, a confidence I am honor-bound to preserve. However, I believe I can say that I consider her mission and her motives both laudable and honorable, and I subsequently volunteered to assist her in achieving her goal."

Mrs. Makepeace's puzzlement was now colored by curiosity. "You surprised her in the library—and thereafter she told you what she was about?"

He felt compelled to admit, "I have a talent that she lacks yet requires in order to proceed with her mission. Regardless, I am not insensible of her trust." He drew breath, went on, "Indeed, my appreciation of her trust played a definite part in what happened next. In short, we were engaged in pursuing her goal when we were discovered in the library by Lord Rothbury, Lady Castor, and Mrs. Atkinson."

Mrs. Makepeace pulled a face. "Rothbury you might have talked your way past, but the other two are inveterate gossips." Her eyes lit. "So you were engaged on a secret mission with Tabitha that resulted in you and she being caught in a potentially compromising situation. What did you do?"

"In order to explain our presence there, alone in private, I declared that Miss Makepeace and I had repaired there to plight our troth—that she had just done me the honor of agreeing to be my wife."

Both Makepeaces' eyes flew wide.

Sebastian hurried on, "As I have assured Miss Makepeace, if, once her mission is complete, she wishes to dissolve our engagement, she may do so in whatever way she chooses. I will abide by her decision, whatever it may be." Searching the elder Makepeaces' faces, he chose his words with care. "However, I will confess that, despite the brevity of our acquaintance, I find Tabitha much more to my taste as a wife than any of the flibbertigibbets inhabiting the *ton*'s ballrooms. I therefore find myself in an unusual situation."

Neither of his listeners made any comment; their attentive expressions encouraged him to continue. "In pursuing her goal, Miss Makepeace will court a certain danger, and while I respect and support her objectives, I cannot in all conscience allow her to be exposed to that danger—not when I can shield her from it. Consequently, regardless of all other circumstances and considerations, I will not step back from aiding and protecting her. I will continue to assist her with her mission until it is concluded and all danger is at an end. For that reason alone, I would ask for your indulgence in allowing our unexpected betrothal to stand, and for your assistance in supporting the protective facade for however long it is required."

Pausing, he met both Makepeaces' eyes. "However, I also wish to declare my interest in preserving the fiction of our engagement—specifically my intention to pursue Miss Makepeace's consent to making what has commenced as a mere facade into a reality. I'm therefore requesting your permission to pay my addresses to her, albeit in an unconventional way. In order to progress with her mission, it will be necessary for me to spend considerable time in her company, and I intend to use that time . . . I suspect the correct phrase is, to woo her."

Both Makepeaces blinked. Before either could speak, he went on, "From comments she let fall, I understand that she views herself as unmarriageable, certainly incontrovertibly on the shelf. I don't agree with that assessment, but I foresee that it might require a certain degree of persuasion to convert her to my view—to convince her that, while she may not be the conventional, perfect wife, she may yet be the perfect wife for me."

He fell silent and, clasping his hands behind his back, waited.

Mrs. Makepeace looked even more fascinated. "You

intend to use the opportunity presented by the situation to woo Tabitha?"

"In a nutshell, yes."

"And," Mr. Makepeace said, "in order to proceed with both courtship and mission unhindered, you're asking us to support and lend credence to the charade of your betrothal."

Sebastian nodded. "With a view to transforming the charade into reality—to convincing Tabitha that we should."

"Excellent!" Mr. Makepeace beamed, then turned to his spouse. "I rather think we ought, don't you, my dear? This scheme sounds like the sort of odd approach that might work." He glanced smilingly up at Sebastian. "And clearly Trantor here will fit into the family."

To Sebastian's relief, after regarding him intently for several moments, Mrs. Makepeace nodded decisively. "Quite." She smiled, looking remarkably content. "I commend you, sir—your approach would do even my husband proud."

Husband and wife exchanged an affectionate glance.

Sebastian didn't make the mistake of thinking either elder Makepeace anything other than exceptionally shrewd. He bowed with real gratitude. "Thank you, ma'am. Sir. I will strive to live up to your expectations."

Mrs. Makepeace's smile was unnervingly understanding. "I believe you will, sir, but that's Tabitha's footsteps hurrying this way, so let us end by wishing you the best of luck."

Mr. Makepeace murmured, "Hear, hear."

Sebastian had presented himself at the front door at precisely nine o'clock—the earliest minute any polite caller could seek entrance to a gentleman's residence. He'd reasoned that the elder Makepeaces would be available, most likely having just finished breakfast, but that Tabitha, having been out until late, would probably still be abed.

His strategy had proved sound. He could only give thanks that his timing had allowed him and the elder Makepeaces to reach an understanding before the advent of his betrothed. His unconventional intended.

He braced himself to meet her again.

The door burst open. Tabitha entered in a rush of air and energy. Her hair a semi-tamed mass of burning curls framing her heart-shaped face, she stared at him, then at her parents, her expression one of outright shock. "Ah . . ." She brought her gaze back to him. "What are you doing here?"

Sebastian arched his brows. "Naturally, I came to discuss our situation with your parents." She was wearing a plain, light green morning gown and looked as delectable as a fresh apple—crisp and tart with an underlying sweetness.

Stunned anew, Tabitha swallowed, then looked at her parents. "I . . . we—had to put it about that we're engaged."

Her mother beamed. "Yes, dear, we know. Mr. Trantor kindly explained all about your mission—well, no details, of course—he wouldn't break your confidence—but that he's assisting you, and to do that, and excuse your presence in Rothbury's library last night, it was necessary to invoke the facade of an engagement."

Before Tabitha could respond, her father remarked, "Quick and nimble thinking. Quite impressive."

She wasn't all that surprised that her father would appreciate such an aspect, but . . . "Unfortunately, as Lady Castor and Mrs. Atkinson were privy to Trantor's declaration, it'll be all over town by now, and as you well know, there'll be repercussions. Talk. Speculation to an outrageous degree."

"Indeed." Her mother smiled with satisfaction. "It'll be delightfully entertaining watching everyone exercising their imaginations—all to no purpose, of course."

Tabitha frowned, trying to interpret her parents' attitude. "You seem . . . remarkably complacent over this."

"Of course, dear—how could we not be? You don't seriously imagine we'd do anything to curtail your mission, whatever it may be. If Trantor believes it to be . . . I believe his description was 'laudable and honorable'—then clearly it behooves us to support you in this, and if assisting in a sham betrothal is what's required, then of course your father and

I will stand behind you. Or behind you and Mr. Trantor, as happens to be the case. Hoodwinking the entire *ton*—not that they'll ever know of it—is well within our scope."

Her mother sent a smiling—approving and amused—glance at Trantor.

Tabitha's wits were still reeling; her stomach remained clenched tight. She could barely credit that Trantor had, unaided, having never met her parents before, managed to not only smooth over the situation—without disclosing the details of her mission—but had succeeded in gaining her parents' support. Their absolutely essential support. And all in fifteen minutes.

Her maid, tipped off by Biggs, the butler, had come rushing up to inform her a gentleman by the name of Trantor—the same gentleman who had driven home in the carriage with her last night—was closeted with her parents in the drawing room. She'd leapt from her bed, and had wasted only the minutes necessary to be decent before rushing down the stairs and into the drawing room.

She stared at Trantor, but he seemed unaware of having achieved any extraordinary feat. He certainly wasn't preening; if anything, he appeared appropriately appreciative of her parents' understanding. Her parents might appear gentle and woolly-headed; in reality they were as sharp as two pins.

Trantor eventually met her gaze, then stirred. He glanced at her parents. "If you will permit it, ma'am, perhaps I might speak with Miss Makepeace privately?"

Her mother graciously inclined her head. "As you are currently engaged, I see no reason why you shouldn't." She glanced at Tabitha, arched a brow.

Tabitha leapt on the chance. "Yes, of course. Sir." She bobbed Trantor a belated curtsy. "If you'll come with me?" To her parents she added, "We'll be in the back parlor."

She led the way to the door and Trantor followed.

The elder Makepeaces watched the pair exit the room. When the door clicked shut behind them, Mr. Makepeace grinned. "Well, that was unexpected."

"Indeed, dear." Mrs. Makepeace patted his hand, then rose. "But then the best things often are."

Tabitha opened the door to the back parlor, held it as Trantor followed her in, then shut it and swung to face him. "What the devil did you tell them?"

He'd walked further into the room. Halting by the sofa, he glanced back at her. "The truth, of course. Carefully edited."

She studied him; last night she hadn't had any real opportunity to. Standing as he was some yards away, the light from the wide windows fell over him and revealed . . . facets she hadn't seen in lamplight. The set of his jaw, the calculation behind his gray eyes, the intent focus that seemed innate. The masculine grace that invested his large frame, that projected a sense of coiled strength waiting to be sprung.

There seemed a great deal more to him than she'd remembered.

Growing restive under her gaze, he shifted, looked forward. Continued in the same collected tone, "Their active participation in our ruse will be essential, so I took the necessary steps to gain it. Among the benefits of being engaged is that we can meet like this—alone." He drew a sheet of paper from his coat pocket, held it up as he glanced back at her. "I've cracked the code. Do you want to see the results?"

She went forward, skirts rustling as she rounded the sofa and sat. She held out a hand. "Let me see."

He hesitated, then placed the folded sheet in her palm. She took it, unfolded it, started to read. He sat alongside her, beside her but not so close she felt crowded.

"As I guessed last night, the locations of all Rothbury's payments—the places he's been instructed to leave his pounds—are churches. I asked my brother's butler if he knew where the churches were. He didn't know them all, but those he recognized were in the City, not in Mayfair."

She read through the entries. "We'll need to check, but the only church I recognize is the one for his upcoming payment—the Church of St. Clement Danes. That's in Fleet Street."

Sebastian nodded. "On the border of the City proper."

Frowning, she turned to him. "But why churches?"

He shrugged. "There are a lot in London, so finding one—or dozens—within easy reach of any particular spot isn't hard. On top of that, churches are not generally inhabited by thieves or others of ill repute. Leaving even cash there for a short time should be safe." He met her eyes. "The choice suggests our blackmailer is intelligent enough to have thought things through. I've not encountered any blackmailers previously, but I wouldn't have expected such careful planning."

She wrinkled her nose and turned back to the sheet. "That seems to confirm that it's someone from the *ton*."

"Not necessarily, although the scheme itself suggests the blackmailer knows the *ton* and its ways very well."

"So Rothbury's to leave his payment in the church at sext—midday? That seems an odd time."

"It's a time most churches—especially those in the city—are likely to be open but not in use. I'm sure our blackmailer will have checked to ensure no service will be imminent."

"Hmm . . . but Rothbury's meeting is still seven days away." She lowered the sheet. "Surely there's something we can do before then, something we can investigate in some way."

He heard her impatience, inwardly smiled. "We can check where all the churches Rothbury's visited are—it might suggest something about the blackmailer. Closer to the date, I'll scout out St. Clement Danes, but beyond that . . ." He waited until she glanced at him, captured her gaze. "As matters stand, we'll need to keep up appearances and shore up the fiction of our engagement." He could use seven days of her company to further his campaign. "We need to behave as a newly engaged couple would."

He saw intransigence build in her expression, and smoothly continued, "I assume you want to be present at St. Clement Danes to identify the blackmailer?"

The look she turned on him answered the question without her, "Of course!"

"Well, then, a sound facade of an affianced couple will allow us to go for drives alone together. And if we happen to travel down Fleet Street, no one will turn a hair."

She grimaced. "They might wonder at what interest takes us in that direction . . . but you're right. Being engaged will allow us—me, particularly—a freedom I couldn't otherwise claim—well, not in town during the Season."

His gaze on her face, he noted the perturbation behind her words. "What is it?" When she glanced at him, he said, "Something's troubling you. What?"

She hesitated. He waited, and again felt a small thrill when she pulled another, quite horrendous, face, then said, "It's the deception." Folding the sheet between her fingers, she rose, walked a few paces, then stopped, staring out of the window at the courtyard garden outside.

He rose, too, watching. Wondering. "You're worried about deceiving the *ton*?"

"Not the *ton*. The Sisterhood." Briefly she glanced at him. "More particularly the young ladies who've joined and look to the older ones among us for guidance in the best way to go on." She gestured weakly and looked out once more. "I feel I'm setting a bad example for impressionable young ladies. For instance, I know next to nothing about you. Everyone will know we've barely met—it'll appear that I've been swept off my feet by a handsome face and masculine charms, which is both not the case and specifically what we at the Sisterhood preach against. We advise that young ladies go into a marriage knowing as much as they can about the man they will wed, if only to protect themselves from nasty surprises later."

"Hmm . . . yes, I see your difficulty."

She looked at him. "You do?"

He nodded, closing the distance to stand alongside her; he looked out at the garden as if in thought. "You're right—we'll need to concoct a story about how we met, how we came to know each other well enough to contemplate matrimony." He glanced sidelong at her. "That, at least, will allow you to hold your head high among the Sisterhood, and not damage your reputation in that regard." He returned his gaze to the shrubs outside. "As for not knowing me . . . we can use the next seven days while we wait for Rothbury's rendezvous to rectify that. Doing so will make you more comfortable, and we have to bear in mind that we don't know how long we'll need to continue this charade—how long it will be before we catch the blackmailer."

Her brow furrowed. "I suppose—"

The chiming of numerous clocks throughout the house cut her off.

The instant the sounds faded, he murmured, "But apropos of concocting a believable tale of how we met—why, when, and so on—I fear we'll need to put our minds to that immediately, because we cannot put off paying another duty visit beyond early this afternoon."

She looked at him. "Who do we need to visit?"

"My aunts, Lady Fothergill and Mrs. Trantor. They live together in a house in Curzon Street. Even if they didn't hear of it last night, they'll hear the news as soon as they come downstairs, but with luck that won't be before luncheon. However, if we don't appear soon afterward to explain, there'll be hell to pay." He grimaced, quite genuinely. "And I do mean hell."

He hesitated, then glanced at her, met her gaze, hesitated again, then let his lips quirk. "Apropos of that visit, of setting the scene, as it were, and I assure you I fully understand this is a charade, but if we're to pull it off—"

Tabitha watched as he drew something from his pocket. He looked down at whatever now lay in his palm, then picked it up and held it out to her. "This was my grandmother's ring. I hope you'll consent to wear it. My aunts will expect to see it on your finger—I can guarantee they'll look."

She hesitated, then reached out and took the ring. It was a simple gold band supporting an oval ruby of a rich, red hue, surrounded by smaller diamonds. The ruby was blood red; the diamonds sparkled. A heart surrounded by light. It was a lovely ring . . . she looked up, met his gray gaze. "I'll feel such a fraud."

He didn't make light of it. "Consider it stage setting—a prop. This is a charade, but if you don't wear it . . ."

She frowned, looked down at the ring, sparkling between her fingers. "If you're sure?"

"I am."

She slipped the ring on her finger.

It fitted perfectly.

"Great heavens, Sebastian! You could have knocked me over with a feather when I heard." Euphemia, Lady Fothergill, a bluff, ruddy-faced woman of imposing size, smiled delightedly at Tabitha, seated on the chaise opposite. "He's been so very cagey about you, my dear. We had no idea his interest was fixed."

"But then," Pamela Trantor said, her soft, die-away voice in sharp contrast to her ladyship's loud and genial tones, "dear Sebastian is nothing if not protective." From her position on the sofa beside her sister-in-law, Pamela smiled fondly at Sebastian, who was standing before the fireplace in the drawing room of the Curzon-Street house. "He's always been very kind to Freddie. Not everyone is, you know."

"Yes, well—no surprise there." Lady Fothergill looked at Sebastian. "Does Thomas know? Surely he and Estelle plan to come down to town?"

"I've sent a message, but I don't expect to see them at this point—apparently Eugenia, the new baby, is colicky."

"Oh, the poor little thing." Pamela's expression grew doting. "I remember when Freddie was that small. He was such a beautiful baby."

Lady Fothergill snorted. "He's just as beautiful now, but sadly no more sensible, and rather less reliable."

Pamela heaved a huge sigh. "He has been slow to mature, but I daresay one day . . ." Her words trailed away.

Lady Fothergill threw her a sharp glance, but refrained from further comment. Much to Sebastian's relief. He didn't need his aunts explaining his need to marry and beget an heir to Tabitha—not now, not ever. If there was any explaining to do, he would do it himself, at the appropriate time. Later.

"Yes, well." He shifted, drawing the attention of all three ladies back to him. Tabitha, a teacup and saucer balanced in her hands, had been regarding his aunts with her customary observant curiosity. "I knew you'd hear the news of our engagement and be badgered for information as soon as you went out, so I came to inform you. The simple facts are that Miss Makepeace and I have a great deal in common, and have decided we will suit."

Euphemia regarded Tabitha with a shrewd eye, then looked up at Sebastian. "Just as well. If what I heard is correct—that you were caught in an embrace in Lord Rothbury's library— then the *ton* will be buzzing." She looked back at Tabitha. "Makepeace, hey? I'm fairly sure I know your mother— Eleanor Crawley as was?"

Tabitha nodded. "Yes, that's right."

"Good—I must send around my card. Bedford Square, did you say?"

While Tabitha gave Euphemia her parents' direction, Sebastian reviewed his progress. He needed his aunts' approval and social support to shore up the facade of their engagement. While Pamela, softhearted and mild, had been easily won over, Euphemia wasn't so readily led. However, she seemed quite taken with Tabitha in an intrigued and rather bemused way, as if she couldn't quite understand how their engagement had come about, and was determined to winkle out the truth.

He was satisfied with that—could work with that.

The letter he'd dispatched to his brother that morning had been brief, merely informing Thomas of his engagement to Tabitha Makepeace and promising to keep Thomas and Estelle apprised of developments. However, in naming

Tabitha, he'd felt compelled to describe her so that Thomas and Estelle might have some hope of placing her. That was the one part of the hastily drafted missive that bothered him. That nagged and niggled. That description had turned quite poetic, and that was so unlike him. He hadn't even known he could think in such terms.

He shook off the unsettling memory, and refocused on what Euphemia was saying.

"—I daresay a dinner. I'll call on your parents later today—we'll sort something out."

Tabitha shot a glance at her coconspirator. She hadn't thought of betrothal dinners and the like. The fiction of their engagement was taking on life, and threatening to get out of hand.

Or, more specifically, to get taken out of their hands.

"I . . ." She willed Sebastian to save them—and was immediately stunned by the thought. She'd done that last night, several times; it was becoming a habit. Since when did she rely on men to save her? "That is"—she looked at Lady Fothergill—"my sister Lydia and her husband Ro are still in the country, and with Sebastian's brother and sister-in-law also out of town, such celebrations will necessarily have to be delayed."

From the corner of her eye, she saw Sebastian nod in agreement.

But Lady Fothergill only smiled. "Very likely, but Pamela and I will call on your parents this afternoon, and see what we can sort out. Don't trouble your head over it—I'm sure your family will be as eager as we are to demonstrate our delight at this development, and that we stand wholeheartedly behind you."

Tabitha saw the look Lady Fothergill sent Sebastian, but was at a loss to adequately account for it. Triumph? Why triumph? And why wasn't her ladyship quibbling about Tabitha's suitability? If she knew her mother, she had to know of Tabitha's reputation. If anything, she should be disapproving . . . although Sebastian was a second son and otherwise, in *ton* terms, the match was an acceptable one.

Before she could think how to probe for answers to the questions piling up in her head, Sebastian glanced at the clock on the mantelpiece. "We really must get on."

Why, she had no idea, but she readily set down her teacup and reached for her reticule. Sebastian stepped forward to offer his hand. She took it and rose, conscious of the warmth of his strong clasp and of his large body as he stood beside her.

Refocusing on Lady Fothergill, she found her smiling benignly.

"Go forth and enjoy yourselves." Her ladyship waved them away. "You may leave all the rest to us."

Tabitha plastered on a smile, curtsied, and they took their leave. Passing Sebastian as he held the drawing-room door for her, she murmured, "That's what concerns me most—them taking charge of things."

As if to echo her comment, Pamela came tripping after them. "No need to try to catch Freddie, Sebastian—I'll send him a note right now."

Their formal engagement dinner was held two nights later.

"I feel like I'm on a runaway horse—one with no reins." A smile permanently affixed to her face, Tabitha paused by the side of her parents' drawing room beside Sebastian, her coconspirator and now formally recognized fiancé.

The room was comfortably filled with family members, both hers and his. From the Makepeace side only Lydia and Ro were missing; Lydia was expecting their second child, and Ro had grown overprotective and didn't like her traveling. Not that Lydia was complaining over missing the Season; she vastly preferred their country home over the bustle of town. Tabitha suspected Ro's attack of overprotectiveness was more a response to Lydia's need for an excuse to remain in the country than anything else. Ro doted on Lydia, and would move heaven and earth to give her whatever she desired. In Tabitha's discussions of marriage with members of the Sisterhood, she often thought of Lydia's happiness—to her mind it illustrated her maturing belief that for some women, marriage truly was the most desirable fate, at least with a man they could trust . . . and therein lay the rub. How many men were trustworthy? Trustworthy enough to marry.

But that wasn't an issue at stake here and now. She and Sebastian weren't truly engaged.

They'd both been circulating, playing their parts; this was the first chance she'd had to exchange a private word.

"Who could have guessed your parents as well as my aunts would take the bit between their teeth and run quite so hard?" His features apparently relaxed, he surveyed the room.

She wasn't at all sure his ease was a pose. He didn't seem anywhere near as perturbed by the rapidity of events as she. Her agreeing to their sham betrothal had triggered an avalanche; she was starting to feel swept away, overwhelmed.

He, on the other hand, seemed to be taking it in his stride.

Somewhat peevishly she remarked, "You don't seem bothered that this is all a sham, and that at some point we'll have to disillusion everyone." That prospect was starting to weigh on her, increasing with every genuinely delighted congratulations tendered by their various relatives.

"I'm more concerned with what I've learned about your blackmailer."

All bother over their sham engagement abruptly vanished. "What?"

"I visited the other five churches the blackmailer has used for Rothbury's payments. All are small local churches in the western half of the City proper. None lies in the more fashionable districts—St. Clement Danes is the most westerly. That suggests the blackmailer is someone who has some connection with the area—the law courts, for instance, are close. Covent Garden and the major theaters are not that far away. To the south lie the docks, but I can't imagine how anyone from there might have learned your friends' secrets."

"Law clerks, actors, and the like—I can't readily see how anyone from those spheres could learn the requisite secrets, either."

"I grant you it doesn't get us much further now, but the information might prove useful later, once we learn more about our villain. It could help us prove they're the guilty party."

"Hmm . . . what about St. Clement Danes? Shouldn't we go and reconnoiter there?"

"I'd thought to go later, closer to the day of the payment, so I can check the church calendar for that week." He trapped her hand, smiled into her eyes as he raised it and brushed his lips across her knuckles. "But now I fear we must do our duty and mingle, before anyone starts to wonder what we're so earnestly discussing. You can continue to interrogate me later."

With effort shaking free of the hypnotic effect of his gray gaze, his mesmerizing voice, and the tingling caress of his lips on her skin, she inclined her head. They parted, both moving into the crowd of guests. Having been reminded of what lay behind their charade, she went readily enough, applying herself diligently to preserving their facade.

She'd just parted from speaking with her uncle William and her aunt Maude when Sebastian's cousin Frederick Trantor—Freddie as his mother called him—appeared at her elbow. Halting, she turned to him, a social smile on her lips.

He fixed her with wide, steady blue eyes. "I just wanted to tell you how happy I am that you're marrying Sebastian." His unbelievably innocent expression fell away as he grinned. "How *especially* grateful."

She'd already taken Freddie's measure. He was as undeniably beautiful as Lady Fothergill had painted him, possessing a choirboylike beauty that glowed and shone, yet equally undeniably, he was immature, unreliable, and impossible to trust. With anything. She raised her brows and, as he clearly expected her to, asked, "Why especially?"

Barely twenty, he was a graceless scamp who seemed unable to concentrate for long enough to properly understand anything at all. Calling him scatterbrained would be a compliment.

A fact he proceeded to acknowledge with a sunny, entirely genuine smile. "Because none of the family, even my own mama, want me to inherit the Coningsby title and the estate—and I don't want to, either." For a fleeting instant, Tabitha glimpsed something that might have been self-loathing slither behind Freddie's blue eyes, but then his smile brightened to a blinding degree. "Can you imagine me in charge of anything, let alone a large estate?" He shuddered. "I could never pull it off—and it would get in the way of me doing the things I like to do. Like racing. Curricles, or even just horses. I like to throw my heart over, and they're always saying I'll come to a sticky end, but I haven't." He grinned. "Not yet."

Before she could respond, he grasped her hand and shook it. "So thank you, Tabitha Makepeace. I don't want to be Sebastian's heir."

Abruptly releasing her, his gaze and his attention shifting away, Freddie moved on.

Tabitha regarded his retreating figure through narrowing eyes. There was something a trifle off about Freddie's "madness." She'd heard some of his more distant cousins refer to him as "Mad Freddie," had gathered from his mother's and his older relatives' comments that he was . . . as he appeared to be. But was that how he truly was or . . . was it his way of coping with some specific difficulty? One thing Tabitha knew about was facades, the masks people constructed to display to the world. She was living behind one now, but even before that night she'd met Sebastian, she'd been living behind another, and had been for years.

The thought wasn't new, yet its clarity shook her. It was always easier to see one's own foibles when they were reflected in someone else.

For a moment she simply stood by the side of the drawing

room absorbing the spark of self-revelation, but then Freddie's words, their actual import, registered—increasingly strongly—in her brain.

"Sebastian's *heir*?" She swung around, located her supposed fiancé, and pinned her gaze on him. With single-minded purpose, she made her way through the crowd, but the instant she reached his side, guests approached to take their leave, to congratulate the pair of them one last time before departing.

She had to grin and bear it, had to keep her expression glowing and happy and make the right noises.

Eventually they followed the last guests into the front hall and waved them off. When Sebastian would have turned to her and taken his leave, she sank her fingertips into his arm and looked at her parents. "Sebastian and I need to discuss some matters—we'll use the back parlor."

"Of course, dear." Her mother waved, tired but clearly satisfied with her night's work. "Good night, Sebastian." Her mother prodded her father. "Come along—we've discussing of our own to do about the engagement ball."

Her father sighed, but he was smiling as he shook Sebastian's hand and followed her mother up the stairs.

Tabitha watched them go. Under her breath asked, "What engagement ball?"

"My aunts, your mother—they've decided we need a formal ball to announce our upcoming union to the world."

"When?"

"Twelve days from now."

"Twelve days! But—"

"Relax." He took her hand and drew her on down the hall toward the back parlor. "Rothbury's appointment in St. Clement Danes is five days away, so with any luck before the ball takes place we'll have discovered we don't suit after all, and that our engagement was all a mistake."

"Speaking of our engagement." Tabitha waited while he opened the parlor door; she went in and waited for him to shut it before turning to face him. She narrowed her eyes on his. "Why didn't you tell me that you're your brother's—Viscount Coningsby's—heir, and that the reason all your family are so delighted to see you engaged to be married is because they're desperate for you to have a son so that there's no chance your cousin, popularly known for good reason as Mad Freddie, ever inherits the Coningsby estates?"

Her voice had risen, yet his expression displayed not a hint of perturbation, let alone discomfort. "Ah—I see. You heard about that."

"Of course I heard about that!" She flung up her hands. "Freddie himself told me about it."

His lips quirked. "I suppose I should have foreseen that."

"What you should have foreseen is that I am not at all amused at being used by you to pull the wool over your family's collective eyes!" Folding her arms, she glared at him. "Correct me if I'm wrong, but are they, or are they not, all currently in alt thinking that shortly after the wedding bells toll and we walk down the aisle, they'll have cause for relief from their worries about the Coningsby succession?"

He pulled a face. "Yes, but—"

"You're supposed to be out in society"—dramatically she pointed outward—"attending balls and parties and finding a young lady to marry, and instead you've decided to embark on our charade knowing it relieves you of pursuing a duty I've already guessed you don't like. Is that true?"

He'd taken a step closer, but then halted. His eyes appeared steely in the weak lamplight. He considered her for a long moment, then—perfectly mildly—replied, "That was my mission—the one I was on that placed me in Rothbury's library when you broke in. I'd already grown bored with it and had decided to put it aside for the night, which was why I was hiding in there with the door locked. And then you walked in, and offered me a much more interesting mission—that of pursuing your blackmailer. I decided to put off my mission of finding a suitable wife until after this mission—the more interesting one I'm pursuing with you—is concluded." He arched his brows, his eyes steady on hers. "I understand the connection you've drawn between the two, but at no point did I intend to use you to mislead my relatives. In terms of my motives in assisting you, that was never a part of the equation."

Arms tightly folded, she glowered at him, yet no matter how much she lectured herself against trusting him, it was impossible to doubt the sincerity in his voice. His hypnotic and therefore untrustworthy, yet compelling and convincing, voice.

Eventually she let her expression ease, let her arms fall, and sighed. "Very well. But now we have to face a major *ton* engagement ball."

His lips twisted in wry resignation. "And between then and now, I've been instructed that we have to attend at least one major ball every night."

She exhaled through her teeth. "Damn it! When I agreed to go along with this sham engagement, I had no idea matters would escalate like this!"

He seemed to consider, then, his gaze still on her, softly said, "I really can't see how we can avoid it."

She humphed, but he was right. She wanted to catch the blackmailer, and this was the price.

Chapter Three

$\mathcal{T}$heir first excursion as a formally affianced couple occurred the following evening when they attended a ball at Carrington House. It was one of the major balls held that evening, and Lady Carrington waxed delighted—nay, ecstatic—on spying them approaching her ballroom door.

She gushed; she exclaimed.

Tabitha kept a socially appropriate smile plastered to her lips. That Sebastian, too, seemed to inwardly wince, mollified her aggravation to some degree. He might have multiple reasons for keeping up their facade, but she, too, had incentive enough to play along.

Parting from their hostess, they joined the throng of guests filling the room.

"Another blasted crush." Sebastian sounded distinctly unamused. "Enlighten me—why do *ton* hostesses consider assembling more guests than can comfortably fit in their rooms a good thing?"

"You'll have to hold me excused." Tabitha inclined her head to a pair of distant acquaintances. "That's something I've never fathomed myself."

The brief glance they shared heightened the sense that in this—in playing their roles and keeping up the charade of their engagement—it was the two of them in league against the fashionable world. Even if the fashionable world didn't know it.

"I fear," she murmured, drawing her eyes from his, "that we'll need to actively mingle."

He gave a soft, disgusted snort, but held his ground by her side as a veritable horde of garrulous and openly curious well-wishers all but lined up to speak with them.

After half an hour of thinly veiled interrogation, Sebastian's temper had eroded to a dangerous degree. He'd never found it easy to abide fools. Musicians had been sawing at their strings on and off for some time, but at last an area of the ballroom was cleared and the opening bars of a waltz reached his ears.

Closing one hand about Tabitha's elbow, he summoned the best smile he was currently capable of and fixed it on the tedious matron and her two giggling daughters currently standing before them. "I fear, ladies, that I must steal Miss Makepeace away. She promised me the first waltz, and I intend to claim the favor."

The glance Tabitha threw him clearly stated she hadn't given the first thought to dancing, but the lure of an escape, however temporary, was difficult to resist.

The three females facing them tittered in unison.

Reinforcing her smile, Tabitha turned back to the trio. "If you'll excuse us?"

A rhetorical question, yet the three gratuitously assured them that they should certainly indulge in the diversion.

Sebastian waited for no further encouragement. With a controlled nod, he drew Tabitha away.

As the crowd parted before them, he lowered his head and murmured in her ear, "You do waltz, don't you?"

"Yes . . . but I haven't in years."

"But you would waltz with your betrothed, wouldn't you? That would be expected."

"Yes . . . that's true."

She made no further demur as he steered her to the floor, then twirled her, stepped closer, and drew her into his arms. They stepped out, and the music caught them. It swirled and swept them up; the other dancers whirled around them, but in that instant they stepped onto a separate plane of existence, or so it seemed.

A plane where their bodies flowed in concert, where he led and she followed . . . effortlessly. The rest of the guests were still there, but distanced, no longer impinging on their reality. He gazed into her eyes, bright hazel and wide, and was lost.

Neither tall nor short, she was the perfect height for him. Slim and slender, almost willowy, she was supple and responsive in his arms. After their first circuit, he murmured, "I'm surprised you don't dance more often—whenever the chance presents." He let his lips curve understandingly. "It's certainly preferable to the alternative."

Tabitha managed a reasonably sophisticated inclination of her head in reply. *I didn't know I could waltz like this*, seemed too risky a confession to make. In truth, she wasn't sure she could speak—her lungs had constricted, not with fear, but with the thrill of excitement. Of pleasurable expectation.

Dancing had always been a chore, something one did because it was expected. She'd never enjoyed waltzing before, yet as the measure continued she only enjoyed it more. For quite the first time on a dance floor she relaxed in her partner's arms; she had complete confidence in Sebastian's skill. If he said he could do something, he could, and it had taken no more than half a minute to be assured that he could, quite definitely, waltz.

So for the first time in her life, she dropped her guard and let herself flow with the dance.

And enjoyed and appreciated as she never had before.

Was it him? Or had she somehow, without being aware of it, changed?

The analytical part of her mind wondered, and wondered if she should waltz with some other gentleman to learn the answer.

But by the time the music slowed and, sharing genuinely appreciative smiles, they halted and he bowed and she curtsied, she'd concluded that pursuing that answer wouldn't be wise. Learning that the only gentleman with whom she shared an affinity on the dance floor was her sham-intended, a fiancé who was that in name only and only temporary to boot, wouldn't make her life easier.

Determinedly smiling, she linked her arm in Sebastian's. "Come on. If we stroll as if on our way to join someone, we won't be quite as besieged."

With a nod, he joined her in projecting that image. Somewhat to her surprise, the next two hours passed in companionable, conspiratorial ease.

The next day they attended an alfresco luncheon at Sion House. Lady Jersey had summoned the cream of the *ton* to assemble at noon and partake of a delicious picnic repast, then explore the delights of her rambling gardens. Well acquainted with the Makepeaces, her ladyship had sent a reminder the day before, which had loosely translated to *Don't you dare not come*. The biggest gossipmonger in the *ton* was not of a mind to be denied their presence, and the associated entertainment.

As Tabitha had always got along well with Lady Jersey, she'd inwardly sighed and obliged, but after two hours of being the cynosure of all eyes, the focus of all attention, when the guests spread out to roam the gardens, she stepped out briskly, ultimately leading Sebastian into the cool shade of the arboretum.

Strolling the path wending among the mature trees, for the first time that afternoon they could speak privately.

After glancing around and confirming no one had yet followed them into the cool haven, Sebastian snorted. "I've fought alongside cannons, but I can't ever recall my head ringing as well as my ears."

Tabitha grinned wrily. "Our hostess does talk a lot, which opens the flood gates for others."

He glanced at her. "I'm surprised you and she get on."

"She's a strong-willed woman who has forged her own place in society, more or less on her terms."

"Put like that, I can see the basis of your mutual appreciation."

"Indeed. I can understand her—she's curious, as always, and senses there's more to our engagement than meets the eye, but she trusts my judgment, regardless. She's intrigued, which is what I expected."

She ambled on; he followed beside and a little behind her.

"What I don't fully comprehend," she went on, "is why everyone else—every last person I've met barring only those who had you in mind for their own charges—is so very happy that you and I are engaged."

Halting, she swung to face him. He halted, too. The slope of the path meant her eyes were nearly level with his.

"I know why your family's in alt, and why my family and connections are, but all the others—especially the parents of other marriageable young ladies—seem thrilled to the back teeth, too." A dark cloud descended over her face. "I've a lowering notion it's a form of relief—that now they can point to me and say, See? Even she is marriageable, so our daughters must be, too."

She paused, then humphed, swung around and ambled on.

He followed. "Are you sure you're reading them correctly? For my part, I'd interpreted their relief being because you, in your previous, unbetrothed, single-lady incarnation, were too compelling a role model for other young ladies—said marriageable but as yet unmarried daughters. You, single and unbetrothed, personified another path, one that did not include marriage, yet you were still recognized and accepted among the *ton.*"

He watched her as she walked slowly just ahead of him. "I, too, see their reaction—their happiness at our betrothal—as primarily fostered by relief. But it's the relief that you'll no longer be there, a living, breathing counterweight to the customary arguments urging young ladies to marry—the alternative incarnate."

She slowed. He slowed as well.

Eventually, she halted, paused, then swung to face him again. With her usual bold openness she studied his eyes, his face, then tilted her head. Eyes on his, conceded, "Perhaps. You may be right."

Other voices reached them. Tabitha glanced back along the path and saw a gaggle of young ladies coming along. She turned and led the way on. "Rothbury's rendezvous with the blackmailer is three days away—we should start making our plans."

"The first thing to do," Sebastian replied, "is to learn what we can about the lie of the land."

The ball that evening proved tedious in the extreme. Tabitha spent a good portion of it mentally distracted, contemplating Sebastian's view of her as a role model for young ladies. It wasn't so much him seeing her as such—she thought of herself in that light; it was one of the reasons she wasn't happy about their charade—but rather that his tone hadn't implied criticism, but acceptance, even a degree of approbation.

The next day, she barely contained her impatience through the morning tea and luncheon she had to attend. If others interpreted her fidgeting as a symptom of unbridled eagerness to meet with her fiancé again . . . well, that wasn't all that far from the mark.

After some argument, she'd agreed to allow him to reconnoiter the Church of St. Clement Danes alone while she continued socially supporting the fiction of their engagement. He'd said he would go to Fleet Street that morning, and had promised to report fully when he called to take her up in his curricle for a turn about the park that afternoon.

He dutifully arrived in Bedford Square at three o'clock. She rushed out from the drawing room where she'd been keeping watch—occasioning a knowing smile from her mother, which she'd ignored—and met him in the front hall.

He smiled when he saw her.

She tamped down the pleasure that rose in response. This was a charade; she mustn't forget that. "So . . . ?"

He took her cloak from Biggs. "I suggest we get going— the wind is chilly and it looks like it's coming on to rain."

She humphed. "This is England—it's always coming on to rain." But she fell in with his transparent wish not to discuss their secrets in front of the staff, allowing him to settle the cloak about her shoulders, then she flipped up the hood, arranging it over her wild mass of hair before swiping up the reticule she'd left ready on the hall table. "Right. Let's go."

He smiled and offered his arm.

She took it and went quickly down the steps beside him. Taking his hand, she climbed into the carriage and sat. He climbed up and sat beside her, the reins in his hands; she held her tongue until the carriage started rolling, then demanded, "Well?"

He grinned and glanced at her. "Patience." He looked back at the road, at the approaching corner. After he'd taken it, he met her eyes. "There's too much detail to relate in traffic. We'll stroll in the park and I'll tell you all without distraction."

So she had to wait some more.

Yet when they were finally strolling the well-kept lawns leading down to the shores of the Serpentine, she couldn't fault his openness, his unrestricted disclosure.

After describing the layout of the church, he told her of this week's calendar of events. "I even checked with the minister. There's an early service that morning, but it'll be long over. The church is always open from dawn to dusk for contemplation and prayer. I stayed from eleven o'clock until midday, just to see what it might be like—only one old lady came into the church, and she stayed for barely fifteen minutes."

She frowned. "That's going to make watching for the blackmailer difficult."

"Indeed. I was going to suggest we watch from outside, but the church's location negates that—there are four exits, and many ways to go the instant they step outside. Watching from outside is hopeless, not if we wish to be certain we've identified the real blackmailer and not just someone who's wandered inside, then come out again by a different door."

"We can't afford not to catch the blackmailer in the act, in the church, but then we'll have to follow them outside, perhaps further, and pick our moment to confront them."

"Precisely. And from what you said, if we don't succeed in identifying the blackmailer at St. Clement Danes, then learning of another rendezvous will be difficult if not impossible. We'll have lost our only real lead."

She nodded, wondering how to achieve all they had to. "Is there anywhere inside we can hide? Some spot from where we can see the whole church. The choir stalls?"

He shook his head. "I looked. There are a number of nooks, but every spot leaves too much of the church unobserved. We would hear someone come in, but if we then emerge to watch them, they'll hear us and very possibly take fright. If they flee without picking up Rothbury's package, there'll be no way we can prove they're the blackmailer and not some unwary soul who just happened to wander in and got unnerved by our presence."

He paused, then went on, "I really don't think there's any alternative but that we go in disguise."

She met his eyes. Saw something of her own—silly, ridiculous, perhaps even puerile—excitement at the prospect shining in his eyes. She grinned. "What should we go as?"

He smiled, caught her hand, and drew her arm through his. Holding her close, he turned them back toward his curricle, parked on the Avenue's verge. "Let's discuss the possibilities."

* * *

Sebastian called at Bedford Square the following morning. Tabitha was—once again—waiting impatiently. He hid a smile at her unrestrained eagerness for his company; even if it was their joint mission that drove it, it was nevertheless balm to his ego.

After greeting Mrs. Makepeace, he offered Tabitha his arm and they set out to walk the short distance to the British Museum. Along the way they entertained themselves with vitriolic observations on the previous night's ball. "At least," he observed, "being engaged, we're now spared the worst of it."

"If we weren't engaged, I wouldn't have attended." She arched a brow at him. "It's you who our engagement has benefited in that regard."

"For which"—he caught her fingers and raised them to his lips, briefly kissed—"believe me, I'm truly grateful."

She humphed, but he detected a faint blush in her creamy cheeks. The museum's gates loomed ahead; they turned in and walked purposefully to the front steps, up, and through the large doors.

"The Egyptian Hall," Tabitha declared, and led the way up the main staircase.

"Are you fascinated by mummies?"

She glanced back at him. "No, but I thought the hieroglyphs might be of interest to you—or at least provide us with a reason for being there."

"True, but my interests lie more in the Assyrian and Mesopotamian systems, not so much the Egyptian."

Her lips quirked as she faced forward. "I'll bear that in mind."

They reached the Egyptian Hall, and found it helpfully deserted.

"There was huge interest some years ago, when things Egyptian were all the rage, but that's largely passed, so . . ." She whirled, arms spread. "We have the place to ourselves, as I'd hoped."

He smiled. "Excellent planning."

"I thought so." She plopped down on a bench before one window. "Now cut line—what about our plans? Rothbury's rendezvous is tomorrow—how are we going to be there and not scare off the blackmailer?"

Assembling his thoughts, he sat on the bench beside her. "Definitely disguises—it's the only way. But they must be the right disguises—the sort that will excuse us being there at that hour, and remaining for more than a few minutes."

Tabitha was relieved that he was still talking of *we* and not *I*; she'd fully expected him to try to insist that she didn't need to be there. She'd been primed to protest and press her case; his lack of resistance to her involvement left her momentarily off balance. She didn't make the mistake of imagining he lacked an active protective streak vis à vis herself; she'd seen evidence aplenty of it through the recent days, especially in the overcrowded ballrooms, where he invariably shielded her from the worst of the crush.

No—his acquiescence to her involvement stemmed from his understanding that being there was important to her, and that as she would fight, and indeed demand, to be present, opposing her would simply be a waste of time.

She appreciated his insight, but was nevertheless stunned. In her experience, gentlemen rarely knew where to draw their protective line.

He'd been mulling something over; now he glanced up and met her eyes. "I was thinking of disguising myself as a drunken tramp. I would pretend to fall asleep on one of the front pews and snore. I should warn you, however, that I won't be fit to be seen with you—well, not you as Miss Tabitha Makepeace."

She raised her brows. "Ah—but what about being seen with a drab and downtrodden woman, slumped in one of the rear pews and weeping silently?"

"Can you pass yourself off as a woman of the lower orders?"

"I've had my maid collect clothes from the other women on our staff. Together they've assembled an outfit from their castoffs. It's utterly drab, dull, and depressing—exactly the sort of attire no one will pay the slightest heed to. In it, I'll be invisible."

He looked skeptical, but didn't argue, merely suggested, "You'll need to dust your hair to dull the shine, and, most importantly, dirty your face—your skin glows like pearl-nacre. If you don't dim it, it will give you away at a glance."

She nodded. "I've got mittens to wear on my hands, so they won't give me away either."

"Good." He paused, then went on, "So our disguises are settled. Now we need to decide how to get there." He glanced at her. "No jarvey will take us up, not looking like that, and I can hardly drive us in my curricle."

"Gifford. He'll be delighted to be a part of this, and he knows the city's lanes well."

Sebastian hesitated, then nodded. "All right. I'll be out-side the rear door of your parents' townhouse tomorrow just after ten o'clock. We'll need Gifford to drive us in a cart—you up on the seat beside him, and me sitting in the bed. He can take us to that part of Fleet Street. I'll slip off the cart before he reaches the church, approach on foot, and go in. You stay with Gifford while he drives past the church, on a little way, then turns and comes back again. You then hop down and leave him. Pretending to be overcome by grief, you enter the church and sit in the back, and weep. That way, we'll arrive independently and should both be in position by eleven o'clock."

Eyes narrowed, imagining it, she asked, "Why so early?"

"Because the blackmailer, too, might come early to take up a position within the church to watch Rothbury leave his payment. If we're already there, they're less likely to imag-ine we have any interest in them."

"Hmm . . ." After a moment, she nodded and refocused on him. "It sounds like between us we have an excellent plan."

He inclined his head. "Dare I say it? We make an excel-lent team."

She grinned, then glanced away, toward a group of young

ladies and gentlemen who came bustling in, the mummies their goal.

He rose and offered his hand. "I believe our purpose here is accomplished."

She sighed, gave him her hand, and let him pull her to her feet. "I'd much rather remain here with the mummies, but we're promised to Lady Hawthorne for luncheon, then your aunts expect us in Curzon Street for afternoon tea."

Winding her arm in his, he turned her to the door. "I admit that when I suggested we use a betrothal as our cover, I had no idea that the social obligations of an affianced couple were so onerous."

"Well now you know." Head rising, Tabitha strolled beside him. "And just think, after this is all over and we dissolve our engagement, you'll have to do it all over again with whichever young lady you choose as your true bride."

Sebastian glanced at her, then faced forward. And grunted noncommittally.

They were both in position in the Church of St. Clement Danes when the city's bells tolled eleven o'clock the next morning. Slumped on his side in the front pew, an empty bottle of blue ruin on the floor alongside, Sebastian breathed heavily, steadily, occasionally interrupting the rhythm with a snort.

He'd been in position when Tabitha had entered. He hadn't been able to see her, but had noted her footsteps. To his surprise, she'd come to the front of the church, to the carved bar at the bottom of the steps before the altar. She'd started to kneel, clearly intending to pray, but then had noticed him lying there.

She'd hesitated.

He'd given a louder, snuffling snort, from beneath his lashes had watched her eyes widen. Clutching an old cloth bag to her middle, all but bowed over it, she'd turned and scuttled back up the aisle.

He'd listened, and as they'd arranged, she'd taken up residence in one of the back pews.

He'd had to grin approvingly, albeit inwardly, at such effective improvisation; it had allowed her to check on him, simultaneously giving her reason—had anyone been already watching—to retreat to the rear.

He was confident they were both thoroughly and effectively disguised. He appeared utterly disreputable, bedraggled, and worn. The old coat Wright had found for him smelled worse with every passing minute. Even the boots on his feet had been resurrected from some junk heap; if it rained, he'd have wet soles.

Somewhat to his surprise, Tabitha was equally unrecognizable. Not content with dusting her hair, she'd frizzed it out so it formed a knotty and unkempt corona about her head, over which she'd jammed a plaid cap that had seen much better days. Her mismatched layers of petticoats, skirts, and threadbare coat screamed lowly seamstress or menial worker. But it was her performance that had most impressed him—her downcast air, the droop of her shoulders, her shuffling walk—the way she held herself as if fearing a blow at any time. If he hadn't known it was an act, he would have felt . . . even more protective than he did.

Every instinct he possessed had urged him to forbid her participation, but . . . he was playing a long game, and gaining her trust was imperative.

Showing her that he could—and would—allow her reasonable leeway to participate in any activity as long as she was adequately safe was essential, and as he was there and had no intention of letting her out of his orbit, she was and would remain safe today.

He lay apparently comatose as the city's bells tolled eleven times. He continued to lie largely unmoving on the hard pew as the minutes ticked by.

As far as he could tell, no one entered the church to surreptitiously take up a watching brief. The floors were stone flags; it was difficult to avoid at the very least scuffing a sole. But no sound beyond the occasional muted sob from the rear pews reached him.

Then the main door of the church was pushed open. Someone hesitated on the threshold. A long moment passed, then the door was pushed shut and heavy male footsteps paced slowly down the aisle.

Rothbury.

Unable to see Sebastian lying in the pew, his lordship walked to the front of the nave, then across, away from Sebastian, to the baptismal font set to one side. If Rothbury had glanced directly behind him, he would have seen Sebastian then, but intent on the font, he didn't look that way. From beneath his lashes, Sebastian watched his lordship glance instead toward the rear of the church, then he swiftly raised the font's heavy lid, pushed an oilskin-wrapped packet inside the bowl, and silently replaced the lid.

Rothbury glanced again at the rear pews. What he saw seemed to reassure him. He looked back at the font, then walked, to all appearances calmly, past it to the church's side door. He pushed it open and went out. The door closed behind him.

Tension rose. Sebastian lay still, slumped and breathing slowly. He heard few sounds from the rear of the church; he pictured Tabitha wearily slumped, eyes closed—waiting as he was.

Minutes ticked past. Fifteen at a guess. The bells tolled midday, then the peals faded away.

He was starting to itch with the need to go and see what Rothbury had left in the font when the side door was hauled open.

Sebastian forced his limbs to stillness, forced his breathing to remain slow and deep.

The door remained open as footsteps—quiet, stealthy—approached the font.

A boy came into view. Maybe twelve years old. He saw Sebastian but was clearly accustomed to such sights; his gaze darted more often toward the rear of the church, but he didn't halt. He climbed onto the stone step surrounding the font, stretched up and shifted the lid.

Reached in and retrieved the packet Rothbury had placed there.

Without examining it, the boy stuffed the packet inside his thin jacket, then shoved the font's lid back on, turned, and hurried for the side door.

He didn't look back as he went through it, barely pausing to shove the heavy door half closed before starting off down the pavement.

Sebastian reached the door before the boy had taken ten paces.

A whoosh of limp skirts heralded Tabitha; she peeked past him. "That's him. Let's go."

He caught her hand and together they walked briskly out of the church, falling in behind the boy. Their quarry didn't run but every now and then he took a few quick steps, as if he wanted to run but had been warned not to do so.

They followed as he made his way, not into the City, but in the opposite direction.

"Covent Garden," Sebastian whispered as the boy headed up Catherine Street. They followed their quarry past the Theater Royal, past the market, closing the distance as he plunged into the labyrinth of narrow lanes beyond.

Eventually he turned down a minor lane, halted outside a door halfway down, and rapped briskly.

Sebastian pushed Tabitha into the deep shadows cast by the overhang above another doorway. The boy glanced back, but didn't notice them. Sebastian doubted he would recognize them even if he did; they were in no way remarkable in that area.

The boy jigged nervously, but then the door opened and he straightened. A woman appeared in the doorway; neither old nor young, she was more neatly and cleanly dressed than seemed the norm for the neighborhood. The boy spoke, then held out his hand.

The woman showed him something in her left palm, then closed that hand into a fist and held it at shoulder height while she extended her other hand, fingers beckoning.

Shifting, the boy drew out the packet he'd retrieved from the font. The exchange—the packet for the coins the woman presumably had in her hand—took place.

Tabitha moved forward.

Sebastian softly swore and hauled her back.

Just as the boy turned to retrace his steps.

Sebastian twisted around, set Tabitha against the door, bent his head and kissed her.

Kept kissing her as the boy's footsteps passed behind his back.

Fought desperately to keep his mind on the job, on this mission, not the other running beneath it. Fought to keep his focus on the lane around them, and not let himself be distracted by the temptation of her delectable lips, by the succulent promise of her mouth.

He wavered, but managed to hold his line. When the boy turned the corner and his footsteps faded, he reluctantly broke the kiss and raised his head.

Even in the dimness, he saw Tabitha blink. Twice. Then she frowned. "What was that for?"

"So he didn't see you—or me—when he passed." Glancing over his shoulder, he saw that the woman had retreated into the house and shut the door.

He felt Tabitha's small hands flatten on his chest. She pushed, and he stepped back.

Her gaze locked on the closed door. Her lips set in a grim line. "Right. Let's go."

Tabitha started forward again, only—again—to be hauled back by Sebastian.

"No." He breathed the word against her ear, sending thoroughly distracting shivers down her spine.

That kiss and its effects had been bad enough. "What now?" she inquired crossly. "That woman is the blackmailer. Let's go and confront her."

His arms snug around her, from close quarters he met her gaze. "Is she? And should we?"

She frowned. "Speak in whole sentences. What do you mean?"

His lips twitched, but he sobered immediately. "I mean, is she the blackmailer, or an accomplice? If we confront her, will the blackmailer have time to escape and flee? Also, if we accost her now, without knowing who she is or how she's connected to the blackmailer—or if she is the blackmailer, how she came to learn your friends' secrets—what are our chances of effectively scaring her off?" He looked into her eyes. "I presume that's what we want—to scare her off so she gives up blackmailing your friends?"

Her hands clasped on the steely arms around her waist, she nodded. "But I would prefer that whatever we do makes her—or the blackmailer—desert their chosen field of employment altogether."

He nodded. "That's my feeling, too. To be sure of doing that, we need to learn that woman's name, learn if she's the blackmailer herself, or if someone else is, then we need to learn the connections between her, the blackmailer, and your friends well enough to understand how she, or the blackmailer, became privy to their secrets. Most important of all, we need to be certain that she, or whoever she's working for, are a single entity, and not part of some wider scheme." He looked down, into her face. "Once we know all that, we'll be able to act, and be sure of achieving our goals without risking your friends' secrets being aired."

She grimaced, but nodded, and reluctantly stepped away from him. She glanced at the closed door across the lane. "So how do we learn her name?"

He grinned and slouched back against the wall beside the doorway. "We wait. It shouldn't take long."

Half an hour later, a woman burdened with a heavy basket halted outside one of the neighboring houses and appeared to search for a key.

"Stay here."

Sebastian left Tabitha on the words and strode quickly across the lane. He gruffly hailed the woman. She turned to him; a low-voiced discussion ensued, then Sebastian gave the woman several coins, and returned to Tabitha. He took her arm and urged her up the lane.

She went, but asked, "Well?"

"Our woman's name is Elaine Mackay. She hasn't lived there long enough for the locals to know much of her— keeps to herself, as her neighbor informed me." He met her gaze. "Does her name ring any bells?"

She wracked her brain, but had to shake her head. "Not even a chime."

Stepping out of the lane they headed back to Fleet Street. Gifford would have returned and would be waiting near the church to take them back to Bedford Square.

Once on Fleet Street, Tabitha spotted the cart drawn into the curb ahead. She glanced at Sebastian, saw he'd noticed, too. "So," she said, "now we know her name, how do we learn the rest?"

Chapter Four

$\mathcal{T}$hey set out in the Makepeaces' traveling carriage early
the next morning. Tabitha had cried off the balls they'd been
scheduled to attend the previous night and the two following on the grounds that she had to—simply had to—make a
dash into the country to speak with four close friends.

"I'm sure," she said, "that everyone assumes that the subject I wish to discuss with them is our wedding."

Seated opposite her, Sebastian murmured, "You're quite
adept at letting people suppose what they will."

"It's easier that way. I just hope Suzanne, Caroline, Jacinta, and Constance can tell us who Elaine Mackay is."

"And how she came to know their secrets."

Tabitha glanced out of the window. "That's Reigate
ahead." Knowing that the Rothburys, mère and père, were
still in London, they'd made first for that family's country
house in Surrey. Suzanne, the Rothburys' daughter, had

reportedly retired there to calm nerves overstressed by her recent engagement.

Half an hour later, welcomed by Suzanne and drawn into a pleasant parlor to partake of refreshments, Sebastian stood looking out of a wide window, taking in the vista of the gardens, and listened while, behind him, seated with Suzanne on the chaise before the fireplace, Tabitha received her friend's enthusiastic congratulations, then doggedly led her to the vital point.

"Elaine Mackay?" Suzanne paused, then said in a breathless, nervy rush, "Oh, yes! The hairdresser Mama hired to do my hair for my engagement ball. She came highly recommended."

Tabitha excused them soon after, saying they had to get on as they had a number of others to call on that day. Suzanne stood on the front steps and waved them off. Glancing back, Sebastian thought she cut a lonely figure.

Tabitha, again opposite, humphed. "Suzanne's something of a social gadabout. Being stuck alone in the country, away from all the fuss and froth of town, is hard on her."

"She's not really suffering from any nervous condition, is she?"

"No. She's suffering because of the blackmailer." Tabitha fixed Sebastian with a direct look. "I've observed that many ladies chatter to their hairdressers, often talking before them without a normal reserve. Elaine Mackay might well have heard enough to guess her victims' secrets, at least well enough for her purposes."

He nodded. "As you say, she wouldn't need to know everything, just enough to make them believe she did."

"She might even have guessed, but not known her conjecture was correct until the victim consented to pay."

"Indeed." He leaned back against the squabs. "As she was the one to whom the payment was taken, and as we now know she was likely to be the source of the illicit knowledge, then it's possible, thank God, that we're dealing only with her—a single blackmailer—and nothing more convoluted."

Tabitha frowned. "But we'll need to check with at least one other victim to be sure she's the only hairdresser involved."

He met her gaze. "We only know of four victims. We'll need to check with them all to confirm that Elaine Mackay is the only blackmailing hairdresser currently active, that she doesn't have a few like-minded sisters also in the business."

Tabitha raised her brows high. "What a thought."

They stopped at Leatherhead for a late luncheon, then she dutifully guided Gifford to the Winden house, near Weybridge. There they learned from Caroline Winden that she, too, had had her hair arranged by Elaine Mackay prior to her engagement ball. It was Caroline who had first told Tabitha of the blackmailer; on thinking back, Caroline recalled a whispered conversation she'd had with her sister while Elaine Mackay had been in the room. Pale, but resolute, Caroline met Tabitha's gaze. "That's when she would have heard of it—I remember Pansy teasing me about how my tastes in gentlemen had changed."

They parted from Caroline an hour later, charged with the task of releasing her from the blackmailer's clutches. Sebastian had been careful not to promise anything, but Tabitha—as usual—had been a great deal more forthright, assuring Caroline that while they would indeed bring an end to Elaine Mackay's illicit enterprise, they would ensure that no public mention of Caroline's past peccadilloes occurred.

Once again in the carriage, Sebastian considered the firebrand seated opposite. Tabitha was very much a dragon slayer. He supposed that made him her knight.

They headed for Burnham. On hearing of their proposed journey, her parents had suggested they spend the night with the Colliers, an older couple, longtime friends of the family who rarely ventured forth and so would be delighted to sustain a visit from Tabitha and her fiancé.

Burnham Lodge became their overnight halt. They spent a pleasant evening wih the Colliers. Mr. Collier was a scholar; Sebastian found no shortage of interesting topics to discuss.

Meanwhile, Mrs. Collier and Tabitha shared family and *ton* news; both seemed to possess a wry appreciation of the absurdity of *ton* fads.

The next morning he and Tabitha set out for Chorley Wood, and the Ellham country house. There they spoke with Jacinta Ellham. She, too, identified Elaine Mackay as the woman hired to dress her hair for her engagement ball. "She's the one everyone must have—much like Mr. Robertson is the best dance master."

They took lunch with Jacinta and her parents, carefully avoiding all mention of the real purpose of their visit. Once back in the carriage, after some discussion they agreed that, having circled around London south to west, they might as well continue on to Harpenden to visit the last of the four ladies who had confided their plight to Tabitha. "If Constance, too, had Elaine Mackay to do her hair, then there really can be no quibble with our conclusion."

"Four out of four." Sebastian nodded. "Certainly that will put it beyond argument."

They found Constance at home, moping in the garden. She brightened considerably on seeing them crossing the lawn toward her. Like the others, she confirmed that Elaine Mackay had been brought in to do her hair. Remembering various other names bandied about in relation to the four engagement balls, Sebastian confirmed that no other outsider—dance master, florist, caterer—had been used in common with Caroline, Jacinta, and Suzanne.

With the prospect of the blackmailer being taken up— quietly and without fuss—a weight seemed to lift from Constance's slight shoulders. She was considerably more chipper when they parted from her.

Back in the carriage, Tabitha all but bounced with impatience. "So it's only Elaine Mackay, the hairdresser, they all had in common—she's the one who received the money, and the person we now know either overheard or encouraged them to share their secrets." She met Sebastian's eyes; hers shone with conviction. "As soon as we get back to town, we'll confront her."

Unlike Tabitha, Sebastian thought that scenario through. He foresaw several difficulties. "Exactly how do you imagine scaring Miss Mackay off?"

"Why, I'll simply tell her that unless she stops her nefarious demands, I'll . . ." She paused, blinked. "Make sure she doesn't work in *ton* households again?"

"And how do you imagine achieving a *ton* ban without divulging the reason why she shouldn't be hired?"

"Hmm . . ."

"Indeed. In short, we need professional advice."

"From the police?" Her tone suggested that was unlikely to be helpful.

"I admit that the police force is still in its infancy and often as riddled with crime as the underworld it seeks to rein in, however, I've heard of a new group being run out of Bow Street. I'll make discreet inquiries, and see if we can't find someone sensible to assist us. I gather Peel is looking to make his force respectable, so perhaps we can present this as an opportunity for him to demonstrate this group's bona fides."

She still looked uncertain, but eventually inclined her head in acquiescence. She glanced out of the carriage window. "It's still light. If we push on, we can reach London tonight. Perhaps Bow Street will still be open."

Sebastian frowned. "We left Harpenden later than expected. I'm not sure we should try for London tonight—I don't fancy crossing Finchley Common in the dark, and I'm quite sure Gifford won't relish the prospect, either."

"Nonsense!" Tabitha waved dismissively. "You shouldn't believe all those tales about highwaymen—I'm sure they're greatly exaggerated."

"Meaning you don't want to believe them because they stand in the way of you and your goal—namely reaching London tonight."

She blinked at him, then struggled unsuccessfully to suppress a grin. "Precisely. Buck up—fortune favors the brave. We'll be perfectly safe. Now we have all the intelligence about Elaine Mackay, blackmailer, that we need, nothing is going to stop me from acting immediately and halting her in her tracks."

Nothing except a stone, a boxing match, and a runaway phaeton. They'd passed through St. Albans and were heading south at a good pace when the carriage jerked as one of the horses stumbled. Gifford immediately hauled on the reins; the carriage swayed wildly, slowed, then came to an ominous halt.

The carriage dipped as Gifford climbed down. Sebastian opened the door, leapt down and went to confer. Tabitha scooted to the window and peered out, but all she could see were Sebastian's and Gifford's backs as they stood beside one of the leaders and talked.

A minute later, Sebastian returned. He climbed back in and sat. "The off-side leader caught a stone in his shoe. We've winkled it out, but the hoof's tender. The horse will have to be rested. Gifford says Radlett's the next town along. We should be able to get a replacement horse there, but until we do he'll have to take it slowly. It'll be late when we reach there."

Tabitha set her lips, firmed her chin. Tipped it a touch higher. "Nevertheless, I see no point in halting at Radlett. Best to get on, even if we reach home at midnight."

Sebastian raised his brows in a resigned manner. "We'll see."

What they saw when they finally limped into Radlett was hordes of carousing young gentlemen weaving about the main street. Tabitha stared. "They're drunk. All of them." That much was apparent. Many were singing, decidedly off-key; others were exchanging insults at the tops of their voices. "What the devil are they all doing here?"

Sebastian had been listening to the chants. Now he

groaned. "A boxing match. There was one held today some-where nearby."

Tabitha viewed his grim expression with concern. "What does that mean for us?"

They discovered the answer when they reached the Rad-lett Arms, the only inn the tiny town boasted. Gifford had trouble merely clearing the way enough to turn the carriage into the yard. Tabitha shut her ears to the swearing and curses issuing from the box above.

Increasingly grim, Sebastian reached for the carriage door. "Stay here."

She shifted to follow him. "Not a chance."

He met her eyes, then looked out of the window at the churning sea of mindless young men filling the yard. His jaw clenched. He nodded curtly. "You may be right. Just stick close—hold on to me and don't let go."

She inwardly scoffed—she was hardly a helpless female—but the instant she set foot on the cobbles she realized her mistake. She seized Sebastian's arm, then he reached back and caught her hand in his. Held it tightly.

Drunken men jostled her on every side. Most were young; she would have had no trouble freezing them in their tracks in a ballroom or in the park. In a poorly lit inn yard in a small country town, with not a *ton* matron in sight . . . that was another matter entirely. Most were nattily dressed, albeit somewhat the worse for wear, but their manners no longer matched their civilized appearance.

Luckily, the boisterous, uninhibited revelers—one step away from drunken louts—seemed to recognize something about Sebastian. They took one look at his face and backed off—enough at least for him to lead her through the throng to the inn's front door.

She glanced back and saw Gifford still on the box, glow-ering at the milling crowd, his long whip held firmly and rather obviously in one hand.

Then Sebastian tugged her through the door and into the main room of the inn. If anything, it was even more crowded than the yard, but he managed by sheer presence and the skillful application of a hard shoulder here and there, to forge a path to the bar.

The innkeeper, while transparently doing a roaring trade, was looking a tad besieged. He spotted them. His eyes widened. He pushed past his serving staff and hurried to the end of the bar. "Sir—it's . . ." He gestured to the mayhem all around. "They're here and won't be leaving until they've drunk my kegs dry. I wish I could help you and the lady, but you'd be wisest to drive on to St. Albans."

"We've just come from there—we're on our way to London. However—"

Watching the melee around them, Tabitha listened with half an ear while Sebastian explained in concise and forceful terms, his crisp accents in sharp contrast to the cacophony of slurring voices, why they could only go on if they could secure another horse.

She turned back to see the innkeeper vigorously shaking his head.

"I haven't a spare horse—this lot has taken them all. But it would do you no good, anyway—the London road's blocked. Some idiot ran his phaeton into the ditch, then another carriage ran into his. All told, six carriages ended locked together—they're saying they'll need a wheelwright to pull the mess apart. Some of my lads are down the road helping—last I heard, they thought it would be dawn before the road's clear."

Sebastian looked at Tabitha, then turned back to the innkeeper. "In that case, we'll need your best room."

"But—"

The innkeeper protested that the room was already let, but Sebastian inveigled and bribed, and ultimately reached an understanding with both the innkeeper and the two youthful sprigs who had originally hired the room. As it happened, both had lost heavily wagering on the boxing match and were happy to recoup their losses by agreeing to sleep in the hayloft.

Throughout the negotiations, Tabitha remained plastered to his side, reassurance and distraction combined. He didn't ease his hold on her hand; he was conscious that her fingers—having curled tightly about his in the inn yard—also hadn't eased their grip. The emotion that provoked was unnerving.

The two sprigs hied up the stairs to remove their bags from the room. Having satisfactorily concluded his business with the innkeeper, Sebastian dismissed the man with a nod, then turned and, once more placing himself in front of Tabitha, pushed into the crowd, heading for the stairs.

Given the density of bodies, some jostling was inevitable, but he kept a glower in place, discouraging any sufficiently inebriated to consider making any sort of try for Tabitha. He'd been young once, long ago, but he still remembered the utter invincibility of youth, and none of those there would have expected to see a gently bred lady in their midst.

It was very likely that, were they able to think, they'd question whether she was gently bred or not.

At least she'd kept her hood up, shielding her face, and with her cloak swathed about her there was precious little of her figure visible . . . but boys would be boys, and lads would be stupid. He was immeasurably relieved when they reached the stairs without him having to defend her honor other than by assisting drunken hellions out of their way.

He drew her forward, around him. Bent his head to whisper, "Go straight up. Don't look back. I'll be right behind you."

Although the majority of those in the inn were young, he'd noticed a few harder eyes, a few older, leaner faces, several predatory gazes that had drifted assessingly over her. He hoped his clear protectiveness would be sufficient to have those more dangerous gentlemen keep their distance. He was perfectly certain they, at least, would be sober enough to correctly interpret his behavior.

They reached the first floor gallery. The two happy sprigs came along, smiling as inanely as only the thoroughly intoxicated can. They tipped salutes his way, then clattered down the stairs.

He urged Tabitha on. "It's the room at the far end of the corridor."

They reached the door. He opened it, glanced inside, then waved her through, and followed.

Tabitha halted two steps into the room and surveyed the amenities. A massive four-poster bed sat against one wall, heavy swags of crimson brocade tied back to each post. Curtains of similar fabric had been drawn over the wide windows, shutting out the encroaching night. Two nicely padded armchairs were angled before the hearth in which a cheery fire blazed.

Walking to the bed, she tested the resilience of the mattress—adequate—noted the creamy linens were soft with age, but spotless. Turning, she sat on the bed and surveyed her partner, somewhat surprised to realize that that was how she now thought of him.

He'd closed the door, but was examining the bolt fixed to it. Apparently satisfied, he glanced at her. "I'll go and fetch our bags and arrange for a meal to be served to us here. I want you to bolt the door after I leave—don't open it for anyone but me, even if they claim to be the innkeeper's son bringing more coals for the fire."

She widened her eyes.

His lips tightened. "Promise you'll do as I say."

He was serious—deadly serious. She nodded. "Of course." It would be ungrateful to tease him, not when he was so tense, and on her behalf. "I'll just wait here until you come back."

He hesitated, as if comprehending that such capitulation was a concession, then nodded. "I won't be long."

Opening the door, he went out.

Tabitha considered the door, then rose, walked to it, threw the bolt, then listened.

Sure enough, his footsteps only then moved back up the corridor.

"Humph!" Turning, she contemplated the bed, then ambled to the armchair facing the door and flopped into it.

She wanted to move forward, was keen to take the next step to stop the blackmailer, whatever that step was. Fate, it seemed, had other ideas.

She grimaced and looked about the room again, searching for distraction. Finding none—even the three paintings on the walls were dull and uninspiring—she fixed her gaze on the flames leaping in the grate. Her lips curved at the thought of some enterprising hellion attempting to gain access by pretending to be the coal-boy.

To her it seemed a fanciful notion, but Sebastian . . . he took what he saw as his responsibilities seriously. He'd been a soldier, had done his duty by his country—had been prepared to give his life for that cause. His family had called on him to save the succession by sacrificing what many men would regard as their well-earned freedom; from all she'd heard, he'd accepted that duty, too, perhaps not happily, yet without complaint. Then she'd involved him in her mission to identify and vanquish the blackmailer, and once he'd committed himself to that endeavor, he'd accorded it his undivided attention.

To the point where he now saw her as someone it was his duty to protect.

In the past, any man seeking to protect her, let alone make a duty of it, would have received short shrift from her. Sebastian, however. . .

Head tilting, she stared unseeing at the flames and tried to pinpoint why he was different. Why she felt no overwhelming need to escape him and his protective tendencies. Indeed, quite the opposite; she'd been grateful more than once.

She saw his protectiveness clearly, yet felt none of her usual violent antipathy . . . perhaps because he hadn't at any stage tried to patronize her, to dictate, or to cast her as an adjunct. He'd never treated her as anything other than a capable adult, an equal.

Perhaps that was why, with him, she was behaving as one—why she was prepared to admit that she'd needed his escort into the inn, that she wouldn't have been comfortable, let alone safe, making her own independent way through the drunken throng. A year ago she would have tried to claim she could. Perhaps the years had finally brought wisdom?

She wasn't entirely sure that was true; beneath her mature exterior beat the undeniable heart of a hellion. Outrageous actions were the province of her branch of the Makepeaces, and in that regard she was her parents' daughter.

Yet no matter what she did, Sebastian probably wouldn't be shocked. He'd taken her breaking into Lord Rothbury's library in his stride, then had included her in the watch in the church, even though she'd had to be in disguise.

In her experience that made him a rare find—a rare gentleman.

One with whom she could be herself, a man who saw her clearly yet didn't feel moved to criticize.

A sharp rap interrupted her reverie.

Rising, as she walked to the door she called, "Who is it?"

"Trantor. Sebastian."

She felt herself smiling as she slid back the bolt and swung open the door.

He entered, carrying her bag and his. "Gifford says he's happy to sleep in the carriage—he wants to keep his eye on the horses. I've arranged for him to eat in the kitchen. The innwife will be up shortly with our meal."

Shutting the door, she turned. "You've thought of everything. Thank you."

He threw her a look, then set her bag beside the bed. He glanced at the crimson counterpane, then took his bag to the other side of the room and set it beneath the window. "You take the bed. I'll sleep before the fire."

She frowned, but before she could voice any protest, a tap on the door heralded the innwife bearing a large tray. Two girls followed, carrying various platters.

They ate before the fire, with the tray on a small table between the armchairs. It was a curiously comfortable meal.

The noise from below was muted by the thick walls, floors, and beams, and the solid oak door. They didn't speak of their mission—what was there to say?—but instead shared entertaining stories culled from their own experiences, or that of friends or family.

It was a relaxing time. As the fire died to glowing embers, Sebastian tried to imagine spending a similar evening alone with any other lady, and couldn't. The realization was unsettling.

A tap on the door proved to be a serving girl come to fetch the tray and build up the fire; with the door ajar, the sounds of the rowdy revelry below reached them. When the girl left, Sebastian held the door for her, then shut it and shot the bolt.

Turning back to Tabitha, he studiously ignored the large and comfortable bed. Reminded himself of the "long" in his long game; this was not an appropriate time or place to press his suit. "Gifford and I think we should leave at first light. The crowd below won't be stirring until later, and we want to be well ahead when they do. So we should get some sleep." He waved her to the bed.

She sighed, rose, and went toward the bed, to the far side, closer to the window. "I'm really not sure about that."

He forced himself to move toward the hearth. "About what?"

"About getting any sleep—not with that crowd below. Who knows what they may take it into their drunken heads to do?"

She was anxious? He hesitated, then, jaw clenching, bent to move the small table out of his way. "I'll be here by the fire. I don't believe any of them will try to force their way in, but if they do, rest assured I'll stop them."

"Hmm . . . perhaps." She stripped off the spencer she'd been wearing over her gown, then set her fingers to the gown's laces.

His mouth dried. He turned to face the flames—tried not to let the image of her sliding off her gown form in his mind.

But he heard the telltale swish of skirts, the soft rustling of petticoats, then the bed creaked. He waited for several heartbeats, then glanced her way.

Sitting propped against the pillows, the covers hiked to her shoulders, she was surveying the expanse beside her. "This is a large bed, and there's a lot of it unoccupied." Across the room, she met his gaze. "I would feel much safer—and will certainly find it easier to sleep—if you weren't so far away."

Even from across the room he saw the faint frown on her face, in her eyes—as if she couldn't quite believe she'd said that.

But then her gaze refocused on him. Her chin firmed. "I'll sleep much better if you're not all the way over there, but here"—she pointed to the other side of the bed—"within arm's reach."

Lust leapt, but he hauled it back, pushed it down. "I'm not sure that's a good—"

A crash reverberated in the corridor, accompanied by the thud of limbs hitting walls and floor. Drunken whispers reached them—more than loud enough to penetrate the oak door.

Tabitha jettisoned what little patience she'd possessed. "Oh, for pity's sake, Trantor—I'm not inviting you into my bed. You can sleep between the covers and the sheet—and keep your shirt and breeches on. That way, if any of those idiots tries to push their way in, you can respond immediately."

Why she wanted him beside her, close, she wasn't entirely sure, but some part of her mind was perfectly certain that that was where he should spend the night. As she'd said, within reach.

Yet even now he hesitated.

She growled and narrowed her eyes at him. "If you won't lie down here, you'll force me to come over there." She gripped the covers as if to push them back and rise—clad, as she was quite sure he'd noticed, only in her chemise. She had a prim white nightgown in her bag, but no degree of necessity would move her to don it, not when Sebastian would see her in it.

As she'd hoped, he held up a hand, staying her. "All right." He didn't sound happy about it, but he glanced at the fire, then crossed to the window and hauled the curtains apart; a wide swath of moonlight slanted across the room. Satisfied, he stalked to the lamp, turned it down, then, features tight, set, approached the other side of the bed.

Satisfied herself, she wriggled down beneath the covers. Steadfastly refused to think of why she'd argued, why, in all truth, she would feel more comfortable with him lying close. Close enough for her to sense his heat, his weight.

She watched as he shrugged off his coat and slung it over the foot of the bed. Then he sat on the edge and pulled off his boots. She heard the twin thuds as they hit the floor. Standing, he turned, glanced at her as he reached for the counterpane; without meeting his eyes, she shifted to her side, giving him her back.

He lay down, then stretched out beneath the counterpane, the sheet beneath him. His weight made the mattress dip on that side. Smiling, she snuggled down, locked her hand in the covers and, still smiling, closed her eyes.

Sleep came swiftly, and claimed her.

Lying supine beside her, Sebastian heard her breathing slide into the telltale cadence of slumber. Told himself that if him lying beside her was what it took to reassure her enough to sleep, then he could hardly argue against being where he was.

Indeed, most of him had no argument with his position at all . . . other than to wish it were closer. With fewer layers of cloth between.

But it was too soon for that. Even if his fantasies had already become ensnared in the possibilities, in the potential she possessed. He, his senses, hadn't forgotten an iota of the passion he'd detected during that burning kiss in Rothbury's library, nor in the too-brief repetition in the lane in Covent Garden.

Most of his senses were preoccupied with the prospect of experiencing that enticing passion again. A good part of his focus remained permanently distracted with plans to make that happen.

"But," he murmured, "I have to survive this first." It was a test. He wasn't entirely sure she hadn't engineered it purely to see how far she could trust him. Regardless, jaw clenched, he vowed to succeed. To lie there and endure, and not touch her.

Obviously he wasn't destined to get any sleep. Closing his eyes, he listened—and was immediately distracted by the soft sigh of her breathing. Gritting his teeth, he forced himself to ignore it, and listen instead for any further commotion beyond the room.

Several incidents occurred, but no boisterous fellow bumbled as far as the door at the end of the corridor.

Gradually, the inn quieted.

Contrary to his every expectation, he slept.

The dream, when it blossomed in his mind, was explicit. He was rolling on a bed half dressed, his partner in passion clad only in an insubstantial chemise. The sheets were a rumpled mass beneath their bodies; a soft cover slung over them kept the night's chill at bay.

Her lips were on his, under his. Parted and open, they lured him deeper into a wild, scorching exchange. Tongues tangled, stroked; like a siren she lured and promised a treasure more precious than gold.

In return, she wanted him.

The passionate nymph wanted her wicked way with him. He saw no reason to deny her.

Saw no reason to stop her unfastening his shirt, then pushing her small greedy hands beneath. She spread them and caressed, setting his skin alight, his senses burning. Just that simple touch, and he wanted so much more.

She pushed and he obliged, rolling onto his back. Hands closing about her waist, he settled her atop him. Lips locked, tongues dueling, she fell on him and claimed him, those wicked, greedy hands possessing with glorious and reckless abandon.

He sank one hand into her curly hair, all but felt its red fire singe him. That his dream nymph should possess Tabitha's characteristics was hardly a surprise; she'd been the woman in his dreams ever since he'd kissed her.

She pressed closer; the firm mounds of her breasts, screened by her chemise, pressed into his chest, the tight buds of her nipples clear evidence of her arousal.

Of her desire, her need, her transparent wanting.

He still had his breeches on, but she'd already bared his chest. No doubt she'd attend to the rest of his clothes shortly. He was looking forward to the moment.

Meanwhile . . . he set his hands to her sleek curves, and set about returning the pleasure she was currently lavishing on him. With hands and fingers, lips and tongue, he caressed; there was no rush, no hurry, only delicious urgency.

The fires between them built. She trembled and shook with the intensity.

Caught her breath when he slid his hand between her thighs and touched her there, found her hot and wet.

Her kiss grew urgently greedy, more needy, more demanding.

Between them, in a flurry of grasping hands, they stripped off his breeches, freed his throbbing staff.

He grasped handfuls of her chemise and wrestled it off over her head. Flung it aside as he reached for her.

And she reached for him. Her fingers closed about his rigid erection.

His breath hitched, caught.

Then he froze.

It wasn't her touch, but the sheer wonder investing it that sent a tendril of warning sliding into his lust-fogged brain.

The tendril became a lash as his reeling senses registered the implication behind that tentative touch. Innocence.

She was innocent. . .

She was real.

He returned to the world—the real world—in a rush. A barrage of sensory information confirmed that it was indeed Tabitha lying naked alongside him. That he and she weren't on some dream plane, but in the here and now.

Then she tightened her grip, stroked.

He bit back a groan, then hauled in a strained breath. "*Tabitha!*"

He might have been asleep, but she clearly hadn't been. For the first time in their acquaintance he was shocked.

The swath of moonlight had strengthened and now beamed across the bed. When she raised her head and looked into his face, in the silvery light he saw her eyes, sultry and seductive beneath heavy lids.

Her lips curved lightly, more wry than surprised. "I didn't mean this to happen. I must have rolled in my sleep—I woke up in your arms . . . and it felt right."

When he didn't respond—couldn't find suitable words—she went on, passion and quiet conviction in her tone, "This feels right. I'm twenty-six and I've never known this—never tasted passion, true passion, before." Her eyes locked on his, her hand still wrapped about his erection, she pressed closer, her breasts to his chest, her firm, sleek, silken thighs sliding over his much harder limbs. "I want you to teach me, to tutor me, to educate me—to show me the wonder I've never known."

He watched the words, her request, her plea, fall from her kiss-swollen lips.

Knew he had to resist. "I can't . . . take advantage of you like this. It's not right—can't be right." He shook his head fractionally. "It's not honorable."

"Even if I wish it?"

"Even then." He forced out the words, struggled to gain some distance; even mental distance would help. "We can't—"

She silenced him by placing a finger across his lips. "Wait. Before you say anything more, consider this."

Her tone remained sultry, alluring, sirenlike. She might be arguing, but he sensed she was confident she'd win.

Her gaze steady, heated yet sure, she continued, "You can't seriously imagine that, having come this far, tasted this much, that I'll be content to never know, to never savor the rest. But I'm the scandalous Miss Makepeace, on the shelf and unmarriageable, so if not here, now, with you, then with whom? I'll have to find some other gentleman to satisfy my curiosity."

Never. Involuntarily, his jaw clenched.

He'd heard that she—all her family—were frequently outrageous. His current position was the epitome of that—if he made her his now, there would be no going back, not for either of them, but she didn't know that.

She didn't know that he didn't consider her unmarriageable, that he was set on taking her off her shelf.

She didn't know that this—her and him rolling naked in a bed—had been slated to happen sometime in the not overly distant future. He'd imagined it would occur soon after the completion of their mission.

Fate—and she—apparently had a different agenda.

Or was it merely a different timetable?

Regardless, this one act—this one night of unexpected passion—would shift the campaign he'd been waging onto an entirely different plane.

A plane he was perfectly happy to further engage on.

Through the shimmering moonlight, he studied her eyes. Mind racing, considered. Even if he could find some way to resist her, was there any point?

Any verbal response risked being too revealing.

Reaching up, he framed her face, slowly drew her down until their lips met, then kissed her.

Slowly, unhurriedly, increasingly deeply.

When desire once more beat its heated wings beneath their skins, he drew back enough to murmur against her lips, "All right. But as in any other dance, I lead and you follow."

He didn't wait for her answer, but kissed her again. Took ruthless command of the exchange, then rolled them both over and settled her beneath him.

And gave her what she'd asked for, all she'd requested, and more.

He showed her what passion was, how it could flare and fill her, raze her defenses and consume every inhibition. Until it burned at her core, a conflagration hot and needy, until she ached to have him join with her and sate their desperation.

Caught in the throes, Tabitha gasped, clung, and greedily absorbed every touch, every stroke. Every possessive yet reverent caress. For all that he took, he gave even more. Through every incendiary exchange he strove to please her, to pleasure her.

To trap her with desire and feed her, appease her, with unstinting passion.

Until she urged him over her and he came, until he parted her thighs with his and with one powerful thrust joined them. Head bent, he drank her shocked gasp, gave her time only to register the feel of him, hard, hot, and solid at her core, then he moved, withdrew, surged anew, and the instant of pain, all memory of it, drowned beneath a tide of swelling pleasure.

A tide that built, that buffeted them, rocked them, and swept them up.

Swept them high.

Skins slick, fingers twining. Bodies merging to a rhythm older than time, they rode on—harder, higher, hearts pounding, senses spiraling. They crested the peak and raced on into glory, into flames and heat, straight into an implosion of sensation that seared every nerve, that scrambled reality with mind-bending pleasure.

That at the last left them breathless, hearts thundering, senses awash and drifting, wrapped in the cocoon of covers, safe in each other's arms.

Ecstasy receded, leaving a warm glow. Reality slowly seeped back into their minds.

He hung over her, his weight supported on his elbows, his head bowed as he struggled to catch his breath. She reached up and, smiling softly, laid a hand against his cheek. "Thank you."

Sebastian heard the words. He turned his head and pressed a kiss to her palm.

Struggled to take in the reality, its implications.

He'd been here before, yet it had never been like this. Never before had the moment had this depth, this intensity of feeling. As if after all his years of soldiering he'd finally come home and found safe harbor.

As if he'd finally found the place he was supposed to be.

The possessiveness that gripped him, that had already sunk its talons deep, shook him.

If he wasn't mistaken—and he knew he wasn't—his long game had taken an unexpected twist.

Summoning what remained of his strength, he lifted from her. Inwardly grinned at her sleepy protest, but she made no further demur when he slumped on his back and gathered her in, settled her against him.

She fell asleep on a sated sigh.

Later, hovering on the cusp of sleep, an earlier thought resurfaced, and he realized he'd been right. Sleeping beside her had been a test, but not in the way he'd thought.

All he could do now was hope that he'd passed, and cope with what came next.

Chapter Five

"Mr. Trantor, sir?"

Gifford's voice, accompanied by a scratching on the door, jerked Sebastian awake.

Warm silken limbs wrapped him in sensual comfort.

"Ah—yes, Gifford." He ran a hand through his hair, gritted his teeth as beneath the covers, Tabitha stirred. "We'll be down shortly." He prayed his leaping tension didn't show in his voice.

"Aye, sir. I'll have the horses put to."

"Good. Excellent."

Straining his ears, Sebastian heard Gifford's footsteps tracking away down the corridor. He fell back on the pillows. An instant ticked by as the events of the night reeled through his brain. Suppressing a curse, he quickly disentangled himself from Tabitha, forced himself to push back the counterpane and sit up.

"We have to get dressed and get downstairs quickly." His

back to her, he ignored the sensual frisson evoked by delicate fingers trailing down his spine.

"Why?" Her voice was all sultry seduction.

"Because we need to leave early before the hordes from the boxing match bestir themselves—remember?"

"Hmm . . . vaguely."

Having shrugged on his shirt and pulled on his breeches, he stood, tucking in the shirttails, then fastening the waistband.

When she heaved a heavy sigh, he finally met her eyes.

She looked deliciously, delightfully rumpled, temptation and outright sin incarnate.

She pouted, but—thank heaven—moved to get out of the bed. "You're serious. And here I thought that we'd had a wonderful time."

She'd turned away so he couldn't see her face. Then she bent over to pick up her chemise and gown; his mouth dried, his eyes wouldn't shift from the perfect, ripely rounded curves of her arse.

Then she straightened and swung to face him. He swallowed, said, "It was wonderful—better than wonderful." He finally glimpsed her eyes, read her expression. Frowned. "As you well know. But we really have to be on our way."

She smiled softly, as if his acknowledgment was all she'd really wanted. "Very well—but you'll have to help me with my laces."

Once again against all his expectations, they slipped out of the inn a mere five minutes later.

Five minutes after that, they were in the carriage and bowling down the road to London.

They reached London just after ten o'clock. Sebastian had Gifford drop him off outside the Coningsby townhouse in Cavendish Square. After promising Tabitha he'd join her in Bedford Square once he was presentable to discuss their next step, he waved the carriage on and went up the steps to his brother's front door.

Thomas and Estelle were still in the country, for which he gave thanks. There was no one there to question where he'd been, or to ask awkward questions. Wright met him in the hall and assured him a substantial breakfast could be assembled within minutes.

An hour later, washed, shaved, dressed in fresh, neatly pressed clothes and fortified by a large breakfast, he set out to walk the few blocks to Bedford Square.

It was tempting to use the moments alone to dwell on what had occurred during the night, but Tabitha's need to "do something" about the blackmailer was tangible; he needed to deal with that first.

Before he let himself consider what might come later—after their mission was complete and he had to convince her not to dissolve their charade of an engagement, but rather let it stand.

The events of the night had only underscored that, for him, that was the right path. His right path. To him, making Tabitha Makepeace his wife had assumed the status of a holy grail.

He wasn't sure whether the events of the past night would make his road smoother, or more difficult.

He wasn't sure he hadn't just dug huge potholes along his path.

But first things first; that had always been his maxim.

He entered the Makepeace residence to learn that Tabitha's parents had already left the house for their day's engagements, and that she awaited him—impatiently, he had not a doubt—in the back parlor.

Absolving Biggs of the need to announce him, he walked down the corridor, tapped on the door, and entered.

Tabitha was seated on the sofa. She looked up; expectation glowed in her face. "Well—what now? Clearly we must stop Elaine Mackay, but how should we go about it?"

She'd washed and dressed, too, and looked distractingly scrumptious in ivory sprigged with spring green.

He sat in one of the armchairs opposite the sofa. "The

first thing I believe we should ensure is the confidentiality of your friends' situations. Mackay must be stopped, but not at the cost of your friends' reputations." Or hers.

She waved. "That goes without saying. So we cannot threaten Elaine with exposure over her blackmailing of any of the four." She fixed him with a direct look. "So where does that leave us? What options do we have?"

He felt insensibly pleased that she was consulting him—truly asking and wanting to know what he thought—rather than just rushing ahead. "The only sure way forward I can see is to trap Mackay—to lure her with blackmail-worthy information about another young lady that is wholly invented and therefore of no real threat to said young lady, and then wait for her to bite. Once she does, we oblige with the payment and watch her receiving it as before, then tax her with it, with the luring, the receiving, and the taxing all done in the presence of a member of the police."

"Hmm . . . I'll leave organizing the police to you, but I believe I can provide just the right bait."

He smiled at the eagerness shining in her eyes, at the quick calculation behind them. "We've already set the perfect stage. Our engagement has been much talked about."

"Exactly! All the grandes dames have declared it a love match, and given the unexpectedness combined with our individual histories, it's been talked of extensively."

"Meaning the gossipmongers have had a field day."

"True, but in this case that's all to the good. The higher the stakes, the more succulent the bait. And even more to the point, our engagement ball is four days away. What could be more natural but that I take my friends' recommendations regarding who to have in to dress my hair?"

She paused, then went on, "And I know the perfect incident to use as the basis for our bait." She met his eyes. "You'll have to trust me as to what it is—I haven't yet worked out how best to present it. But I assure you, once she hears of it, Elaine Mackay will not be able to resist blackmailing me."

* * *

With their engagement ball only four days away, they had no time to lose. They consulted Mrs. Makepeace; as she already knew and approved of their mission, convincing her to assist them took no time at all.

However, as Mrs. Makepeace pointed out, there were procedures to be followed. "You cannot simply summon such a person to attend you on the day. She will expect to be interviewed ahead of time, and to discuss and consider styles, then to have her fee negotiated and agreed. We had a lovely young man in to dress Lydia's hair, but in the interests of justice, and as this woman's work is clearly acceptable, I see no reason we shouldn't summon her for a consultation tomorrow."

So it was that the following morning Sebastian sat beside Tabitha on the sofa in the drawing room, with Mrs. Makepeace seated in an armchair to his right, and watched Elaine Mackay walk calmly into the room.

Her gaze swept them, then she curtsied demurely.

"Please do sit, Miss Mackay." Mrs. Makepeace waved to the straight-backed chair set before them.

With an elegant nod, Elaine Mackay came forward. She was of above average height, with smooth brown hair sleeked back in a neat bun at her nape, and well set greeny-brown eyes. Beyond that, she was unremarkable; there was no feature of face or person that might induce anyone to pick her out in a crowd.

She halted and nodded to them before she sat, perching on the edge of the chair and clasping both hands on the plain brown reticule she balanced on her knees. "I'm honored to be considered for your upcoming event, ma'am." Her glance took in Sebastian, and the easy way he held one of Tabitha's hands. She looked back at Mrs. Makepeace. "I take it it's an engagement ball?"

"Indeed. We've heard that your work has proved most satisfactory, and in some instances seen the results." With a regal wave, Mrs. Makepeace indicated Tabitha's wild curls; for the occasion, she'd left them free—they formed a vibrant corona about her head. "As you can see, my daughter will pose something of a challenge. Do you think you're up to it?"

A spark of purely professional interest lit Elaine Mackay's eyes. After a moment's consideration, she said, "I've faced more difficult tasks—if I might point out, Miss Makepeace's coloring is excellent, and while any tightly structured form would be a struggle, I believe that by careful choice of style, a most sophisticated result could ensue." She turned back to Mrs. Makepeace. "What style did you have in mind, ma'am?" She glanced at Tabitha. "Miss?"

Tabitha merely smiled eagerly and clasped her other hand over Sebastian's; they'd agreed she needed to project an image of scatterbrained innocence.

"We thought Grecian might suit," Mrs. Makepeace replied. "But I would like to hear something of your background in the field—what brought you to it, and how long you've been practicing."

"Oh, I've always been good with hair—since I was a little girl in Edinburgh."

Her brogue was so faint, Sebastian concluded she'd left Scotland a great many years ago.

"As to my experience, I've been dressing hair in the theaters for many years. I realize it's not appropriate to compare young ladies making their come-outs, or at their engagement or wedding balls, to great actresses, yet both are examined very closely and constantly while they are on their stage, on their particular day."

Mrs. Makepeace raised her brows. "Very true. It is an apt analogy." She paused as if considering, then went on, "I believe we might come to some arrangement, but if you would, I would like to get a better idea of what style you would suggest for dear Tabitha"—Mrs. Makepeace paused to glance approvingly at the picture both Sebastian and Tabitha were endeavoring to present of a besotted young lady and her possessively attached fiancé, then looked meaningfully at Elaine Mackay—"on the occasion of the ball to celebrate her engagement to Mr. Trantor."

Elaine Mackay turned to study Tabitha. Sebastian noted that she also surreptitiously studied him, taking in the subdued elegance of his attire, no doubt evaluating his wealth and consequent worth to the Makepeaces. He'd dressed for the occasion, down to the ornate gold-and-diamond pin anchoring his cravat.

Eventually, Elaine Mackay rose, and indicated the straight-backed chair. "If Miss Makepeace would oblige me by sitting here, I can give you some idea of what I think would suit."

Tabitha eagerly leapt up and sat, smiling at Sebastian in a thoroughly giddy way as she did. He had to fight to suppress a grin. Elaine Mackay had an actress as her client, even if she didn't know it.

"And if I could view the gown . . ." Elaine Mackay darted a glance at Sebastian. "That is, if it's not being kept a secret."

Tabitha waved the notion aside. "I have no secrets from dear Sebastian." She all but glowed. "None. Our union will be based on the utmost trust, you see."

She kept her bright gaze on Sebastian's face, so didn't see the sly smile that, for a fleeting instant, curved Elaine Mackay's lips. "Well, then." All business, she turned to Mrs. Makepeace. "If I could see the gown, we can confirm the style. But while it's being fetched . . . let's see."

For the next five minutes, Elaine Mackay bunched and pinned Tabitha's hair, talking continuously about curling tongs and irons, hair padding and ornaments. Mrs. Makepeace held her own, displaying a knowledge Sebastian hadn't thought she would possess. When Tabitha's maid arrived with a delicate gown of sea-green silk, Elaine broke off to admire it with a knowing eye, and compliment the selection.

Watching her performance, Sebastian had to admit that she used sincerity to great effect. The overall impact was of a helpful and knowledgeable artiste, one who was an expert in her field and appreciated the artistry of others in theirs.

Only the calculation that hovered behind her eyes gave any hint of her untrustworthy nature.

Eventually, Mrs. Makepeace declared herself more than satisfied. Tabitha bounced up and rushed to a mirror; turning this way and that, she examined the roughly constructed style. Elaine Mackay quickly followed to point out various elements and explain how it would look when properly done on the day.

With everyone happy and satisfied, Mrs. Makepeace made a generous offer, one Elaine Mackay accepted with the barest of hesitations.

After she'd gathered her reticule and departed, that sly smile again playing about her lips as she turned away, Sebastian held up a hand to halt any exclamations, waited until he heard the front door close, then smiled at Mrs. Makepeace. "You were inspired." He looked at Tabitha. "And if I didn't know better, I would think you a fluff-brain intent on nothing more than pleasing me." His smile widened. "You were brilliant. You were both brilliant. That last hesitation of hers was just for show—she'd already taken the bait."

"Excellent!" Mrs. Makepeace declared, jaw firming, a militant look in her eye.

"Now for our next step," Tabitha said.

Looking from mother to daughter, taking in the feminine resolution etched in their features, Sebastian could only be glad that Elaine Mackay couldn't see them now.

The day of their engagement ball rolled around surprisingly quickly. With Sebastian, Tabitha had filled the intervening two days with the typical social events a newly affianced couple would attend. Keeping up appearances, as they dubbed it, yet she was a trifle unnerved by how easy it was to hang on Sebastian's arm and pretend to be his lady.

After their night at the Radlett Arms—which they hadn't yet had any chance to discuss—she was aware that their interactions had taken on a new depth, a subtle shading she suspected arose from that intimacy. Beyond that thought, she steadfastly refused to let her mind wander further and dwell on what had occurred. Not yet—not while their mission was under way and she had to keep her wits about her.

What hours she'd spent apart from Sebastian had gone in polishing her story, the secret she would, when suitably encouraged, divulge to Elaine Mackay. She'd lied often enough in her youth, and had generally been successful; she'd long ago absorbed the successful liar's code: stick to the truth as far as possible. In this case, that wasn't difficult.

Two years before, her sister Lydia and Tabitha's now-brother-in-law Ro Gerrard had retrieved a letter she'd unwisely written in her late teens to the then-imagined love of her life. The contents of the letter would have been embarrassing enough for even the giddiest young lady, but for Tabitha, with her widely known views on marriage and her position in the Sisterhood, publication of that old letter within the *ton* would have reduced her to a laughingstock.

That was the fabric of truth she intended to embroider. All she needed to do to create a highly sensitive secret was change the names and overemphasize the details.

Elaine Mackay was due to wait on Tabitha at four o'clock in Bedford Square. Their ball was to be held at Ro and Lydia's London home, Gerrard House in Grosvenor Square. It would be preceded by a formal dinner, also at Gerrard House.

By half past three, Tabitha had bathed and, swathed neck to toe in a voluminous wrapper, her hair a frizzy halo about her head, stood in the first-floor gallery of her parents' house and watched Sebastian ascend the main stairs, another man following close behind.

Reaching the top of the stairs, Sebastian turned toward her. His lips curved; his gaze raced over her, then returned to her face. "Good afternoon, my dear." He took her hand, briefly raised it to his lips, then turned to introduce the other man. "This is Inspector Stokes. He's recently taken up a position in Peel's new force, and is eager to see what he can make of our case."

"Miss Makepeace." Stokes inclined his head politely.

Tabitha was agreeably surprised. She'd heard a great many tales of policemen, most highly uncomplimentary. Stokes, however, was neatly and unobtrusively dressed, well enough to appear abovestairs in a gentleman's home without causing undue comment. His manners, too, while reserved, seemed natural; he was an inch or two shorter than Sebastian, dark haired and dark featured, and otherwise perfectly presentable. And if she'd interpreted Sebastian's introduction correctly, Stokes was ambitious for success, which boded well for his commitment. She deigned to bestow a welcoming smile upon him. "Good day, Inspector." Glancing at Sebastian, she waved down the corridor. "Let me show you our stage, and your hide."

Turning, she led the way down the corridor to an open door. Entering the room beyond, she paused in the center, waited until both men joined her, then waved at the large dressing table set against one side wall. "That is where I will sit. Miss Mackay will stand behind me as she dresses my hair. We chose this room because, while it has a lady's dressing room to that side"—she pointed to where another door stood open, revealing a welter of skirts and bandboxes—"it also has a gentleman's dressing room on this side." She indicated a matching door to the right of the dressing table; that door stood slightly ajar, with the room beyond in darkness. "Naturally, as this is supposed to be my bedchamber, that gentleman's dressing room would be expected to be unused. If you stand in there and make no sound, there will be no reason for Miss Mackay to suspect you are there, yet you'll be close enough to hear every word she and I exchange."

Stokes, who, now she could see him clearly, appeared quite young, looked eager. "If I may . . . ?" He pointed to the door. When Tabitha nodded, he pushed it open, looked in, then stepped inside. He glanced back at them around the door. "If you could sit at the table, Miss Makepeace—and Trantor, perhaps you could stand behind her?"

They dutifully took up those positions. Stokes closed the door until it was an inch away from being shut. "Trantor—can you see me?"

Sebastian looked, as did Tabitha. After a moment, he shook his head. "Not really. If you don't move, your clothes merge into the shadows—as she won't know you're there, even if she looks that way, it's unlikely Miss Mackay would detect you."

"Excellent!" Stokes opened the door and came out. He inclined his head to Tabitha. "I applaud your arrangements, Miss Makepeace." He looked at Sebastian. "It appears our stage is set."

"Now all we need is our principal player." Sebastian raised his brows as the front doorbell peeled.

They all listened, heard Biggs cross the hall, then his stentorian voice carried up the stairs. "I believe Miss Tabitha is ready for you—I'll send for her maid. She'll take you up."

Tabitha waved her hands at both Sebastian and Stokes. "Into the dressing room. We arranged for my maid, Tilly, to bring Miss Mackay up, then Tilly will stay and fuss for a few minutes, then leave us alone."

"Very good." Stokes led the way into the dressing room.

Sebastian grinned at the excited anticipation in Tabitha's face. He bent his head and pressed a swift kiss to her lips. "Good luck." Then he followed Stokes into the darkened dressing room.

Tabitha pressed her hands to her cheeks, then drew in a deep breath. She did indeed feel as if she were stepping onto a stage. One on which she'd have to improvise to a large degree. She had to hope Elaine Mackay would give her the opening she needed to impart her secret, and that she wouldn't do anything to make the woman suspicious.

Hearing footsteps approaching, she checked the almost closed door of the dressing room, then, satisfied there was nothing to give the men away, she sank onto the stool before the dressing table, and schooled herself to play her part. She had to build on her earlier appearance before Miss Mackay and pretend to a naivety she'd never possessed.

"Oh! There you are." She swung to beam at Elaine Mackay as Tilly ushered her into the room. Swinging back to face the mirror, she plumped up her flyaway hair. "I've been thinking . . . do you really think the Grecian style will be best?"

With a confident smile, Elaine Mackay set a package containing her implements down on the dressing table and smoothly moved into what Tabitha mentally dubbed her reassurance mode. Tilly bustled about, then went into the lady's dressing room. She came out with Tabitha's petticoats over one arm. Laying them out on the bed, she turned to Tabitha. "I'm just going down to check over your ball gown—it might need the iron put to it."

Tabitha, engrossed in Elaine Mackay's transformation of her hair—she really was a gifted hairdresser—waved Tilly off. "Take your time and make sure every last crease is gone—I want everything to be perfect for tonight."

"Yes, miss." With a bob, Tilly was gone.

Tabitha waited. Minutes ticked by with nothing more than a comment here and there about this curl or that. She was starting to feel anxious, but then Elaine Mackay murmured, "It's such a wonderful time in a young lady's life—getting engaged."

Eyes wide, fixed on her own reflection, Tabitha made a breathless sound of agreement. In the corner of her vision she caught the sly, measuring look Elaine Mackay sent her way.

"Why," the hairdresser said, paying attention to a stray curl, "in many ways it's as if you leave your old life behind, all the mistakes and stumbles, and start afresh as a soon-to-be new bride."

Tabitha nodded emphatically. "Yes, exactly . . . oops—sorry."

Her smile a touch strained, Elaine reset the curl Tabitha had yanked out. "It must be such a relief not to have to worry anymore about past indiscretions. I know many of my young ladies have said that."

"Oh, yes!" Tabitha gushed. "I know just how they feel."

"Indeed?" Polite skepticism colored Mackay's voice. "But I wouldn't imagine you had any truly worrisome episode in your past."

"Oh, but I have! You have no idea." Tabitha lowered her voice. "I'm just so relieved that once I marry Mr. Trantor I can forget all about the letter."

"Letter?"

"Hmm. It's such a silly thing to have done." In the tone of a naive girl recounting a past incident to someone she trusted without any true appreciation of the potential for harm vis à vis her current situation, Tabitha babbled, suitably disjointedly, through her embellished tale of a highly inflammatory letter explicitly alluding to a lover's tryst—she allowed the implication that the tryst had culminated in intimacy to slide through—ultimately explaining in an airy way how such a letter surfacing now would shred her reputation.

As the tale that she had once believed herself utterly, romantically, and most definitely physically, in love with the gentleman now popularly known as Addison the Spineless Wonder truly would play havoc with her image, she substituted Addison with a blameless young gentleman who she knew had been with the army in Spain over the time her supposed indiscretion had taken place.

Elaine Mackay was an excellent listener; even knowing her motives, Tabitha found it remarkably easy to blab her secret.

The exercise, however, brought home to her how betrayed and lost her friends must have felt when the blackmailer's demand arrived. The conversation with Elaine remained so inconsequential, constantly interrupted by details about her hair and with Elaine giving the impression that she wasn't really listening, Tabitha finally understood how her friends might have revealed their secrets, then forgotten that they had.

A hairdresser, after all, was one of those people one didn't truly see. They came, they did one's hair, they went—and had no other connection to their clients' lives.

But although she hid her interest well, Tabitha was certain Elaine Mackay drank in every detail she revealed.

She knew it was a ploy, a staged act—not real—yet in thinking ahead, imagining how she would feel when the demand arrived and threatened her future with Sebastian . . . she felt nauseous.

As if she felt truly threatened . . . as if she truly had a future with Sebastian. . .

Oh, God. She truly did want a future with Sebastian.

Elaine was busy with the back of her head.

Shocked by the insight, nearly frantic, Tabitha consulted her true feelings . . . Her heart sank.

How had this happened?

But then Elaine straightened. Tabitha hurriedly bundled the startling truth from her mind and plastered on a suitably vacuous smile. "It looks lovely. I adore those bouncy little curls on top."

With a smile and a few words, Elaine encouraged Tabitha's focus on her creation.

Five minutes later, Elaine packed her implements. Tabitha rang for Tilly, who appeared and briskly escorted Miss Mackay downstairs.

Reseated on the dressing stool, but now facing the open door, Tabitha waited until she heard the front door shut, then slumped back against the dressing table. "You can come out—she's gone."

Stokes came out, followed by Sebastian.

Stokes nodded approvingly at her. "That was an excellent performance, Miss Makepeace."

Sebastian's approbation shone in his eyes. "An inspired performance."

Tabitha felt wrung out, but manufactured a smile. "Thank you."

"Now all we have to do," Stokes said, "is wait for Miss Mackay to take the bait."

* * *

Tabitha smiled into Sebastian's eyes as they circled the ball-room in Gerrard House to the strains of their engagement waltz. "I can't quite believe we're doing this." Couldn't believe how genuine it felt, how much she wanted it to be real.

"We are—and if I say so myself, we're highly convincing." His eyes locked with hers, his lips lightly curved, he whirled her swiftly—exhilaratingly—through the turn at the bottom of the long room. As they precessed back up the polished floor, other couples joined them—Ro and Lydia, Sebastian's brother Thomas and his wife, Estelle, who had arrived in London only the previous night. Tabitha's parents joined in, then a host of guests stepped out; two minutes later the floor was crowded.

Sebastian slowed their progress so they merged with the other couples.

Tabitha forced her thoughts back to their charade. "We survived the dinner better than I expected. Coping with our families was one thing, but keeping our facade intact before the grandes dames . . . I wasn't sure we could pull that off."

"But we did, and not one of them doubted. I overheard several say what an exceptional couple we make."

"I hadn't expected they'd all be so interested in my imminent nuptials, but if anything, their avidity is even greater than it was with Lydia and Ro." She lightly grimaced. "I suppose because they'd given up hope of me ever marrying."

Sebastian caught her gaze, held it.

She got the impression he was considering what to say, frowned lightly. "What is it?"

After a further moment of hesitation, he said, "I admit it's necessary for us to put on a good show—to give everyone what they expect to see—but there's no reason we shouldn't enjoy the moment, exactly as if it were real."

Something inside her quivered. "But it's not."

"It's as real as we wish to make it. Tonight, we're an engaged couple." He glanced at the hand she had resting on his shoulder. "You wear my ring, and I think—" He broke off, then smiled and met her eyes. "I think you're the most mesmerizing lady I've ever had the pleasure of holding in my arms."

"Oh." She couldn't deny the frisson of delight that shot through her. As it faded, she lifted her head. "You're right. We should enjoy tonight for what it is, and leave tomorrow and whatever comes for tomorrow."

"Precisely." He gathered her in for the next turn. As they emerged from it, he murmured, "Incidentally, don't be tempted to dance with Freddie. He has two left feet and will almost certainly tread on your hem."

She laughed, and accepted his advice, let the role she'd agreed to play take hold—and for that one evening gave herself over to being . . . the lady Sebastian wanted in his arms.

Sebastian eventually had to yield to the press of requests and allow other gentlemen to dance with his betrothed. The degree of discipline he had to exercise to smile and permit it was merely the latest symptom of his evolving possessiveness—an emotion of which he was increasingly aware.

He made an effort not to stand and brood, or, worse, glower, and forced himself to make a circuit of the room, stopping to chat with various guests, as he suspected he should. His aunts were thrilled. Tabitha's parents were smiling. Her sister Lydia beamed and kissed his cheek—then whispered that she hoped he would triumph.

As the look in her fine eyes conveyed that she understood his true goal was to convince Tabitha to marry him, he took her encouragement as a good sign.

Despite his good intentions, he'd come to a halt by the side of the room, his gaze fixed on Tabitha as she whirled about the floor in the arms of some dandified sprig, when Robert Gerrard—Viscount Gerrard, or Ro as the family called him—strolled up. Halting beside Sebastian, he, too, looked out at the dancers. Said, his deep voice low, "Mr. and Mrs.

Makepeace explained the situation—your novel tack to winning Tabitha's hand. I feel compelled to wish you luck—and to tell you that if you hurt Tabitha, I will hurt you."

Sebastian, his gaze still on the fiery head of his betrothed, merely raised his brows. "If I hurt Tabitha, I hurt myself even more."

Ro turned his head and looked at him.

Sebastian obligingly glanced his way, saw his putative brother-in-law's eyes widen slightly, then Ro's lips curved and he inclined his head. "Good answer."

They both looked back at the dancers, at Tabitha.

"Incidentally," Ro said, his tone warmer, conversational, "Lydia thinks your quest is highly romantic. Me, I'd call it as eccentric as anything any Makepeace ever did—putting the betrothal before the wooing." He caught Sebastian's gaze, tipped his head to him and grinned. "Welcome to the family."

"Thank you," Sebastian dryly replied. "I'll do my poor best to fit in."

Chapter Six

$\mathcal{F}$or the next four days, they played the part of a rapturous, newly betrothed couple—a necessary strategy to ensure Elaine Mackay had good reason to act. They were seen at the most select balls every night, and strolled in the park at least once a day, receiving the accolades of their peers and the blessings of the most haughty of the *ton*'s matrons.

But the grandes dames kept their eagle eyes on them. Strolling beside the Avenue on Sebastian's arm, Tabitha leaned close to murmur, "It's as if they want to ensure there's no backsliding."

She straightened, after a moment added, her tone cooler, "I wonder what they'll say when we cry off."

Sebastian glanced at her, then covered the hand resting on his sleeve, squeezed lightly. "Let's go for a drive—there's something I want to show you."

Raising his arm, he signaled to his tiger, who'd been holding the black gelding harnessed to his curricle.

Lengthening her stride to keep up with his increased pace, Tabitha glanced at his face, saw determination of a sort she couldn't place in his features. "What is it, this thing you wish to show me?"

"You'll see when we get there." He briefly met her gaze. "It's a recent acquisition on which I'd like your opinion."

As he clearly didn't wish to tell her more, she held her tongue and let him help her up into the curricle. He joined her on the box seat. The diminuitive tiger swung up behind as, with an expert flick of the reins, Sebastian set the black pacing.

He drove out of the park, then tacked through the early afternoon traffic. He turned up Orchard Street, then continued northward along Baker Street. Far ahead, beyond the end of the street, Tabitha could see the greenery of Regent's Park. She glanced at Sebastian curiously, but he was busy managing his horse; it didn't seem wise to attempt to probe.

Eventually, he turned into the carriage drive that circled Regent's Park, veering left along the facade of the various recently completed terraces.

To her surprise, he slowed the curricle, easing the carriage into the elegant curve of Nash's celebrated Sussex Place. Sebastian halted the curricle outside Number Twenty. Handing the reins to his tiger, he stepped down to the gravel, then rounded the back of the curricle to hand her down.

Her hand in his, he pushed open the wrought-iron gate and led her up the path to the front door.

A cherry tree wept blossoms in the narrow front garden. She looked up at the elegant lines of the facade. "Who lives here?"

Then she realized he'd pulled a key from his pocket. Fitting it to the lock, he glanced back at her. "I do."

He set the door open, then waved her through. Surprised, she stepped across the threshold into a narrow, airy hall lit by a skylight high above. The floor was all polished boards; her footsteps echoed. She turned to face him as he followed her in, shutting the door behind him. "I thought you lived at your brother's house while in London."

He pulled a face. "I did. Thomas and I originally thought that, as we both spend at least half the year in the country, we could share the ancestral abode while in town. But then he arrived with Estelle and their five young daughters. I did mention that the youngest was barely three months old, I believe?"

She smiled. "You did."

"You'll recall I also mentioned I'm something of a scholar, that I like deciphering old scripts and ancient codes?" When she nodded, he smiled wrily. "Once my nieces arrived, Thomas and I realized our idea of sharing the family town-house wasn't going to work."

He glanced around. "So I bought this. I haven't had a chance to furnish it yet—I thought I'd wait . . . but here." He waved her to the first door on the right. "I bought one piece, just to see how it would suit. Take a look, and tell me what you think."

She walked in. Her gaze was immediately caught by the elegant lines of the white marble mantelpiece framing the hearth directly opposite the door. From there, she looked up, walking further into the room as she took in the finely wrought decorative moldings on the cornices and ceiling. A delicate chandelier depended from the central rose.

The floor beneath her feet was richly polished oak; the ceiling was painted white, as were the doors, architraves, and window frames. The walls were a soft dove gray; the color reminded her of his eyes.

She swung to the window, and caught her breath. The long panes framed the weeping cherry tree and its pale pink and white blossoms, with the green lawns of the park across the carriage drive and the glint of light on the water of the boating lake in the distance.

Her gaze lowered and fastened on the one piece of furniture in the room—a sculpted chaise longue. The honey tones of oak gleamed in the delicately shaped and carved frame. The upholstery was gray silk, a subtle shade darker than the walls, finished with white piping.

Placed before the window, before that view, the chaise was perfection incarnate.

"It's . . ." She searched for words. "Exquisite."

Turning her head, she studied his face, then met his eyes. "You're a man of many talents, Sebastian Trantor. Some of them unexpected." She moved closer, raised a hand to his cheek. "The lady who marries you will be lucky indeed."

She'd never meant any words more.

But she gave herself and him no time to dwell on them—to dwell on the fact that whoever he eventually married, it wouldn't be her. That once Elaine Mackay made her demand and they trapped her retrieving the payment, their mission would be complete, and their betrothal would end.

She kissed him. Boldly. With all the sultry passion he'd taught her she possessed. With an intent she hadn't even paused to consider, but simply knew was right.

With a desperation she felt to her heart, to her soul, throughout her being.

If she was fated to never again know passion, then she'd take what she could, with him, now. And if it might be thought unfair to the lady whose drawing room this delicate, perfect room would eventually be, she nevertheless felt that hypothetical lady owed her this much. Owed her this afternoon of pleasure in return for letting him go.

Setting him free.

Sebastian found himself enthralled all over again. Caught in the web of her desires, trapped by his need to respond. To trace, to take, to savor.

To pleasure her until she gasped and clung.

To caress her until she writhed and demanded.

Until, with her hair burning the gray silk of the chaise, she drew him down, took him in, and loved him.

Drew him into her heat and saved him. Claimed him.

Both of them wanted with a powerful need, but both

strove to hold the urgency at bay. To instead take the slow path, and fill the afternoon with their sighs.

To explore, and learn, and know. To take pleasure in giving, and in receiving.

To challenge, then submit. To lead, and then to follow.

To let the journey take them as passion rose and desire burned and need inexorably climbed.

Until they surged as one and reached for the stars.

And the spiraling glory caught them, shattered them, and drowned them in ecstasy.

Later, Tabitha refused to let him speak. She had a dreadful suspicion that her desperation had been all too evident, that he'd seen too much, read too accurately, and now knew the panicked yearning in her heart.

She didn't want to hear excuses; explanations would be tedious.

She didn't think she could bear to hear him being kind.

So wrestling with her petticoats, ignoring her half-dressed state, she put her foot down and imperiously declared, "*Do not* say a word. Don't spoil the moment. Let it be what it is and accept it for that."

His breeches still unbuttoned, his shirt gaping, Sebastian met her gaze; his eyes were stormy—she could tell from the set of his lips that he didn't agree with her decree. But she'd judged him correctly. He nodded curtly. "If you wish."

He looked down and laced his cuffs. She wriggled into her gown, then presented him with her back. "If you could help . . . ?"

He humphed, and rapidly did up her laces. Five minutes later, they were back in the curricle and heading back to Bedford Square.

Sebastian had hoped to make more headway toward his ultimate goal—perhaps even admit to his true agenda—but her decree . . . then again, he couldn't regret those moments in what he already thought of as their drawing room. The house, the chaise, all had gone as he'd planned—better than he'd planned. He hadn't imagined she would react as she had, that the place would move her in that way, but he couldn't in all honesty complain. If nothing else, the interlude had confirmed just how perfectly suited they were in every way.

He'd simply have to find another opportunity to break the news to her that their sham betrothal was to him no sham.

He drew rein outside her parents' townhouse. Leaving his tiger with the reins, he escorted Tabitha up the front steps. Biggs opened the door to them; Tabitha went in and he followed, intending to take his leave of her in the back parlor. And preferably steal another kiss while he was at it.

But after closing the door, Biggs lifted a salver from the hall table. "A letter for you, miss—a boy brought it around an hour or so ago."

One glance informed Sebastian that the letter wasn't merely another invitation card. Alert, he waited as Tabitha looked back, then retraced her steps.

She lifted the letter from Biggs's salver, then glanced at him. "Let's go into the parlor."

He followed her down the hall.

In the parlor she walked to the window, broke the seal on the letter, smoothed out the single sheet. Angled it to the light and read. She met his eyes as he joined her. "This is it—the blackmailer's demand."

She offered him the sheet.

He took it. The few lines required less than a minute to read. "We need to send for Stokes."

Tabitha crossed to the bellpull. When Biggs answered the summons, she asked for a footman to be sent to Bow Street.

Stokes didn't keep them waiting. Within the half hour he was standing on the parlor rug scanning the missive. "Tomorrow at ten in the morning." His eyes narrowed. "That doesn't give you much time to think."

"It was the same with Rothbury's payments," Sebastian said. "The first demand gives the target a day, but subsequent demands—which escalate in amount—give increasing notice."

Stokes nodded. "Because after the first payment is made, she's sure the target is hooked, and she's smart enough not to scare her targets off at the first jump—just look at this sum. A pony. Significant, but not that much when all's considered. Tempting enough to think that the easiest way out is simply to pay."

"So." Seated on the sofa beside Sebastian, Tabitha fixed her gaze on Stokes. "What will we do?"

Stokes looked again at the letter, then at Sebastian.

Sebastian turned to Tabitha. "We do precisely as she asks, and give her her due."

Chapter Seven

𝒯he following morning at half past nine, Sebastian handed Tabitha down from her parents' town coach at the eastern end of Fleet Street. St. Bride's Church stood in a quiet court between two buildings to the south of the bustling thoroughfare. On Sebastian's arm, Tabitha held up her skirts as they crossed the street, then entered the churchyard.

At the center of its court, the church could be approached from virtually every direction; there were countless alleys and shadowy runnels from which someone might have been watching them.

They halted a few steps from the church door. Any watcher would have interpreted the ensuing charade as Tabitha wanting a private moment alone inside the church, possibly to pray or to remember some dead relative. Sebastian agreed with a shrug. Slipping his hands into his pockets, he settled to wait, looking idly back at the traffic thronging Fleet Street.

Tabitha entered the church alone. Their plan was relatively simple. Follow the instructions in the note and put the package containing the money—they were taking no chances; Sebastian had produced twenty new five-pound notes—into the pocket for music sheets carved into the side of the first choir stall on the right, then Stokes and his constables would keep watch and follow whoever fetched the money until the package reached Elaine Mackay's hands.

Entering the shadows of the church's foyer, Tabitha looked around. To make a charge easy to prosecute, Stokes had to see her put the package into the choir-stall pocket, then see whoever came to get it pick it up, and keep them in sight as they—they assumed the courier would be another young lad—ferried it to Elaine Mackay's house, and ultimately placed it in her hands. It was, apparently, highly preferable for Stokes to keep the package, or whoever was carrying it, in sight at all times.

Moving into the nave, Tabitha was reassured to see Stokes lounging in one of the rear pews. He saw her and nodded, but it might have been merely a polite acknowledgment rather than a greeting. Not, Tabitha noted as she continued more confidently down the center aisle, that at that hour there was anyone else about to see.

But they'd agreed to behave as if Elaine Mackay herself was watching; even though they'd come early, for all they knew, when she took on a new "client," Elaine might take a more personal interest in the proceedings.

Tabitha made her way to the first choir stall on the right. After glancing once more around the church, she drew the packet from her reticule, and deposited it in the music-sheet pocket.

Her part played, she turned and walked briskly back up the aisle. Drawing level with Stokes, she surreptitiously gave a little wave. He responded with a stern look, but she saw his lips twitch.

When he'd met her and Sebastian in Bedford Square an hour ago, he'd brought two young constables with him to keep watch and assist as needed; she didn't know where the pair were, but they'd been dressed as laborers the better to blend with the many thronging the pavements.

Stepping out into the sunshine, she saw Sebastian waiting on the path ahead. He'd been watching the street, but as if sensing her presence, glanced back at her. She smiled, walked forward and slid her arm into his. "All done. Stokes was there and saw all as required."

"Good." Sebastian closed his hand over hers on his sleeve as they walked toward the street. "I suggest we take his advice and depart. We can repair to the other end of Fleet Street. If, as we expect, she sends another boy to fetch the packet, he'll almost certainly pass that spot on his way to deliver it."

"How will we know which boy to follow?" As they stepped onto the street, she waved at the hordes busily bustling in every direction. "There's boys of all sorts everywhere."

"Only one will have Stokes and his lads on his heels."

"True." Without further argument, she climbed into the carriage.

He gave Gifford their direction, then followed.

At two minutes past ten o'clock, they left the carriage pulled up at the curb in the Strand, and strolled arm in arm to take up a position on the pavement on the north side of the western end of Fleet Street. They pretended to be admiring the spire of St. Clement Danes.

"It seems appropriate," Tabitha said, "that the payment that will allow us to stop Elaine Mackay will go past here, the spot where the payment that led us to her was made."

"Indeed." Sebastian glanced over her head, back down Fleet Street. "And here comes our courier."

When she tried to whirl about, he prevented it. "No—don't look." Turning her, he strolled westward, in the same direction as the courier. "I'm not sure which boy it is, but Stokes is coming this way, and he's clearly got someone in his sights. Let's amble and give them a chance to overtake us."

She nodded decisively. "Then we'll follow."

He could see no way of preventing it. Neither he nor Stokes was eager to have Tabitha present when they confronted Elaine Mackay, but as it was her mission, as it had been she who'd persevered and brought the blackmailing scheme to light to the point where an arrest was looming—and given her determination, let alone her intransigence—they'd had to give way on that point.

Within a minute, one of Stokes's constables came striding past, whistling a cheery tune. A few paces behind him, a young lad—a messenger boy indistinguishable from the hundreds of others who ran errands in that part of the city every day, ferrying papers between solicitors' offices, law courts, various registries, banks, and countless businesses—strode along.

Stokes, his eyes alert, his attention fixed, moved smoothly in the boy's wake.

Sebastian allowed Stokes to get several paces ahead, then yielded to Tabitha's insistent nudging and followed.

"If that messenger boy knows what he's carrying, I'll eat my best bonnet."

"I doubt you'll be put to that masticatory feat—I suspect most messenger boys learn to have no knowledge of or interest in the packets they carry."

After a moment, she said, "Too much temptation?"

"Too much danger."

They remained behind Stokes, who cleaved through the teeming crowds like a tracking hound. He was tall enough that his black hat showed clearly above the throng.

As they'd expected, the boy led their procession around Aldwych and into the streets about Covent Garden, eventually turning down the narrower lanes, taking a direct path to Elaine Mackay's door. For most of the distance, one of Stokes's constables ambled ahead of the boy; Sebastian didn't sight the second constable until he joined them in the shadows of an alley opposite and a little way short of Elaine Mackay's door.

When Sebastian arched a brow the man's way, he grinned and held up a finger to enjoin their silence. Then, much to Tabitha's irritation, the constable turned and took up a position in front of her. Sebastian saw her glare at the poor man's back, then she shifted to peer around him.

Their plan was nearing its culmination.

Having reached his destination, the boy paused to pull the packet from inside his jerkin. The constable who'd been ahead of him earlier had continued ambling, but more slowly, along the lane, scanning the doors as if searching for a particular house. Stokes had halted in the middle of the lane, looking down it, apparently surveying something in the distance. He paid no attention to the messenger boy, only a yard or two away.

Packet in his hand, the boy faced Elaine Mackay's door and rapped smartly.

A minute ticked by, then the door opened, revealing Elaine Mackay.

She saw Stokes, but as he wasn't looking her way, she ignored him and looked at the boy, focusing on the packet he offered her.

She smiled, smugly satisfied, and reached for it.

She didn't see Stokes's head turn, didn't see the rest of them watching.

Grasping the packet, she passed the boy a coin she'd had ready in her hand. "Good. Off you go."

Packet in hand, she turned to go inside and the boy turned away.

But Stokes was there. He seized the boy, pushed him into the arms of the young constable who'd swiftly returned up the lane.

Whirling, Elaine Mackay saw Stokes coming after her. Her expression shocked, aghast, she tried to slam the door shut, but Stokes reached it in time and forced it back. Elaine released the door and fled deeper into the house. Stokes followed.

The constable in the alley had raced out to support Stokes. Tabitha had shot after him; Sebastian had gone straight after her.

On Stokes's heels, the constable rushed in through the open door.

A heavy thud and a string of curses halted Tabitha and Sebastian on the threshold. In the gloom within they saw Stokes and the luckless constable rolling in a narrow corridor desperately trying to untangle themselves from a large amount of washing that had been slung in their path. Both had fallen, their legs trapped in damp sheets.

Beside them, the messenger boy was still frantically wrestling. Sebastian turned to help the other constable assure him that he was wanted only as a witness and not suspected of any crime.

That took a mere instant—a single forcefully delivered sentence—but when Sebastian looked back, Tabitha was gone.

He glanced around and caught sight of her skirt whisking down an alley alongside the house. He swore and raced after her.

Tabitha wasn't about to let Elaine Mackay escape and continue to make hay from other people's misery. Especially not Tabitha's friends' misery. She rushed down the alley to the back of the house, barreled around the corner—

Came to a teetering halt—facing Elaine Mackay holding a pair of sharp hair shears leveled at Tabitha's face.

"You!" Elaine spat the word. "How dare you!" Her eyes blazed, fury and hatred an incandescent mix. "You're nothing but a pampered idiot. Get out of my way!"

Tabitha might have obliged, but there was no place for her to go—the back wall of the next house stood close to the back of Elaine's; the space they stood in was a few feet wide.

Lips curling, face contorting, Elaine jabbed the shears viciously at Tabitha's face.

Heart pounding, she weaved back.

A steely arm looped about her waist and hauled her back and to the side of a hard male body. From the corner of her eye she saw a fist flash past at head height.

Then Elaine Mackay howled.

Tabitha heard the clatter as the hair shears hit the ground.

Wriggling in Sebastian's grasp—he was holding her off the ground—she looked and saw Elaine Mackay—still yowling—with both hands clapped to her nose and blood pouring down.

Tabitha glanced up at Sebastian; he was frowning and looked thoroughly uncomfortable. "What?"

He watched, lips thinning, as Elaine Mackay's howls subsided to sobs and she crumpled to sit on the ground. "I've never struck a woman before."

Tabitha looked at Elaine Mackay, then back at him. "Well, just remember not to do it again."

Stokes, who'd appeared through the back door, grunted. "Not unless they're villains like this one—then you're excused."

"There, see?" Tabitha gestured at Stokes as without compunction he hauled Elaine Mackay to her feet. "You're absolved." She paused, then, when Sebastian didn't respond, added pointedly, "You can put me down now."

He glanced at her, then, as if only then registering that he held her still, grunted and complied.

Tabitha wondered what was it about men and grunting. As a form of communication, it left a lot to desired.

They followed Stokes and his captive inside the small, poky house. Stokes had sat Elaine in the single chair by a rickety table in the tiny kitchen. Over the tops of the hands still clasping her nose, the hairdresser's eyes shot daggers at Tabitha. "I'm going to ruin you!" The words were muffled, yet still venomous. "You haul me up before a beak and I'll tell everyone what I know about you and your precious letter." She transferred her gaze to Sebastian. "Your engagement will be over faster than you can blink."

Tabitha heaved a dramatic sigh, reclaiming Elaine's attention. "What you don't understand is that it's all a lie—a sham. There's nothing you can do to harm me or Mr. Trantor— everything you think you know was a fabrication, a trap to make sure we caught you."

For an instant, Elaine Mackay looked utterly shocked, then her malevolence returned. "I'll tell all about the others, too. How do you think they'll treat you then—when it'll be your fault that the *ton* learns all their silly secrets?"

"Oh, there's no risk of that." Stokes grinned wolfishly when Elaine looked up at him. "Now you've helpfully admitted your involvement with blackmailing others, too, and in front of several members of the force"—he nodded at the two constables who were standing in the doorways—"as Mr. Peel has no intention of setting the *ton* against him by unnecessarily airing their scandals, you'll face a closed court. No chance to tell anyone but the judge all about the things you've learned while dressing young ladies' hair." His grin grew intent. "You're nicked."

He glanced at the constables; the messenger boy was hanging back in the hallway, round-eyed. "Take her back to Bow Street, and you can take the boy, too. Lad," he said to the messenger boy, "once you tell the sergeant what you did today, you'll be free to go."

The boy bobbed his head.

Leaving his men to see to their charges, Stokes waved Tabitha and Sebastian out of the crowded kitchen. Stepping into the rear yard, Tabitha led the way down the alley and back out into the lane.

Sebastian joined her.

Stokes halted before them. "Thank you both. I assume you'd rather you heard no more of this episode?"

Sebastian agreed.

Tabitha hesitated, then said, "Only if she escapes."

Stokes smiled at that. "Rest assured, she won't."

"One question," Sebastian said. "How will the others— those she truly blackmailed—know they no longer need to fear exposure? Admittedly they'll no longer receive any demands, but they may well grow anxious over what the sudden silence portends."

"Hmm." Stokes frowned. "I'll have a word to my superiors. It seems like that's something Mr. Peel himself might like to undertake—discreetly putting it about that Miss Mackay the hairdresser had been blackmailing various *ton* clients, but as she's now to be transported, her victims need no longer fear her. No need to single out any clients, and no need to explain your part in it, either."

Tabitha nodded. "That should do it."

They parted with handshakes and congratulations all around.

Stokes turned back to the house, to where his men were leading out their prisoner.

Taking Tabitha's arm, Sebastian turned her toward Aldwych, beyond which Gifford and their carriage would be waiting. "It's too early for a celebratory luncheon." And he had to clear one last major hurdle before he could celebrate anything at all. "In the interim, might I suggest we adjourn to the park?"

Tabitha glanced at him, then nodded. "If you wish."

Tabitha couldn't understand why she felt so . . . deflated. She'd succeeded in her mission. Brilliantly, even if she said so herself. Yet instead of bubbling and effervescing with delight, she felt as if some huge, dull weight was dragging her down.

Gifford drove them into the park. It was not yet noon and the carriages of the matrons and grandes dames were drawn up along the Avenue, the *ton*'s matchmakers making use of the pleasant morning to parade their charges on the lawns. She really didn't feel like socializing, but Gifford pulled in to the verge nearby; inwardly sighing, she followed Sebastian from the carriage.

Although he wound her arm in his, to her surprise he didn't lead her toward the fashionable throng but rather cut a path parallel to the Avenue, within sight but a little way apart from the clusters of young ladies and gentlemen strolling and avidly chatting under the matrons' watchful eyes.

She glanced across the lawns at the courting couples—and the reality that had been hovering, the dark cloud at the back of her mind, came rushing to the fore and swamped her. "Ah . . . yes. Of course."

Her mission was complete—and their engagement was at an end.

Sebastian glanced at her, puzzled.

She forced herself to lift her chin, to draw in a tight breath and state, "Now we've solved the riddle of the blackmailer and put an end to her schemes, we need to address the question of how to dissolve our engagement."

That was why he'd brought her there, so they could work out their next—and last—plan. How to bring their association to an end.

He cleared his throat. "Yes—I wanted to speak to you about that."

He didn't immediately go on. Glancing down, not knowing how—what tack to take, what words to use—to move the moment along, yet desperate to do so—she hadn't imagined it would hurt so much—she noticed the glimmer of his grandmother's ring on her finger. The betrothal ring his family had expected him to give to the lady he'd chosen as his bride.

She halted. Drawing her hand from his arm, she reached for the ring. "I should give this back to you."

She grasped the band, started to wriggle it free.

Sebastian reached out and closed one hand over hers. Waited until she looked up and met his eyes. Hers were strangely dull, unusually somber. He held her gaze, quietly said, "Actually, I wanted to ask if you could see your way to keeping that on your finger."

When she stared at him, just stared, he clarified, "If you would keep wearing it."

She blinked. Looked down at his hand, clasped over hers, at the ring still glowing all fire and light on her finger. "But—"

"We make a good team." Desperation forced the words from him. He'd meant to formulate some sophisticated plea, rehearse an eloquent proposal, but . . . he shifted to face her. "I know this mission is over, but we could find other missions—do other things. Together." That was the important thing—him and her together. He caught her gaze as she looked up at him again, held to it as if it were a lifeline and he was drowning. Closed his other hand with the first about her hands, clasped them between his as he said, "I know you think you're unmarriageable, and that you weren't—aren't—looking for a husband, that you aren't enamored of the married state at all, but we suit so well, and I like all your odd quirks—all the ways you're so different from other young ladies. I appreciate your unconventionality. We've rubbed along together tolerably well and . . . we're compatible in so many ways . . ." Holding onto her hands, he hauled in a tight breath. "I would be honored if you would leave my ring on your finger."

Tabitha stared into his face, and still couldn't take it in—couldn't accept that what her dazed and rattled mind was screeching at her was indeed the true interpretation of his words. In her life, in her experience, things she'd longed for had never fallen into her lap. So, her fingers clinging to his every bit as tightly as his were to hers, she forced herself to ask, "What exactly are you saying?"

She was distantly aware that the strollers by the Avenue were watching; none were near enough to hear, but they all could see—enough to know some discussion of great moment was occurring. She didn't need to look to know they were waiting with bated breath to observe the outcome.

She cared not a jot. For her, in that moment, only Sebastian mattered.

He was frowning—she thought with self-disgust—as he stared down at her. "Damn!" Pulling one hand free, he ran it through his hair, thoroughly disarranging it. "I've done this wrongly."

Before she could react, he went down on one knee, both hands once again clasped about hers as he gazed up at her, his gray eyes locked on hers. "Tabitha Makepeace, will you do me the honor of being my wife, to have and to hold for the rest of my life?"

She blinked. "You want to marry me?" She had to be sure. "You really want to marry me of your own volition—this isn't some form of duty that you feel you must honor, is it? Your duty to your family, or because of our . . . closeness at the inn, and at your house?"

She couldn't bear it if it were.

"No." His lips twisted. "I realize that the notion might seem strange, but I really, truly, in all honesty, and with absolute sincerity, want to marry you. Just you—no one else. No one else will do. And I rather think that my trials and tribulations in searching for a suitable wife proved beyond question that I am not that much of a self-sacrificing saint that I would marry out of duty. I tried, but I couldn't. The simple truth is that I couldn't imagine marrying any young lady." He held her gaze. "Not until I met you."

Tabitha believed him. She trusted him; she always had. She'd somehow recognized from the first that his heart was true . . . and now it was hers. Truly hers.

She looked down at him, felt her features soften, felt her expression slowly transform as her heart filled and filled, then overflowed with joy. . .

He saw; he searched her eyes, her face, and read her answer there. His own expression lit—he waited, waited . . . then abruptly winced. Muttered, "For pity's sake, say yes and put me out of my misery. This grass is damp, and my knees will cramp, and—"

"Yes." The word was weak, her voice faint, but she repeated it. "*Yes*." Slipping her hands free of his, she grasped his shoulders and tugged. As he rose, she laughed joyously, then caught his hands in hers, held them as she looked into his eyes. "Yes, Sebastian Trantor, I'll marry you."

Releasing his hands, she reached up and framed his face. He, his eyes, were all she could see. "I'll marry you and we'll make our marriage, our future life, our next mission."

He smiled. "That's all I ask."

She smiled back. "And that I can do."

She stretched up and kissed him—kissed him and was kissed as no other young lady in living memory had been kissed in the park, in full view of the goggling matrons and grandes dames all but hanging out of their carriages along the Avenue.

They adjourned to her parents' house to convey the good news, both that the blackmailer had been caught and removed without fuss, and that, contrary to their earlier intention, they would not be dissolving their engagement.

His hand locked around hers, Sebastian smiled proudly at Tabitha. "We've decided we'll make a good team in the wider sphere of life, too."

She arched her brows at him. "There'll be challenges, of course."

Mrs. Makepeace smiled contentedly. "We always knew you were well matched. And challenges, my dear, are what adds spice to a marriage."

Mr. Makepeace smiled at Sebastian. "So my dear lady keeps telling me."

Sebastian grinned, and looked at Tabitha again, drank in the sight of her—the joy and sheer happiness shining in her bright eyes and radiating from her. "You may be sure, sir, that I'll appreciate those challenges as I ought."

"Oh, I don't doubt it," Mr. Makepeace said. "You're no fool."

They remained in Bedford Square for a private celebratory luncheon, over which they discussed and agreed that their change of heart necessitated no further public confirmation.

At the end of the meal, Sebastian caught Tabitha's eye.

"We should call on my aunts—before they hear of our scene in the park and start speculating as to what it might mean."

"Goodness, yes." She laid aside her napkin, exchanged a glance with her mother. "We'd better go and reassure them straightaway."

Her mother nodded benign approval. Her father waved them on their way.

They called at Fothergill house to discover that his aunts had already heard the news.

"Great heavens, Sebastian! What was that all about?" Lady Fothergill raised her quizzing glass and observed the pair of them through it. "You haven't been giving dear Tabitha any reason to doubt your affections, have you?"

Standing beside Tabitha, her hand in his, Sebastian heard her choke. "No—of course not. We were . . . discussing our wedding."

"Oh?" Pamela Trantor's eyes lit. "Weddings are such *wonderful* affairs—yours, I predict, will be the highlight of the Season."

"Indeed." Lady Fothergill nodded sagely. "The *ton* always enjoys a good wedding, especially one they weren't expecting. Takes something extraordinary to stir us out of our ennui these days, but I predict your wedding will do it. Bound to raise all sorts of interest. Daresay even the scribblers will be there—they love to report on all the details these days. Rather unrestrained, of course, but at least you'll know you've made your mark."

"Ah . . . yes." Tabitha took in Sebastian's blank expression—had no difficulty reading the horror behind it. She plastered on a wide smile and beamed it at his aunts. "I've just remembered—we have to rush around and tell Lydia and Ro. They'll be cross if we don't involve them in the planning."

Lady Fothergill indulgently waved them away. "Go, go! We'll call on your mama in the next few days and start the ball rolling. The date—that's the first thing to decide on. We'll have to look into when St. Georges can be had—you'll want it held there, of course."

Tabitha just smiled and waved over her shoulder as Sebastian—who had waited for no further encouragement beyond his aunt's wave—towed her out.

"What possessed you to mention our wedding?" Tabitha asked the instant they were back in the town carriage.

"It was the only thing that sprang to mind. Did you really want to call on Lydia and Gerrard?"

"No—that was just an excuse to allow us to leave." She stared at him, felt his horror infect her. She slumped back against the seat. "They've got the bit between their teeth and God only knows how we can rein them in. What are we going to do?"

"I'm thinking. Bear with me for a moment."

His moment lengthened to include the time it took for Gifford to drive them to the townhouse in Sussex Place. He dismissed Gifford, saying they were going for a drive in his curricle. Somewhat to Tabitha's surprise, that proved to be true.

"Where are we going?"

"There's someone I know who can help us with this. We're going to see him."

He didn't volunteer anything more, but concentrated on guiding his pair of highbred blacks steadily north through the traffic.

When they joined the Great North Road, she glanced at him. "You've got a plan, haven't you?"

He nodded. "I'm not sure you'll like it, but it was all I could come up with. And before you ask, the reason I haven't told you is that if you don't know, then when we next see our dear families you can claim complete innocence."

She smiled, slid her arm in his. "We're in this together, remember. This is our new mission, and we'll face it together."

He drew in a deep breath, let it out as he said, "I thought

that, as we'd made your family, and mine, and everyone else involved—even your friends and their families, and their husbands-to-be, too—so happy and relieved and pleased, that it was time we attended to our own happiness and relief, and pleased ourselves." He glanced at her, met her eyes. "You don't want a big wedding and neither do I. Underneath our glib exteriors, we're both rather private people, and enduring such an event would place a strain on both of us—one we don't deserve. So . . . I thought we should elope."

When he looked back at the road, Tabitha gathered her giddy wits enough to ask, "To Scotland?"

"No—just to Lincoln. My maternal uncle is bishop there, and he doesn't get on with my aunt Fothergill. He'll be thrilled to grant us a special license and officiate, too. Then I thought we might take refuge at my home—Grimoldby Abbey. You haven't seen it yet and you should." He glanced at her briefly. "I hope you'll like it."

Expectation and exhilaration returned in a rush. Tabitha felt as if she were glowing. She hugged his arm. "I'm sure I will."

Sebastian nodded. "So that's my plan, but if you don't like it, you only have to say, and I'll turn the horses around and we can book St. Georges and have a big *ton* wedding . . . if that's what you'd rather have." Again he met her eyes. "Your choice, my love."

She held his gaze, then slowly smiled. Radiantly. For one instant he thought she might be pleased because he'd given her the option—that she would take him up on it because of some misguided notion that they should please others rather than themselves even in the matter of their wedding—but then her eyes—those bright eyes that had drawn him from the first—lit, too, and he knew she'd never disappoint him. That regardless of whatever challenges came their way, she'd always be with him, by his side.

"Lincoln," she declared, and her expression conveyed her rapturous happiness.

He swallowed, felt humbled.

Knowing she was desired for herself had transformed her; knowing he'd achieved that transformation had transformed him—he literally felt like a different man, the sort of man he'd been waiting to become.

Then she hugged his arm, leaned against his shoulder as he looked ahead once more.

Stated, in her usual determined and impatient way but he could hear the delight bubbling through her voice, "I want more than anything to get started on our new mission. Drive on, my love—and don't spare the horses."

Only Love

MARY BALOGH

Cleo Critchlord

Jock Critchlord

Chapter One

*H*aving dismissed her maid from her dressing room, Cleo Pritchard confronted her own image in the dressing-table mirror and made a few frank admissions to herself. And came to a firm decision. It was high time.

First, she would never be married. No one wanted her.

Second, she would never have a lover. For the same reason.

Third, she would never have a suitor. She had never had one, not once in her life, and she was twenty-seven years old.

There.

The facts were out in the open at last, even if she had not spoken them aloud. She felt better now. Well, not really perhaps, but she would. It was always the best policy to be honest with oneself.

Of course, some might say that she must have had at least one suitor in her life, for she had once been married. For five long years, in fact. She had also been widowed for five.

But Colonel Aubrey Pritchard had never been her suitor.

Twenty-three years her senior, he had not deemed it necessary to woo her or court her or propose marriage to her in person or even really to want her. He had wanted Elizabeth, her elder sister, but at the time Elizabeth had agreed to marry Charles Darbyshire and too many people knew about the impending betrothal for a stop to be put to it. Not that Elizabeth had *wanted* to stop it, even though the colonel, as the second son of a viscount, was considerably more eligible. Aubrey had offered for *her* instead, though she was only seventeen. She would actually suit him better, he had told her father, as she was young enough to be biddable and plain enough not to be a distraction to his men. He needed another wife, he had explained, because an officer was entitled to have someone besides just his batman to minister to his needs.

The late Mrs. Aubrey Pritchard, Cleo had discovered later, *had* been a distraction to her husband's men and had had to have biddability disciplined into her. But at the time Cleo did not know this, and perhaps it would have made no difference even if she had. She had made no objection to the proposed marriage even though she had not set eyes upon her prospective husband more than twice and had never exchanged a word with him. At that time in her life she would have married anyone who would have her. Her elder sister was both pretty and vivacious and her younger sister was clearly destined to be a beauty. Her brother was good-looking and pleasant natured. She was plain. And short. And overweight. And painfully shy. It was already glaringly obvious to her that she was never going to take the eye of any of the neighborhood young men—not that she ever raised her eyes from the ground before her feet when there was a young man within a hundred yards of her. Yet she had had all the needs, all the hopes, all the dreams of any normal girl.

She had been ecstatic, if the truth were told. Married at *seventeen*. Even before Elizabeth. The colonel had been a fine figure of a man, even if not exactly handsome.

Gazing into the glass now, her elbows propped on the dressing-table top, her chin in her hands, Cleo wondered if she had learned from bitter experience or if she was just as foolish now as she had been ten years ago. But there was no way of knowing, was there? No one was asking her to marry him. No one was even showing any interest in her though she lived in London and had faithfully accepted all her numerous social invitations during each Season for the last three full years. This was well into the fourth.

The only gentlemen who danced with her at balls were acquaintances of Elizabeth's or their brother Alfred's. Men who felt obliged to give her half an hour of their lives.

The fault was not entirely her looks, perhaps. It was more her manner and behavior. She so *expected* to be found dull and unattractive that she found it difficult to look any man in the eye. She always feared they would think she was being *forward*. And she avoided any conversation beyond the merely mundane lest she bore her partner. And then, of course, she always *did* bore him. She knew it was foolish, self-defeating behavior. But knowing a thing and doing something about it were two entirely different things.

Being shy was a positive curse. She *so* envied people who could walk into a room, head high, eyes meeting everyone else's, as if they *expected* to be welcomed and to be liked.

Though there *were*, of course, her looks, which had not improved with age. Cleo always thought of herself as *square*. There was the shape of her face to prove the point and the short, stocky body beneath it. Well, no, that was no longer true, was it? There had been a time in the Peninsula when she was with Aubrey and the British army as they fought against the forces of Napoleon Bonaparte that she had taken consolation for her unhappiness in food and had indeed become stocky. But after Aubrey's death and her return to England, she had taken herself in hand and lost the excess weight and even the unnecessary weight she had put on as a girl.

But she still thought of herself as square.

She had so *hoped* to find happiness in a new marriage. She had been only twenty-two when she was widowed, twenty-three when she put off her mourning. Little more than a girl, actually.

Her expectations had never been impossibly high. She had never expected *love* in any future marriage, not the passionate love of high romance that one read about in storybooks, anyway. She had not expected to attract any very handsome or magnetically charming suitor. All she had hoped for was happiness, which to her was synonymous with contentment. A home of her own with a kindly man and a few children and neighbors and a garden and. . .

Well. It was not to be, was it? None of it. And it was time she accepted reality.

Ah, but she had known that passionate sort of love once, though it had been a foolish thing, entirely one-sided and impossible for every imaginable reason. But there had been a moment. . .

Only, alas, a moment.

But she would hug it to herself for the rest of her life like a priceless jewel, just as she had for six years.

He had probably forgotten within a day.

How pathetic she was.

But she was not usually self-pitying. There was *nothing* more unattractive than self-pity.

Cleo removed her head from its resting place on her hands, gave it a little shake, and drummed the fingers of one hand on the dressing table. This was her younger sister's year. Gwinn—Guinevere. Their father had named all his children after prominent kings and queens of history, but while with Alfred and Elizabeth that fact was not glaringly obvious, the same could not be said of Cleopatra and Guinevere. Gwinn was nineteen and making her come-out under Elizabeth's sponsorship. And when Cleo went along to balls and other entertainments with the two of them, she felt relegated quite firmly to an older generation.

Yet another impediment to her very modest dreams.

There was another ball tomorrow evening, Lady Clare-mont's, and finally Cleo was admitting to herself that she *hated* balls. She *hated* being a wallflower. She *hated* having to stand or sit in full view of half the *ton,* smiling and fanning her face and pretending to be having a rollicking good time among the mothers and chaperons of the pretty young things who were dancing every set.

And this was where her firm decision came in.

She was not going to do it any longer. Not after this year, anyway, when she felt obliged to give Elizabeth her company while Gwinn was being made much of by hordes of young, eligible gentlemen. After this year she would retire from society. It was not as if her life would be empty and meaningless. Quite the contrary. She had several worthwhile activities in which to immerse herself and numerous hobbies and a few good friends. And there was nothing obviously pathetic about a widow choosing to live out her life alone in faithfulness to the memory of a long-deceased husband.

Living a quiet, dignified life of good works and busy industry would be her new goal.

It sounded dreadfully dull.

But she had decided. She *must* dream up a new, more modest, dream. The old one was not serving her at all well. She would never marry again. She would never have a suitor. Or a lover. No one was interested.

The more fool they.

Cleo was now drumming the fingers of *both* hands on the dressing-table top. She looked with firm resolve at her image and then, after a few seconds, she crossed her eyes and poked out her tongue.

There. That felt *immensely* better.

She laughed—at herself.

And by now Alfred's carriage must be waiting outside her door to fetch her for dinner. She was to attend the opera afterward with him and Megan, her sister-in-law. She was looking forward to the evening.

She got to her feet and reached for her shawl and reticule.

* * *

Jack Gilchrist felt somewhat overwhelmed by the greeting he received when he arrived at Waterton House on Portman Square in London late one afternoon. He must have arrived mere moments after the children returned home from a walk with their mother and their nurse.

Charlotte, Countess of Waterton, his sister-in-law, was pulling off her gloves while the nurse bounced an infant in her arms. A small child was complaining that her bonnet ribbons were in a knot, and a considerably older one was assuring her impatiently that the knot would only get worse if she kept pulling on it. Meanwhile a child between the two of them in age was bending over the younger one and batting her hands away so that she could undo the knot herself.

They all stopped to look at Jack as he stepped inside the front doors, which were standing open.

"Jack! There you are!" Charlotte exclaimed, and she stepped forward to hug him, while the baby popped a thumb in her mouth and hid her face against the nurse's shoulder, the eldest girl curtsied and instructed the others to do likewise in a voice that could only be described as bossy, the younger one rushed at him to show him her new white gloves—which she had *kept* white throughout their walk— and the one who was younger again burst into tears and resumed her fruitless tugging at the bonnet ribbons.

Matthew, Earl of Waterton, Jack's older brother, appeared from somewhere, and stood in the background, his hands behind him, and—wise man—waited for either his wife or the children's nurse to impose order on the girls again.

It happened within a minute or two, and all four children disappeared upstairs with the nurse.

Matthew nodded his head.

"Jack," he said. "You are looking well."

He was not *feeling* particularly well. Oh, health-wise, he was fine. He had recovered from his war wounds long ago. He was actually one of the fortunate ones since he still had all four limbs and both eyes and ears, and his scars were not in obviously visible places. But he had not recovered from his aversion to being in public and risking a resumption of the adulation that had so bewildered and embarrassed him five years ago. Heroism was a ridiculous notion when it came to war. One did one's duty, and as an officer, one looked out for one's men and one's superiors. If one happened to be in the right place at the right time—or the *wrong* place at the wrong time, depending upon one's perspective—then sometimes one could be of real service to someone, even if only the lowliest enlisted man, at the same time as one furthered the cause for which one fought. It was what anyone would do under the circumstances. There was nothing *heroic* about it, unless one saw all soldiers as heroic.

He had used his slowly healing wounds as an excuse to withdraw from all the admiration and adoration to which he had found himself subjected when he returned home from the Peninsula. He had gone to live in the old steward's cottage on a far corner of his brother's secondary estate in Dorsetshire. He had made a home of that cottage for almost five years, neither avoiding company nor courting it. Company had largely avoided him, though he did not believe there was anything deliberate about it on the part of his neighbors. He had, he supposed, gained something of a reputation as a recluse.

He had not minded. He had never intended to make it a lifelong state, but it had suited him while he healed. And one thing he had learned from war was that not all wounds were physical and that those that were *not* actually took longer to heal.

He had been called out of seclusion before he was ready to come out of his own volition. Matthew had invited him to come to London. No, actually he had *summoned* Jack. He had informed his younger brother in a terse, formal letter that he was sending the carriage from London to fetch him and that he would be needing the carriage again within a week.

Jack might have refused to come, of course, but that would

be making too much of a point of his reclusiveness. He was *not* a recluse. He was merely a man enjoying a long stretch of solitude and peace while he learned to be comfortable again within his own body and mind and soul.

His arrival, first in London, and now here at Waterton House had been somewhat jarring. He had not realized just how quiet and solitary his life had become.

"So are you, Matthew," he said in response to the comment upon his looks. And he advanced toward his brother, his hand outstretched. "Your girls are growing up."

"Even the baby is walking already," Charlotte said. "When she chooses to, that is. You will wish to settle into your room, Jack. But do come up to the drawing room for tea first. That journey all the way from Rigdon Hall is a tedious one, as I discover afresh every time we go down there."

"Jack would prefer something a little stronger than tea, I am quite sure, my love," Matthew said. "And somewhere quieter than the drawing room if Rose and Anne are to be allowed down as they usually are. Come into the library, Jack, and sample some superior brandy."

Jack smiled apologetically at his sister-in-law and, in some relief, followed his brother into the library. He closed the door behind him and took one of the leather chairs beside the hearth. Matthew poured two glasses of brandy, handed him one, and took up a stand before the unlit coals with the other. He swirled the brandy, took a taste, and gazed down into his glass.

He was about to discover, Jack concluded as he rolled a mouthful of the smooth liquor over his tongue, why he had been summoned. Matthew was not going to waste any time. Jack sat back in his chair and crossed his legs. He hoped it was something that would allow him to return home soon. Spring in the countryside and by the seashore was his favorite time of year.

"Charlotte had a difficult time of it with Lily's birth last year," Matthew said, still gazing into his glass. "The labor was long and intense. I thought I was going to lose her. So did the physician. He finally had to rip Lily out. By some miracle, both she and Charlotte survived."

Jack felt himself flushing. This was more information than he needed to hear.

"They both look well now," he said.

"Rathbone informed us at the time," Matthew continued, "that there would be no more children, that it would be dangerous to try and impossible to accomplish."

"I am sorry," Jack murmured.

"We both hoped," Matthew said, "that by this year, after everything had healed and Charlotte had recovered her health, Rathbone would discover that after all there could be another child. But examinations have been made—all of which Charlotte bore with admirable fortitude—and the judgment was handed down just last week. Nothing has changed. We will have no more children."

Jack shifted uncomfortably in his seat and lifted his glass to his lips again. He was genuinely sorry. But what did this have to do with him? Had he been brought here to cheer them up? He was surely the wrong person to do that.

"Jack," Matthew said, changing position abruptly and sitting on the edge of the chair at the other side of the fireplace. "The title has descended in the direct line for five generations. If there is no heir of the direct line, the title and the property will pass to Hugh."

Their second cousin, who had been a bully as a boy and both a bully and a rake of the worst order as a man.

Jack began to have an inkling of where this was leading.

"You are only thirty-six," he said. "Hugh is two years older. And maybe his sons will improve with age. You may live to be eighty and Hugh to be sixty-two. *I* may live to be ninety."

His poor attempt at a joke did not draw a smile from his brother.

"And I may die at thirty-seven," he said, "and Hugh at sixty-two, or eighty-two. And you at thirty-one."

Next year. Jack frowned.

"*Might* you die at thirty-seven?" he asked.

His brother did not answer the question.

"You know," he said, "that almost all the property and fortune are tied up in the entail. There is very little I am free to leave to Charlotte and the girls. Lily is *one*, Jack, Emily *four*. Even Rose is only ten. It will be eight years or more before she marries. And how can she marry well if there is virtually nothing for a portion?"

"Matt," Jack asked, "*is* there a chance that you might—?" His mouth felt suddenly dry.

"There is *always* the chance," Matthew said impatiently. "I could drop dead within the next minute. So could you. But yes, Rathbone did find something to concern him when he examined me last week along with Charlotte. Some sort of . . . *murmur* was the word he used, about the heart. Nothing serious in all probability, he told me. But he wishes to keep an eye on it. I am not going to dwell upon it. What will be will be. But, Jack . . ."

He paused to set down his glass and run the fingers of one hand through his hair.

"You must marry," he said abruptly. "Without delay. You must produce a son. *Sons.* If I could order you to marry, I would. I cannot, of course. But I *can* beg you, appeal to your sense of family duty and honor, do whatever I need to do to get you to agree. You must marry. And this is the perfect place and the perfect time to do it. This is the Season, the great marriage mart, and a few months of it still remain."

Finally he looked up into his brother's face.

Jack felt as though he were turned to stone.

Marry? It was something he supposed he had always intended to do eventually. But . . . in such haste? Within two months? Matthew was expecting him to join in all the hectic madness of the London Season in order to choose a *bride* from the hopeful young things who thronged the ballrooms and drawing rooms? And marry and impregnate her without delay?

All to stop Hugh and his sons from succeeding to the title

after both Matthew and he were dead—which of course could conceivably happen long before all Matt's daughters were safely grown up and married.

Yes, good Lord, it *could* happen.

Besides which, the thought of Hugh ever owning Rigdon Hall and controlling everyone dependent upon it for their livelihood was a ghastly one. Not to mention Mayfield Park, Matthew's principal seat in Berkshire, where they had both grown up.

But . . .

He was expected to *marry? Now? This year?*

His face felt suddenly cold as if all the blood had drained out of it. There must be an alternative. But Charlotte could have no more children. And even if she could, she might have yet another daughter. And Matthew could not simply put her from him, Henry VIII style, in favor of a more fertile alternative.

"Lady Claremont's ball is tomorrow evening," Matthew said, picking up his glass again and swirling the contents. "It is always one of the biggest squeezes of the Season."

"You expect me—?" Jack stopped. Of course Matthew did.

"Yes," his brother said. "Yes, I do, Jack. Please."

It was Jack's turn to run a hand through *his* hair.

"I think I have forgotten how to make conversation with a lady," he said. Or with anyone, for that matter.

"You will not need to," his brother said. "No one will have forgotten exactly who you are, Jack. Especially *this* year, when the great victory of Waterloo is still fresh in everyone's mind. And you always were impossibly attractive to the ladies anyway."

Jack winced and drained his glass.

The silence stretched. He was the one who broke it eventually.

"It would seem, then," he said curtly, "that I am going to Lady Claremont's ball tomorrow evening."

Chapter Two

"He is a very decent fellow," Alfred said. "Shall I bring him over here and introduce him?"

The very decent fellow was Mr. Pike, a gentleman from the North of England who did not come often to London but had come this year in order to seek a wife. Or so he had told Alfred in a recent conversation at White's Club. He was a tall, slim young man with blond good looks and—if Cleo could judge from this distance—blue eyes. He was at present in conversation with two pretty young ladies while an older lady hovered protectively nearby. All three of the young people were laughing. Two fans were fluttering merrily.

"No, of course not," Cleo said hastily. It always embarrassed her that her brother felt obliged to try to prevent her from being a total wallflower. "I am quite happy sitting here watching everyone else."

"The second set is mine," he said, "after I have danced

the first with Megan. I insist upon it. Don't go promising it to anyone else."

He grinned at her, and she smiled back.

"I shall reject all the dozens of offers I shall receive in the meanwhile," she said.

"It is a waltz," he told her.

"Oh, good." She beamed. She *loved* the waltz, even when she must dance it with her brother.

He made his way back to Megan's side and led her onto the floor, where the opening sets were beginning to form. Elizabeth was out there with Charles, and Gwinn with Lord Kerby, who was becoming one of her many regular beaux. Cleo smiled at Lady Naismith and her sister as they passed in front of her, arm in arm, tall plumes nodding above their heads.

The ballroom was already crowded, and more guests were trickling in, late though it was becoming. Cleo knew almost everyone by sight. One did, of course, tend to see the same people over and over again during a Season and even from year to year. There was almost never anyone new except for the fresh crop of very young ladies fresh out of the schoolroom each spring and of very young gentlemen newly down from Oxford or Cambridge or newly up from their fathers' estates in the country.

Though there was someone now, just inside the ballroom doors.

He was a tall, powerfully built gentleman with very erect bearing. Cleo recognized it instinctively as *military* bearing though he was not wearing a uniform. He was with the Earl and Countess of Waterton and was facing away from Cleo.

He was new.

And then he half turned and she saw his face.

Her hands clenched in her lap, her right closing hard about her fan, her left bunching the lace of her gown inside it. She felt as though she were looking down a long, dark tunnel to a distant point of light. The air felt cold in her nostrils. She forgot to breathe.

Major Gilchrist! *Jack* Gilchrist, though she had never called him by his given name.

She had not even known for certain that he was still alive. She had never asked anyone. It had seemed better not to know for certain. But she had feared the worst. She had not set eyes on him since her return from the Peninsula. And he had been horribly wounded when he was invalided home.

He was the only man, apart from her father and brother, ever to have kissed her. The *only* one. Including her husband.

His head kept turning as he looked about the ballroom. And then his eyes alit upon her—before she could recover herself and look down. Then she could *not* look away, for his eyes held hers, looking puzzled for a moment as though he felt he ought to recognize her but did not, and then lighting up with full recognition and . . . pleasure?

He turned back to the Earl of Waterton, who was, of course, *his brother,* presumably to say something to him, and then came striding toward her, looking only at her, glancing neither to left nor to right, smiling.

Cleo remembered to breathe again only because her survival depended upon it. She sucked in a deep, ragged breath.

Oh! He was actually *happy* to see her.

She rose to meet him. He held out both hands as he drew close, and she lifted her own and placed them in his. They were large, warm, capable. They closed tightly about hers.

"Mrs. Pritchard," he said.

"Major Gilchrist."

"I cannot tell you," he said, "how intimidating it was walking in here tonight to a roomful of strangers. And then to see a familiar face. Particularly when it was yours."

It was one of the loveliest things anyone had ever said to her.

She was half aware that the orchestra had started playing and the dancing had begun.

"You did recover from your wounds, then?" she said. "I did not know, but I often wondered. I am so glad."

"Thank you," he said. "I believe my life hung in the balance for a while, but fortunately I was only half aware of the fact while it was happening, and here I am with all my body parts in good working order again. And you—how are *you* doing? Have you remarried? Did I call you by the right name?"

"I have remained a widow," she said. "I am always busy. Among other pursuits, I have nieces and nephews to entertain whenever they are in Town. And this year my younger sister is making her come-out and I am helping our elder sister chaperon her at all the busiest entertainments. I am never idle."

She was being too defensive.

Their hands were still clasped between them. He seemed to realize it at the same moment she did. He squeezed hers once more and released them.

"I am delighted to hear it," he said. "I will call on you at home if I may. I really know no one, you know. I was in the army for seven years, and I have been living in the country for five. All this really *is* intimidating, is it not?" He indicated the room about them with one arm.

He looked as solidly built as he always had even though he was not wearing a uniform now. He looked more handsome than ever. His face was perhaps a little leaner, but the leanness suited him. His dark eyes had always looked very directly into those of the person to whom he spoke—her in this case. It was something he had learned as a commander of men, she supposed, though it was very attractive. His hair was still thick and dark. He was one of the most handsome men she had known. Perhaps *the* most handsome, though she could, of course, be biased.

"One becomes accustomed to it," she said. "I have grown used to the crowds. I endure them for the sake of my family, though it does sometimes become a little tedious."

And now she was overdoing the ennui.

"You must dance with me," he said. Then he laughed

softly. "You see how my manners have grown rusty over the years? Mrs. Pritchard, would you do me the honor of dancing a set with me? The next one?"

The next set was Alfred's. The *only* one she had promised. The only one she would dance tonight. Perhaps Major Gilchrist would wait for the third if she explained. But the next set was to be a *waltz*. And Alfred was merely doing her a kindness. He would not mind if. . .

"It is to be a waltz," she said.

He grimaced and then grinned.

"I believe," he said, "I can manage it without putting your toes in any great peril. *Will* you dance it with me?"

"Yes," she said. "Thank you."

But instead of striding away, as she expected him to do until the end of *this* set, he indicated the chair from which she had risen, waited for her to seat herself, and then took the empty chair beside her.

"My brother will despair of me," he said.

She looked across the ballroom to where the Earl of Waterton was in conversation with a few other gentlemen.

"Will he?" she said, opening her fan to cool her hot cheeks. "Why?"

"I am supposed to be seeking introductions to eligible young ladies," he said. "I am supposed to be beginning an earnest search for a bride. The succession needs to be secured, and the countess has produced only daughters. It is why I have been hauled to London when I would have been perfectly happy to remain in my little cottage by the sea. Life can sometimes be tiresome, can it not? The campaign is supposed to begin tonight. But I would far prefer to sit here talking with you, and then dancing with you."

Happiness was a treacherous thing. Cleo had been feeling totally, mindlessly happy for . . . how long? Five minutes? Ten? And yet now she felt as wretched as she had been happy.

It was all illusion, of course. There had been nothing in

seeing an old acquaintance again to cause her anything but a moment's mild pleasure, as it had caused him. There was nothing now to cause her despair. Nothing had changed. Her life was as it had been fifteen minutes ago, when she had felt neither happy nor wretched.

"There will still be plenty of the evening left after the second set has been completed," she said. "You may pursue your quest then and make your brother proud of you." She smiled and fanned her face. "And you may even begin looking about you at some leisure while we are sitting here and while you are dancing with me."

His head turned sharply toward hers, and she could sense that he was looking very directly at her.

"My manners may be *rusty,* Mrs. Pritchard," he said, "but they have not crumbled away altogether. I will do no such thing. Besides, how could I pay any attention to any other young lady while I am becoming reacquainted with *you*? You are looking well. You have lost weight."

She turned her head and met his eyes the moment before they closed and he grimaced.

"And there," he said. "My manners have grown *very* rusty. I do beg your pardon. But you really are in good looks. Which is not to say that you were not when I knew you before."

She laughed.

"You ought to stop now, Major Gilchrist," she said, "before your tongue is in such a knot that it will take you the rest of the evening to untie it."

And they *both* laughed. Right into each other's eyes.

Cleo felt quite dizzy. And happy again. But very aware that after their dance he was going to go in search of an eligible *young* lady to court.

Twenty-seven suddenly felt very ancient indeed.

Jack had forgotten all about her until he saw her again this evening.

But after his surprised pleasure had abated slightly, he

wondered if perhaps the truth was more that he had sup-pressed the memory of her. For it was a guilty memory. Also embarrassing. And more than a little puzzling.

He had always liked her though he had never really known her. She had dealt with her life in the Peninsula with the British army with a quiet dignity no matter what the condi-tions. And the conditions, he had always suspected, were not *just* difficult terrain and frequently appalling weather conditions and billets rarely if ever what she must have been accustomed to. Pritchard had always been a brute with his men and was hated and feared in equal measure. The men, Jack included, had guessed that he was a brute with his wife, too. She had never appeared openly timid or cringing, it was true, but the fact that her eyes were always downcast when she was around the men, even the officers, was suggestive of a need to avoid instigating any jealous rage.

Not that the men had looked much at her. She was a small, dumpy woman with a plain face. But Jack had liked her anyway. He had found himself seeking her out with his eyes more often than he could reasonably explain to himself.

And then, during the Battle of Bussaco, Jack's men had brought word that Colonel Pritchard had been killed in a fierce scuffle; though when the fighting was all over, his body was nowhere to be found. It had been assumed he had been burned up in one of the many raging grass fires the guns had caused. There had been enough hopelessly charred bodies to give credence to the theory. It had been Jack's un-enviable duty to take word back to Mrs. Pritchard.

She had been alone in the colonel's billet. When she had turned pale and almost collapsed at the news, Jack had stepped forward and set his arms protectively about her and held her tight against his chest while she drew ragged breaths and recovered herself. And then she had tipped back her head and gazed up at him with large, unexpectedly beau-tiful eyes and . . .

Well, then had come the puzzling part. He had lowered

his head and kissed her. And she had kissed him back even though he had come to her in all the grime of battle. Before their embrace ended, it had turned hot and passionate and undeniably sexual.

He had apologized profusely when it was over, promised to send one of the other officers' wives to bear her company— something which, of course, he ought to have done *before* calling on her—and left the house without further ado.

That was all. Word had come the next day that the colonel had been taken prisoner and that the French were willing to ransom him for a large sum. The sum had been paid with some dispatch, and he was back with the regiment within a week of the battle.

Jack did not believe he had exchanged a word with Mrs. Pritchard since that day. Or seen her eyes since that day. Until now.

If he had remembered that incident as soon as he saw her this evening, he doubted he would have stridden across the room to greet her with such enthusiasm.

What must she think of him?

And yet she appeared as delighted to see him as he was to see her. And he still was delighted despite a slight discomfort. Perhaps it was because she looked so familiar and he was feeling more than a little self-conscious. People were beginning to look his way with recognition, and he suspected that word was spreading that the officer who had deliberately taken a bullet intended for Wellington at the Battle of Fuentes de Oñoro after first distinguishing himself in the action was back in London.

Time had been kind to her. She was no longer dumpy but had a neat, almost slender figure. And her plain face looked far different when her eyes were raised and she smiled. Her laugh was low and infectious.

She might as well have worn a veil in the Peninsula for all he or any of the men had seen of her modest attractions.

They were waltzing, and he was performing the steps with

only marginal competency. She was nevertheless following his lead and felt light and supple in his arms. Her eyes were on his and her cheeks were slightly flushed.

He wondered if she remembered that embrace with as much embarrassment as he did. But he could hardly ask her, could he?

"You obviously do far more dancing than I do," he said. "I do apologize for my clumsiness."

"You have not stepped on even one of my feet—*yet*," she said, giving him one of her transforming smiles. "And I do not dance a great deal. I am a very sober widow, you know."

She surely could not have loved Pritchard. Jack was rather surprised she had not remarried by now. But perhaps one experience of marriage had been enough for her. Perhaps freedom brought happiness enough into her life.

"Then I am honored that you have danced with *me*," he said. "What have you done with your life since you returned from the Peninsula? Apart from playing with your nieces and nephews, that is."

She had a small house in London not far from Hyde Park that had been her husband's, she told him. She was involved in a few charities. She had friends among the ladies who were similarly employed. She had learned to play the pianoforte since there was an instrument in the house and she hated to see it go unused. She liked to paint though she had no great skill with a brush. She embroidered and knitted and tatted. She read. She told it all with great enthusiasm, and he marveled that it all brought her happiness. But then his own life for the past five years would sound pathetically lacking in excitement if he were to put it into words.

"And what have you done with *your* life, Major Gilchrist?" she asked.

And there, he did indeed have to put it into words—the walking through the woods and along the beach, the swimming in the sea, the gathering and chopping of wood for the fire, the whittling that had produced pieces of furniture that pleased him and would probably horrify any connoisseur, the reading, the cooking—yes, *cooking,* he repeated when she raised her eyebrows—the sitting, both indoors and out, merely enjoying the silence.

"Which, like the color white," he explained to her, "is not the absence of anything but the containment of everything. I sometimes believe that if only I could understand *nothing,* I would know *everything.* And sometimes I feel I am about to grasp it—and then it eludes me."

He laughed suddenly.

"And now you will think me a mad fellow," he said, "a hermit who has lost his wits."

"Not at all," she said calmly. "I would like to hear more. I will think about *white* and *silence* and *nothing* and try to understand what you mean."

"And become mad like me?" he said. "What a strange conversation to be holding in the middle of a waltz."

And, grown bold after several minutes of waltzing without any mishap, he twirled her about one corner of the dance floor, and she tipped back her head and laughed aloud.

He really did like her. He was glad they had met again.

"*May* I call on you?" he asked her. "Perhaps tomorrow?"

"Perhaps *tomorrow,*" she said, "you will be escorting one of the young eligible ladies now in this ballroom to a garden party or taking her for a drive in the park. You must not procrastinate, must you? It is time you took a bride, Major Gilchrist, and set up your nursery."

He grimaced. Good Lord, he had already forgotten his very reason for being here.

"But I would be delighted," she said, "to have you call whenever you have a spare moment. I may have questions about nothing."

This time when she smiled, her eyes sparkled with merriment, and he thought, with a shock of understanding for his behavior in the Peninsula, *She is actually attractive.*

"I may have nothing for answers," he said, and they both laughed.

He twirled her again and allowed them both to enjoy the rest of the set without the distraction of conversation.

And enjoy it they did. Perhaps she did not much care for dancing, but he could feel the pleasure she was taking from *this* dance. And he enjoyed it because *she* did.

He was glad Pritchard had died in the very battle that had wounded him and ended his career in the army. He had never mourned his colonel, whom he had hated as much as any of the enlisted men had, but he had never been actively *glad* of his death until now.

Mrs. Pritchard deserved to be free of him. She deserved her quiet, happy life.

Chapter Three

It was a beautiful warm, sunny day, and Gwinn was strolling along beside the waters of the Serpentine in Hyde Park with Lord Kerby. And so Elizabeth was strolling there too, a discreet distance behind them, and, since she had not wished to do so alone, she had invited Cleo to accompany her.

Cleo did not resent the summons even though she had intended to spend the afternoon mastering a Bach fugue that had been tying her fingers in knots for weeks. The pianoforte could wait for another day, when it rained. Besides, she doubted she would have been able to concentrate fully upon a difficult piece of music.

It was difficult to concentrate upon *anything* today. Her thoughts had been whirling about inside her head since last night and simply would not be stilled. And the worst of it was that she was likely to see a great deal more of Major Gilchrist in the coming weeks—just as she had been forced to see a great deal of him after that day when they had thought

Aubrey was dead. Seeing him had been torture then, and it was going to be torture now.

She had been forced to pretend even more than usual last evening after the second set was over that she was enjoying her own solitude amid the dancing. And it had all had to be done while she was aware of him being introduced to a series of pretty young girls and smiling at them and conversing with them and dancing with them.

Soon he would be married to one of them.

Oh, it had hurt. And it had been no consolation to tell herself with firm good sense that she had absolutely no reason to feel pain. He had been pleased to see her, and he had enjoyed dancing with her. He wanted to continue their acquaintance. He wanted to call upon her at home one day when he was not busy with more important matters.

All that would change soon, of course.

And she would be left with another sweet, bitter memory to add to the first.

A mother sat on the bank of the Serpentine hugging her knees while her three children played about her and their father was crouched on the grass looking intently at something one of the children was showing him. He tweaked the brim of her bonnet and got to his feet, laughing—and revealed himself to be Major Gilchrist.

"Oh, look," Elizabeth said, "there is the handsome hero of Fuentes de Oñoro who was good enough to dance with you last evening."

As though it had been a gesture of pure charity. It had *not* been.

He had seen her and was smiling and raising his tall hat.

"Mrs. Pritchard," he said.

The mother on the grass, she could see now, was the Countess of Waterton. A nurse nearby was rocking a baby in her arms.

"Major." Cleo smiled. "May I present my sister, Mrs. Darbyshire? Major Gilchrist, Elizabeth."

Gwinn and Lord Kerby had strolled on ahead, but they

stopped and waited when they realized their companions were delayed.

The weather was soon exhausted as a topic, and Cleo and Elizabeth would have resumed their walk, leaving Major Gilchrist with his sister-in-law and nieces. But Elizabeth had mentioned that they were with their sister and Lord Kerby, and he had glanced toward them and then back.

"Perhaps, Mrs. Pritchard," he said, "since they will not be left without any chaperon, I may escort you home?"

Elizabeth looked at him in obvious astonishment. Cleo felt her cheeks grow hot.

"You will be all alone," she said to her sister.

"No, of course I will not," Elizabeth assured her. "I shall join Gwinn and Lord Kerby. It is time we went home anyway. I will be saved from having to call out the carriage for you if you go with Major Gilchrist. Not that I would mind, of course."

"Then I would be delighted," Cleo said, turning back to him.

And she was given all the novel pleasure of slipping her hand through the offered arm of a tall, handsome gentleman for all the world to see.

"Why are you not strolling here with a pretty young lady?" she asked as they walked away, back in the direction from which she had just come. She injected mock severity into her voice.

"I beg your pardon," he said, looking down at her. "But I thought that was precisely what I *was* doing."

Cleo laughed and felt suddenly and deliriously happy again.

"It was a fortunate coincidence, meeting you here," he said. "I had just come from your house, where I was told that you were out."

"You came to call upon me?" she asked. "Oh, Major Gilchrist, your brother will be in deep despair again today."

"Perhaps not," he said, and for a mere moment he set the fingertips of his free hand lightly over the back of her hand as it rested on his arm.

She would be very surprised if she did not discover five

small scorch marks there when she got home and removed her gloves. What a foolish fancy!

"I was wondering, Mrs. Pritchard," he said, bending his head closer to hers, "if you would be good enough to marry me."

He had not intended to come out with it quite as abruptly as that. He had had very few dealings with ladies even before he retired to the country five years ago, and no experience at all with courtship. It even occurred to him now that perhaps he ought to have spoken with her brother first.

But he had been agitated since last night.

Since two o' clock this morning, to be more precise.

He had been lying awake, his hands laced behind his neck, gazing up at the canopy above his head as he relived the evening's events. He had met a number of young ladies, all of them eligible, most of them pretty, most of them seemingly happy to be introduced to him and to dance with him. All of them appeared to know who he was—apart from just Mr. Jack Gilchrist, that was. A few of them gazed admiringly at him. One or two gazed adoringly. One asked him how it had *felt* getting shot and knowing that he had saved the life of the great Duke of Wellington—who had been simply Viscount Wellington at the time, of course, but Jack had not pointed that out.

It had seemed to him that any one of those young ladies would welcome his suit. In addition to his supposed heroism, there was, of course, the fact that he was heir to an earldom.

And there were a number of other eligible young ladies with whom he had not danced, simply because there were not enough sets in one evening.

Surprising and ridiculous as it seemed to him, it appeared that he was very eligible indeed. He would have no difficulty at all in accomplishing the task Matthew had set him.

But the trouble was, he had found as his eyes followed the pleats of silk over his head to the rosette behind which they all met in the center of the canopy, that he was having a hard time remembering the faces even of the young ladies with whom he *had* danced, though he had spent about twenty minutes with each. And if he *could* remember, then he could not recall the name that went with the face. And he could not recall what made each young lady different from all the others.

They all seemed the same to him in memory. Which was quite unfair to them, of course, for they were all individuals with lives and hopes and dreams of their own. They *deserved* to be remembered.

He could remember everything about Mrs. Pritchard. He had even noticed her *gown,* which had been of pale blue silk or satin overlaid with a silver net tunic. He could remember the way her brown hair had been piled high with tendrils of curls trailing over her temples and before her ears and along her neck. He could remember how her smile had softened the rather severe squareness of her face. He could recall the low sound of her laugh and the glow of happiness on her face as she waltzed. And he could remember thinking that he had not mistaken the matter on that embarrassing day in the Peninsula—she really *did* have startlingly beautiful blue eyes. It was a pity she kept them lowered much of the time.

Intimidation had caused that during her marriage, of course. And surely a natural shyness, too. But she had forgotten her shyness last evening. She had been genuinely glad to see him. If she remembered that embrace, then she had forgiven him.

He was spending too much time thinking of her, when he ought to be trying to remember if there was something about one of the young ladies with whom he had danced that would help him choose which one to court.

And then the answer came like a fist out of the darkness to punch him beneath the ribs, almost literally robbing him of breath.

Of course!

Mrs. Pritchard was young. The fact that she was a widow

whom he had known for so long had clouded his realization of that fact. He did not doubt she was several years younger than his own thirty. She was free. She liked him. They knew each other. Well, perhaps that was something of an exaggeration, but at least they were acquainted with each other, and they had been relaxed in each other's company last evening. They had talked with ease. They had laughed together. They had even been comfortably silent together.

They could be friends, he had sensed while they were together. He had planned to cultivate her friendship, to keep alive their acquaintance.

Why not marry *her*?

There was only one impediment. She had declared herself to be happy with her life. And he could believe that after a marriage that surely could not have brought her much happiness, she was glad to be free and intended to remain free.

Would she marry him?

There was only one way to find out, he had concluded, swinging his legs over the side of the bed, resting his elbows on his knees, and running the fingers of both hands through his hair.

He would ask her.

He did not know her well, but he was sure she would suit him.

And perhaps he would suit her.

And so, when he saw her in Hyde Park after the setback of finding her from home, he was so delighted and then so pleased that she agreed to allow him to escort her home that he blurted out his question without giving her any chance at all to guess where his conversation was leading and prepare herself mentally to deal with his proposal.

Dash it all, he was still just a gauche military officer, even though he had sold out more than five years ago.

"*If* it would suit you to do so, of course," he added to what he had already said.

He had shocked her. She had stopped walking, snatching

her hand from his arm as she did so. She looked up at him with wide, startled eyes. Her lips were parted.

"Marry you?" she said in a near whisper. She cleared her throat. "*Marry* you?"

"I hoped you might." He clasped his hands at his back and leaned slightly toward her, noting in some relief that they had drawn clear of the crowds about the Serpentine and were not likely to be overheard. "Indeed, I *hope* you *will,* though I ought not to have blurted out the question as I did. I ought to have waited until we had reached your house. Shall we wait and discuss the matter there?"

"But whyever," she asked, looking bewildered now, "would you wish to marry *me,* Major Gilchrist?"

He felt embarrassed—as he deserved to. She might as well have asked why he thought *she* would want to marry *him.* That was what she surely meant. He had been presumptuous. And he had been arrogant, assuming that any woman would be *glad* to marry him. Though he was not normally an arrogant man. At least, he did not believe he was.

"It occurred to me last night," he said, "that if I *must* marry, I would rather marry you than anyone else I met at Lady Claremont's ball or anyone else I am likely to meet at the next ball. Indeed, I would rather marry you than anyone else at all."

"If you *must* marry," she said.

"And it seems I must," he said, but suddenly he understood her meaning. He was offering for her, she was telling him, *only* because he must marry.

And the devil of it was that she was right.

Though he *did* like her. And now that he had thought of marrying—something he had always intended to do one day anyway—he really could not think of anyone he would *rather* marry. Or, since he did not know many ladies, he really did not think he would ever meet anyone he would rather marry than Mrs. Pritchard.

"*May* we discuss this further at your house?" he begged

her. "If you will allow me inside, that is. If you will not dismiss both me and my suit out of hand. In which case, I suppose there is nothing to discuss anyway. *May* I take you home now?"

"I shall positively die," she said, "if I do not have a cup of tea soon."

And when he offered his arm, she took it, and they resumed their walk to her house at a slightly brisker pace than before.

They walked in silence.

All she could think about was *tea*?

It was all she *wanted* to think about, and all she *would* have thought about if other thoughts had not been buzzing about in her head like a swarm of angry, trapped bees.

He wanted her to *marry* him.

She was *parched*.

No, he did not *want* it. He *needed* to marry, yet he did not relish the process of choosing a bride from among the myriad strangers he had seen in the ballroom last evening. He had a previous acquaintance with her and so it seemed less daunting simply to choose her.

When she swallowed, there was nothing *to* swallow. She almost choked on dryness.

He wanted to discuss his proposal further. She must concentrate her mind upon what she would say.

She had *no idea* what she would say.

Mrs. Evans usually kept a full kettle humming on the fire in the kitchen. It was to be hoped there was one there this afternoon, that her housekeeper had not used the hot water for something else, that she had not forgotten to fill the kettle. Or put it on the fire.

It was with such flitting, fluttering thoughts that Cleo occupied herself while she walked home with Major Gilchrist. And she wondered if she would wake up soon. But she must be awake already. She did not remember any dream *this* bizarre.

Mrs. Evans *did* have the kettle on to boil. She brought a tray of tea and sweet biscuits into the parlor a scant five minutes after Cleo and Major Gilchrist had entered the house. Cleo had busied herself in the meanwhile, removing her bonnet and gloves and arranging them neatly on the chair just inside the parlor door though usually she took them straight upstairs.

Major Gilchrist meanwhile had gone to stand close to the fireplace, his back to it. He clasped his hands behind him and stood with his booted feet slightly apart, like a soldier at ease on the parade ground.

Though she did not suppose he *was* at ease.

Mrs. Evans set down the tray, glanced curiously at the visitor, and left the room, shutting the door quietly behind her.

Cleo seated herself behind the tray and busied herself with pouring the tea and setting a few biscuits on each of the small plates. She handed one and a cup and saucer to the major.

"Thank you," he said, taking them and going to seat himself opposite her.

It was against Cleo's nature to take the initiative in a social situation. But on this occasion it was what she must do. *Some* sensible thoughts had been mingled with all the bees.

"Major Gilchrist," she said, "have you forgotten your main reason—indeed, your *only* reason—for wishing to marry? Is it not for the production of an heir?"

"Yes," he said, "though—"

She did not let him finish.

"I was married to Aubrey," she said, "for five years. I had no children with him. And no miscarriages. Would it not seem foolish even to consider marrying me under the circumstances?"

She did not look at him. She rearranged the teapot on the tray and remembered that she had not asked him if he took milk or sugar.

There was a short silence.

"I did not hear of Colonel Pritchard having *any* children," he said. "Yet you were his second wife, I believe. How long was he married to the first?"

"Twelve years," she said. "And no, there were no children."

She raised her eyes to his.

"It is altogether possible, then," he said, "even probable, that you are not barren."

Cleo felt her cheeks flush.

"But it would surely be unwise to take the risk of marrying me," she said, "when I was married all that time without once conceiving."

"There are no guarantees with any marriage," he said. "Any lady I choose to marry may prove barren. Or she may produce only daughters. Or *I* may be incapable of begetting children."

She felt suddenly dizzy at the intimate nature of their conversation. They had never conversed at all before last night. They were really little more than strangers.

"I wish to marry *you,* Mrs. Pritchard," he said. "I realize that it is perhaps selfish of me to ask when you made it clear last evening that you lead a full and happy life as a widow. It has occurred to me that you may intend never to give up your freedom again, that your happiness *depends* upon that freedom. And if that is so, I will not pester you. I hope we may be friends, but I may have made that impossible now. I decided to take the risk of asking you anyway. You would do me a great service as well as an honor by marrying me."

A service. Major Gilchrist certainly did not have a golden tongue. But she was glad of it. He spoke plainly, and so she could plainly understand.

He needed a wife. She was available, and he knew her slightly and did not have to start at the very beginning with her. He needed a son, and she might be fertile if the fact that neither she nor Aubrey's first wife had conceived was not simple coincidence. He was willing to take the risk since marrying her was more convenient than embarking upon any other courtship.

Did any of it matter?

She could be married. She could marry the only man she had ever loved. She knew him to be a kind man. As an officer, he had been everything he needed to be. He could be a firm disciplinarian when occasion called for it, but mostly it had not been necessary. His men had worshiped him and obeyed him simply out of their perfect trust in him and their desire to please him. In return, he had loved them and protected them and risked their lives only when it was absolutely necessary—as it often was in war, of course.

And he was a handsome man and an attractive one too—and there *was* sometimes a difference. His kiss had been by far the most wonderful experience of her life. She could have far more than his kisses for the rest of her life.

There was only one problem—well, two really.

The first was that she feared dreadfully that perhaps she *was* barren, that she would not be able to provide him with the one thing for which he had married her. Yet he would be stuck with her for life. And she with him. It would be dreadful indeed to know that there was no foundation left upon which to build anything positive—affection, friendship, a shared life.

But far more important than that fear was her second problem. He did not love her. He did not pretend to. He was not marrying for love and he was being quite open and honest about it. She might have accepted that fact, knowing that he was a good and kind man and that she might expect a comfortable marriage with him. But the trouble was that she *did* love him. And she did not know if she could bear to be married to him when there was no hope of having her feelings returned and when she must spend every day and every night disguising the way she felt.

It might be better not to be married to him at all.

Or maybe she was being very foolish. Was it better to be without him for the rest of her life when she might be *with* him?

Might she spend the rest of her life bitterly regretting her decision if she refused? And knowing when he married and *whom* he married? And knowing about their growing family?

Of course she would bitterly regret her foolishness.

But perhaps she would bitterly regret marrying him if that was what she decided to do.

How was she to decide?

A rather lengthy silence had fallen on them.

"I am a clumsy fellow, Mrs. Pritchard," he said. "And not just at the waltz. I ought to have spent some time cultivating your acquaintance and gradually making my intentions known to you. Do forgive me. Would you like some time to consider your answer? Or is it simply no? Do tell me if it is. I would not distress you."

She had been running one finger over the handle of the teapot and watching its progress. She raised her eyes to his again.

"Yes," she said. "I *would* like some time, Major Gilchrist. My answer ought to be no and perhaps will be no. But I— yes, I would like some time if you are prepared to give it."

He got to his feet.

"May I return tomorrow?" he asked her. "Or is that too soon? Two days from now? Three?"

"Tomorrow," she said. "At this time. I will remain home."

Taking longer would not help her decision. She would merely think herself in circles, as she probably would even with only one day in which to do it. She really *did* ought to say no. And she probably *would*. But she was also horribly tempted. And part of her was amazed that she hesitated at all, that she did not simply jump at the chance to be deliriously happy. Happily-ever-after happy.

Perhaps she *had* learned something from experience. Perhaps she was not such a pathetic, abject creature as she used to be.

This time she was *choosing* whether to marry or not.

The very sensible thought did not help at all.

He was bowing to her.

"Tomorrow, then," he said. "Good afternoon to you, Mrs. Pritchard."

And he strode from the room without looking back.

Her biscuits were still on her plate, Cleo realized. There was a grayish film of coldness over the untouched tea in her cup.

He had not touched either his plate or his cup either.

Chapter Four

*C*harlotte, in anticipation of Jack's arrival in Town and of his agreeing to Matthew's plea, had organized a dinner party for that evening. And, as might have been expected, each group of invited guests included at least one unattached, eligible young lady. Two of them were seated on either side of him at dinner, and in the drawing room afterward he found himself, at Charlotte's suggestion, over at the pianoforte, turning pages of music for another as she entertained the company. He danced incessantly after the carpet was rolled back and all the young persons took to the floor while the mother of one of them supplied the music.

It was all very informal, very jolly, and very *obvious*. It was soon perfectly clear to Jack that each young lady and each parent was well aware that he was in Town to choose a bride, who could in time expect to produce a future Earl of Waterton. It was equally clear that the almost awed admiration with which he had been greeted five years ago on his return from the Peninsula really had not abated to any marked degree in the interim. The Duke of Wellington was by now, of course—since the Battle of Waterloo last year—the most famous, most venerated man in England. And Jack had once saved his life. He could not even deny it. It was true.

But that did not make him a *hero*. Any soldier would have done the same thing if he had been in that particular spot at that particular time. And Wellington had always had a habit of moving coolly about a battlefield, well within firing range.

Jack found it all very wearying. He longed for his cottage and his solitary life. But both were, alas, no longer attainable. When he married, Matthew was already insisting, he would reside in the main house at Rigdon. And when he married, of course, he would no longer be alone.

He made his way on foot the following afternoon to Mrs. Pritchard's house. He was still castigating himself for rushing her when he ought to have spent at least a week or two taking her for walks and drives, dancing with her at balls, speaking with her at concerts and soirees, and so forth. He ought to have let her see—and everyone else too—that he favored her. He ought to have given her time to prepare herself for his offer. And he really ought to have spoken to her brother. And possibly to his.

He was nervous. What had she decided? More than ever he hoped she *would* marry him. The thought of having to choose and court someone else was daunting, to say the least. He did not *fancy* anyone else.

He *did* fancy Mrs. Pritchard. The realization had taken him somewhat by surprise during the night—yet another one in which he had got precious little sleep. He had realized that, even apart from the necessity of getting married, he actually *wanted* to marry her. Something about her . . . soothed him, if that was the word his mind sought. He liked her. He sensed that they would deal very well together, that they could have a good life together.

No, *soothed* was not the right word. Neither was *liked*. He felt a definite attraction to her. And what was more, he suspected he always had.

It was strange, really considering the fact that she had never said or done anything to draw anyone's attention her way, much less to *attract* anyone. Quite the contrary.

But there had always been something about her. It was something he had never tried to explain to himself before now, for of course she had been another man's wife. And even when he had finally kissed her, it had been such a dreadfully inappropriate response to the occasion that he had been consumed with guilt and embarrassment afterward. He had embraced—and sexually wanted—another man's wife when she was at her most vulnerable.

And so all thoughts of the incident—and of her—had been firmly suppressed. Very successfully, as it had turned out. Until he saw her again two evenings ago, he had forgotten her to all intents and purposes.

He had arrived at the house. He knocked on the door and waited. If she refused him today, he would always wonder whether her answer would have been different had he wooed her with greater care. But such thoughts were pointless. It was too late to do things differently now. And he had promised not to pester her if her answer was no.

The door was opened by the servant who had brought the tea tray yesterday. She appeared to be expecting him. She took his hat and gloves and showed him into the parlor.

Mrs. Pritchard was seated where she had sat yesterday. She was in the process of setting aside her embroidery. She was all cool poise as she got to her feet and indicated the chair where *he* had sat.

"Good afternoon, Major Gilchrist," she said.

It was impossible to read anything in her face.

"Mrs. Pritchard," he said, inclining his head.

She sat back down, and he took his seat. She picked up her embroidery again and bent her head to her work.

Good Lord, this was awkward.

"The sun is shining again," he said. "It is actually quite warm outside. Perhaps you would like—"

She did not let him finish.

"I have thought since yesterday," she said. "I have thought and thought. But thoughts can move in endless circles and settle nothing. Eventually a decision must be made."

"I am deeply sorry," he said, "if—"

"I believe I gave you the wrong impression two evenings ago," she said. "Indeed, I know I did, because I did it deliberately. I let you believe that I am happy in my widowhood, that my life is busy and fulfilled. That is not actually the case."

Ah. Perhaps he ought to have guessed it. But he knew so little about her. Indeed, he knew very little about *women*.

"I am not *un*happy," she said. "And my life is not empty of meaning or activities or friends. I do not *need* a man in my life. I can live alone with some contentment, for the rest of my days if necessary. But I would *like* to have a man, preferably as a husband but not necessarily so."

He gazed at her bowed head in some shock. Had she just said what he *thought* she had said?

"Mrs. Pritchard," he said, "I hope I have not given the impression that my intentions are anything less than honorable?"

She looked up at him, her eyes huge and calm.

"No, of course you have not," she said. "You need to *marry*. I do not."

Her eyes went back to her work, and her hand pushed the needle through the cloth again and drew it back out. They were graceful, elegant hands.

"The trouble with marriage," she said, "from my point of view anyway, is that it is so very permanent. I cannot try it and then decide that after all it is not what I want. I know that from experience."

"If you marry me," he said, "I will spend the rest of my life seeing to it that you do not regret your decision. That is no idle promise."

"No, I know it is not." She set her work down in her lap again, the needle still in her hand, and looked at him once more. "But you would be powerless to prevent my regretting the decision if I discovered after a few months that I cannot conceive a child. *You* could not fail to regret it if that happened, though you would, of course, behave for the rest of our lives with scrupulous honor and courtesy. It would not be a happy marriage, Major Gilchrist, for either of us, and the only type of marriage that could lure me away from my freedom is one that gives some promise of being at least mildly happy."

"In all probability," he said, "you *can* have children, Mrs. Pritchard. In all probability, so can I. But there are no guarantees. There never are. There never *can* be."

"Yes," she said quietly, looking down to thread her needle through the cloth before setting her hands, one on top of the other, over it, "there can be."

He frowned in incomprehension.

She looked up at him again.

"I realized in the end last night," she said, "that despite all the arguments against accepting your offer, I would nevertheless say yes except for one thing. Only one of those arguments was a stumbling block I could not see my way past. I may be barren. You cannot know how long five years can seem to a woman who waits in hope at each month's end before pinning her hope on the *next* month. I always longed for a child. It would have validated my hasty decision to marry Aubrey. It would have enriched my life."

He opened his mouth to speak, but she held up a staying hand and he closed it again.

"If it could be proved that I am not barren," she said, "then I would marry you, Major Gilchrist. Gladly. There are two months or so of the Season remaining. If that proof could be made during that time, then I would marry you. Indeed, I would have no choice *but* to marry you. But if there were no proof, then my answer would be no. For both our sakes."

He was on his feet, Jack realized. His hands were clenched into fists at his sides.

"What are you suggesting?" he asked, though he would have to be an imbecile not to understand.

"It is really quite the accepted thing, you know," she said, "for a widow to take a lover, provided the affair is conducted discreetly and does not cause any open scandal. I believe I would like to have a lover for a couple of months. It is four years since Aubrey died. "

"*Mrs. Pritchard*," he said, using a voice he had not used since selling his commission, "enough of this. You are suggesting that I *debauch* you? It is something I would not do in a million years."

"Well, then," she said, "my answer must be no."

He might have turned and stridden from the room and the house had not her eyes filled with sudden tears a moment before she hid them by lowering the lids over them.

Fatally, he hesitated.

Tears?

Why?

"I thank you for your kind offer," she said. But her voice was no longer the calm, flat sound it had been until now. It shook. She stopped and swallowed. When she spoke again, she sounded breathless. "But I must decline it, Major Gilchrist. I do wish you well in your search for a bride. I am quite sure you will have no trouble at all. I wish you happy."

He frowned down at the top of her head, hesitated again, and then closed the distance between them. She did not look up. He went down on one knee before her and possessed himself of one of her hands. It was, as he expected, as cold as marble. He dipped his head and saw that her eyes were still swimming with tears.

"You were *serious*?" he said.

"Yes," she agreed. "And it had nothing to do with debauchery or immorality. It is *not* immoral for a widow to take a lover. Whom would I be likely to harm? It is not as if you are a married man. And it would be over before you married someone else."

"Or," he said, "it would result in our marriage if I were to impregnate you."

"Yes," she said.

"I would feel as if I were insulting you," he said, "and treating you like a broodmare."

"Nonsense." She sniffed. "The suggestion was mine, not yours."

He handed her his handkerchief and waited while she dried her eyes and blew her nose. She crumpled the handkerchief, hesitated, and then shoved it behind her on the chair.

"Will you not reconsider?" he asked her. "Will you not marry me without conditions? I really do *wish* to marry you, you know. There is no one else, and I would really rather there not be."

"You are kind," she said.

"I am not offering out of *kindness*," he told her as he got to his feet.

"No, I know." She seemed more in command of herself again. "And it is for that reason I would need to be sure."

She was looking steadily at him now.

"I would like to be married to you, Major Gilchrist," she said. "But only if I were sure that I could offer you sons or at least the *chance* of sons."

He wished he had never mentioned to her his reason for marrying. He ran the fingers of one hand through his hair.

"But where . . . ?" He tried again. "When . . . ?"

"Mrs. Evans's regular day off is tomorrow," she said. "She is my housekeeper and cook. And this morning I insisted that my maid take paid leave for a month or longer. Her father is very ill, probably dying, and her mother is nursing him while coping with eight other children."

She had thought this through before his arrival, Jack could see.

They stared at each other, her cheeks gradually flushing.

This was *not* something he ought to do.

"I shall come again tomorrow, then?" he said.

"Yes." She clasped her hands together. "If you will."

He bowed to her and took his leave.

If you will. As if he had offered to take her for a drive in the park or for a visit to some gallery.

Would he? He strode down the street, pondering the question. Would he go back there tomorrow to bed her? And continue to do so daily until she was with child or until it became clear that it was not going to happen? But the test period was to be only two months. Surely it often took longer. . .

This was madness.

But he wanted her. Despite everything back there at her house, despite his shock and discomfort at what she suggested, he had felt the stirrings of desire. Perhaps because she was the last person he would have expected to make such an improper suggestion.

Tomorrow he could act upon his desire.

Would he?

Did *she* desire *him*? She wanted to marry him. She had made that clear. Perhaps she also found him attractive.

He was going to have to think. Long and hard.

One thing he knew. He wanted to marry her. Even if Matthew were to inform him when he arrived home that everything had changed and he could return to Dorsetshire and his cottage, he would not go. Not before he knew beyond all hope that she would not have him.

But of course Matthew would *not* release him from the obligation. And Mrs. Pritchard knew of it and would not release him from it either. She would marry him only if she was satisfied that she was capable of helping him fulfill that obligation.

Dash it all, he was going to have to *think*.

Cleo sat at her dressing table the following afternoon, brushing her hair. She gathered it into a jeweled clip at the neck and let the length of it fall loose down her back. She liked to wear it this way when she was home alone and was not expecting visitors. Without all the curls and ringlets that were necessary for a woman to be properly dressed, her face looked less large, less square.

Today, of course, she *was* expecting a visitor.

She had thought everything through with deliberate care. She was still pleased with the very sensible solution she had found to a dilemma that had seemed at first to be without solution.

This way she could both ensure that neither she nor Jack Gilchrist was forced to live through the disappointment of a childless marriage *and* avoid the bleakness of saying an outright no to his marriage proposal. If he was right and she *could* have children, then this way she would be able to both marry him and present him with the child he needed—assuming, that was, she would have a son. But nothing could be absolutely guaranteed.

And, if she could *not* have children, or at least if she did not conceive within two months, then she would remain free of a marriage that would have brought her nothing but ultimate pain and him a quiet frustration. In the meantime, she would enjoy him as a lover for two whole months.

It all still made perfect sense to her.

She was *not* going to start feeling guilty. It really *was* unexceptionable for a widow to take a lover. And if *unexceptionable* was perhaps a little too strong a word, then certainly *accepted* was not. She was free to take a lover without having to feel a qualm of conscience.

And if the thought had crossed her mind, as it inevitably had, that losing him after two months if she failed to conceive was going to be too excruciatingly painful to be borne, then she ignored the thought. She would deal with it when the time came.

If the time came.

She might just as possibly be getting married in two months' time, or even sooner.

Cleo got to her feet and went to stand at the window of her bedchamber to look down at the street outside. And there he was in the distance, striding purposefully toward her house, five full minutes early.

Her stomach lurched. She looked back over her shoulder. The bedcovers were neatly turned down, the two pillows plumped up side by side. She looked down at herself. She was fully dressed since she had not liked the thought of answering the knock on the door in her dressing gown. She was not wearing stays, though, since it was difficult to lace herself into them.

She squared her shoulders and lifted her chin, schooled her features, as she had done yesterday afternoon, into calm placidity, and started downstairs. There was a firm knock at the door before she reached the bottom. She almost lost her courage at that point and scurried back upstairs to wait until he had gone away again.

But her life had been one long exercise in timidity.

She finished descending and hurried to the door to let in her lover.

Her first thought was that he looked like Major Gilchrist. Which was patently absurd, for of course that was precisely who he was. But . . . he looked like *Major* Gilchrist. Like a soldier, an officer—cold, commanding, self-possessed.

And then their eyes met and his softened. He smiled.

"Mrs. Pritchard," he said.

She stood aside to let him in and shut the door after him. Now already they were in the realm of impropriety, a single man and a single woman alone in a house together. She took courage now that it had started.

"Call me Cleo," she said, turning to look at him. "It is short for Cleopatra, but fortunately, no one except my father has ever called me that."

He removed his hat and gloves and set them down on the hall table.

"Cleo," he said. "I am Jack. Short for John." He grinned. "But no one has ever called me that."

She clasped her hands at her waist and smiled back at him. She had smelled cologne as he passed her—very subtle and very masculine. It had made her feel slightly short of breath.

"Mrs. . . . *Cleo*," he said, and he looked at her with his very direct gaze. He clasped his hands behind his back. "I have taken the liberty of informing my brother and sister-in-law that I intend courting you."

Her eyes widened in shock and some horror.

"I deemed it necessary," he said, "since I will not be courting anyone else during the next month or two and I would not have them think that I was not doing what I had promised to do."

"Oh," she said, "you ought not to have told them, Major Gilchrist. They must be *horrified*."

"Not at all. Why should they be?" he said. "They were a little surprised, perhaps, that I have chosen a widow rather than a girl fresh out of the schoolroom. And a little surprised too that they do not know you, though Charlotte did catch a glimpse of you in the park two days ago. Matthew does know Sir Alfred King, your brother, however, and considers him a worthy gentleman. Once I had assured them that I knew and liked you in the Peninsula and that you are, in fact, younger than I, though I do not know your exact age, then they were quite delighted to know that I have already fixed my choice sufficiently to embark upon an actual courtship."

"But," she said, "you are *not* courting me."

"Indeed I am," he said. "What do you call it?"

"An affair," she said.

She was still, she realized, standing just inside the front door. He was still only a few steps into the hallway.

"With a view to marriage," he said. "The proposal has already been made, and you have already given a conditional acceptance. Courtship is the right word. An affair is an open-ended thing, one that either or both the participants fully mean to end as soon as the pleasure has gone. It is a trivial thing, something in which I am not interested. Not with you."

"I *wish*," she said, "you had not told anyone."

"They want to meet you," he said. "This evening, in fact. They have a private box at the theater and plan to go there this evening. They have invited us to join them."

Her eyes had widened again.

"I cannot *go to the theater* with the Earl and Countess of Waterton," she said, aghast. "Not *this evening*. Not after *this afternoon*."

His eyes looked away from hers for a few silent moments, and then he sighed and looked back.

"Whatever happens this afternoon," he said, "need not affect this evening. Not unless, after all, you believe this afternoon will transform you into a fallen woman instead of a widow exercising her freedom to take a lover. But, Cleo, why put that to the test? You told me yesterday that you are *not* as happy in your aloneness as you led me to believe at Lady Claremont's ball. You told me you would *like* to marry me and that you *will* if I can get you with child before the end of the Season. Why not leave the whole possibility, or probability, of conception and its outcome to nature, as the vast majority of couples do, and marry me anyway?"

"No," she said after only a moment's hesitation.

She could not give him an explanation. Perhaps she could not even give herself one that made proper sense. If she only *liked* him, and if she only wanted to be married again, she surely would accept his offer gladly. But she *loved* him. She was not even sure why that fact made all the difference, for of course, even if she *did* conceive and *did* marry him as a consequence, she would still be facing a marriage in which she loved while she was only liked in return. But at least they would both have a child to love equally.

The fact that she loved him *did* make a difference, however illogical the idea sounded.

"No?" He raised his eyebrows.

"No," she said again.

"Well, then." He reached out a hand for hers, and his eyes moved over her from head to toe.

She was acutely conscious of her casually dressed hair, of

the fact that she was not wearing stays beneath her dress and must look plumper than she normally did, of—

But she was mortally tired of feeling unattractive and inferior. And he was *not* Aubrey, who had used her with tedious frequency even while constantly complaining of her lack of all claim to beauty. He was *Jack*. And if he did not like what he saw or what he got in the bed upstairs, then he could simply go away and she would forge contentment out of the rest of her life alone.

She set her hand in his, and his fingers closed warmly and strongly about it.

"Where—?" he asked.

"Upstairs," she said. But she took a firm step toward him. This was *not* in any way going to be like what she had known and endured with Aubrey. "Kiss me first. Before we go up. As you did once in the Peninsula."

His eyes looked arrested.

"You *do* remember," he said.

"Of course I remember," she said. And then, very rashly, before she could choose her words with more care, "It was my first kiss. And the only one. Ever."

His head snapped back as though he had been punched in the chin. And then his eyes softened and moved to her lips.

"I am so sorry," he said.

"I am *not*," she assured him. "Kiss me again."

And he did, his mouth touching hers, lips slightly parted. And then his arms came about her waist and drew her against him while *her* arms twined about his neck and clung tightly.

It was the same and yet different. This time he did not smell of sweat and dust and blood and smoke. He smelled of soap and his subtle cologne. And this time there was none of the fierceness of that first kiss. He kissed her softly, warmly, opening his mouth over hers, tasting her lips with his tongue, exploring inside when she parted her own lips and sliding deep when she parted her teeth, slow enjoyment giving place to something warmer, to the promise of a far greater heat to come.

And yet there was the same flaring of what, if she had been forced to put a word to it, she could only have described as *joy*. Joy and yearning and desire and *rightness*. The feeling that she *was* worth this, that she had as much to give as she had to receive.

That she was an equal partner in the encounter.

He lifted his head from hers but did not move it back more than a few inches. He gazed into her eyes, his own heavy with . . . desire. It was unmistakably desire, but not the sort she was accustomed to, the sort that preceded the order to lie on her back and was followed by a swift one-sided journey to grunting, animal satisfaction. This was. . .

Well, sometimes there were no words.

Sometimes there were not really even thoughts.

"Take me upstairs, Cleo," he said, his voice a low caress.

"Yes," she said.

Chapter Five

The bedchamber had been prepared for the occasion, Jack could see as soon as he stepped inside and closed the door behind him. The covers had been turned back neatly on the bed, the pillows nicely plumped. The curtains were half drawn across the window. Pots and brushes were lined up in orderly fashion on the dressing table, books pushed into a tidy pile on one of the bedside tables. Nothing had been left lying around, though apparently there were no servants in the house to clean up after her.

A single shaft of sunlight shone through the window and slanted across the foot of the bed.

Curtains, carpet, bedcovers, wallpaper—all were in varying shades of green, like a spring garden. It was both surprising and pleasing for a bedchamber.

But Jack took it all in at a glance. His attention was focused upon Cleo—Cleopatra. The latter was about as inappropriate a name as any her father might have given her.

She was all small, soft womanhood. Strangely appealing. Strangely desirable. Strange because she was not the sort of woman who was obviously beautiful. Though there were, of course, her eyes.

They gazed into his now a little uncertainly. She did not know what to do next now that she had brought him here. She had had five years' experience at marriage but did not know how to proceed with a lover.

She had had a husband who never kissed her. And it was hard to imagine that he had shown her tenderness in other ways instead.

The man had been a vicious soldier. The sick joke had sometimes circulated in the officers' mess that Colonel Pritchard had killed more of his own men for various misdemeanors than all of Napoleon Bonaparte's soldiers combined had done in combat.

Cleo Pritchard had been kissed only once in her life until a few minutes ago. And she had remembered the embrace and had wanted it repeated.

Jack framed her face with his hands, ran his thumbs lightly across her lips, and lowered his head to kiss her again. And he was instantly engulfed again in the warm fragrance of her. He was not sure if it was soap or perfume he smelled. It was so faint a scent that it seemed more the fragrance of *her*.

He moved his hands over her head while he deepened the kiss, feeling the soft smoothness of her hair. Her hands rested on either side of his waist.

This was wrong, he knew, even though his treacherous body disagreed with him. He had hoped to prevent it happening by telling Matt and Charlotte that he was courting her and then telling *her* that they were cautiously pleased. But she had held to her strange sense of honor. She would not marry him unless she could be sure she was capable of bearing his children.

Though he had the feeling now that there was more than just that. He had the feeling that she needed this, that she craved the touch of a man who would *kiss* her before he used her. Perhaps it was herself she protected by insisting that they have an affair before they married. Perhaps the fear of another marriage in which there was no tenderness was too much for her to bear.

He raised his head and gazed into her eyes again. They were deep and defenseless now.

"There will always be tenderness," he said softly.

A small frown of incomprehension creased her brow for a moment.

"It will never be just for a slaking of appetite," he said, "and never just for procreation. There will always be tenderness. There will always be you and me, never just me."

Her eyes told him that she understood though she said nothing.

"Let me help you off with your dress," he said, and she turned obediently for him to undo the hooks at the back of it. He wondered briefly how she had managed to do them up if her maid was not here. She swept her hair forward over one shoulder and bent her head.

Ah.

She was wearing no stays, as he had suspected, and nothing else either, beneath her dress. He nudged it off her shoulders, and she held it in place with her hands spread over her breasts. But she released her hold as she turned toward him, and the dress slid to the floor. She was wearing no stockings, either. When she stepped free of her dress and her slippers, she stood naked before him. She looked at him with those large, calm eyes, and he realized for the first time that it was an expression she must have cultivated long ago to hide a tumult of feelings. She was a woman who had hidden very effectively inside herself for a long, long time, he suspected. At least since her marriage.

His eyes moved over her. She was not excessively slender. She had pleasing curves and sturdy, nicely shaped legs. Her hair was in a thick cloud down her back. He had not noticed her freeing it from the clip at the back of her neck.

He reached out both hands and slid them lightly down over

her breasts before cupping them from the undersides and touching her nipples with his thumbs. Her skin was warm and soft and silky. Her nipples hardened under his touch.

The blood was humming through his body, catching at his breath.

"Cleo," he said softly, "you are beautiful."

And he spoke the simple truth.

She bit her lip, and there was uncertainty in her eyes. Vulnerability. She did not believe in her own beauty. Had Pritchard not discovered it? Was that why she had allowed herself to grow plump in the Peninsula?

"Lie down for me," he said, "while I undress."

And she turned without a word and did as she was told. Unquestioned obedience. He drew a slow breath as he divested himself of his coat and waistcoat and pulled his shirt free of his pantaloons. This was all by her choice. It was what she wanted, what she had insisted upon if she wished her to marry him.

Why had he accepted her conditions?

Why had he not simply walked away and found someone else?

Because it was she, and she alone, whom he wanted? Was he *in love* with her, then?

But how could he be? He scarcely knew her. Though he was about to get to know her a good deal better.

She watched him quietly as he undressed. And finally, as his pantaloons and his drawers dropped to the floor, she spoke, and the illusion of quiet submissiveness went away, much to his relief, though her words both amused him and touched him.

"You are beautiful too, Jack," she said. "Truly beautiful. With your clothes and without them. Not many men are, I suspect, though I have not seen many men unclothed, of course."

And as she looked up into his eyes, suddenly her own were filled with merriment while he grinned back at her, and they both burst into laughter.

A certain uncomfortable tension had been broken, and she reached out her arms to him. She had not covered herself with any of the bedclothes.

"Come, then," she said. "Be my lover, Jack."

And it seemed to him that for the moment she had forgotten *why* he was to be her lover, that she wanted this merely for the pleasure of it. For the *mutual* pleasure. It seemed to him that she had accepted her own attractions and believed herself to be beautiful.

Had he been able to do that much for her? To convince her?

He lay down beside her on the bed, turned onto his side, and propped his weight on one elbow. He leaned over her and kissed her, and she surged over onto her side to face him, pressed her body against his, wrapped her arms about him, and kissed him back with hot ardor.

He would have taken it slowly. He wanted to give her tenderness, the experience of knowing a lover who would make the time to give as well as to take. He wanted to make love to her. He wanted to give her all the pleasure of knowing sex as it could be with a man who was not simply a brute. And perhaps he wanted it for himself too, a slow building of sensual pleasure before the driving need of sexual appetite took over. He too was ending a long sexual dearth.

But she would have none of it, and he understood the reason within moments, for he found that he shared it. She was hungry. Starved, rather. And it was not tenderness she needed. Not now. Not this first time. It was the wonder and power of her human sexuality. She needed to celebrate her own beautiful womanhood.

And he needed the corresponding affirmation of his own manhood.

He would not have been able to put all this into words if he had been called upon to do so. But he felt her need and his own instinctively, and because she would be his wife if he could convince her, and also the mother of his children, and because he cared for her, he could give her only what she needed and wanted. What *he* needed and wanted.

She was all hot, sensual woman and he was . . . By God, he was on fire too. It had been a long time. Too long. And never with her. Never with Cleo.

Tenderness be damned!

And so within minutes he rolled her to her back and came on top of her, pressed his knees between her thighs—not that she needed any encouragement, slid his hands beneath her buttocks, and pressed deep and hard into her.

Her arms were iron bands about his body. Her legs twined tightly about his. And firm inner muscles clenched about him, causing sweet, hot agony.

"Jack." Her voice was low. "Ah, Jack."

He withdrew to the brink of her and thrust back inside and began to work her as slowly, as thoroughly as his control would allow. There was not a great deal of it left, by God. She met and matched his rhythm and clung tightly to him until incredibly, before his control went, she crashed into release, calling his name again as she did so.

He plunged gratefully after her, spilling his seed and the last of his energy into her and collapsing his weight onto her while he recovered his breath.

Good God!

Like a randy schoolboy.

And yet not.

Good God!

He disengaged from her and lay beside her, waiting for his heart to slow. For his breath to become less audible. He felt cool and slick with sweat. He laid the back of one hand over his eyes—that shaft of sunlight had moved up the bed and found his face.

He realized a few moments later—though it was probably somewhat longer than *just* a few moments—that he must have dozed off. He turned his head sharply to look at her.

She was gazing back, her head turned to the side, her eyes calm again. She had pulled the covers up over them both. Her arms were on the outside, but the sheet decently covered her breasts.

She suddenly looked like Mrs. Pritchard again.

"I hope," she said placidly, "that has done the job, though it would be too good to be true if it happened the very first time, I suppose. Thank you for making it a pleasant experience, Jack."

Pleasant? Done the job? What the devil?

"Pleasant?" He raised his eyebrows.

"You made it seem," she said, "as if it was not *just* about proving whether I can conceive or not, and I am grateful for that."

Good Lord, she really was firmly back within her fortified defenses.

He raised himself on one elbow again and propped his head on his hand.

"If that was only *pleasant,* Mrs. Pritchard," he said, "I think perhaps I ought to go home and shoot myself."

Her eyes widened with shock, then clouded with uncertainty, and finally twinkled with merriment. She laughed— that low, merry sound that so attracted him.

"I think perhaps I ought to save your life," she said, "by telling the truth."

"I think you ought." He looked steadily back at her.

Her smile faded and her cheeks grew pink.

"It was a great deal better than *pleasant,*" she said, her voice hesitant. "At least for me it was."

"Was he a terrible brute?" he asked softly, his eyes never leaving hers.

"Aubrey?" she said. "No. He never beat me."

"Is that the best you can say about the way he treated you?" he asked.

"He told me frequently that I was not beautiful," she said. "But he was telling no more than the tr—"

He pressed a finger across her lips.

"He was a filthy liar as well as a brute," he said. "Or *I* am a liar. Take your pick."

"Oh, Jack," she said against his finger.

"Take your pick," he said again.

She sighed.

"You are beautiful," he said. "I was not a virgin before today, Cleo. I have had many liaisons, though none since my return to England. Until now, that is. I am sure it is extremely bad manners to compare one woman with another in the hearing of one of those women, but I am just a rough soldier and would not recognize good manners if they were to stand toe to toe with me and jab me in the nose. In comparison with the others, you are so superior that you make the comparison ridiculous. Like comparing the sun to a speck of dirt."

Her smile was slow until it lit up her face.

"Oh, Jack," she said, "you are wonderful."

And she raised both arms and pulled his head down to hers again.

It was more wonderful the second time. No, that was not right. *Wonderful* was a word like *perfect*. It was a superlative. Nothing could be more wonderful than wonderful.

The second time was *different*. It was far slower. It was more tender. It was more . . . personal.

They took time to explore each other with hands and lips and tongues—and even teeth. They murmured soft words to each other, though Cleo could never afterward remember exactly what they had said. They looked at each other, gazing into each other's eyes while they made love. And when they finished, they finished together and sighed out their contentment against the side of each other's face. And when he moved off her, he kept one arm beneath her head and she snuggled against him while she gazed out of the window at a clear blue sky.

It was only then that she felt a little uncomfortable. Oh, not physically. She probably felt cozier, more relaxed than she ever had. She could easily nod off to sleep.

But it was not supposed to be this way. When she had thought things through yesterday morning and the night before that, she had come to a clear understanding of how she might proceed, of how *they* might proceed. It had all made perfect, rational sense. They would discover one way or the other whether she could have children and decide their future accordingly. Nothing could be simpler.

Or more pleasing to her. For however things turned out, she would have Jack for two months out of her life. It would be better than nothing.

She had expected it to be pleasant, the process of finding out, that was. Yes, she really had even though it had never ever been pleasant for her before. She had expected it to be quiet and sedate—though that second was not *quite* the word her mind sought. She had expected to feel happy afterward. She had expected her thoughts to be centered upon the question of whether she *had* or whether she had *not* conceived.

She would not be feeling uneasy at all, she thought now, if everything had proceeded according to her expectations.

It had not been pleasant at all. Oh, it *had* been, but only in the way a spectacular sunset might be described as *nice* or the way a mouse in comparison with an elephant might be described as *smaller.*

She had been shaken to the roots of her being. And being in love with Jack—which she had been for years—had suddenly taken on a wholly new dimension. For though she had looked forward to going to bed with him and had certainly not expected it to be an ordeal, it had not occurred to her that the physical act could be such a powerful, integral expression of her love.

And why had he not simply proceeded to business?

She was going to be severely punished for her immorality if she did not conceive, she thought. She would be forced to live out the rest of her life on memory alone.

Punishment. Immorality. Was that how she was thinking now, then? She was no longer an independent widow, for whom it was quite acceptable to take a lover?

All because she had *enjoyed* the act?

Would she feel less sinful if she had *not* enjoyed it?

And *why* had he not simply performed the act?

He had made her feel . . . cherished. Attractive. Even beautiful.

He had made her feel *wanted*. She had never felt wanted before. *Needed,* yes. Aubrey had needed to use her since he was surprisingly fastidious in his personal habits and feared contracting some dreaded disease from prostitutes. Yes, he had actually told her that.

But he had never *wanted* her.

It had felt as if Jack *had*.

He was smoothing a hand over her head and lowered his mouth to kiss her at the hairline.

"A penny for them," he said.

Her thoughts? She tipped back her head and smiled at him. His face was only inches from her own. Ah, he was so very handsome. And there was a look of lazy contentment in his eyes.

"I was thinking how . . . *pleasant* this is," she said, and his eyes smiled back into hers. "I am not great with words."

"Only with feelings?" he said. "Tell me about your feelings, Cleo. What makes you happy? What are your hopes? Your dreams?"

You, to all three. But it was not what she said.

"I am not a wild dreamer," she said. "I never have been. I am a dull creature. Little things make me happy—flowers, sunshine, birds singing. I hope to have a home in the country again one day, though I am not ungrateful that Aubrey left this house to me. I would have had to go live with Alfred if he had not, and that would have been a burden to him and to Megan. I dream of a cottage with a garden. And with a thatched roof and whitewashed walls and roses growing over the lintel."

"And other people to share that home with you?" he asked.

She hesitated. But why not speak the truth?

"It is only a dream," she said. "A kind man and a few children. A little dog. I am not an adventurous creature, am I?"

"I would imagine," he said, "that you have already had quite enough adventure for one life."

"Yes," she agreed. "Some women have envied me my years following the drum. They have *no idea.*"

"I believe I must be a dull creature too, Cleo," he said. "I found my cottage after I had recovered sufficiently from my wounds to live alone. It is on one corner of my brother's second estate and is, by most people's standards, rather run-down. It has no thatched roof, no lintel, no roses, no garden. The woods are the back garden, the beach and the sea the front. I might have lived at the main house, and all sorts of people believe either that Matthew was cruel for denying it to me or that I am more than a bit peculiar. I loved that cottage. I still do, but it will never again be my home, alas. I must live at the main house after I am married." He kissed the top of her head again. "After *we* are married."

She sighed and burrowed closer to him. She did not want to pursue that line of thought.

"It sounds idyllic," she said, "your cottage. I have seen the sea, of course, but I have never spent time beside it. Is it a little frightening?"

She had not enjoyed any of the sea voyages she had undertaken.

"It keeps me reminded," he said, "of the vastness of all life, of its constant rhythms. It keeps me reminded of eternity, which *could* be frightening, I suppose, if one feared death. I do not. I have come eyeball to eyeball with it. I would even have welcomed it in the early days after I was wounded. My close brush with death has actually been my greatest gift. Eternity is just the endless, steady rhythm of all that is. It soothes me. I have walked for hours on the beach. I have *sat* for hours merely gazing into the flowing or ebbing waves. I am indeed a very dull man, Cleo."

"Yes," she said, "I suppose you are."

And she laughed softly against his chest before he found her mouth with his own and kissed her. She could tell that his mouth was smiling.

Oh, this was very treacherous indeed. This was *not right*. It was as though he had read her mind.

"Cleo," he said, "what happens tomorrow when your housekeeper has returned?"

She could not say she had not thought of it. Of course she had. She had not thought of any solution yet, though. She supposed she had assumed that one would present itself when the time came. Perhaps she could send Mrs. Evans on some errand that would keep her away from the house for a few hours. Perhaps if she shut the sitting-room door, Mrs. Evans would believe they were in there and not realize that they were upstairs in the bedchamber. Perhaps. . .

Well, there really *was* no good idea, and even if she found one, it would not work well for every day of two months.

"I thought so," he said when she did not answer. "I think you had better just marry me and be done with it."

"No," she said, though she could no longer quite understand why she was being so stubborn. He had *enjoyed* their lovemaking. She was sure he had. He liked her. He had called her beautiful. He had compared her with other women with whom he had been and had said . . . how had he phrased it?

In comparison with the others, you are so superior that you make the comparison ridiculous. Like comparing the sun to a speck of dirt.

Why *not* just marry him and be done with it? And he was right in what he had said a day or two ago. There were never any guarantees in any marriage. Even with the Countess of Waterton. Neither she nor the earl could have known that she would have only daughters.

"Silence again," Jack said, kissing her once more. "My stubborn Cleo. Very well, then. I shall lease a house for a couple of months. I'll do it today or tomorrow morning, and I will come tomorrow afternoon to take you there. I daresay your housekeeper will come to wonder why you are going out driving with me every afternoon. I daresay your brother and sisters will wonder too, as will my brother and sister-in-law. But I am sure we will learn to be endlessly inventive in our explanations."

"Yes." She tipped her head to look back at him. "Thank you, Jack. But I must share the expense with you. Or bear it all myself."

"Nonsense," he said, and he slid his arm from beneath her head, swung his legs over the side of the bed, and sat up. "I must be going."

She lay where she was and watched him while he dressed, standing unself-consciously before her. The flesh on the left side of his chest was unnaturally pink and puckered where the bullet intended for Wellington had struck him. It looked to be right over his heart. How the bullet could have missed defied explanation. His right leg was badly scarred. There were the white lines of old saber wounds in various places over his body. It seemed a miracle to Cleo that any man survived warfare.

He was beautiful despite it all. And now, instead of killing and risking being killed every day of his life, he lived in a dilapidated cottage with woods, a beach, and the sea for his garden.

Had lived.

Now he must marry and move into a large house.

He looked down at her when he was dressed.

"You will come to the theater this evening," he said. It was not a question. She answered it anyway.

"Oh, no," she said. "Definitely not. Not after this afternoon. It would not be right."

"And yet," he said, raising his eyebrows, "I will be going. After this afternoon."

"That is another matter altogether," she said. "I will not go, Jack."

"Matthew's carriage will be outside your door at seven o' clock sharp," he said. And then he grinned. "And the Earl of Waterton does not take kindly to being kept waiting, Cleo. Or, even worse, to being kept waiting *in vain*."

And he turned on his heel and left the room. He even closed the door behind him.

"Jack," she cried in panic.

She could hear his booted feet on the stairs.

Oh, the wretched, wretched man. How could she run after him? She was *naked*.

She could not possibly go to the theater this evening as a guest of the Earl and Countess of Waterton. Not when she and Jack had become lovers this afternoon.

It just would not be right.

But—she could attend the theater this evening as the guest of an *earl*. With the earl's brother and heir as her escort. The very handsome brother. The hero whom the whole *ton* admired, even adored. The man she had loved for years and would love all her life.

She could have this one evening to cherish in memory for the rest of her days.

And perhaps, after all, she was not barren. Perhaps even now she was with child. Perhaps she and Jack would marry and have children—plural—and live with a measure of contentment, even happiness, in that large house. Perhaps he would take her sometimes to the cottage by the sea. Perhaps they would stroll on the beach together and dream together of peace and beauty and eternity. Perhaps. . .

Cleo swiped at her cheeks with the heels of her hand.

Good heavens, *tears*?

She would cause him horrible embarrassment if she was not ready to leave when the earl's carriage came for her at seven. Though it would serve him right, wretched man. She had said no, but he had ignored her.

She threw her legs over the side of the bed and sat up.

She would go, she supposed. She might tell herself and tell herself that she would not, that he could not make her go, that he ought to be taught that no meant no. But in the end she would go anyway.

How could she *not*? Life had suddenly grown dazzlingly bright, and it would be foolish of her to withdraw to the shadows before she must.

Chapter Six

*J*ack was very much afraid as he rapped the knocker against the door of Cleo's house that evening that she would refuse to answer or else come to the door patently *not* dressed for an evening at the theater. It had been wrong of him to ignore her protests this afternoon and not to go back when she called to him.

It was just that he suspected Cleo did not have much confidence in herself and none at all in her own beauty. Pritchard had destroyed what little she might have had as a girl. She *was* beautiful even if she did not have an obviously pretty face—though even *that* was lovely when it was animated and her eyes were raised. She had the most attractive smile of anyone he knew. He was a little biased, of course. He could no longer see her objectively. She was *Cleo,* the woman with whom he had come vividly alive again this afternoon for the first time in many years.

He felt whole again in ways he could not put into any satisfactory words. But he did not *need* words. What he *did* need was to persuade her to do likewise, to step confidently out into life again—or perhaps for the first time, to recognize herself as an attractive, sexual woman who could look anyone in the eye in the full expectation that she would be liked, even loved.

But, he thought ruefully as he stood outside her door and glanced back to the carriage, inside which Matthew and Charlotte waited, he ought not to have ignored her very firm no to this evening's invitation.

He heard the lock turn on the other side of the door and it opened to reveal, not the housekeeper back from her day off, but Cleo herself, looking very smart in a sea-green evening gown of fine muslin, her hair dressed in a smooth chignon at the back of her head. She was looking at him with large eyes that held a hint of reproach.

"Ah," he said. "You cannot know how anxious I have been, Cleo. It would have been more than a mite embarrassing to have to return to the carriage with the news that you refused to come when it was only this morning I informed them that I intended to pay court to you. It would have been no more than I deserved, though. You look lovely. I like your hair dressed that way."

Her cheeks warmed with color, and her eyes grew more luminous. It was the look of a woman seeing a man for the first time since he became her lover. He smiled back at her, though a little ruefully.

"The flattery," she said, "is unnecessary. I am coming, as you can see."

"Flattery, of course," he said. "You have exposed my lying tongue. I actually like your hair *much* more the way you wore it this afternoon."

He saw understanding dawn in her eyes, and she smiled slowly back at him before stepping out of the house and turning to close the door.

He felt suddenly, absurdly happy. He took the key from her hand, locked the door himself, and waited while she tucked it away inside the small evening reticule she carried. He offered his hand and she set her own on top of it as he led her down the steps and across the pavement to the carriage.

Matthew was standing outside the open door. Charlotte was still seated inside, but she was leaning forward so that she could see out. They were curious to meet Cleo. They had been unable to place her in their minds even though they were sure they must have seen her a dozen times and Charlotte had actually been there beside the Serpentine when he bore her off home two days ago. They both remembered her brother and sisters, even the young one who was just making her come-out this year.

Cleo, Jack realized, had made an art out of being invisible. Even now he could feel her withdrawing inside herself, and when he glanced at her, he could see that her eyes were downcast and fixed on the pavement before her feet.

"Charlotte, Matt," he said, "may I present my dear friend, Mrs. Pritchard? My brother and sister-in-law, Lord and Lady Waterton, Cleo."

He squeezed her hand as she curtsied without raising her eyes.

"How do you do, ma'am?" Matthew said. "I understand you knew my brother in the Peninsula."

"I was there with my husband," she said.

"If I had known," Charlotte said, "that you knew Jack, that is, I would have secured an introduction to you long ago, Mrs. Pritchard. For now I have a clear look at you, of course I know that I have seen you many times before. I had not even realized you were Sir Alfred King's sister. Do come and sit beside me. If you are like me, you hate riding with your back to the horses. We will leave *that* seat for the men."

And she moved to the far side of the seat while Matthew handed Cleo up the steps and Jack took his place opposite with his brother.

"It was a good thing," Matthew said, "that Jack had a previous acquaintance with you, Mrs. Pritchard, and discovered you the very evening we cast him to the lions. We invited him to join us in Town, you see, because we judged he had spent quite long enough rusticating after recovering from his wounds, and we insisted that he join us at the very first ball following his arrival to *enjoy* himself. But of course, we had not taken into account the fact that he knows almost no one."

They were, Jack realized with a rush of gratitude, going out of their way to set her at ease. It was not difficult to see that she was tense and nervous.

"You must tell us," Charlotte said, laying a hand on Cleo's arm, "what Jack was like in the Peninsula. We have heard all sorts of wonderful things from other people about his exploits there, but he is far too modest to tell us anything himself."

Cleo looked up at last. She met Jack's eyes first and then turned her head to look at Charlotte as the carriage rocked into motion.

"I did not know Major Gilchrist well," she said, "but I *was* aware that his men were devoted to him. That did not happen with all officers or indeed with many at all."

Apart from that one time, when he had brought her word of Pritchard's supposed death, Jack would have thought she was quite unaware of his existence.

"You must come to tea at Waterton House one afternoon, Mrs. Pritchard," Charlotte said, "and we will have a comfortable coze over tea. I long to know of your own experiences following the drum too."

"She doubtless will not tell you, Charlotte," Jack said, "of her own heroism. She endured appalling conditions along with all the men, but while we all cursed and complained volubly, I never once heard Mrs. Pritchard utter a word of complaint."

"Oh, that is because you could never hear my *mind*, Jack," Cleo said, looking at him with a smile.

And then she bit her lower lip and looked down at her hands in her lap again. She must have realized that she had spoken aloud and smiled and called him *Jack*. Which was shocking indeed when Matt and Charlotte both knew that he was planning to make her his bride.

He gazed fondly at her lowered head, and then he looked from his brother to his sister-in-law in the semi-darkness of the carriage interior. What were they thinking? Doubtless he would hear in the morning at breakfast, or tonight after the theater.

But there was the whole evening to live through yet.

And he did not, of course, care what they thought. Well, he *did,* but their opinion would not weigh with him. He had chosen to take upon himself the duty Matt had begged him to consider, but how he fulfilled that duty was his concern, and his alone. And that of the woman he chose too, of course.

He was rapidly coming to realize something. He already liked Cleo Pritchard. He already knew he was fond of her too. He found her more than appealing as a bed partner. But it seemed to him now that he could fall in love with her without any effort at all.

The carriage was slowing again. They were arriving at the theater, he could see.

Her life had suddenly become almost unrecognizable to Cleo.

Last evening at the theater had been unlike anything she had ever experienced before in her life. The Earl and Countess of Waterton had treated her like an honored guest. The countess had seated her beside herself in the earl's box until just before the play began, when she had relinquished her seat to Jack and taken her place beside her husband. During the intermission, the four of them had strolled in the corridor outside the boxes and taken refreshments and stopped to chat with several people.

It had all been more wonderful than anything she had

experienced in her life before it. For one evening she had been part of that small family group and had been made to feel as if she belonged. And yet it had all been very public. The earl and countess had attracted attention, of course, but Jack had attracted even more. And she, Cleo, had been *with* him. There must surely have been some speculation—the *ton* thrived upon gossip.

She could *be* a part of all that for the rest of her life.

And she would be if she conceived.

She had lain awake half the night, turning from one side to the other in a vain attempt to find comfort and oblivion. But it had been no good.

Everything felt *wrong*.

Her own carefully thought out scheme had been made to seem cheap rather than noble. And the glamour of the evening's events, which had so enthralled her at the time, made her distinctly uneasy in retrospect.

She had not intended to make such a public appearance with Jack. She had not consented to it. It had been forced upon her—though she could have simply refused to go, of course. In going she had *given* her consent.

She had expected that while she discovered whether or not she could conceive, her life and Jack's would proceed along separate lines. She had expected her own to continue much as it had been for the past five years—with the exception of their regular afternoon trysts, that was. She had expected him to continue with his social life among the *ton,* perhaps getting to know some other young ladies as he did so.

He had not asked her if he might inform his brother and sister-in-law that he was courting her. But why would he? He might court whomever he chose. The lady concerned would still have the freedom to refuse to be courted.

By this morning Cleo felt that she was being drawn again into something that threatened to move outside her control. She had had no control whatsoever over her life or even her person while Aubrey lived. She had been her own mistress since his death. She had a home and just enough money to live comfortably and keep two servants. She had her dreams, even her hopes, but she also had a firm grasp on reality. She was not actively unhappy and knew how to cultivate contentment.

All that had been disturbed, shaken up, made rather public, and she was beginning to feel something very close to panic.

But whom was she trying to deceive? What was so very wonderful about her present life apart from the fact that it was within her control? And was even that so? She had hoped for marriage, and marriage had eluded her. Until now.

Her life was *not* a happy one and had not been for five years. Or ever, in fact.

She was just a coward. She was *afraid* to be happy.

No, she was not. She just did not want Jack to be trapped in a childless marriage. His need for children was his only reason for giving up the freedom he seemed to value. And *she* did not want to be trapped in a marriage that could not offer her what she craved. Though it was only with Jack that she craved love.

Cleo sat on the bench of the pianoforte, running her fingers aimlessly over the keys, not even depressing them. She sighed aloud. Why were some decisions so difficult to make?

When in doubt, say no.

When in doubt, say yes.

The pessimist versus the optimist.

The realist versus the dreamer.

The coward versus the valiant.

Nothing helped.

Jack would be coming this afternoon to take her to the house he was going to rent for a few weeks.

It all suddenly seemed a little sordid.

A Puritan conscience was a horrible thing to have.

And then her sisters came to call. Cleo assumed they had come to persuade her to go shopping with them, and she got gladly to her feet before they were ushered in.

When in doubt, buy a new bonnet.

It was instantly clear that they were both brimming over with excitement.

"Cleo!" Elizabeth exclaimed. "You dark horse, you. You danced with Major Gilchrist at Lady Claremont's ball, and you accepted his obliging offer to walk home with you when we met him in Hyde Park the following day. But you said *nothing* about the fact that he is actually *paying court* to you."

Cleo stared at her, aghast.

"He is not—" she began.

"It is all here," Gwinn said, waving a newspaper in her hand. "You have actually appeared in the society pages this morning, Cleo. You were a guest in the Earl of Waterton's box at the theater last evening, and you were being escorted by the handsome hero of Fuentes de Oñoro. Word has it that the two of you were acquainted in the Peninsula, and that Major Gilchrist came out of seclusion recently in order to find you again now that your mourning period for Colonel Pritchard is decently over. Word also has it that as the Earl of Waterton's heir, the major is planning to take a bride in order to secure the succession. One particular bride, it would appear. There will be many disappointed young ladies this morning."

"Let me see that." Cleo snatched the paper from her sister's hand and scanned the passage in growing dismay. Gwinn had not exaggerated in her paraphrase. "Oh, how dare they."

Elizabeth laughed and clapped her hands.

"Cleo," she said, "I could not be happier. It is disrespectful to speak ill of the dead, I suppose, particularly when he was your husband, but I felt badly for you throughout your marriage. I always felt that I ought to have married him myself and so saved you. You deserved far better. And now you are going to get it at last."

"Major Gilchrist is very handsome," Gwinn added. "As well as being *famous*. How splendidly brave he was in risking his own life in order to save the Duke of Wellington's. And there is a strong chance that he is to be your *husband*, Cleo?"

Cleo closed her eyes briefly. Could life possibly get any more unreal?

"We had a passing acquaintance in the Peninsula," she said. "Because he was a military man for so many years and has lived in the country since being so badly wounded, he knows very few people in town despite the fact that he is the son of an earl. I daresay he knew no one but me at Lady Claremont's ball apart from his own brother and sister-in-law. It was natural that he dance with me. And it was understandable that he invite me to the theater last evening. I was delighted to attend. The play was very well done."

And I may at this very moment be with child by him.

Elizabeth and Gwinn exchanged amused glances.

"Methinks the lady protests too much," Gwinn said, "or whatever that quote actually says."

"Methinks you are right," Elizabeth said as she smiled fondly at Cleo.

Fortunately, Mrs. Evans chose that moment to bring in a tray of tea, and they all took seats and enjoyed a visit together until Elizabeth got up to leave. Nothing more had been said about last evening or the very foolish little passage in the paper.

"We have the Severidge garden party to dress for, Gwinn," she said. "You are coming too, Cleo? We will come by with the carriage."

"Oh," Cleo said. "No. I have other plans, I'm afraid."

"Let me guess," Gwinn clasped her hands to her bosom. "Major Gilchrist."

Cleo thought of lying. But it was too late. Her cheeks felt suddenly hot, and she knew she was blushing.

"He is taking me for a drive," she said. "Will you mind terribly much—?"

They assured her they would not and went merrily on their way.

Was this how Pandora felt, Cleo was left to wonder, after she had opened that famous box? Had she despaired of *ever* replacing all its contents before closing the lid and restoring tranquility to her life?

But, Pandora aside, did she want to restore tranquility to her life?

The inner debate resumed.

Chapter Seven

*W*hen Jack arrived at Cleo's house that afternoon, he was on foot. And it was just as well, he saw when he was shown into the parlor. She was not dressed for the outdoors. She was standing before the fireplace, her hands clasped at her waist, a determined look on her face, as though she had steeled herself to say something and was not to be deterred.

Which fact rather deterred *him,* for he had something to say too.

He took a few steps into the room and waited until he heard the door click shut.

"Cleo," he said.

"I will not be coming with you," she said. "I am truly sorry for the trouble you must have gone to in renting a house. I hope you will be able to cancel any lease agreement you made. I must insist upon sharing any expense with you—or even paying it all if you wish. I will not be coming, either this afternoon or any other."

"Good," he said. "There is no house. I did not rent one—or even look for one."

"Oh." She looked suddenly mortified. But she replaced the determined look almost immediately. "I ought to have added that we will not remain here either. I mean—"

He held up a staying hand.

"There is no affair between us, Cleo," he said. "One afternoon does not qualify for the name, does it?"

"No," she said after a brief silence, and her eyes slipped from his to focus upon his chest. "No, it does not. Not at all. I thank you for your . . . your kindness to me. I hope you find a suitable bride soon. I hope she will be someone who can make you happy. You need to be happy. You need not feel obliged to stay any longer. I—"

"Cleo." He took a step closer to her.

She stopped talking and looked up into his eyes again. Her own looked huge and . . . *wounded*? Her cheeks were flushed.

"If you have no other plans," he said, "will you fetch your bonnet and come walking in the park with me? Not in any of the fashionable parts of the park, though. I am not in the mood for crowds, and I daresay you are not either. I do not suppose either if us ever is, in fact. There are areas that are more like secluded countryside. Come walking there with me?"

"Why?" she asked. "You do not need to—"

"Yes," he said, "I do, Cleo. Please come. Unless you would really rather not, that is."

He held his breath while she examined the backs of her spread hands for a few moments.

"Very well," she said at last. And she moved past him without another word and left the room.

Five minutes later she was back, wearing a straw bonnet and a blue spencer one shade darker than her dress.

They remarked upon the unseasonably warm weather as they walked to the park, and discussed last evening's play. He wondered if she had seen the morning paper and decided that yes, she must have. He did not ask.

And then they were in the park, strolling among trees along a path that was wide enough only for pedestrians but was not being used by any of those, it seemed, except themselves.

They had been silent for five minutes or more.

"Cleo," he said at last, setting his free hand lightly over hers on his other arm, "talk to me. Tell me why."

"There are so many reasons," she said after a minute more of silence, "that I do not know quite where or how to begin. I just cannot do *that* again, Jack, what we did yesterday afternoon. I thought I was woman of the world enough to do what many other widows do without a qualm of conscience. Not that it is exactly conscience with me. I do not believe that what we did was wrong—morally wrong, that is. It just was not *right*. I cannot explain it better than that."

He patted her hand.

"I cannot marry you," she said, "without being sure that I can offer you the one thing for which you are ready to sacrifice your freedom. And yet I have understood today that I have actually been afraid that I *would* conceive if we had an affair that lasted two months. Then I would be forced to marry you."

He winced inwardly and they walked onward, slightly uphill. To his right he could see the open fields of the park spread slightly below them.

"For five years," she said, "I was actively unhappy. I had no one but myself to blame. I was not forced to marry Aubrey. I *wanted* to. I was the first of my family to marry when I had expected not to marry at all. Aubrey was not really cruel to me. He did not *beat* me. But—"

"He was cruel," Jack said, cutting her off. "He destroyed your sense of self, Cleo. He convinced you that you are not beautiful."

"Oh," she said, turning her head to look at him briefly, "I did not need *him* to convince me of that. I have always had access to a mirror. But that is beside the point. I married and was unhappy because he was *unkind* to me. And now I have been offered the chance to marry again, and this time I would be unhappy because you would be *kind*. Children or no children, you would be kind. I know that. Indeed, if there were no children, you would be even kinder than if there were. I could not bear it, Jack. I am sorry. I really ought not to have come to the park with you."

"I hope," he said, bending his head closer to hers, "I could never be less than kind to anyone who was in my care."

"I know," she said, and her voice sounded hopelessly bleak. Her head was down. He could not see her face around the brim of her bonnet.

He glanced quickly about. There was no one in sight. He turned sharply off the path, taking her with him, and then he swung her around in front of him, her back to a tall tree trunk. He hemmed her in with his arms, and dipped his head until he could see her face clearly. Her eyes were startled and were looking directly back into his.

"Why do you think," he asked her, "I want to marry you, Cleo? Apart from the fact that I must marry, that is, if I am to do my family duty. Why do you think I chose *you* over every other lady I might have asked?"

"Because you knew me," she said. "Because you are rather shy, I believe, or at least reserved in manner, and it was easier to offer for me than to—"

He rested his forearms up to the elbows along the trunk on either side of her head. Her body was half pinned between him and the tree.

She fell silent.

"That," he said, "is a little insulting to me, is it not, suggesting as it does that I chose without any real care either to your feelings or indeed to mine?"

"I did not choose my words carefully," she said. "I meant no insult. I have been flattered. I—"

"*Flattered,*" he said. "You are not worthy of me, then, Cleo? Is that what this is all about? You are not *worthy* of me? You are worthless, unlovely, dull, ineligible, *old*?"

Her eyes brightened with tears, but almost simultaneously sparked with anger.

"Of course I am worthy," she cried with more vehemence than he had ever heard from her before. "I am a *person*. I am *me*. And perhaps beneath the skin I am as beautiful as the most lovely person you could name. *Of course* I am worthy. Stand back. You are too close. You did not rent a house as you said you would. You were going to end our affair. You have had second thoughts about it. You no longer want me after yesterday afternoon. It does not matter. Maybe *you* are not worthy of *me*. Stand *back*."

He kissed her. Hard and open-mouthed. But she did not relent.

He raised his head, took a step back, and clasped his hands behind him.

"Yes," he said, "I would have ended the affair even if you had not, Cleo. I could not do it. There was no moral objection. There is no reason in the world why you and I cannot enjoy each other if we choose. Except for one. I want you as my *wife,* not my lover. And I want that for only one reason that matters. Having children with you is not that reason. The fact that I love you *is*."

She blinked back tears again, though the anger had not gone from her face.

"You see what I mean?" she said. "*Kindness*. Do you not *see* that this is worse than bluntness? Cleo must be reassured. She must not be made to feel rejected. She must not be made to feel that she in not worthy of a good man's regard. I do not need this, Jack. I am strong enough to live my life my way. I always have been. Aubrey made me unhappy, but he did *not* destroy me. Meeting you again and loving you again will not destroy me either. I *will not* have you feeling guilty."

He regarded her silently, and she looked defiantly back.

"Meeting me again and *loving me again*?" he said softly.

She bit her lower lip.

"A slip of the tongue," she said. "But you must have known. It must have been painfully obvious. Of course I loved you. I always have. And I probably always will. But that is my concern. It need not concern you."

"I am to believe you, then, am I?" he asked her. "But you will not believe me? I am insulted again."

"Don't, Jack," she said. "Don't be *kind*."

"What a mass of contradictions you are, Cleo," he said. "Strong, independent, stubborn, invulnerable, and as ignorant of your own worth as it is possible to be. Cleo, believe me because you *must* believe. All of my future happiness depends upon it. And it would seem that yours does too. I *love* you. I believe I loved you without realizing it from the time I first knew you, though I *did* know it after that day I kissed you. And then I ruthlessly suppressed the feelings as rather horrifyingly inappropriate. I could not love another man's wife. It took me a few days after we met again this year to realize that those feelings had always remained dormant, just waiting to bloom again when I saw you again. I *love* you, and it must be marriage between us or nothing."

One of his hands was splayed beside her head again. The other he kept behind his back, and he realized suddenly that two of his fingers were crossed—a long-forgotten superstition of childhood.

"But what," she asked him, "if I am barren?"

"Then I will be disappointed," he said. "I daresay you will be too. We will deal with it if that is what happens. I will never stop loving you and striving to remain happier with you than I have ever been before in my life. I don't believe you will stop loving me. It is not in your nature not to love with your whole heart. I *know* that about you without any tangible proof at all. Sweetheart, Matt and Charlotte have not stopped loving each other because they cannot have more children and the four they do have are all girls. Surely you could see last evening that they are a happy, loving couple."

She swallowed rather awkwardly.

"Say you will marry me," he said. But he pushed himself away from the tree even as he said it. "No, wait a minute. Let me do this properly."

And he went gingerly down on one knee, noting the uneven ground and the exposed tree roots as he did so, and took her right hand in both of his.

"Cleo, will you marry me? On the understanding that my motive is entirely selfish and concerned solely with my own happiness and yours? That love is my only motive even if it was not when I first began my search for a bride? But then I saw you, and how could anything else matter except love and the chance to reach for happiness for the rest of both our lives? *Will* you say you will marry me before I go rambling on even more and make an even greater ass of myself?"

And then they were both laughing and she looked quite dazzlingly beautiful as she bent over him and kissed his up-turned face.

"How could I possibly say no now?" she said. "You would surely die of embarrassment."

And he surged to his feet, wrapped both arms about her waist, and swung her about in a complete circle while she shrieked and laughed.

He set her feet back on the ground and kissed her again. As he had that very first time. As he had wanted to yesterday before lust got in the way.

Not that he would rule out lust for their wedding night and every available night after that. Lust was a healthy expression of love, though by no means the only or even perhaps the most important one.

Now, because they were in the middle of Hyde Park, even if they *were* in a secluded part of it, there was no place for lust.

Only love.

And so he kissed her with all the love and yearning in his heart. And he knew that she kissed him back the same way.

"Was that a yes?" he asked against her lips after a long while.

"It was a yes," she said, her beautiful eyes shining back into his.

"Good," he said. "Let's go and tell Charlotte and Matthew. I promised to bring you for tea if you had no other engagements. They were very taken with you last evening and congratulated me on making such a wise choice. And lest you become suspicious of that word *wise,* let me explain that they consider you warm and mature and capable of giving me the companionship and care and love that I apparently so richly deserve. I have very *kind* relatives."

"Well," she said as she took the hand he offered and allowed him to lace his fingers with hers, "*of course* I am warm and mature and capable of all those other things and more. *Of course* I am beautiful and wonderful and—"

But she had to pause to laugh. Her eyes sparkled into his as they began to walk back down the path together.

Epilogue

*J*ack walked alone on the beach at Rigdon. The sunset created an orange-and-yellow band of exquisite beauty across the still water. He wished Cleo was beside him so that they could share it.

But she was not.

She was at home, sleeping.

At least, he hoped she was still asleep. She had earned the rest. She had been hard at work for almost twenty-four hours.

Hard at *labor*.

And, shockingly, it was only eight months since the grand wedding at St. George's on Hanover Square in London that Matt had insisted upon.

It was surprising how large premature babies could be.

Jack smiled across the water.

A son.

And perfect in every imaginable way despite the anxious

assurances the physician had given them that the child's head would look less distorted and the skin of his face less patchy tomorrow.

Their son was perfect as he was. Jack had never seen a more beautiful baby, in fact.

He had left the house to come to the beach because he had been afraid that he might use his time while mother and son slept pestering all the servants with his enthusiasm.

But he was going back now.

Perhaps Alexander needed to be held.

Or perhaps he needed to hold Alexander.

And perhaps Cleo would wake soon and he would see in her eyes again, as he had seen earlier, tired though they had been, that her happiness was complete, that all lingering anxieties had been put to rest.

Foolish Cleo. With her head she still sometimes entertained doubts about herself and his happiness with her. With her heart, of course, she knew the truth.

The heart would eventually rule the head completely.

He turned from the sunset toward the brighter light of home.

And Cleo.

And their son.

Hope Springs Eternal

JACQUIE D'ALESSANDRO

Penelope Markle

Abe Testwell

Prologue

Dear Sir:

Per your request to keep you informed on the where-abouts and activities of Miss Penelope Markham, I am writing to inform you that she has returned to England from the Continent. As you know, she wasn't scheduled to do so for another two months; however, an unfortunate situation arose in Italy, one involving her making a sculpture of a most inappropriate nature, embroiling her in a scandal that resulted in her being dismissed as art instructor to Lord and Lady Bentley's children. Given the lurid circumstances regarding this matter, I fear it will be impossible for Miss Markham to find another position, especially as she will most emphatically not receive a recommendation from Lord and Lady Bentley. Indeed, they have informed everyone in their circle of Miss Markham's disgrace, and word of the incident has spread like wildfire, casting her in a most unfavorable light. A shame, as I understand Miss Markham possesses great artistic talent. Sadly, she clearly also possesses a rebellious, wayward streak, much to her detriment. Miss Markham arrived in London yesterday and has taken lodging at Exeter House in Covent Garden. Her future plans are unknown at this time, although given Lord and Lady Bentley's determination, it is safe to surmise that whatever they are, they hold little promise.

I shall await further instructions from you and remain at your disposal.

Sincerely,
Harold P. Wheeler, Solicitor

Chapter One

*A*lec Trentwell stood in the doorway of a dilapidated coffee house and stared across the cobblestone street at Exeter House. The faded brick facade and peeling, dull paint lent the boarding establishment a tired, worn air, much like the haggard, hollow-eyed prostitute assessing him from the adjacent alleyway. She tugged her bodice lower in invitation, filling Alec with a combination of pity and revulsion. He shook his head and she shrugged, then sank into the shadows.

He thought of Penelope Markham and his hands tightened into fists. Bloody hell, this was no place for an unmarried, unescorted woman. In spite of—or perhaps because of—the crowds frequenting the nearby market, danger lurked in every doorway, every shadow. The area was *maybe* marginally safe during the day, but at night thieves, footpads, prostitutes, and pickpockets made their living preying on the hoards of theatergoers. He shuddered to think of what could happen to a lone woman. Especially to the one particular woman he sought.

Penelope Markham. Although he'd never met her, through the strong bond he'd shared with her brother, Alec felt as if he knew her. Certainly he felt a deep sense of responsibility toward her. In spite of the gut-churning emotion that gripped him at the prospect of facing her, he'd intended to do so upon her return to England—an occasion he'd believed was still months away until this morning, when he'd read his solicitor's note. He'd planned to spend those months in seclusion in the small cottage he'd purchased in Little Longstone—another of his plans that had sadly gone awry. He should have known that his well-meaning but interfering family would find a mere three-hour buffer between himself and London far too easy to breech. One minute he'd been existing in the solitude he craved, then the next his brother had descended and Alec's life had changed. Again. And not for the better. Again.

Damn it, he was tired of change.

In truth, he was simply tired. Of everything.

But there were promises to keep. And he intended to keep them, no matter how much he dreaded the prospect of doing so.

The door to Exeter House opened and Alec stilled at the sight of the woman who emerged. Based on Edward's description of his sister, and her unmistakable resemblance to Alec's former sergeant, he was certain the tall, bespectacled, dark-haired woman was Penelope Markham. Dressed in a plain brown walking gown and matching spencer, she clutched what appeared to be an oversized sketch pad. She glanced in both directions, as if aware of the dangers lurking about and debating which route was safer.

She frowned and pushed her glasses higher on her nose, a gesture that tightened Alec's throat. How many times had he seen young Edward doing that exact same thing? He didn't know. Only knew he'd give everything he owned to see his sergeant do it again.

But dead men didn't push up their glasses.

Just then, Miss Markham's gaze caught his and nailed him in place. Her eyes seemed to pierce him, making him feel as if she could see his soul. His secrets. And the countless lies that writhed in the empty darkness there.

For the space of several heartbeats he couldn't move. Couldn't breathe. Couldn't do anything save stare back at her. A wave of hot shame washed through him, making him feel as if he stood in a ring of fire, burned by the guilt that had been his constant companion for the past ten months, since that horrific day at Waterloo.

She blinked several times, then turned away. Clutching her sketch pad to her chest, she walked with a purposeful stride toward the muted sounds of the nearby Covent Garden Market. Alec shook his head, jerking himself free of the stupor into which he'd momentarily fallen, and started across the street. He'd taken less than a half dozen steps when a shabbily dressed man emerged from a shadowed alleyway and blocked Miss Markham's path.

"Where's a pretty piece like ye off to in such a hurry?" the man asked with a leer.

Miss Markham gasped and stepped back. Outrage and disgust ripped through Alex. In a single, swift motion he pulled his knife from his boot and sprinted across the street. The man reached out to grab Miss Markham's arm, but before he could touch her, Alec stepped between them.

"You have precisely two seconds to disappear," he said in a deadly voice.

The other man narrowed his eyes. His lips curled back, showing rotted, broken teeth. "And if I don't?"

Alec pressed the point of his blade under the man's ribs. "Then I'll gut you like a fish. I may do so anyway, just because you sicken me. I definitely will if I ever see you so much as look at this woman again." He pressed the knife in harder and the man sucked in a quick breath. "Any questions?"

A combination of hatred and fear flickered in the man's

eyes. He shook his head, stepped back, then disappeared into the shadowy alleyway from where he'd first appeared, his footfalls echoing, then fading to silence.

Alec released a breath he realized wasn't quite steady and ruthlessly shoved aside the mental pictures bombarding him, accompanied by the terrifying echo of men's and horses' screams . . . images and sounds he normally only experienced in the dark of night while lying alone in his bed. But the threat of bloodshed and the feel of a knife hilt gripped in his hand had brought the vivid memories sneaking out into the light of day, rendering them even more starkly horrifying. He needed several seconds to compose himself before turning around. When he did, he found himself staring into startled gold-flecked brown eyes magnified by spectacles. Miss Markham stood less than a foot away, wide-eyed and pale.

"Are you all right?" he asked.

She moistened her lips. "Y . . . yes. Thank you, sir. I—"

"We need to get you away from here, Miss Markham." He lifted his hand and whistled for his carriage, which waited at the end of the street.

Her eyes widened further. "How do you know my name?"

Alec had imagined this moment when he'd meet her countless times over the last ten months. He'd prepared for it, the scenario running through his mind over and over again. He'd introduce himself, then tell her what he had to say. Quick, impersonal, emotionless. Then he'd return to his solitude. And try to forget the unforgettable.

Never once had he considered that he'd be standing on the street, a cold sweat covering his body, stomach knotted, heart and head pounding, gripping a knife after scaring off a man who would have done God knows what to her.

Nor had he imagined the impact of looking directly into those gold-flecked eyes. Or of her standing close enough for him to notice the pale freckles dotting her nose. Close enough to detect the subtle scent of flowers rising from her skin . . . skin that looked like velvet cream. Nor had he even once considered that a wayward curl of glossy mahogany hair might blow across her cheek, begging his fingers to tuck the spiral back into place. Or that her mouth would look so lush, yet so vulnerable at the same time, making it nearly impossible to tear his gaze away from it when she moistened her lips.

He needed to pull himself together. Escort her to his carriage. Yet his legs felt like stone. He needed to speak, but all the words he'd planned to say fled his mind.

Wariness filled her gaze and she retreated a step. The movement jerked him back to his senses and he cleared his throat. "Please don't be alarmed. My name is Alec Trentwell. I knew your brother. In the army. I was—"

"—Edward's commanding officer," she broke in. Her expression cleared. "I know your name well, Captain Trentwell. Indeed, given how frequently Edward mentioned you in his letters, I feel as if I already know you." Confusion again clouded her features. "But how is it that you are here and know who I am?"

"I . . ." Once again Alec found himself at a loss. "I heard you'd returned to England and I wished to see you."

Crimson bloomed in her cheeks. "Oh, dear. Clearly, word of what happened in Italy has reached London. Truly, the entire incident was misunderstood—"

"Miss Markham, I wish only to talk about your brother. I was with him that last day at Waterloo, and there are . . . things you should know."

His carriage halted beside them and he nodded toward the black lacquer vehicle pulled by two matched bays. "As this is not the safest place, would you consent to accompanying me somewhere else? Somewhere we can talk?"

Her gaze roamed his face, and he was struck by the intelligence shining in her eyes. "Of course, Captain Trentwell. Edward thought the world of you. I'd be very interested to hear anything you have to tell me about my brother." Her voice quavered and a shadow of unmistakable grief crossed her features. "I miss him terribly."

She averted her gaze, but not before he saw her blink back tears. His hands clenched inside his gloves. Bloody hell, this was going to be so much harder than he ever imagined. He forced himself to move, to open the carriage door bearing the Earl of Crandall's seal, grateful that he'd opted to use his brother's carriage rather than hiring a hack. He held out his hand to help Miss Markham inside. She set her gloved hand in his and he frowned at the odd tingle of warmth that shot up his arm. Before he could fully examine the puzzling sensation, her fingers slid away and she sat on the pale gray velvet squabs. Alec shook his head, then looked up at the coachman. "Hyde Park," he instructed.

"Yes, sir."

Before entering the carriage, Alec scanned the area. When he was satisfied no immediate danger threatened them, he slipped his knife back into his boot, then entered the carriage and settled himself on the seat opposite Miss Markham. And stilled at her expression. Bloody hell, there was no mistaking the gratitude shining in her eyes.

"I haven't properly thanked you for your intervention, Captain Trentwell."

"What were you thinking, going about unescorted—especially in Covent Garden?" The question came out far more brusquely than he'd intended. Certainly far more brusquely than could be considered polite. But damn it, tension still gripped his entire body.

Color flooded her cheeks, but instead of shrinking into her seat at his rebuke, she hoisted a brow and raised her chin. "A woman of my age hardly requires an escort to walk to the market. While I never would have ventured out alone at night, I believed I'd be safe enough during the day. Clearly I was mistaken."

"Clearly."

"You quite saved the day and I'm most grateful for your bravery. Not that I'm surprised—Edward always referred to you as a hero in his letters."

The knot in Alec's stomach cinched tighter and he barely

swallowed the bitter sound that rose in his throat. *Hero.* Bloody hell, was there a word in the entire English language he detested more than that one? No. In the first few weeks following his return from the war that damn word had been relentlessly heaped upon him, a weight falling upon his shoulders until he'd felt crushed. Until he couldn't stand it any longer and had escaped to Little Longstone. To obscurity. And solitude. To a place where he didn't have to live a lie. Or pretend he was something he wasn't.

Like everyone else who'd anointed him a hero, Miss Markham was wrong. But she would soon know the error of her ways. The gratitude and admiration currently glowing in her eyes would quickly dissipate after he told her what he'd sought her out to say. After she knew the truth. The truth that ate at him every day. The truth she deserved to know.

That he'd killed her brother.

Chapter Two

$\mathcal{P}$enelope sat across from Captain Trentwell and pressed her sketch pad more firmly against her lap lest she give in to the nearly overwhelming urge to fan herself with the tablet to relieve the heat scorching her.

Good heavens, it felt as if her skin were afire and her skirts ablaze. Obviously the aftermath of her encounter with that horrible man, but still no less confounding, especially given that thanks to Captain Trentwell's swift intervention, she'd barely suffered any fright at all. Indeed, from the moment she'd first seen the tall, arrestingly handsome man standing across the street, before she'd even known who he was, her every thought had been reduced to two words: *oh, my*.

Those same two words reverberated through her mind now as his height and the breadth of his broad shoulders reduced the spacious carriage interior to what felt like the size of a hatbox. Heavens, the man took up a great deal of space. And clearly he used up a great deal of air as well, because there seemed to be a sudden dearth of oxygen. Just as well that she couldn't pull in a deep breath, otherwise she'd most likely humiliate herself by involuntarily heaving the sort of gushy, feminine sigh she had, until this moment, believed herself quite immune to heaving.

Of course, such a sigh would only result from pure artistic appreciation, as Captain Trentwell's countenance was the most compelling she'd ever seen. Even if she didn't know him to be a war hero, his bearing had instantly marked him in her mind as a military man. His features seemed hewn from granite, from his blade-straight nose to the slash of his high cheekbones to his square jaw. Deep lines bracketed his firm mouth, one which she could easily imagine barking out orders on a battlefield. A mouth that appeared utterly uncompromising and made her wonder if it ever tilted upward in a smile.

Creases radiated from the corners of his eyes, lines she imagined were the result of squinting into the sun as opposed to indulging in fits of unbridled laughter. A thin scar bisected his left brow, an imperfection that only served to fascinate her further. His hair was thick and wavy, and she wondered if the sun-streaked brown strands would feel as soft as they looked.

But it was his eyes she found most compelling. When their gazes had met outside Exeter House, even across the span of the street, she'd been pinned in place by the intensity of his gaze, so much so it had been nearly impossible to look away from him. And then when he'd turned around after dispatching that hooligan, rather than her first thought being about her safety, it was, *Blue . . . his eyes are blue.* The deep, mysterious azure of the sky at twilight, just before darkness completely swallowed the daylight. His eyes had once again pinned her in place with what flickered in their depths. Pain. Dear God, so much pain. The kind that haunted a person and ate at their soul.

That flash of pain had disappeared, replaced by a detached expression she recognized very well as she'd seen it frequently in Edward's eyes—as if a curtain lowered, purposefully blocking out all emotion. Even though Captain Trentwell was a stranger, seeing that raw pain followed by that blank expression grabbed Penelope by the heart, and it had been all she could do not to reach out and touch him and offer him her sympathy. When he'd asked if she was all right, she'd sent up a silent prayer of thanks that he'd rendered her momentarily mute for otherwise she might well have given in to her bad habit of saying precisely what she was thinking: *Actually, I don't believe I'll ever be the same again, and I fear it's entirely your fault.*

He'd stunned her by knowing her name, yet when he identified himself as Captain Trentwell it somehow made perfect sense that the arresting man with the intense eyes and military bearing who'd bravely rescued her was the same courageous man Edward had written to her about at length. Certainly it was a surprise to meet him so unexpectedly. Clearly he'd sought her out and she cringed at the thought of him knowing about the scandal that had forced her to leave Italy in disgrace and return to England to contemplate a future that looked very bleak indeed.

"Are you certain you're all right, Miss Markham? You look flushed."

His deep voice yanked her from her thoughts, and although she prayed for her skin to pale, she knew she was doomed to both failure and further embarrassment when more heat rushed into her face at the realization she'd been caught gawking at him. The gawking was for artistic purposes, of course—her fingers itched to draw him, paint him, sculpt him in marble—but that didn't make being caught any less humiliating.

"I'm fine, Captain Trentwell. I possess a most robust constitution. It's merely warm in here." Anxious to change the subject lest she inadvertently confess that *he* was the source of her flaming cheeks, she asked, "Do you reside in London, sir?"

"No. I live in Kent, in a small village called Little Long-stone."

"I see. So you traveled all the way to London to see me?"

"Actually, I was already in Town, visiting my brother and his family, who are here for the Season, when I learned of your arrival."

"Your brother is the Earl of Crandall."

He seemed surprised. "Yes. Do you know him?"

"No. Edward mentioned in one of his letters that the earl was your older brother."

He merely nodded and silence fell between them. Although he didn't speak, his gaze remained on her and a frown creased his brow, as if she were some sort of puzzle he was attempting to solve. It was nearly impossible not to fidget under his unwavering regard and once again Penelope had to fight the urge to fan herself. Botheration, she was normally most self-possessed, but something about this man completely flustered her. Which was quite vexing as she considered herself quite . . . unflusterable.

"Your brother wrote to you frequently," he finally said. "Whenever he had a free moment he took pen to paper."

She gratefully grasped the subject. "I loved hearing from him, knowing what was happening with him."

"He enjoyed receiving your letters in return. They always made him laugh."

An image of Edward's smile flashed in her mind and hot moisture pushed behind her eyes. "I'm glad. There wasn't usually anything of great interest to report. My position as art teacher to Lord and Lady Bentley's three children wasn't rife with excitement."

"On the contrary, he found your stories most diverting. As did I. He often read passages of your letters aloud to me. My favorite was your retelling of an art lesson with Lord Bentley's children at the lake on his country estate."

Penelope winced. "Oh, dear. Edward told you about that?"

"He did. Bit of a . . . difficulty you had there."

"You are kind to describe the incident as such, sir, for in truth it was a Debacle of Gargantuan Proportions, especially since the children were supposed to be completing drawings as gifts for their grandmother's birthday celebration that evening. But it was such a lovely day, and really, how was I to know the rowboat would spring a leak?"

Captain Trentwell raised a brow. "A leak? I believe you wrote that it sprung a half dozen."

"Yes, and very inconveniently not until *after* I'd rowed into the middle of the lake. Fortunately, the water was no more than waist deep and the children were all able swimmers—not that you'd have known it from all their yelling and splashing about. I learned that day that even the most gently bred, polite children turn into unruly, boisterous imps when lake water is involved."

"If I recall correctly, you were also guilty of splashing about."

"Only to defend myself from the veritable walls of water those little devils flung my way," Penelope replied in her most prim tone.

"Naturally. Although I feel compelled to inform you that your brother often referred to you as Imp."

"I'm certain he did," Penelope said gravely. "It is an old family nickname. Goes back generations. It means, um, 'one who possesses great decorum.' " She gave a decisive nod, which sent her spectacles sliding down her nose.

One corner of Captain Trentwell's mouth quirked upward. "Indeed?"

She pushed up her glasses and forced her gaze to remain on his eyes rather than that fascinating upward flick of his stern mouth. "Yes. *Great* decorum. That is, after all, how I was able to get myself and three extremely bedraggled, wet children back into the house, redressed and freshly coiffed, and with finished drawings in time for the party that evening without Lord or Lady Bentley knowing about our, er, adventure."

"I believe that would take dexterity and ingenuity rather than decorum, Miss Markham."

"Perhaps. But mostly luck."

"And the bribing of several servants, if I remember the story correctly."

Penelope raised her chin. "Bribery is such an . . . ugly word. I prefer to call it a trade entitled 'I'll Sketch Your Portrait in Exchange for Your Silence in This Matter.' "

Captain Trentwell nodded in an approving manner. "Most effective, I'd wager. One can only wonder what fate might have befallen you without your artistic talent."

"I would have sunk even more quickly than that leaky rowboat." No need to add that she'd inadvertently managed to do just that in Italy, a most unfortunate situation that had left her in her current dire circumstances—disgraced, unemployed, not likely to be employed, and alarmingly short of funds.

"Edward showed me several samples of your work—small illustrations you included with your letters to him. You're very talented."

An embarrassed flush crept up Penelope's neck. "Thank you, however those were just idle drawings."

"If so, then you are very talented indeed. Edward told me your work belonged in a museum."

"My brother was my greatest champion." A sad smile tugged at her lips. "If only Edward had been a museum curator and I'd been born a male so my work would be taken seriously."

He studied her for several seconds with an indecipherable expression. Then he cleared his throat and said, "Ever since that day . . . since Waterloo . . . I've wanted to meet you and personally extend my condolences on your loss. Edward was an extremely fine young man. A brave and exemplary soldier. An inspiration to others, including myself. I'm sorry, so very sorry for your loss."

His hoarse rasp, coupled with the palpable tension emanating from him, made it clear his words were not only heartfelt, but difficult for him to speak. Emotion swelled Penelope's throat, and to her mortification a tear slipped down her cheek.

Before she could reach for her handkerchief, Captain Trentwell muttered something that sounded like *bloody damn hell* then yanked a snowy linen square from his pocket. "Here," he said in a gruff voice, holding out his hand.

"Thank you." Penelope slid off her glasses, set them atop her sketch pad, then dabbed at her eyes, which continued to leak a seemingly unending stream of tears. "Forgive me, Captain Trentwell. Contrary to all evidence, I'm not normally a weepy female. But hearing you—a man Edward so greatly admired—speak so highly of him, well, it just touches me. And reminds me how much I miss him." A watery laugh escaped her. "If he were here right now he'd roll his eyes, tell me to stop being such a nodcock, and perform his brotherly duty by reminding me what a red-eyed, blotchy fright I look when I cry."

"I didn't mean to upset you."

She shook her head and squinted at him. Without her glasses it was difficult to make out his expression, but surely he was horrified to find himself trapped in a coach with a crying female. Determined to pull herself together, she gave her eyes a rigorous swipe, her nose a gusty blow, then slipped her glasses back on.

"You didn't upset me, Captain."

His grave gaze flicked to his wet handkerchief she clutched, then returned to her eyes, which she knew looked red and puffy. Heavens, he did indeed look as if he'd rather be facing the fires of hell than sitting across from her. Botheration, why couldn't she be one of those women who looked adorable and dewy when they cried rather than swollen and blotchy?

"There's no need to spare my feelings, Miss Markham."

"I'm not. Truly, I'm not upset. Indeed, I'm honored. That you would take the time to seek me out. To pay tribute to my brother. In spite of the hardships involved, Edward loved being a soldier, and a good deal of that had to do with you, with being under your command. It would please him no end that you came to see me. And said such nice things about him. I, of course, thought he was brave and wonderful, but as his sister, that was rather expected of me." Without thinking, she reached out and rested her hand over one of his clenched fists. "Thank you, Captain Trentwell. You are indeed as kind and fine a man as Edward said."

She sensed him go perfectly still. Then his lips pressed into a thin line and a frown creased a deep crevice between his brows. His gaze shifted downward, riveting on her hand resting upon his. Penelope stared as well, struck by how small her cream-colored glove looked compared with his. At how intimate the sight of her fingers curved over his appeared.

A heated tingle raced up her arm and her breath caught at the sensation. His tightly clenched fingers flexed beneath hers, and although her inner voice screamed at her to pull her hand away, she found she couldn't move. Couldn't draw a breath. Couldn't do anything save stare at her hand atop his.

For several seconds it felt as if time stopped and the entire world existed inside the confines of his carriage. Then he broke the spell by gently taking her hand and setting it back on her lap.

A wave of embarrassment washed through her and she mentally chastised herself. Touching a man she'd just met was completely inappropriate, yet it had felt so natural to do so. No doubt because, although they were strangers, she felt as if she knew him. She raised her gaze and discovered him looking at her with an intensity that curled her toes inside her leather walking boots. "Miss Markham. There is something I need to tell you." His deep voice sounded harsh. Urgent. "You need to know that . . ." He frowned and cleared his throat. "That is to say, I—"

His words cut off when the carriage jerked to a halt.

"Hyde Park, sir," came the coachman's voice.

Captain Trentwell blinked, then shook his head, as if coming out of a trance. He appeared about to say something, then pressed his lips together. He sat still as a statue, looking at her, his eyes bleak. Penelope clearly sensed he was struggling with . . . something. She longed to help him, but didn't know how.

"You were saying, Captain?" she prodded gently.

He exhaled a slow breath, then shook his head. "Nothing." His frown deepened. "Nothing," he repeated. He then inclined his head toward the window. "Shall we walk?"

Penelope swallowed her curiosity and nodded her consent. Obviously she'd have to wait to discover what he'd wanted to tell her. Clutching her sketch pad to her chest, she exited the carriage and together they entered the park.

Chapter Three

Tell her! Bloody hell, tell her now. Then send her on her way and be done with this torture.

The words screamed through Alec's mind as he and Miss Markham entered Hyde Park—the same mantra that had pounded in his brain from the moment he'd first seen her. But for some reason he didn't understand, he couldn't force the words from his lips. Why couldn't he say it? Just four bloody words: *I killed your brother.*

Was it because that by uttering that sentence he'd then be forced to explain what had happened? To relive the horror of that day? Perhaps, although that couldn't be the only reason, as the horrific events of Waterloo played through his mind every night like a discordant melody. Still, he'd never actually spoken of them. To anyone. God knows he didn't want to now, but damn it, he felt an honor-bound duty to tell her the truth about Edward's death and his role in it. Yet when the moment to tell her had arrived in the carriage, he'd failed. Sweat had coated his skin, the words had jammed in his throat, and just as he had on that ill-fated day last June, he'd hesitated. He well knew the disastrous results of hesitation. So why had he done so?

You are indeed as kind and fine a man as Edward said. Those words she'd spoken in the carriage had tightened the noose of guilt around his neck until he could barely breathe. And then she'd laid her hand on his. And for the space of several heartbeats everything inside him had simply . . . stopped. His blood, his heart, his breath.

The gesture had caught him completely off guard. It had been so long since anyone had touched him. His choice—he lived alone and didn't encourage familiarity—and clearly over the ten months of his self-imposed exile he'd forgotten how powerful a gentle touch could be. In spite of the two layers of gloves separating their skin, warmth had suffused him, filling him with an overwhelming urge to clasp her hands tightly in his to soak up all the kindness and compassion and admiration glowing in her eyes. He didn't deserve it, but God help him, it had felt so incredibly *good*.

The way that single touch had made him feel now forced him to admit why he'd hesitated—because her opinion of him would change once she knew the truth. *Admit the truth, you selfish bastard*, his inner voice sneered. *You don't want to see the admiration and warmth glowing in her eyes turn to disgust and loathing.*

Bloody hell, he couldn't deny that. During the three years Edward had been under his command, Alec had come to admire Miss Markham through her brother's stories of her and the letters she sent. Even without benefit of meeting her, Alec knew her to be witty and intelligent. Kind, generous, and caring. Talented. And more than a little mischievous. Ridiculous as it was to like someone he'd never met, to view a stranger as a friend, there was no refuting that's how he felt. Surely if she was completely unfamiliar to him his task would prove easier.

But she wasn't unfamiliar to him. And he knew as soon

as he told her she'd turn away in disgust. And he'd never see her again. And that prospect filled him with a confounding, profound sense of loss he couldn't put a name to.

So he'd wait—just for a little while. He'd waited all these months she was traveling on the Continent, so what were a few more minutes? Besides, there were other things he needed to discuss with her first, before she banished him as he knew she would. No matter how much she might come to loathe him, he still felt a responsibility toward her, and that wasn't something his battered conscience would allow him to dismiss.

"This is my very favorite sort of day," she said.

Her statement jolted him from his brown study and he realized to his chagrin that they'd walked in silence for quite a distance along the path meandering through the park's verdant lawns. He glanced at her and was struck by the way the bright sunshine coaxed reddish highlights from the curls that had escaped her bonnet to brush her cheeks . . . cheeks that once again bore a becoming blush.

"Your favorite in what way?" he asked.

"I adore it when the sky is so vividly blue it almost hurts your eyes to look at it, and the clouds are so fluffy they resemble stuffed pillows, and the air bears just enough coolness to offset the heat of the sun." She smiled. "It's the perfect sort of day to spend outdoors."

Unlike some people whose smiles were nothing more than a slight curving of their lips, Miss Markham's smile engaged her entire face, completely transforming her—lighting up her eyes, showcasing perfectly straight, pearly white teeth, and denting a pair of shallow, beguiling dimples in her cheeks that hinted at the deviltry sparkling behind her spectacles. It was, Alec decided, the most enchanting smile he'd ever seen, and he found himself unable to look away from her. Edward had said other children in their village where they'd grown up had referred to her as Plain Penelope, and that she'd never had a suitor. But surely he was mistaken about the latter, or that was by her own choice. For while Miss Markham might not be beautiful in the classic sense, her smile was surely enough to grab any man's attention.

Indeed, now that he looked closely, he realized her eyes were quite remarkable—like fine brandy sprinkled with flecks of gold. And her lips . . . yes, they were quite remarkable as well. Certainly much fuller than was fashionable, but then he'd never particularly cared about the latest rage.

She tilted her face toward the sun, let out a deep breath, then dazzled him with another smile. "A lovely day, is it not?"

"Lovely," Alec agreed, although he realized he wasn't speaking of only the pleasant weather.

"The sort of day that inspires me to sketch." She tapped her pad. "Would you mind if we sat for a moment? I'd like to commit some of what I'm seeing to paper."

"Of course." He indicated a bench set beneath a trio of soaring elms. "Will that do?"

"Perfectly." They moved to the bench and he watched, transfixed, as she pulled off her gloves, then opened her pad to a clean page. Heat suffused him at the sight of her bare hands, a reaction he was at a loss to explain, especially as they were merely capable and sturdy-looking, her fingers bearing several faint ink stains. Certainly they weren't pale, slim, elegant hands, yet he couldn't tear his gaze from them. She pulled a length of charcoal from her pocket and slowly circled her finger around the tip, a gesture that made his cravat suddenly feel too tight.

He cleared his throat and pulled his gaze away from her hands. "What are you going to sketch?"

"That couple." She nodded down the path, her eyes glowing with amusement. "The pair with the trio of misbehaving dogs."

Alec spotted the couple she indicated—a tangle of people, dog leads, and boisterous canines, one of which was no larger than a teapot, another that looked like a small, fluffy bear, while the third was the size of a small horse. "Quite the interesting assortment of pets they have," he remarked.

"Indeed." Her hand flew over the page and he barely managed to refrain from craning his neck to see her progress. "Do you have any pets, Captain?" she asked as her gaze flicked back and forth between the scene and her sketch pad.

"A horse," he replied, although he considered Apollo more of an old friend than a pet. "You?"

She shook her head. "No. Lord Bentley owned a mastiff I adored. His name was Hugo. He looked very much like that couple's largest dog."

"The one that should be saddled?"

She laughed. "Yes. Hugo possessed the sweetest disposition and infinite patience with the children, even when the boys dressed him as a pirate or little Lady Annabelle turned him into a princess."

"A princess?"

"Yes. Definitely not his favorite outfit, but he loved Lady Annabelle so he bore the indignity with stoic resignation. He much preferred the pirate costume." She grinned. "He enjoyed chewing on the sword."

"No sword for the princess?"

"Sadly, no. That came with a tiara and feather boa. Hugo learned from experience that feathers don't make a good chew toy. Would you like to see a picture of him?"

"Very much."

She stopped drawing and flipped back several pages, then turned the tablet toward him. The illustration showed a tremendous dog with a tiara perched on its head lying across the entire length of a sofa, his huge paws resting on a young girl's lap. A feather boa adorned the dog's neck. And were those . . . *ear bobs* dangling from the beast's ears? A chuckle rumbled in Alec's throat. By God they were.

"The child nearly buried beneath Hugo's paws is Lord Bentley's youngest, Lady Annabelle," Miss Markham said. "Hugo didn't quite understand that he wasn't a lap dog."

"A very substantial lap would be required for that beast."

She laughed, then turned the tablet back to herself. She stared at the picture for several seconds and he watched all the amusement seep from her eyes, replaced by unmistakable sadness. "I miss the children—and Hugo—very much. Indeed, I would love to have a Hugo of my own some day." She gave a decisive nod, then said, "I shall add 'get a Hugo' to my list."

"Your list?"

"Yes. It's filled with things I wish to do, places I'd like to visit—that sort of thing."

"You keep an actual, written list?"

"Oh, yes. Otherwise I'd forget. In fact, I'd best write down my latest wish while I'm thinking of it." She once again flipped pages in her book, this time to the last page and made a notation. "'Get a Hugo,'" she read when she'd finished.

He caught a brief glimpse of what appeared to be a long inventory of items, several of which had lines drawn through them, before she turned back to her sketch in progress and continued working.

Unable to curb his curiosity, Alec asked, "What else is on your wish list?"

She kept her gaze on her sketch pad and shrugged. "Lots of things. Some of them simple, some of them silly, some of them impossible."

"If it's impossible, why wish for it?"

"Spoken like a pragmatic military man." She lifted her gaze and stared at him through very serious eyes. "But I believe it's important to wish for, hope for your heart's desire, even if it seems unattainable. Miracles do happen, Captain Trentwell. And if we give up hope . . . well, then there is nothing left. 'Hope springs eternal in the human breast,'" she quoted softly.

"Alexander Pope," he murmured.

She smiled and nodded. "Yes. You're familiar with his work?"

"Very. He is my favorite poet." When her brows shot upward, he said, "You look surprised. Even pragmatic military men enjoy reading."

Color washed over her cheeks. "I'm certain they do. I'm

merely surprised because Mr. Pope is my favorite poet as well."

"And you've taken his words about hope to heart."

"Yes. Therefore, although it is highly unlikely that the Prince Regent will commission me to paint his portrait, that remains on my wish list. Right along with riding a horse, having my own garden, and finding the perfect skipping rock."

Now it was Alec's turn to raise his brows. "You've never ridden a horse?"

"Not yet. But, as Mr. Pope said—"

"Hope springs eternal," they said in unison.

She flashed him a quick grin, then returned her attention to her sketch. Alec watched her, fascinated by the way her hand lightly moved across the page while a furrow of concentration creased between her brows. Her glasses slowly slid down her nose, something she ignored until they balanced perilously close the tip. Then, without missing a stroke, she gave them a quick push upward, the movement leaving a small streak of charcoal on her chin. He was about to tell her, but the words died in his throat when she pursed her full lips and gently blew on her sketch. His gaze riveted on her lush mouth as she blew several more times, her lips puckered in a perfect imitation of a kiss. A perfect kiss from those lovely, moist lips. . .

Heat shot through him—but this time of a far different sort than the cozy warmth he'd experienced when she'd rested her hand on his. No, this heat, fierce and unexpected in its intensity, all but incinerated him. While he hadn't felt such a strong rush in a long time, it was unmistakable and there was no denying what it was.

Desire.

She glanced up. Her lips remained pursed for several seconds, then she pressed them together, jerking him from the heated stupor into which he'd fallen.

"The dust . . . it gets in my way," she said.

He bludgeoned back the shocking carnal images crowding his mind . . . of those plush lips crushed beneath his own. Of them kissing their way down his naked torso. Of them surrounding his—

He shook his head and forced his gaze away from her distracting mouth. Bloody hell, what was *wrong* with him? Clearly he desperately needed sexual relief, although he hadn't realized just how desperate that need was until several seconds ago, when the sight of her pursed lips had set him on fire and robbed him of his wits.

He felt the need to say something, but damned if he knew what. He knew she'd said something to him, but damned if he remembered what. He tugged on his suddenly tight cravat and cleared his throat. "I beg your pardon?"

"I just said that the charcoal dust gets in my way. So I was blowing it away." She flashed a grin and her dimples winked at him. "Based on your somewhat stunned expression, I thought perhaps you feared I'd taken leave of my senses and was kissing my work."

Kissing . . . kissing . . . Bloody hell, the word was imbedded in his brain. Thank God his expression hadn't given away what he'd really been thinking. "A, um, hazard of using charcoals, I gather."

"Yes. I'm finished with the preliminaries. Would you care to see?"

"Absolutely."

She handed him the sketch pad and another bolt of heat shot up his arm when her fingers brushed his. He snatched his hand back as if she'd burned him, which it bloody well felt as if she had. Thoroughly disgusted with himself, he lowered his gaze to the sketch.

And was instantly charmed by the depiction of the laughing couple entangled with their zany dogs. "You perfectly captured the moment."

"Thank you. I'll put the finishing touches to it when I return to Exeter House."

Alec handed her back the tablet. The mention of her lodgings reminded him of the other topic he needed to discuss with her. "Surely after what happened this afternoon you're not planning to remain there."

"Actually I am."

Alec shook his head. "No. The area isn't safe."

"Perhaps not completely, but it is safer than many parts of London. There's no need for you to worry on my behalf, Captain Trentwell. I own a pistol and I'll be careful."

"Are you carrying your pistol now?"

"Well, no, but—"

"Have you ever shot anyone, Miss Markham?"

"No, but—"

"Have you ever fired your pistol?"

"Once."

"Did you hit your target?"

"Well, no, but—"

"Then I feel it is my duty to inform you that the only way a pistol can serve as effective protection is if you carry it on your person and are able to hit that at which you're aiming."

"Obviously. However, it hadn't occurred to me that I'd require protection during the day. Now I know, and I shall act accordingly."

"Miss Markham, a pistol won't help you if it's not used properly. In fact, it's more likely that you'll either shoot yourself or be disarmed and shot with your own weapon."

Before she could argue, he rushed on, "For your own safety, I insist you lodge elsewhere."

Twin flags of color stained her cheeks. "I'm afraid that's impossible."

There was no reason to ask why—the only possible explanation would be a lack of funds to lodge anywhere better. As he had during his years in the military, Alec quickly assessed the problem from every possible angle—including the fact that he still needed to discuss Edward with her—and arrived at a resolution.

"Miss Markham, I have a solution."

She raised a brow. "I wasn't aware there was a problem."

"Regarding your lodgings."

"As I said, Captain, there isn't a problem."

"I disagree. You shall stay at my family's townhouse in Mayfair. My brother, his wife, and his children are in residence, so you will be well chaperoned."

Her complexion now resembled the setting sun. "Captain Trentwell. While I appreciate your concern, I cannot accept."

"Of course you can." He consulted his pocket watch and inwardly groaned. Damn it, where had the time gone? If he wasn't home in a half hour's time, William would have his head, and given that he planned to bring Miss Markham home with him, this wasn't a good time to risk vexing his brother. He stood and tugged his coat into place. "Come. We'll get you settled and I'll send a footman to the Exeter to gather your things."

She remained seated and stared up at him for several seconds, then huffed out a laugh. "I'm not certain if I'm more amused or aggravated."

"I cannot imagine why you'd be either."

Clearly amusement won out, because her eyes twinkled behind her lenses. "Captain, clearly it's necessary to remind you that I am not a soldier and therefore barking orders at me will not win the day."

Alec's brow collapsed into a scowl. "I wasn't barking orders. I was merely—"

"Telling me what to do. In a very commanding way."

"Because I'm concerned for your safety. If I seem abrupt, it's because time is of the essence. My brother and his wife are hosting a party in my honor and it begins in precisely twenty-seven minutes. I gave my word I wouldn't be late."

"Then by all means you must go without further delay. I appreciate your concern. While I do need to carefully watch my finances, I am not destitute and cannot accept charity."

Bloody hell, he should have known she'd react this way.

He again quickly assessed the situation, then said, "I'm not offering you charity. I'm offering you employment."

"Employment? What do you mean?"

"I mean an exchange of your talent for payment. I realize I'm far from the Prince Regent and we're not the royal family, but I'd like to commission you to paint my portrait, and a family portrait as well."

She rose and pressed her hand to her chest. "I . . . are you certain?"

"Of course. You're immensely talented."

"Thank you. It's just . . ." she hesitated, then said in a rush, "I cannot be less than completely honest with you, Captain, especially given your kindness to Edward, and to me. Do you know why I was relieved from my position with Lord and Lady Bentley?"

"It doesn't matter—"

"I'm afraid it does. As you will hear about it at some point, I'd prefer you hear it from me."

"Very well, I'm listening."

She moistened her lips with the tip of her tongue, a flick of pink that had Alec fisting his hands inside his gloves. "I found the artwork in Italy fascinating. So fascinating, I was moved to attempt a sculpture in the, er, Renaissance style."

"Meaning?"

"A nude." She lifted her chin. "A *male* nude. Human sized. Of, um, human proportions."

An image instantly rose in Alec's mind . . . of her bare hands fashioning such a sculpture . . . her fingers gliding over a nude male form . . . that looked exactly like—

Him.

Bloody hell! He blinked to dispel the disturbing mental picture, but its effect lingered, heating him to his core and forcing him to shift his feet to relieve the pulsing ache in his groin.

"I kept the sculpture in my bedchamber, away from the children," she continued, "but Lady Bentley learned of its existence from one of the maids, stormed into my chamber and flew into the boughs. She dismissed me on the spot—quite a shock as she didn't so much as bat an eye during our visit to the Uffizi Gallery and there were more nude male sculptures in there than I could replicate in ten lifetimes. She refused to give me a reference, and informed me that she'd see to it that I was never hired again. In my own defense, I can only say that it was *art*—and not in any way lewd or intended to be construed as such. Still, you deserve to know the full truth—that this scandal surrounds me and that you certainly risk Lady Bentley's wrath if you hire me." She hiked her chin another notch. "I quite understand if you withdraw your offer now that you are in possession of all the facts."

You deserve to know the full truth. It clearly was humiliating for her to tell him, yet she had, doubling his admiration for her. And his guilt. *Tell her. Tell her now. Give her the same courtesy she just gave you.*

But he couldn't. If he did, she'd never consent to work for him, and then where would she be? Unemployed and lodging at Exeter House and a target for every footpad in the area. No, he couldn't allow that. He'd tell her—*after* the portraits were done and he'd paid her handsomely enough to keep her financially secure for the foreseeable future.

With his conscience as assuaged as it was going to get, he said, "I appreciate your honesty, Miss Markham, and am sorry you were dismissed from your post. But Lord and Lady Bentley's loss is my gain and I've no fear of their possible wrath. My offer stands."

She regarded him steadily and he could almost hear her internal debate, weighing her uncertain future against an employment opportunity she clearly suspected was manufactured purely for her benefit. Finally she said in a quiet voice, "I accept, Captain Trentwell. And I thank you."

Relief, and something that felt suspiciously like anticipation but surely wasn't, rippled through him. "You're welcome. Now that that's settled, let us make our way to the townhouse lest I'm late and truly incur some wrath—that of my brother."

They started down the path leading back toward the park entrance. "This party in your honor you mentioned . . . is it to celebrate your homecoming from the war?"

Alec bit back the humorless sound that rose in his throat. "No. The party is to celebrate my upcoming marriage."

Chapter Four

$\mathcal{P}$enelope looked around the elegant grandeur of her bed-chamber in Lord Crandall's townhouse and pinched herself on the arm to make certain she wasn't dreaming. The sting on her skin assured her the pale green silk-covered walls, ornate canopy bed with its gold velvet counterpane and lace-edged pillows, and marble fireplace where a cheery fire crackled were all real. Yet it was difficult to grasp that a mere few hours ago she'd faced dire, unemployed straits at the Exeter and an uncertain future and now she had a commission for at least two portraits and accommodations in a beautiful guestroom in the most exclusive section of the city. Indeed, she felt more like a guest than an employee.

She'd briefly met the earl and countess. Their surprise was evident upon learning Captain Trentwell had hired her, but both had made her feel welcome. Clearly they hadn't yet heard of the Italy debacle, for if they had her employment would have ceased before it even began. Would Captain

Trentwell still wish to hire her if his brother had objected? Probably not, so she prayed he wouldn't change his mind. For while she'd told him she wasn't destitute, in truth her situation was quickly approaching desperate. Her funds would last her no more than two months—and only that long if she were extremely frugal and skipped meals. Captain Trentwell's offer had indeed been a godsend.

An image of the darkly handsome captain flashed in her mind and this time she wasn't able to suppress a feminine sigh of appreciation. Based on Edward's writings she'd already known Captain Trentwell to be kind and heroic—she just hadn't realized *how* kind and heroic. He'd not only rescued her from that dreadful man, he'd also saved her from the financial calamity looming on the horizon. He was, in every way, a hero.

And an extremely attractive one. Attractive? More like spectacular. Her fingers itched with anticipation at the prospect of sketching him for his portrait. It would prove a challenge to perfectly capture his expression to convey everything he was—a brave military leader, yet a kind, generous man. A man who lived with inner pain and secrets.

A man who was getting married.

An unexpected, utterly ridiculous and completely inappropriate sense of loss had swept through her when he'd announced tonight's party was to celebrate his upcoming marriage. Botheration, what sort of person was she? She should be delighted for him. He deserved every happiness life had to offer. Yet rather than well wishes, her first reaction had been crushing disappointment.

Which was laughable. Even if he wasn't soon to be married, a man like Captain Trentwell—devastatingly attractive war hero and brother to an earl—would certainly never look at her twice. He could have any woman he wanted, so of course his future wife would be a young, beautiful society diamond, whereas Penelope knew all too well that at nine and twenty she possessed neither youth nor beauty, nor did she have any connections to recommend her. Even a decade ago, when her parents had been alive and money wasn't scarce and she'd spent a Season in London in the hopes of attracting a husband—well, even then she'd faded into insignificance amongst all the peers' daughters and gorgeous young women of the *ton*.

He hadn't offered any details regarding his fiancée or the wedding, and she hadn't asked. She'd merely congratulated him, then focused on beating back the unacceptable, unwanted, and overwhelming envy she felt toward a woman whose name she didn't even know.

The muted strains of a waltz drifted into the room, pulling her from her thoughts. To her surprise the Captain had invited her to attend the party, but she'd demurred. Even if she'd owned a gown appropriate for the occasion—which she did not—she had no wish to court disaster by showing herself at a soiree filled with people who undoubtedly knew Lord and Lady Bentley.

But the Captain had also invited her to explore the house and roam the corridors to peruse the extensive artwork and portraits of generations of Trentwell family members, an offer she intended to take advantage of.

Tucking her sketch pad under her arm, Penelope quit the room and entered the corridor. The music swelled louder, mingled with the hum of conversation, laughter, and the tinkle of crystal glasses, evoking memories of the elegant soirees she'd once attended. She moved slowly along, her kid boots sinking into the thick dark blue carpeting, and examined each painting of the former Earls and Countesses of Crandall and assorted family members lining the paneled walls. Some were formal portraits, others of gentlemen on horseback, ladies sitting in the gardens, or children surrounded by dogs, all dressed in the fashions of the time.

As she neared the end of the corridor, the sounds of the party increased in volume. When she turned the corner, she found herself near a small gallery that overlooked the party below through a narrow stone archway. Unable to resist, she approached the wrought-iron railing and looked down. She judged that more than one hundred elegantly dressed people mingled in the spacious room, some conversing in small groups, some partaking of the refreshments set up on a long table against the far wall, while others swirled around the parquet dance floor in time to the waltz being played by the quartet of musicians near the French windows.

Dozens of candles blazed in the gleaming crystal chandeliers, bathing the partygoers in a golden, prism-filled glow. Her gaze panned over the crowd, halting when she caught sight of Captain Trentwell.

He circled the dance floor with a beautiful, petite, blond young woman dressed in an exquisite pale blue gown. Given the naked adoration glowing on the young woman's face as she gazed up at him, she was clearly his fiancée—and exactly the sort of exquisite female Penelope had imagined he'd choose. Certainly no one could fault his taste, or the bride-to-be for looking so dazzled. Dressed in perfectly tailored formal black that accentuated his broad shoulders and muscular physique, Captain Trentwell looked big and dark and dangerously handsome.

The young woman said something, and Captain Trentwell, who towered over his petite fiancée, bent his head, clearly trying to capture her words. No doubt he didn't want to miss a single syllable of whatever pearls fell from her perfect, bowed lips. Although Penelope had long ago stopped the pointless practice of lamenting her average looks, the sight of that stunning young woman waltzing with Captain Trentwell squeezed her in a vise of envy and made her uselessly wish she'd been born blond and beautiful. What would it feel like to be held in his strong arms? To have him bend closer so as not to miss a word she said?

You'll never know. So stop being a nodcock and cease thinking about it. Exactly. It was one thing for hope to spring eternal for the unlikely—it was quite another to wish for the utterly impossible.

Even as her mind commanded her to turn away and continue her perusal of the Trentwell ancestors before she was caught gawking, she opened her tablet to a fresh page and pulled her charcoal from the pocket of her gown. Her hand moved swiftly across the page, capturing the image below. The waltz ended and Penelope watched in an agony of envy that utterly irritated her as Captain Trentwell escorted his stunning fiancée from the dance floor. When they passed beneath the gallery where she stood and she lost sight of them, she turned her full attention to completing the rough outline of her drawing.

"Idiot. That's what you are," she scolded herself under her breath. She blended the charcoal with a practiced finger, then blew away the dust. "Jealousy and envy are naught but wastes of time and energy." She knew it, yet still her heart ached with a yearning she couldn't squelch.

Which was truly vexing. "Good heavens, it's not like you to moon over a man," she muttered. She frowned at the likeness of Captain Trentwell she'd drawn. "Why do you have me so unsettled? I command you to stop it at once. I'm confused and thrown off balance and I don't like it one bit."

"Don't like what one bit?"

Penelope gasped at the sound of the quiet, deep voice that came from directly behind her. She whirled around and found herself face to face with Captain Trentwell.

Chapter Five

$\mathcal{P}$enelope pressed a hand to her chest where her heart thumped hard and fast and pressed her lips together lest she say the words that rushed into her throat. *You were attractive at a distance, but up close . . . Dear God, up close you are utterly breathtaking.* Her gaze fastened on his and her mind instantly emptied, her last thought being a combination of reluctant admiration for his fiancée for retaining her wits enough to converse while being held in this man's arms and a heartfelt, *Oh, my.*

Answer him! her inner voice shouted. Yes, she needed to answer him, but God help her, she'd completely forgotten the question. She cleared her throat, then managed, "I beg your pardon?"

"I was wondering what you didn't like. The party perhaps?"

Sanity returned with a slap, accompanied by a rush of heated embarrassment. "Of course not," she assured him quickly. "The party looks lovely. I was, um, referring to my sketch."

His gaze dropped to the pad she held. "What don't you like about it?"

She shoved the tablet behind her back. "I . . . I failed to capture the mood correctly."

"What were you drawing?"

"Just an image of the party."

Unmistakable interest flared in his eyes. "May I see it?"

"No!" Penelope gave a nervous laugh. "I mean, it's not finished yet."

"I don't mind."

"Don't you need to return to your guests?"

One dark brow lifted. "Are you trying to get rid of me, Miss Markham?"

Yes! "No! It's just that, well, surely your guests are missing you."

He flicked a gaze toward the gathering below and an expression that looked like a grimace, but surely wasn't, passed over his features. "I'm certain the festivities can carry on for a few minutes without my presence. And clearly you've forgotten that you are a guest here as well." He craned his neck and shot a pointed look at the tablet concealed behind her back. "May I?"

Botheration, to refuse him again would make her appear both childish and churlish. Swallowing her dismay, she handed him the tablet.

Alec studied the image of himself and several other couples waltzing and was once again amazed by her talent. "This is extremely well done, Miss Markham. You captured the movement of the dance perfectly. I can almost hear the rustling of the ladies' gowns."

"Thank you, Captain. You and your fiancée make a striking couple."

His gaze shot to hers. "Fiancée?" He shook his head and handed her back the tablet. "The young lady I was waltzing with is not my fiancée." Indeed, he couldn't even recall her name. As far as he was concerned, she'd been interchangeable with every other woman he'd met and danced with this evening. They'd all been beautiful, yet nothing about any of them had captured his interest.

Fire raced into Miss Markham's cheeks. "Forgive me, sir. I just assumed——"

"I don't have a fiancée."

She blinked. "You don't? But . . . but I thought you said this party was to celebrate your upcoming marriage."

"It is."

"I'm afraid I don't understand."

Alec flicked another glance at the soiree below. While he didn't particularly relish discussing the details of his situation, it certainly won out over the alternative of returning to the festivities right away. He returned his attention to Miss Markham and his heart skipped in the most unexpected way at the sight of her. The very welcome sight of her—a woman who wasn't staring at him as if he were a prize to be won.

He lightly grasped her arm and led her around the corner where they were away from the gallery, and the noise of the party faded to a quiet hum. "The purpose of the party is to find me a fiancée," he said. "My brother has five daughters and no son. After his wife nearly died four months ago giving birth to their youngest, the doctor advised them that she cannot have any more children. He asked me to marry—preferably as soon as possible as at two and thirty I'm not getting any younger—in order to produce a male heir to inherit the title. I agreed to do so."

She nodded slowly. "I see. Well, based on my brief glimpse of the festivities, you have your pick of beautiful young ladies."

"Yes. None of whom I know, none of whom know me, and all of whom—along with their matchmaking mamas—are looking at me as if I'm a bauble in a treasure chest."

"Surely that cannot surprise you, Captain."

He shrugged. "I suppose not, as the woman I choose will be the mother to the future Earl of Crandall."

She blinked, looking nonplussed. "Oh. Yes, I hadn't thought of that."

"Indeed? Then what did you mean? Why else would I be viewed as a bauble in a treasure chest?"

Even in the dimly lit corridor he could see the scarlet that stained her cheeks. A nervous-sounding laugh escaped her. "You are casting about for compliments, sir."

His brows shot upward. "I am?"

"Aren't you?"

"No. Just an honest answer."

"In that case, I would say that it's because you're very . . . dashing. Any young lady would gaze at you adoringly, as she would a bauble, because you're, well, a treasure."

Something seemed to shift inside Alec at her words—words he knew all too well weren't true, yet they still ridiculously, inordinately pleased him. "I assure you I'm nothing of the sort. And no one was gazing at me adoringly—that was calculation in their eyes."

Miss Markham shook her head and her glasses slid down her nose. She pushed them back up, then said, "I don't know about anyone else, but the young lady I sketched you dancing with was looking at you as if the sun rose and set upon you alone. It was one of the reasons I was moved to draw that scene."

"*One* of the reasons? Why else?"

She hesitated, then said, "The dancers, the candlelight, the elegantly dressed guests . . . it was all so lovely, I couldn't resist." Mischief flickered in her eyes. "And of course because you looked especially bauble-like."

His heart sped up at her words. "I thought you said I was 'dashing.' "

"You are." She grinned. "In a very bauble-like way."

He stared at that smile, at her laughing eyes and the dimples flanking her lush mouth, and felt a bit of the tension that had gripped him all evening fade away. Not that he felt in the least bit relaxed in Miss Markham's company. No— quite the opposite, actually. But the tension he felt with her was somehow exciting and welcome—an eager anticipation of what she'd say next, if their hands would touch, if she'd smile at him, as opposed to the dread he'd felt from the moment the party began.

With his gaze steady on hers, he offered her a formal bow. "Dashing in a bauble-like way . . . thank you, Miss Markham. That is the nicest thing I've heard all evening."

She laughed, a warm, husky magical sound that enveloped him like a heated blanket. "And I know a Banbury tale when I hear one, sir. I'm certain you've been smothered with compliments all evening."

A humorless sound escaped him. "I can't deny I've felt smothered all evening."

Her amused expression changed to one of confusion. "You're not enjoying the party?"

"In truth, no. Actually, I couldn't wait to escape for a few minutes and seized the first opportunity to do so." He didn't add that he'd immediately made that opportunity happen when he'd seen her in the gallery. "I don't particularly care for crowds."

"Nor do I. Thus my skulking about in the corridors."

"Are you enjoying the paintings?"

"Very much. There are some exceptionally fine portraits here."

"And also some rather hideous ones." He moved a bit further down the corridor, then nodded toward a large gilt-framed painting. "This one, for example."

Miss Markham joined him and leaned forward to peer at the painting of Alec's great-great-great-grandfather. Her shoulder brushed his and he pulled in a quick breath—one that filled his head with her subtle floral scent. Unable to stop himself, he bent his head closer to her and breathed in again. Bloody hell, she smelled good. Like summer in the country—flowers and sunshine with a bit of spice thrown in.

"He is quite . . ." She turned toward him and her words trailed off. Her face was less than a foot away from his. If he leaned forward just a little bit, he'd be able to touch his lips to hers, a realization that hit him like a steamy slap. She took a quick step back and her shoulders bumped the wall next to the painting. A lifetime of manners demanded he step back as well.

Instead he stepped forward and planted one hand on the wall next to her head.

Her quick intake of breath sent a dark thrill through him, one he couldn't explain and was apparently helpless to control because in spite of his better judgment and common sense, both demanding he move away from her, he instead leaned closer.

"He is quite what, Miss Markham?"

She moistened her lips, a gesture that had him fisting his hand against the paneling. "He is quite . . . formidable."

He nodded slowly. "Yes. And forbidding. As a child I always found that painting frightening. I hated walking down this corridor alone. The image seemed to watch me, and every time I walked by I feared he'd reach out and grab me."

"You've obviously overcome your fear."

"True. But I'm not alone." No, instead he stood improperly close to a woman to whom he needed to confess his darkest secret, his deepest shame. A woman whose nearness had his heart pounding hard enough to bruise his ribs. Bloody hell, not one of the more than two dozen society diamonds he'd danced and conversed with this evening had affected him like this . . . like he'd been walloped in the head. And set on fire.

He'd received many smiles tonight, but only one had enchanted him. Heard many compliments, but they'd all merely sounded like empty words until he'd come to the gallery and heard this woman call him dashing. Every gorgeous woman he'd danced with had lips, but only this woman's fascinated him. And tempted him beyond all reason. She hadn't been out of his thoughts all evening. He couldn't explain his reaction to her, but by God, there was absolutely no denying it.

"No, you're not alone," she whispered.

"You're not afraid he'll reach out and grab you?"

Her gaze searched his, and Alec forced himself to remain still, to not give in to the craving clawing at him to press her against the wall and find out if she felt as soft and luscious as she looked.

"No," she whispered. "I'm not afraid."

"Perhaps you should be."

"Perhaps. But I'm not."

The need to touch her could no longer be denied and Alec reached out and ran a single fingertip down her cheek. Soft. God, she was indeed soft. Her eyes appeared huge behind her spectacles, but he saw no sign of fear. Rather, he saw a vulnerable longing. And a trembling desire. Both of which set him afire—a flame that burned even hotter when her moist lips parted slightly and he could hear her quickening breaths.

The muted party sounds coming from the drawing room below filled with the young women from whose ranks he was expected to choose a wife all faded away, replaced by the potent need roaring through him, a raw desire unlike anything he could recall ever before experiencing. A need he simply could not ignore. One that incinerated every reason why he shouldn't, couldn't kiss her.

With his heart beating so loud she surely could hear it, he cupped her face between his hands, then leaned forward and brushed his lips over hers. If he'd been capable of doing so, he would have laughed in disbelief at the inferno that whisper of a touch ignited in him. He heard a thump, and it vaguely registered that she'd dropped her sketch pad. She stilled beneath his hands, and for several agonizing seconds he thought she meant to push him away. End this madness. Because God knows, he wasn't capable of doing so. But then she expelled a shaky breath, wrapped her arms around his neck and parted her lips. And sealed her fate.

Alec settled his mouth on hers and everything faded away, everything except her. He deepened the kiss, his tongue exploring the delicious, silky warmth of her mouth. A growl rumbled in his throat and he clasped her tighter against him.

God, it had been so long since he'd held a woman. Kissed a woman. And this woman tasted so damn good. Warm and sweet and seductive. And she felt so bloody damn good. As if she'd been cast from a mold to perfectly fit in his arms.

Any chance he might have had of listening to the bit of sanity attempting to fight its way through the fog of lust engulfing him was obliterated when she squirmed against him and opened her mouth wider beneath his.

Need shuddered through him and without breaking their kiss he turned them. With his shoulders pressed against the wall, he spread his legs and pulled her into the *V* of his thighs. It felt as if she melted against him, wax to his burning flame. With a groan he plunged his hands into her soft hair, scattering pins, releasing a mass of curls that unfurled down her back. He wrapped the silky tresses around his fist and gently urged her head back. Kissed his way along her jaw, then trailed his tongue down the gentle slope of her neck.

Although his conscience yelled *Stop!* the demand was drowned out by the mantra of *More!* pounding through him. His mouth founds hers once again, and one lush tongue-mating kiss melded into another. He ran one hand down her back to her buttocks and press her more firmly against his erection while his other hand came forward to cup her breast. She gasped and arched into his palm. Even through the layers of her clothes he could feel her hard nipple. Bloody hell, he wanted to strip away every bit of her clothing. With his teeth. Then simply devour her. Somehow a modicum of sense prevailed, warning him that if he didn't stop this—immediately—that's precisely what he would do.

It required every ounce of his will to lift his head. Breathing hard, he looked down. And groaned again at the sight of her. Ragged breaths puffed from between her kiss-swollen lips. Shiny dark curls lay in wild disarray around her shoulders, and he could clearly see the outline of her hardened nipples through her gown. Her glasses sat slightly askew on her nose, and their lenses were completely fogged over.

He reached out a less-than-steady hand and slipped off the spectacles to reveal that her eyes were closed. Her eyelids fluttered, then slowly rose to half-mast, as if she were awakening from a long slumber. She looked flushed and aroused and delightfully undone by his impatient hands and by God, it took all of his will not to kiss her again.

Somehow, without even trying, this woman had obliterated a lifetime of gentlemanly breeding and the fierce control under which he'd operated as an army officer. Shame hit him like a blow to the head. Bloody hell, he didn't know what had come over him. He'd never treated a woman with such a shocking lack of finesse. Had never lost command over himself like that.

An apology was in order, but he couldn't form the words. Not when the only word reverberating through his mind was *again*. Gritting his teeth against the need still hammering him, he took her by the shoulders and firmly set her away from him. Forced himself to release her. And say the words she deserved.

"Miss Markham, I owe you an apol—"

She cut off his words by touching her fingertip to his lips. "Please don't say you're sorry." Her voice sounded soft, husky, and not quite steady. She took her glasses from him and slipped them back on. "If you'll excuse me, I wish to retire."

She turned to leave. Alec reached for her hand, but she eluded him. "Miss Markham, I—"

"It's time for you to return to your party, Captain Trentwell," she said firmly. "Good night."

Alec watched her hurry away, then stared at the corner where she turned long after she'd vanished from his sight. Finally he roused himself from the stupor into which he'd fallen and looked down. And saw her sketch pad. He picked it up and again studied the drawing of him dancing with a young woman whose name he couldn't have recalled even if his life had depended upon him doing so. As if on cue the sound of the string quartet striking up another waltz broke through the haze engulfing him.

As Miss Markham had stated, it was time for him to return to his party. To find a wife. Among the dazzling array of society chits lining the drawing room like a banquet feast.

The problem was that the only woman who'd piqued his hunger tonight wasn't part of the menu.

Chapter Six

The next morning Alec strode into his brother's private study and halted in front of the enormous mahogany desk. "We need to talk, William."

William looked up from the *London Times* spread before him. His sharp gaze assessed Alec and while Alec knew his brother would see signs of the sleepless night that had plagued him, it was clear William hadn't slept well either. Dark circles shadowed the light blue eyes he'd inherited from their father, and his thick blond hair—another gift from their father—looked as if he'd tugged his hands through it. "I'm surprised to see you up so early after last night's party," William said.

"Army hours are ingrained, I'm afraid. What is your excuse?"

"A great deal on my mind. As it happens, I need to talk to you as well."

Although Alec was anxious to speak his mind, he said, "All right. You first."

William indicated the chair opposite him. "You should sit."

Alec's brows rose at his brother's serious tone and expression. At eight and thirty, William was six years his senior, and as such had always felt an obligation to look after Alec. While Alec loved his brother and appreciated his concern, he didn't require looking after. Ever since his return from the war, all he wanted was peace, quiet, and solitude. William, however, filled with well-meaning but misguided intentions, was determined to drag him back into Society. Thus Alec's escape to Little Longstone. Where he would be right now had William not needed and asked for his help.

After seating himself Alec said, "Clearly something is amiss."

"I'm afraid so." William folded his hands on the desk and regarded Alec through troubled eyes. "It concerns Miss Markham. There's a . . . problem."

Alec gripped the wooden arms of his chair. Damn it, this undoubtedly had to do with their encounter last night. "Is she . . . ill?"

"No."

Relief flooded Alec. "Then what is wrong?"

"I heard some disturbing news about her last evening."

Alec's relief turned to frustration with the realization that news of Miss Markham's Italy scandal was clearly already making the rounds. "I see."

"You don't seem surprised, Alec."

"If the news is regarding the incident in Italy that led to her dismissal from Bentley's employ, I'm not."

William nodded. "Yes, the story was on everyone's lips last night, so of course you would have heard."

He hadn't taken note of any gossip. No doubt because he'd paid little attention to the party chatter before his interlude with Miss Markham, and absolutely no attention whatsoever to it afterward.

"Quite the debacle," William continued. "Lord and Lady

Bentley are most set against her." He let out a long, tired-sounding breath and dragged his hands down his face. "This places us in a most awkward situation as she naturally cannot remain in our employ in light of this disturbing news. Of course you couldn't have known when you commissioned her to paint our portraits—"

"On the contrary, I knew all about it."

"How?"

"Miss Markham told me herself—before I employed her."

William blinked, then frowned. "Then why did you hire her?"

"Many reasons."

"Indeed? Since I cannot fathom even one why you'd ever consider bringing scandal into our home—not to mention the ire of Lord Bentley, a man I know and respect—I'd be interested in hearing them."

"I disregarded any talk of impropriety as I believe Miss Markham was dismissed unfairly. The sculpture in question was not intended to be lascivious in nature. It was *art*, and no more scandalous than the statues produced by Michelangelo."

"Surely you're not comparing Miss Markham's work with that of Michelangelo—who, by the way, was a *man*."

"Yes—and if Miss Markham was a man, her talent would be celebrated rather than denigrated. And no, she isn't Michelangelo, but she is extremely talented."

"Be that as it may, if Jane and I had been aware of the situation, we would not have agreed to your hiring Miss Markham or allowing her to stay here." William blew out a tired sigh. "You should have told us, Alec."

"So you could react as you are now? No." He leaned forward and kept his gaze steady on William's. "You know her brother was my sergeant. He was all the family she had in the world. I feel a duty toward her."

Concern mixed with frustration clouded William's eyes. "Alec, you're not responsible for the family members of every soldier who died at Waterloo."

I am for those I killed. "I know. But in this case, her ability to support herself as an art instructor is now lost to her and I wish to help."

"Then give her money and be done with it."

"She would never accept charity. But she *would* accept a commission to paint my portrait. If you no longer wish for her to paint yours, that is your prerogative. However, I still intend for her to paint mine."

William frowned. "It's not that I'm unsympathetic to her plight, but given the circumstances, she cannot paint it here. I cannot allow any hint of scandal to touch Jane or the girls."

"I understand. And not to worry. I've already decided upon other arrangements for Miss Markham."

A bit of the tension eased from William's face. "I trust these arrangements will be done in a timely manner?"

"My plan is that she'll be gone from the house by this evening," Alec assured him.

There was no mistaking William's relief. "Excellent. Now that that's settled, what did you wish to speak to me about?"

"Our family's future. You'll be happy to know that I've decided upon a bride."

William's expression cleared and his lips curved up in a satisfied smile. "I am indeed happy to know that. I knew that party would get the job done."

"It did indeed."

"Would have been impossible for you not to find *someone* amongst all those beautiful young women." He chuckled. "I'm not certain I'd ever have been able to choose. Good thing you've always been the decisive sort."

"Actually, the decision wasn't all that difficult."

William's eye gleamed with a knowing look. "Ah. So one young lady in particular captured your interest."

"Yes, she did."

"I knew it! Jane and I discussed this last night after we retired. We both suspected Cupid's dart had found you, but we couldn't agree with whom you were smitten. We made a wager, one I'm certain I've won." William rubbed his hands together. "Heh, heh, heh. I'm going to greatly enjoy collecting my forfeit from my lovely wife. So tell me, who is the lucky lady?"

"Who do you think?"

"Lady Sarah Weston. I saw the way you looked at her during the quadrille."

Alec didn't bother to point out that whatever his expression may have been, it was merely to mask his boredom. "Sorry, no."

William's face fell. "Blast. So I suppose Jane was right. She picked Lady Melanie Springton."

"No, not her either."

William's brows collapsed. "Well. Then it must be Miss Emily Fernbank."

"I'm afraid not."

"Miss Adeline Bailey?"

"No."

"Lady Caroline Worthington? Miss Elizabeth Chapman? Miss Helena Grainger?"

"No, no, and no."

William tossed out several more names and Alec shook his head at each suggestion. Finally William blew out a quick laugh. "I officially surrender. Whom have you chosen?"

"Miss Penelope Markham."

Alec watched confusion flicker in William's eyes, followed by shock. Several seconds of the loudest silence Alec had ever heard swelled between them. Finally William said, "I beg your pardon?"

"You heard me, William. I'm going to ask Miss Markham to marry me."

William shook his head. "No. You're joking."

"I assure you I'm perfectly serious."

"Then you're foxed."

"I'm also perfectly sober."

"Then you're insane. It's completely impossible."

"May I ask why?"

A humorless sound huffed from between William's lips. "In what way *isn't* she impossible? First there's the scandal in which she's embroiled. That would taint not only you, but the entire family."

"Once she and I are married the talk will cease. No one is going to speak ill of the Earl of Crandall's sister-in-law."

"Even if that's true—which I'm not conceding, by the way—there is the issue of her age. The entire reason I asked you to marry is to produce an heir. Miss Markham is hardly in her first bloom of youth."

"Neither is she in her dotage."

"What if she is unable to conceive?"

"There is no reason to believe she can't. Nor is there any guarantee that any of the younger women at last night's soiree would be able to."

William dragged his hands down his face. "Good God, Alec. Why *her*? I paraded a roomful of beauties in front of you last evening."

Alec wasn't certain how to explain something he was at a loss to understand himself. "I don't feel anything for any of those women."

"Given your promise to marry as soon as possible, had you believed you'd make a love match?"

"No. But I'd hoped to at least feel *something* for my future wife. And I feel something for Miss Markham."

"Yes—a misguided sense of responsibility."

"It's more than that, William."

"How can that be? You just met the woman yesterday. You've known Lady Sarah and some of the other party guests for years."

"I may have only been introduced to Miss Markham yesterday, but through my relationship with her brother I feel as if I know her very well."

"You claim you feel more for her than responsibility. What else could you possibly feel? Unless it's pity?"

"I cannot deny I am sympathetic toward her plight. But it's more than that. I feel an undeniable . . ." His voice trailed off, uncertain what to call the raging heat she inspired in him.

William studied him through narrowed eyes. "You don't mean . . . surely you can't mean *lust*?"

Somehow *lust* seemed too tame a word for the inferno that had incinerated him last night, but as Alec couldn't think of another, he nodded. "Yes."

William's jaw dropped. "Now I know you're jesting."

Alec's jaw tightened. "You're implying Miss Markham isn't the sort of woman to inspire lust?"

"I'm not implying it at all—I'm saying it outright."

"I disagree."

"But . . . but . . . how can that be?"

"I don't know," Alec said in a chilly tone, "but it is. And you should be glad for it as it will certainly aid in the heir-begetting activities. I'll also remind you that you are speaking of my future wife and the future mother of the next Earl of Crandall."

Color rose on William's cheeks. "I was not trying to be insulting—"

"Yet you were."

"I'm certain that except for the scandal she's a very nice woman—"

"She is."

"But—"

"No 'buts,' William. It is my choice and she is who I want." Alec looked into his brother's eyes, then asked quietly, "Do you want my happiness?"

William raked his hands through his hair. "Of course I do."

"Then accept my choice. While I appreciate the party and your efforts to find me a bride, I wouldn't be happy married to a society chit whose life revolves around Town and soirees. I want to live quietly in the country. With someone who shares my interests." *And whom I cannot keep my hands off of.*

William leaned back in his leather chair and studied him for several long seconds. Finally he blew out a deep breath and nodded. "Very well, Alec. It's not the choice I would make, but it's not my choice to make. I know it wasn't your preference to even marry and that you're only doing so because I asked it of you. Therefore I'll respect your decision—especially since it's obvious you won't change your mind."

"You're correct—I won't."

"Which means I've lost my wager with Jane, blast it all."

Alec nearly grinned at his brother's disgruntled tone. "You're forgetting that Jane also lost her wager with you."

William brightened a bit at that reminder. "Yes, she did, didn't she?" He rose and held out his hand. "Congratulations, Alec. I wish you every happiness. And many sons."

Alec shook his hand. "Thank you. Now about the wedding . . . I was thinking of this afternoon, if that's convenient for you."

William blinked. "You wish to get married *today*?"

"Yes—provided I am able to secure a special license this morning, although I'm not anticipating any problem in doing so. And provided that Miss Markham agrees." He rose. "I'll speak to her now, then hopefully be off to the Archbishop's office at Doctor's Commons for the license."

"And what if Miss Markham wants a fancier wedding and for the banns to be posted?"

"Then that is what she shall have. But I don't believe that will be important to her." At least Alec prayed it wouldn't be. The mere thought of waiting three weeks to finish what they'd started in the gallery last night clenched his hands into fists.

"Very well. While you're proposing and procuring the license, I'll speak to Jane about transforming the drawing room into a wedding chapel."

"Thank you, William. Perhaps Jane would also agree to arrange for Miss Markham to have whatever it is brides require to ready themselves for their wedding."

"Consider it done."

They shook hands again, then Alec quit the room. After closing the door behind him, he pulled in a bracing breath. He'd convinced William.

Now all he had to do was convince the bride.

Chapter Seven

$\mathcal{T}$hank you for seeing me so promptly, Miss Markham," said Captain Trentwell.

Penelope stood in the library and faced the man responsible for her sleepless night. The man who had kissed her senseless and opened a floodgate of feelings and sensations, of wants and desires she had no idea how to dam up. A massive mahogany desk stood between them, a fact for which she was grateful as the more distance separating them the better, lest she give in to the nearly overwhelming temptation to rush into his arms and beg him to make her feel that incredible magic again.

However, any hopes she'd harbored that he'd welcome another opportunity to kiss her withered at his stern, serious expression and stiff posture, and the fear that lurked in the back of her mind raced to the forefront—had his brother heard of the Italy scandal? Was she about to be dismissed?

Forcing a calm she was far from feeling and one she

prayed disguised the full-body blush heating her skin, she said, "Your note indicated you wished to speak to me as soon as possible."

"Yes." He nodded at the chair next to her. "Please sit."

Even though her knees felt less than steady, she shook her head. "I'd prefer to stand."

"Very well. I'm sorry to inform you that word of what occurred in Italy is the latest gossip fodder."

Penelope's stomach dropped and she grasped the back of the chair to steady herself. "I see." She drew a deep breath, then raised her chin. "I'm afraid I suspected as much. And of course I fully understand the ramifications, Captain Trentwell, of the impossibility of you and your family risking any hint of the scandal surrounding me attaching itself to you." A crushing sense of loss pressed down on her, and to her mortification hot tears pushed behind her eyes. "Naturally I release you from your offer to paint your portraits. And now if you'll excuse me, I'll see to packing my things."

She turned to leave, anxious to quit the room before she suffered further humiliation by him seeing the tears she wasn't certain she could keep at bay much longer. She'd barely taken a step toward the door when his voice halted her.

"Miss Markham."

Penelope briefly closed her eyes and fought for composure. Remaining facing away from him, she asked, "Was there something else, Captain Trentwell?"

"Yes. I wished to give you this."

Damnation, now she'd have to face him. She drew a deep breath and turned. And found him standing a mere arm's length away. "You dropped this in the corridor last night," he said.

She looked down and saw he held her sketch pad. Heat rushed into her face. Clearly she'd dropped it when he'd kissed her. She hadn't noticed it was missing, nor had she given it a single thought. No doubt because she'd been unable to think of anything other than him and their kiss since the instant he'd touched his mouth to hers.

She took the pad, ignoring the warmth that sizzled up her arm when their fingers brushed. "Thank you. And now if you'll excuse me—"

This time he stopped her by lightly grasping her arm. "Actually, there is more I wish to discuss with you."

Penelope prayed he didn't feel the tremor of delight that ran through her at his touch. She had to lock her knees to keep herself from leaning toward him like a flower seeking sunlight. "Very well, I'm listening."

"You may recall I mentioned last night my intention to marry."

Given the pain that had knifed through her at the news, she wasn't apt to forget. "Yes. In order to hopefully produce a male heir."

"Yes. I wanted to tell you that I've decided upon a wife."

An ache she couldn't name suffused Penelope. Her hands tightened around her sketch pad and she swallowed hard. Dear God, she wanted, needed to get out of here. Now. Before the tears she valiantly held back burst forth.

"Congratulations, sir. I hope you and the future Mrs. Trentwell enjoy every happiness."

"Thank you. As do I." His gaze searched hers with an expression she couldn't decipher other than to know it weakened her already unsteady knees. "Do you think I could make you happy, Miss Markham?"

Confusion assailed her. "I don't understand—"

Her words chopped off when he lowered himself to one knee before her and slipped a square velvet box from his waistcoat pocket. He opened the box's hinged lid to reveal a slim gold ring set with a single perfect pearl. "Miss Markham, will you do me the honor of becoming my wife?"

Penelope could only be thankful her jaw was attached as it otherwise would have dropped to the floor. She stared into his very serious dark blue eyes and blinked, certain he and this entire scenario was a figment of her desire-addled imagination. When he still remained kneeling before her after half a dozen blinks, she managed to say, "I beg your pardon?"

"I asked you to marry me."

Dear God, she *had* heard him correctly. Which could only mean one thing. She leaned toward him and sniffed.

One dark brow shot upward. "Do I . . . smell?"

Utterly confounded, Penelope shook her head. "No."

"You sound surprised."

"Frankly, I'm shocked. I thought for certain you'd reek of brandy."

He muttered something that sounded suspiciously like *Why does everyone think I've been drinking?* "I am *not* foxed."

"Then I cannot imagine why you would ask me to marry you."

"Can't you?" Before she could speak, he rose to his feet. After slipping her sketch pad from her nerveless fingers and setting it and the ring on the desk, he lightly clasped her hands, entwining their fingers. "I am in need of a wife. You are without means, income, or a place to live. It is a perfect solution to both our problems."

"But we only met yesterday! We barely know each other." Yet even as she said the words, her heart rejected them. For thanks to Edward's letters she felt as if she did know this man. And had known him for years.

His gaze searched hers. "Did we just meet? It doesn't seem that way. I feel as if I've known you for years."

His words that so clearly mirrored her thoughts tingled heat down her spine. "I fear you haven't given this matter sufficient thought, Captain. What of the scandal surrounding me and the fact that Lord and Lady Bentley are dead set against me?"

"The gossip will cease once we're married."

A humorless sound escaped her. "Surely you don't believe that. If anything, a hasty wedding will only increase the gossip and rile Lord and Lady Bentley further."

"The talk will eventually die down, and what they or anyone else thinks of is no significance to me. The only opinion that is important to me in this matter is yours. Therefore, I shall ask you again. Will you marry me?"

It actually frightened her how much she wanted to say yes. He was offering her all the dreams she'd set aside years ago—for a husband, a home of her own, a child—yet how could she accept? While he'd made light of the scandal, she'd lived with Lord and Lady Bentley long enough to know how vicious gossip could be amongst the *ton* and how entire families could suffer from the behavior of one member. Captain Trentwell's honor, his loyalty to Edward had driven him to make this rash offer, one she was certain he'd regret once he had time to think about it. Therefore, although her heart yearned to accept him, she shook her head.

"Your offer is uncommonly generous, Captain, and I cannot tell you how much I appreciate it. It only further proves you are worthy of the deep admiration Edward felt for you, a high regard I assure you I share. Clearly you feel a responsibility toward me, but there is no need for you to do so."

Something that looked like guilt flickered in his eyes, but was gone before she could decide. "I am not proposing out of a sense of responsibility. I am doing so because I need a wife and I believe that we are well suited. I need an heir and I believe you will make an excellent mother."

His words, while certainly more practical than romantic, touched something deep inside her. Still, she forced herself to say, "Thank you. However, I cannot allow you to make such a sacrifice."

"I assure you I'm sacrificing nothing."

"How can you say that? You should be proposing to one of those beautiful young women you danced with last night."

"I'm proposing to the beautiful woman I kissed last night."

Disappointment slapped her that he'd resort to insincere flattery and to her horror her bottom lip trembled. "Captain Trentwell, I beg you cease this nonsense. I realize you are only trying to be kind, however it is not necessary to utter such absurdities."

"I am being neither kind nor absurd. Rather, I am being practical as us marrying is the perfect solution to both our situations. And I'm being honest. I find you delightful. Fascinating. And extremely attractive. Has no one ever told you that your eyes are extraordinary and your smile is absolutely dazzling?"

"Perhaps my mother, but aside from her, no."

"Then you weren't listening, because I just told you."

Whatever she might have said in response died in her throat when he released one of her hands and stroked a gentle fingertip down her cheek. " 'Beauty in things exists merely in the mind which contemplates them,' " he quoted softly.

Penelope swallowed to locate her missing voice. "David Hume," she murmured.

He nodded. "The fact that you recognize the words of my favorite philosopher is just one of the many things about you I find so attractive."

A blush warmed her cheeks. "Anyone would know that, Captain."

"You're wrong. Not one of those supposed beauties from last night engaged my interest. But you . . ." He brushed the pad of his thumb over her lower lip and Penelope's heart jumped. "You captivated me with your smile. Your laughter. Your talent and intelligence. I had no desire to kiss any of those women, yet I couldn't *not* kiss you." He regarded her gravely. "You should know that I don't care for Town life, therefore we would live quietly in Little Longstone. My home there isn't a grand estate, but I think you'd find it very comfortable. Would that meet with your approval?"

"Of course. But—"

Her words halted when he stepped closer and their bodies lightly bumped. "You should also know that because the goal is to produce an heir, preferably as soon as possible, it will of course be necessary to consummate the marriage."

He leaned forward and nuzzled her neck with his warm lips. "Preferably as soon as possible."

Her heart stuttered. Since her voice seemed to have gone missing, she did the only thing she could—tilt her head to give him better access.

"And as frequently as possible," he murmured, drawing her closer until they touched from chest to knee.

"H . . . how frequently?" she asked, her words ending on a soft gasp of delight when he touched his tongue to the base of her throat, then lightly sucked on her skin.

He kissed his way up her neck to her jaw, then brushed his mouth over hers. "Every day. Several times. At least."

Oh, my. Everything inside her screamed for her not to question this opportunity further, to grab it before he changed his mind. She'd long ago given up hoping for a marriage proposal, let alone one from a handsome, heroic, dashing man who could wobble her knees by the simple act of breathing.

He ran the tip of his tongue over her bottom lip. "Do you think you could do that . . . Penelope?"

The sound of her name whispered in the husky rasp had her fingers curling into the soft wool of his jacket. *Could she?* Dear God, did he even need to ask? Surely there wasn't a woman in the entire kingdom who wouldn't give a limb to be bedded by this man. Every day. Several times. At least.

"Yes, but—"

"Excellent." His mouth came down on hers and with a groan she couldn't contain Penelope rose on her toes and wrapped her arms around his neck. And in a heartbeat found herself crushed against him. Since that was precisely where she'd ached to be since the moment she'd walked away from him last night, she eagerly parted her lips, a silent plea to deepen the kiss which he immediately answered, caressing her tongue with his.

Dear God, he tasted so delicious. Like mint and cinnamon with a dash of danger mixed in. The heat that seemed to pump from his body surrounded her, saturating her with warmth and his woodsy, clean scent. Closer . . . she wanted, needed, to be closer to him and his thrilling hardness that pressed between her thighs in a manner that had her clinging to him as if her life depended upon it. The folds between her legs felt swollen and heavy and she squirmed against him in an attempt to relieve the pulsing ache.

With a low moan, he lifted his head and Penelope forced her heavy eyelids open. The fire burning in his eyes scorched and utterly amazed her. "Say you'll marry me," he demanded in a low, intense voice.

"Captain Trentwell, I—"

"Alec. Say you'll marry me, Penelope."

That heat blazing from his eyes melted away whatever bit of resistance she might have retained. He obviously didn't love her but he claimed to admire her, and there was no refuting the confounding yet obvious evidence of his desire.

Even before seeing him in person she'd liked and respected and admired him—feelings that had only increased upon their meeting. And as for desire . . . never had she dreamed she could feel such aching want. Certainly many marriages were based on far less than what they already shared, and she didn't doubt that given time she could, and would, grow to love him. Could he, would he grow to love her?

Did that really matter?

Her heart said yes, but her practical mind said no. It didn't matter. What mattered was he'd offered her a future. And she'd be a fool to turn him down.

She moistened her lips and whispered the words that would change her life.

"I will marry you."

He briefly closed his eyes. When he opened them, the intensity of his gaze simultaneously froze her in place and heated her to her core. He released her and moved to the desk, returning with the pearl ring. "It was my mother's," he said quietly. "I hope you like it."

Penelope gazed at the beautiful ring and blinked back tears. "It's the most beautiful ring I've ever seen. I've always loved pearls. They remind me of the moon."

"I'm glad you like it. I also hope you don't want a long engagement."

"A long engagement is not necessary."

"Excellent. So you've no objections to the wedding taking place today?"

Penelope blinked. *"Today?"*

"This afternoon. The carriage is waiting to take me to Doctor's Commons so I can procure a special license."

A nervous laugh bubbled in her throat. "Heavens. You weren't jesting when you said you wanted to get started on your heir as soon as possible."

He pulled her tighter against him and leaned down to brush his lips over the bit of skin behind her ear—skin she hadn't known was so delightfully sensitive until he'd touched it. "Is that a problem?"

"N . . . no. Merely a surprise."

He raised his head and she caught her breath at the smoldering look in his eyes. "I'm going to greatly enjoy convincing you how desirable you are, Penelope. And I'll make certain you enjoy it as well."

Heavens. Surely the thought of doing *that* should fill her with apprehension rather than overwhelming anticipation. "I shall do my utmost to please you . . . Alec."

He brushed a wisp of hair from her cheek and frowned. "I know you will. You already have. And I'll do everything in my power to make you happy."

She offered him a half smile and repeated his words. "I know you will. You already have."

His frown deepened and he appeared troubled. "Penelope, I want you to know, that is, I need to tell you . . ."

"Yes, Alec?" she prompted when he continued to merely frown.

He opened his mouth, then shut it, then shook his head. His expression cleared, although his eyes remained troubled. "Nothing. Certainly nothing that can't wait. Right now I must be off to Doctor's Commons. I've already apprised my brother about the wedding and he's informed his wife, who will assist you in my absence." He leaned forward and pressed a chaste kiss against her forehead. "I'll return soon."

She watched him walk toward the door and couldn't quite hold in the sigh of appreciation that rose in her throat. He looked as marvelous exiting a room as he did entering one. The instant the door closed behind him with a quiet click, Penelope moved to the nearest chair and sat down heavily. She stared at the luminous pearl adorning her left hand and marveled at the miraculous turn her life had taken since yesterday.

So many hopes she'd believed were beyond her reach had suddenly come true. A laugh of disbelief escaped her, followed by a sense of joy unlike anything she'd ever before experienced. Her gaze fell upon her sketchbook, and suddenly unable to sit still, she rose and crossed to the desk. Opened the tablet to the last page, then reached for the piece of charcoal she always carried in her pocket. She skimmed her finger down her wish list and drew a single line through three entries she'd never thought she'd cross off: Be kissed. Own a pearl. Get married.

And it was all because of Alec. A man who'd touched her heart long before she'd physically met him. A man whose eyes told her he was tortured by his war experiences. A man she wanted to help heal—not only because he'd taken care of her brother during the war, but because once she had met him, he'd touched her soul. A man whose kiss turned her knees to porridge.

A man she was determined to make happy. Because he was a man who deserved every happiness.

Chapter Eight

$\mathcal{A}$lec was trying his damnedest to think of something, *anything* other than his new wife, who sat opposite him in the carriage, but the task proved utterly impossible. How could he when he had only to reach out a hand to touch her? When her delicate floral scent filled his head with every breath? When she just looked so damn desirable and he wanted her so damn badly and bloody hell, she was now *his* and had been for an entire two hours and sixteen minutes and would this damn carriage ride *ever* end?

No, it wouldn't—at least not for another two hours. Jesus. He'd survived more battles than he cared to recall, but not touching her for the remainder of this torturous ride to Little Longstone was going to be the death of him. And he didn't dare touch her, because if he did, even once, he knew he wouldn't be able to stop. And she certainly deserved better than having her skirts tossed up in a carriage. He was a man of control. A man of patience. He could wait.

He stared out the window and forced himself to take several slow, deep breaths. The first hour of this seemingly end-less journey had crawled by at a snail's pace, an exercise in torment during which he'd mentally recited the alphabet backwards—one hundred and four times—then run dozens of math sums in his head.

But nothing worked. All he could think about was how damn much he wanted his *wife*. Bloody hell, he couldn't stop thinking the word. In his mind's eye he saw his *wife* as she'd entered the drawing room for the simple wedding cer-emony, wearing an unadorned pale yellow gown, carrying the small bouquet of pink roses he'd purchased for her on his way back from Doctor's Commons. Her only jewelry was the pearl ring he'd given her, but to him she didn't require anything else—the shy glow in her beautiful bespectacled eyes, coupled with her sparkling smile rendered her far more radiant than any jewels.

With William and Jane standing witness, he and Penelope had exchanged the vows that bound them for life. A life he unexpectedly couldn't wait to begin, a surprise, as he hadn't anticipated the stirrings of hope and happiness seeping into him. Indeed, it had been so long since he'd felt either, he almost hadn't recognized them.

A life you should *have begun by telling her the truth about how Edward died, you selfish bastard.*

Alec squeezed his eyes shut and bludgeoned back his con-science, which had been flaying him alive. Damn it, yes, he should have told her. After failing to do so as soon as he'd met her yesterday, he certainly should have last night. But then the urge to touch her, kiss her, had driven every other thought from his head. And of course he should have told her before marrying her, but while he'd opened his mouth to do so in the library, after she'd accepted his proposal, he'd been unable to pry the words from his throat. What if she'd changed her mind? It was a chance he hadn't been willing to take.

No, since he'd waited this long, there was no point now in not waiting until they were settled into married life. After she'd hopefully come to care enough for him so that forgiveness wasn't beyond the realm of possibility—both for what he'd done and his failure to immediately confess it. *A few weeks . . . a month or two at the most*, he assuaged his scowling conscience. Then he'd tell her. And pray that this tiny ray of light he'd been given wasn't snuffed out.

"Alec . . . are you all right?"

His eyes popped open at the sound of her voice and he turned toward her. And stifled a groan. Bloody hell, there was no logical reason why, dressed in the same prim yellow gown she'd worn for the ceremony, topped with an equally prim dark blue spencer and matching bonnet, she should look so damn delectable, but by God she did and his fingers literally itched to muss up all that primness. To discover every soft curve his very active imagination envisioned beneath her clothing.

He shifted in his seat in a completely unsuccessful attempt to relieve the strangulation occurring in his breeches. "I'm fine," he lied in a voice that sounded as if he'd swallowed gravel.

"You look . . . flushed."

No doubt because he felt as if he were roasting over a roaring flame. "It's a bit warm in here."

"You seem . . . preoccupied. Is something amiss?"

Only that I want you so badly I can barely sit still. "No."

The word came out sharper than he'd intended and he felt like a complete bastard when twin scarlet spots stained her cheeks. "I don't believe you."

"You think I'm lying?"

Another layer of color stained her cheeks. She raised her chin and said, "I think you don't wish to hurt my feelings by saying what you're thinking."

"And what am I thinking?"

She bit down on her bottom lip, a gesture that fisted Alec's hands. "You have regrets," she whispered. "Over our hasty marriage. I knew you would, yet still I selfishly—" her voice hitched and she cleared her throat. "I'm so sorry."

Alec forced his attention away from her ripe mouth and met her distressed gaze. "Any regrets I'm feeling have absolutely nothing to do with marrying you."

"It is not necessary to spare my feelings."

"It is not your feelings I'm attempting to spare."

Confusion filled her eyes. "Then what?"

Bloody hell. Well, best he tell her. He certainly didn't want her to think he was sorry they'd wed. "It's your virtue and maidenly sensibilities I'm trying to protect."

She blinked. "I don't understand. I believed our marriage would be, um, consummated."

"Yes. But—" Damn it, his cravat felt like a noose. He impatiently tugged on the linen knot and said, "It shouldn't be consummated in a *carriage*."

Her eyes widened. "You mean you want to . . . *here*? *Now*?"

A humorless sound escaped him. "So badly I cannot think properly."

Realization dawned in her eyes. "So the reason you've been brooding and preoccupied and ignoring me isn't because you don't want me, but rather because you . . . do?"

He ground his teeth and prayed for strength. "Yes."

"So badly you cannot think properly."

"That is actually a grossly lukewarm description of how much, but yes."

"I see."

He turned to look out the window, unable to watch her recoil from his blunt words. Damn it, confessing he longed to fall on her like a rabid dog had probably not been a wise thing to do.

She cleared her throat. "Would it help to know that I feel the same way?"

Alec snapped his attention back to her and his heart damn near stopped at the desire glittering in her eyes. "You do?"

Crimson flooded her cheeks. "Yes. And I'm wondering . . . is there any reason why our marriage *shouldn't* be, um, consummated in a carriage?"

A half dozen reasons flew into his mind starting with the fact that she was a virgin and at least deserved a bed, and ending with the carriage not offering the utmost in comfort, but he swatted them away as he would an insect. "No, no reason at all . . . Mrs. Trentwell."

Feeling as if his skin was on fire, he reached out and plucked her from her seat, then settled her across his lap. The relief he felt at finally touching her, holding her, was incinerated by the feel of her soft curves pressing against him. "Just so you fully understand," he said, impatiently tugging on her satin bonnet strings, "your virtue is about to be completely, thoroughly compromised."

"Thank goodness."

She yanked her bonnet from her head, tossed it to the floor, and wrapped her arms around his neck. With a groan Alec buried his face in her fragrant neck. "God, you smell so damn good." He traced his tongue down her throat while his fingers slipped the pins from her hair.

She gasped and tilted her head. "I'm delighted you think so. In the future, in the interest of saving time, I believe it would be best for you to simply tell me what you want. Not only will I be happy to oblige you, but chances are favorable that I want the same thing."

"Excellent. Have I mentioned that I greatly admire your practical, logical nature, as well as your adventurous spirit?"

"No, I don't believe you have."

"A dreadful oversight on my part. Please consider yourself told. And I am happy to comply with your request— provided you return the favor and tell me what *you* want." He raised his head and sifted his fingers through her loosened hair. "As for me—I want to touch you." The mass of shiny mahogany curls tumbled over his hands, releasing a soft floral scent that made his head swim.

"I want you to kiss me."

"Thank God." He cupped her head in his palms. "To use your exact words, not only will I be happy to oblige you, but chances are favorable that I want the same thing."

"To use your exact words, thank God," she murmured.

Alec settled his mouth on hers and groaned at the sensation that swamped him . . . that of a man who'd just discovered shelter after a grueling journey through a horrific storm. Their tongues met, and need unlike anything he'd ever before experienced gripped him. Even while his mind commanded him to go slowly, gently, his hands attacked the fastenings on her clothing with a lack of subtlety and finesse he'd have found appalling if he'd had the wherewithal to think properly. And what little control he still possessed was disappearing at a rapid rate because his *wife*, his delectable, luscious, surprising wife was impatiently tugging at his clothing and squirming on his lap.

He opened her spencer, yanked away her lace fichu, and slipped his hand inside her bodice. Warm, soft breast topped with a pebbled nipple filled his hand. She gasped against his mouth and her head fell limply back, affording him the opportunity to drag his mouth along the pale column of her throat.

More . . . damn it, he needed, wanted more. With a growl of frustration he shifted them until she lay back on the velvet squabs and he reclined on his side next to her.

She looked up at him through eyes hazy with desire. His inner voice whispered at him to tell her how beautiful she looked, flushed with arousal, but before he could form the words she reached up, fisted her fingers in his hair and pulled his head down to meet hers in another lush, open-mouthed kiss.

Desperate, aching need filled him, one that demanded to be satisfied. He tugged down her bodice and skimmed his open mouth along her jaw, over her collarbone, then lower, until his tongue circled her taut nipple.

"Alec . . ." his name whispered past her lips, then trailed off into a groan when he drew her nipple into his mouth. She strained upward, offering more of herself, an invitation he instantly accepted. She ran her hands through his hair, over his shoulders, her breathing growing more erratic with each deepening pull of his lips on her nipple.

He coasted one hand down her body and slipped it beneath the hem of her gown, dragging the material upward as he kissed his way back to her mouth. "Spread your legs," he demanded in a rough whisper against her lips. Her thighs fell open without hesitation, her choppy breaths hitching when his fingers glided over her folds.

A long groan escaped him. "You're wet. So beautifully wet." Her eyes slid closed as he teased her with a slow, circular motion, then slipped a finger inside her. "And tight." His erection jerked in anticipation and he prayed he'd last long enough to bring her pleasure.

"You're driving me mad," she said, her words ending on a breathy moan.

"As you are me."

"I . . . I don't see how." She laid one hand against his chest and he knew she felt his heart pounding against her palm. "I want to touch you. As you're touching me. But I'm not certain how. I don't know what to do."

The fire inside him burned hotter. "It's simple. Don't be afraid to tell me if I do something you like."

She strained against his hand. "I like . . . *ahhh* . . . that. Very much."

"Or anything you don't like."

"I suspect that isn't going to be necessary."

"And know that if you enjoy being touched in a certain way, chances are extremely good that I'd enjoy being touched in the same manner. But we'll save that for next time as my control is on a *very* short tether. Believe me, if you touch me now, this will be over before it's begun."

"I . . . I'm not certain how much longer I can wait. I feel so achy." She spread her legs wider. "And . . . desperate."

Bloody hell, he knew all about desperate. Unable to wait any longer, he slipped his fingers from her body, yanked his shirt from his waistband, then jerked open his breeches. His erection sprang free, an instant of relief that ended on a harsh hiss when she brushed her fingertips over him.

Her gaze flew to his face and she pulled her hand away. "Did I hurt you?"

Alec pulled in a ragged breath and gave his head a single quick shake. "No. Do it again."

Curiosity gleamed in her eyes. He looked down and watched her hesitantly glide her fingers over the head of his arousal.

"You're wet as well," she said, dragging a single fingertip through the pearl of moisture leaking from the tip.

He slammed his eyes shut and groaned. And even though he stood in grave danger of being a hell of a lot wetter, he grated out, "Again."

She stroked him again, then again, each pass of her fingers growing less hesitant, propelling him toward the brink of insanity. "That feels so incredibly . . . good." Helpless to remain still, he rolled his hips and thrust into her hand. She wrapped her fingers around him and he knew he was done.

He wordlessly grasped her wrist, eased her hand away, and settled himself between her splayed thighs. Supporting his weight on his forearms, he slowly eased inside her, watching every nuance of her expressions. Arousal. Need. Desire. But no fear. Thank God, because he wasn't certain he was capable of calming her.

"I don't want to hurt you," he ground out.

She gripped his shoulders and undulated beneath him. "You'll only do so if you stop."

Alec gritted his teeth and thrust. And sank deep into the tight, wet heaven of her body. Her eyes widened for a single heartbeat, then closed.

"Oh, my," she whispered.

Alec forced himself to remain still, to allow her to grow accustomed to him, but bloody hell, the effort nearly killed him. She was so tight and so hot . . . sweat broke out across his back and beaded on his forehead.

Her eyes fluttered open and she stared up at him with an expression of wonder that squeezed his heart as snugly as her body gripped his. "I feel so delightfully, deliciously . . . full," she murmured. "Full of you. Is this as wondrous for you as it is for me?"

Alec had to swallow to locate his voice. "I've never felt anything so incredible," he said, meaning every word. He drew halfway out, then sank deep again, the slick friction dragging a groan from both of them.

"Alec . . . I want you to do that again."

He obliged her, this time withdrawing nearly all the way from her body before taking the slow deep glide that buried him to the hilt. Her inner walls gripped him like a hot, wet fist and he clenched his jaw against the intense, blinding pleasure.

"Wrap your legs around me," he demanded in a hoarse rasp.

She instantly obeyed, and with his gaze locked on hers, he stroked inside her, each thrust increasing in speed and force. Her movements were awkward at first, but she quickly caught the rhythm. He was helpless to further delay the climax bearing down on him, and he knew he was only a few heartbeats away from exploding. Her fingers bit into his shoulders. "Alec," she panted. "I feel so . . . *ohhhh.*"

Her body clenched around him and with a groan that felt dragged from the depths of his soul, he crushed her to him. His release pounded through him, the intense shudders wracking his entire body. When they subsided he dropped his forehead against her shoulder and fought to catch his breath.

God help him, he couldn't move. Couldn't so much as make a fist. He wasn't certain how long he remained immobile, still buried inside her, before he garnered the strength to lift his head. She lay beneath him, her mussed hair spread around her in wild abandon, her skin stained with a delicate rosy glow, her parted, moist lips resembling plump, ripe cherries. His gaze slid down, noting the pale golden freckles that dotted her chest, an enticing trail that led to her soft breasts, topped with hard, coral nipples whose taste and texture lingered on his tongue.

How in God's name had she never had a suitor? He didn't know—it defied logic—but by God he was glad for it. The thought of another man kissing her, touching her, making love to her filmed a red haze over his vision. He raised his gaze back to hers and saw she'd opened her eyes. And that they were wet with tears.

Panic raced through him and he made to push off her. "I hurt you. I'm sorry—"

His words cut off when she tightened her arms and legs around him and shook her head. "You didn't hurt me at all. Indeed I've never felt so marvelous in my entire life." A pair of fat tears leaked from the corners of her eyes.

"Then why are you crying?" He brushed his thumbs over her temples, but that just seemed to bring more tears. "Bloody hell, *please* stop crying."

A noise that sounded like a half laugh, half sob escaped her. "I'm not crying."

"Well then you're doing a damn fine imitation of it." He reached between them and managed to wrestle his hand-kerchief from his waistcoat pocket, then gently dabbed her eyes. "Tell me why you're crying," he said quietly.

"That was just so . . . you were just so . . ." She heaved an unsteady breath. "Incredible. Lovely. I always wondered what it would be like, but never thought I'd know. And now I do." She reached up and lightly traced the scar that bisected his eyebrow. "Thank you, Alec."

Something shifted in his chest, as if whatever anchored his heart and lungs in place broke loose of its moorings. How could he explain that while he'd believed he'd known what passion felt like, the last half hour had proved him utterly wrong? "*You* were incredible and lovely. Beautiful." He skimmed his fingertips over the blush staining her cheeks. "Absolutely beautiful."

She appeared about to argue and he silenced her with a kiss. When he raised his head he said, "Since you cannot see yourself and I can, you are absolutely not allowed to gainsay me on that point."

"Very well. But then you cannot object to me saying the same thing to you."

"Thank you—which, for future reference, is the proper way to acknowledge a compliment. Although I believe men are normally referred to as handsome rather than beautiful."

She framed his face in her hands and, with her tear-dampened eyes steady on his, whispered, "Some men are handsome, but others—and they are very rare—are beautiful. And you, Captain Trentwell, are beautiful."

Bloody hell, he felt . . . undone. Humbled. And wracked with guilt. *She wouldn't think you so bloody beautiful if she knew the truth.*

He shoved the thought back into the crypt from which it had slithered and touched his forehead to hers. "It is I who should be thanking you," he said quietly. "I'd forgotten how it felt to touch someone. To be touched in return."

"You've been alone for a long time."

His damn throat swelled shut and all he could do was nod.

Her hands gently stroked his hair. "You're not alone anymore, Alec."

A sense of relief washed over him, like a cleansing spring rain, bathing him with a calm he hadn't felt in a very long time. He lifted his head and brushed his lips over hers, then looked into her eyes. "Neither of us is alone anymore, Penelope."

A slow grin curved her lips, spreading until it lit her entire face. It was impossible to resist and he felt his own mouth stretch into an answering smile. Outlining his lips with her fingertips, she said, "You should smile more often."

"I have a feeling I'll be doing so with ridiculous frequency."

Her own smile widened. "I believe our marriage is off to a very good start, Captain Trentwell."

"I agree, Mrs. Trentwell."

He just prayed she would continue to think so after he told her the truth.

Chapter Nine

"Bloody hell, Penelope, this is pure torture."

"Perhaps, but you promised." Penelope bit back a smile as she dipped her paintbrush into the flesh-tone color she'd mixed by blending several oils together. It perfectly matched Alec's skin tone, lending the painting a realism that made it seem as if his naked body leapt off the canvas. Of course, she'd hidden his identity by disguising him as the Greek god Adonis. No point in bringing more scandal down upon her and the Trentwell name.

Not that she wouldn't deserve it this time. Before Alec, she'd drawn the naked form—and attempted that one sculpture in Italy—purely from an artistic standpoint so as to develop her talent. However, now that she'd been married to such a perfect male specimen for the past two months, she had to confess, she painted him nude solely because of how their sessions . . . came to an end.

"You realize you'll be repaid for this," he said.

His low, hoarse voice, coupled with the scorching heat sizzling from his blue gaze tingled anticipation down her spine. "Is that a threat?"

"Threat, promise, vow—call it whatever you wish. Just be assured that the torture you give, you shall receive in return."

"You'd best be careful, sir. With a single stroke I can change your nose so that it resembles that of Cyrano de Bergerac."

"In case you haven't noticed, it isn't my *nose* that has grown."

Penelope pushed up her spectacles. "Oh, I've noticed." Given how her hard nipples pressed against the thin silk of her dressing gown, her own arousal was impossible to miss. Which meant it was time for this session to conclude. She glanced at her painting and sighed at her dismal progress. At this rate it would take her a year or two to complete. Oh well . . .

Setting aside her palette, she dragged her gaze from her husband—no easy task—and picked up a clean brush. Putting a deliberate sway in her hips, she approached him slowly and said, "Due to your persistent lack of cooperation by *growing*, I'm not sure I've captured you accurately. Therefore, I need for you to remain very still so I can make certain I have the correct feel of things."

She stopped directly in front of him, and with her gaze locked on his, trailed the brush down the length of his jutting arousal.

He hissed in a sharp breath. "Penelope."

That single word, ground out through his clenched jaw, rippled a dark thrill straight to her core.

"Yes?" She trailed the paintbrush over his erection again, this time finishing with a slow swirl around the engorged tip.

For an answer he yanked her against him and crushed her lips beneath his. His tongue invaded her mouth as his impatient hands jerked her robe down her arms. The garment pooled at her feet, leaving her as naked as he. Without breaking their frantic kiss, he hoisted her up and moved forward, until her shoulders hit the wall.

"You're going to want to hang on," he warned. Penelope wrapped her arms and legs around him, then gasped when he entered her in a single deep, hard thrust. Her pleasure-filled moans mingled with his choppy breaths as he relentlessly stroked her. Her climax screamed through her, her fingers digging into his shoulders as he followed her over the edge into release.

Thank goodness his strong arms remained wrapped around her, otherwise she'd have slithered to the floor in a boneless heap. Gathering her close, peppering her face with kisses, he carried her to their bedchamber where he deposited her on the bed with a gentle bounce. He disappeared for several minutes, and when he returned he carried the paintbrush she'd teased him with—and a jar of honey.

"You're about to learn that you are not the only member of this household who can wield a paintbrush," he said with a wicked smile.

To her delight, he proved he was indeed an accomplished artist, painting an intricate swirling design that curled from the base of her throat all the way to her toes, a work of art he then licked away with long, leisurely laps of his very talented tongue. Penelope returned the favor, reveling in his every groan, and deep shudders of his release.

The following morning, she awoke and indulged in a leisurely, full-body stretch, savoring the feel of the soft sheets against her naked skin. What would she and Alec do today? Make love after a rousing game of backgammon? Or perhaps steal away to the warm springs at the edge of the property and enjoy a long soak, followed by a repeat of last night's sensual activities? Or perhaps a picnic in the garden? He'd so far kept the promise he'd made on their wedding day, and they'd made love every day. Several times. At least.

With a soft sigh of utter contentment, she reached out a languid hand for Alec. When her fingers encountered his empty pillow, she opened her eyes and discovered she was alone.

Concern flooded her. Had he suffered a nightmare after she'd fallen asleep? She prayed not, but given that today marked the one year anniversary of Waterloo, it wouldn't surprise her if he had.

Indeed his nightmares were the only shadow over their lives. As the anniversary of the battle neared, the horrible dreams grew worse and she was at a loss as how to help him. She knew they stemmed from his war experiences, but the few times she'd broached the subject, he'd immediately spoken of something else. While she felt profound sadness about losing her brother to the battle, her heart broke for Alec, who had survived and still bore the internal scars of that day. The pain in his eyes ate at her, but without his cooperation, all she could do was try to soothe him, hold him, when he thrashed in the night and awoke shaking and bathed in sweat.

Before arising, she rolled over onto his side of the bed and buried her face in his linen pillowcase and breathed deep. The material was cool, indicating he'd been gone for a while, yet it still bore a slight trace of woodsy sandalwood mixed with that elusive scent that belonged to Alec alone.

Determined to see if he was all right, she slipped from the covers and began her morning ritual. As she washed and dressed in a simple day gown, her mind remained filled with her husband. Her husband, who, for the past two months, had pleased her just as much outside the bedchamber as in it.

She simply loved living with him, loved the experience of discovering something new about him every day. He enjoyed reading, especially with his head resting in her lap while she stroked his hair—which she didn't mind at all as she sought any excuse to touch him. He adored blueberries, hated broccoli, possessed uncanny luck at card games, and was completely unbeatable at chess. He enjoyed long walks in the woods, and was patient to a fault, proven when he taught her to ride his horse Apollo, helped her plant flowers, and searched for hours for a perfect skipping stone so she could cross those items off her wish list.

He claimed to enjoy her efforts at the pianoforte, to which Penelope could only conclude he was either the politest man in the world or utterly tone deaf for she was an abysmal pianist. Still, he'd sit for an entire afternoon listening to her as if she were a virtuoso while she butchered song after song, and each time she looked up from the music she'd find his heated gaze resting on her—and soon afterward, much to her delight, his heated hands.

He was keenly intelligent, could discuss any subject, never tired of hearing the stories of her life, and told entertaining tales of his childhood. He frequently asked for her opinion, especially with regards to an addition he wished to add to the cottage. And as the weeks flew past, she was gratified to note that his formerly rare smiles appeared much more frequently, each one feeling like a gift, and they were usually accompanied by a rumble of deep, rich laughter. She enjoyed the sound so much she'd made it her private mission to see to it that he laughed every day.

After donning her gown, she pulled her hair back into a simple chignon and decided that as soon as she found Alec she would tell him the two pieces of news she carried in her heart, the first of which she'd held there for weeks—while she'd already liked and admired him when they married, those seeds had taken root over these past two months spent in his exclusive company, days and nights filled with discovery and intimacy, and had bloomed into a deep, abiding respect. And, to love.

She'd fallen in love with her husband.

She'd been initially reluctant to examine her deepening feelings too closely, to acknowledge them, even to herself. After all, Alec hadn't married her for love. But with each passing day her feelings had grown until ignoring them was impossible, as was pretending they were merely admiration and respect.

For weeks now the words *I love you* had ached in her

throat, yearning to be said, but as Alec had never broached the subject of love, she'd remained silent, although it had grown increasingly difficult to do so—and after last night, after the profound passion they'd shared, she simply couldn't do so any longer. And it seemed somehow fitting that she do so today, on the anniversary of the battle that haunted him. She prayed that knowing he was loved would help chase away the ghosts. And that her other news would make for happy memories of this day to help temper those that plagued him—the news that she was certain she was with child.

She settled her hands on her abdomen, envisioning the life she knew in her heart was growing there. Her monthly courses hadn't appeared since her marriage and up until then they'd always occurred regularly. In her mind's eye she imagined the scenario that was her fondest wish—Alec looking at her through love-filled eyes, cradling his newborn son.

With that picture embedded in her mind, Penelope quit the bedchamber and went in search of Alec, determined to tell him of his impending fatherhood as well as her love for him—one bit of news he'd been waiting to hear, and one she prayed he'd be happy to hear.

Chapter Ten

*A*lec paced the length of the library. Damn it, he couldn't put it off any longer—he had to tell Penelope the truth. Today. His conscience, which had been eating him alive for weeks, could no longer be bludgeoned into submission. Especially not today, a day he'd been dreading more and more as it slithered inexorably nearer. The day that marked one year since Waterloo. One year since Edward's death.

He paused his restless strides at the sound of a floorboard creaking overhead, announcing Penelope had arisen. An image of her slipping from beneath the covers, hair tousled, eyes sleepy flashed in his mind. He'd wanted nothing more than to remain in bed with her this morning, holding her against him, breathing her in, but she needed her rest and he'd needed time alone to gather his thoughts.

He dragged his hands down his face and cursed himself for allowing two months to pass without telling her. Especially as the delay was the result of pure selfishness on his part—a trait he disliked in others, yet had managed to rationalize in himself. All because he'd been so damn happy. Bloody hell, he hadn't expected that. Any more than he'd expected to fall in love with his wife.

His sweet, witty, talented, passionate wife who constantly either amused, excited, delighted, or surprised him—sometimes all at once.

Oh, he'd tried mightily to deny the feelings that had been building over the past eight weeks, but every moment spent in her company only confirmed and deepened what he'd felt for her the moment he first saw her. He loved her so damn much he just ached with it. Ached for her to know. Ached for her to love him in return. And that couldn't happen until he told her about Edward. Penelope deserved the truth and he didn't want any more secrets between them.

Would she forgive him? His stomach tightened at the very real possibility that she wouldn't. That the companionship and intimacy, passion and camaraderie they'd shared for the past two months would be irreparably broken. The thought of that suffused him with a pain that damn near crushed his heart—the sensation that was at the root of him not telling her already. But he couldn't lie to her anymore. She cared for him—he knew she did. She showed it every day, in myriad ways, every time she smiled at him, touched him, took him into her body, held him after another nightmare. But did she care enough to forgive him? He didn't know. He could only hope to God she did.

He moved to the window and looked out at the tranquil garden blooming with a profusion of color thanks to Penelope's efforts. He'd thrived under her loving touch just as his weed-ridden, neglected garden had. One year ago today he'd stood on a battlefield and fought for his country, his life, and the lives of his men. Today he would fight again—for the unforeseen gift of this life he'd been given with Penelope. He hadn't asked for it, hadn't expected it. Yet he wanted it more than he ever would have believed possible.

He heard the light tread of her footfalls in the corridor and he turned. Seconds later she appeared in the doorway, and as it always did when he gazed into those magnified bespectacled eyes, his heart skipped a beat.

Without a word she crossed to him. Put her arms around his waist. Fitted her body to his and nuzzled her face against his neck. "Good morning," she whispered in his ear.

His arms went around her and he pressed his lips to her fragrant hair, wondering how it was possible that her touch, her mere presence managed to simultaneously excite and calm him. "Good morning."

She leaned back and her eyes searched his. "This is a difficult day for you."

They hadn't talked about it, but the fact that she knew was merely another facet of her to love. "For you as well."

"Not like it is for you. I haven't seen Mrs. Watson this morning, but she left breakfast in covered dishes on the sideboard. You must be hungry—"

"I'm not. At least not yet." He eased himself back a step and clasped her hands. "I told Mrs. Watson to take the rest of the day off," he said, referring to the kindly, plump woman from the village who served as their cook and maid. "There's something I need to tell you and I wished to do so privately."

"I've something to tell you as well."

"And I very much want to hear it, but I need to tell you now as I've already allowed far too much time to pass without doing so." He led her to the settee in front of the fireplace and indicated she should sit. After she'd settled herself, he perched on the edge of the cushion, forced himself to look her in the eyes, and drew a bracing breath.

"It concerns Edward."

A frown formed between her brows. "What about him?"

"I need to tell you about Edward's death. About Waterloo."

Dozens of images suddenly burst into his brain. Blood, death, the sound of artillery fire. Something warm touched his hand and he looked down. She'd wrapped her fingers around his.

"I can see this is painful for you, Alec. You don't have to tell me."

"Yes, I do." He cleared his throat and gripped her hand, an anchor in the storm of the horrific memories. "There was a small chateau, Hougoumont, that was in a key position for our army. Two of our companies, including mine, garrisoned the chateau and the surrounding woods. We fortified the buildings and blocked all the gates except one to provide access for ourselves and our Allies."

He drew a breath, shoved aside the images pounding through his head and continued, the words coming faster as he spoke. "The battle for Hougoumont was fierce. Bloody. The French were everywhere, rushing the main gate, surging around the outbuildings. We had to keep them out but the gate sustained damage. We were determined to close it, but they were just as determined to force their way through. We managed to shut the gate and one brave solider slammed the bar in place. But not before a number of French had penetrated. I was the officer in charge of hunting down those French soldiers. I selected several men to assist me. Edward was one of them. It was during that mission he was killed."

He paused. His jaw tightened at the sympathy, the concern in her eyes. And hoped this wouldn't be the final time he'd see them shining there for him. "Edward's death was my fault, Penelope. I killed him." He briefly squeezed his eyes shut. "God help me, I killed him."

A layer of color leeched from her face. "What do you mean? Did your weapon mistakenly discharge?"

"No."

"An accident with your bayonet?"

"No." Unable to remain still, he stood and paced in front of her. "The men I chose fanned out, with Edward and I heading toward the most distant outbuilding at the rear of the chateau. When we entered we discovered a Frenchman lying on the floor, his leg bleeding." He paused at the fireplace and turned to face her. "We were not there to gather prisoners."

She nodded slowly. "You had to kill him."

"Yes. As I raised my weapon the Frenchman looked me in the eyes and begged for his life. Said he had a wife. Children. And wanted to live. And I hesitated." He turned back toward the fireplace and stared into the low burning flames. Braced his fisted hands on the mantel. Then squeezed his eyes shut. And relived that horrible moment so vividly it was as if he stood in that outbuilding once again.

"I hesitated," he repeated, forcing the words from his raw throat. "And in that split second of hesitation, the Frenchman fired the weapon concealed beside his injured leg, hitting Edward. I immediately killed the Frenchman, but it was too late. Edward was dead."

He swallowed and turned to face her once again. "He died because of me. I killed him."

She rose and moved to stand in front of him. "You didn't kill him, Alec—"

"He died because I hesitated," he said, his voice as flat and bleak as he felt. "If I'd killed the Frenchman instantly, as I should have, he wouldn't have been able to discharge his weapon. I killed Edward as surely as if I'd pulled that trigger myself."

He dragged a hand through his hair. "It was always my intention to tell you—it is why I sought you out immediately upon your return to England. I went to Exeter House to tell you, but then I . . . didn't. Couldn't. You were so lovely and looked at me with those beautiful eyes . . . as if I were a hero. I knew it wasn't true, knew I had to tell you, yet I couldn't force out the words. I was overwhelmed by how much I wanted you. And if I told you right away, you'd go away and I'd never see you again. Never have the chance to explore the extraordinary way you made me feel."

Her expression had gone blank and something very close to panic clutched his heart. "And then we married, and I swore to myself I'd tell you, that I'd just wait a bit longer, until you perhaps came to care for me, at least a little, enough to consider forgiving me, not only for the careless act that killed your brother, but for not telling you. My only excuse is that until I met you, I'd forgotten what happiness felt like and I selfishly wanted to prolong the feeling for as long as possible."

He reached for her hands. They felt cold and lifeless in his. Looking into her eyes, he prayed she could see the depth of his regret when he said, "I'm sorry, Penelope. So bloody damn sorry. Sorry Edward died. Sorry I killed him. Sorry I didn't tell you before now. And I hope—no, God, I pray—that you can somehow find it in your heart to forgive me."

She didn't move, didn't blink. Just looked at him through blank eyes that reminded him of snuffed-out candles. He forced himself to remain equally immobile, because he knew if he moved, it would be to fall on his knees before her and beg her to forgive him.

Finally she raised her chin in that show of bravery and determination he loved so much. "I wish you had told me this two months ago, Alec."

"So do I."

"I'm certain you do, but I suspect not for the same reasons I do. It's clear you've borne an enormous burden of guilt, not only these past two months, but this entire year. I'll say to you now what I would have if you'd told me when we first met—and I'm certain my brother would echo these sentiments. You did *not* kill Edward. Edward was a soldier, and as horrible as it is, as much as we may detest it, soldiers die. It could just have easily been you who perished."

"If I hadn't hesitated—"

"He might very well have died anyway. Everyone knows how heavy the casualties were that day. The point is, you are not only human, you are *humane*. That Frenchman begged for his life. I cannot imagine anyone not hesitating under similar circumstances."

She gently squeezed his hands, a gesture that swamped him with such hope, his knees nearly buckled. "It breaks my heart that you have suffered such torment over Edward's death, and also on my behalf these last two months. You asked for my forgiveness and I give it to you readily as I do not blame you for Edward's death, nor would anyone else. The person who needs to forgive you is *you*. And I pray you do so, Alec. You are a brave and noble man. Edward respected and admired you, sentiments I echo and that you deserve."

For several long seconds Alec couldn't move. Couldn't speak. Her words reverberated through his mind, pounding in tandem with his thumping heart. She forgave him. Didn't hate him. *Forgave him*. The future he'd believed would be ripped from his fisted hands spread before him like a sun-dappled ocean.

He had to swallow twice to locate his voice. "Thank you—although those two words feel extraordinarily inadequate. Such kindness, understanding, compassion, and unconditional forgiveness are far more than I deserve and gifts I'll treasure forever." He raised their joined hands to his lips and pressed a fervent kiss against her fingers. "*You* are a gift, Penelope."

He tried to draw her into his arms, but she shook her head. The warmth in her eyes dimmed, replaced with what appeared to be dawning dismay, and she withdrew her hands from his. He felt her slipping away and he tightened his grip, but again she shook her head and he forced himself to release her.

"You lied to me," she said.

Guilt along with confusion slapped him at her accusatory tone. Had he misunderstood when she'd said she forgave him? "Yes. I've admitted that."

"Not about Edward. About why you married me. You assured me your proposal was not due to a sense of responsibility toward me, but clearly it was." All the color drained from her face and she pressed her hands to her midsection. "All these weeks I believed you. Thought your proposal stemmed from some liking of me, but it was only because of your misguided guilt about Edward. I should have known better, but I allowed myself to think . . . to hope . . ." She squeezed her eyes shut and lowered her gaze to the floor. "Dear God, what a fool I am. What a fool you must think me."

Alec stepped forward and grasped her upper arms. "I don't think you're a fool. I think you are the most amazing, incredible, beautiful woman I've ever known."

A noise that sounded like a half laugh, half sob escaped her. She raised her head and his insides clenched at the defeated humiliation in her eyes that swam with unshed tears. "Stop. Please. I understand now why you acted as you did. Why you married me rather than one of those society beauties. There is no more need for further pretense."

He barely resisted the urge to shake her, but his fingers tightened on her arms. "You *don't* understand, damn it, and I am *not* pretending."

There was no mistaking the disbelief in her eyes. "I understand perfectly. You weren't wracked with guilt over the death of a brother of any of those other women. You cannot possibly expect me to believe that your marriage proposal sprang from anything other than a sense of responsibility and obligation."

He hesitated, and instantly saw that once again, a hesitation cost him dearly as her eyes went bleak. "I never denied wanting to help you out of the difficult situation in which you were involved. You needed help, I needed a wife. Marriage was the perfect solution for us both."

"Perhaps. But I had a right to know the true reason behind your proposal. I deserved the unvarnished truth from you— that I was nothing more than an obligation and responsibility and that you wouldn't have spared me a second glance otherwise. Of course I should have known that without you telling me. Why else would a man like you have paid attention to a woman like me, especially when you had a pick of society beauties at your disposal?"

"The second glance I gave you had nothing to do with

Edward and everything to do with *you*. I didn't want any of those other women. I wanted *you*."

"Because you felt a duty to look after me because of Edward."

He huffed out a frustrated breath. "Yes, but it was more than that. And even if I did feel responsible for you, is that so terrible?"

"Not if you'd admitted it. Instead you denied it. And showered me with compliments. Which I stupidly believed." She released a shaky breath. "In truth, I'm more upset with myself than I am with you. For allowing myself to believe pretty words."

"Any pretty words I said were sincerely meant."

She merely shrugged. "For wanting things I should have known were beyond my reach."

"Such as?"

"A man who wouldn't purposely mislead me to believe he wanted to marry me for any reason other than because he felt obligated to do so."

The hurt in her eyes ate at him like acid. He lifted a hand to touch her cheek, but she stepped back and his hand fell to his side. "I never meant to mislead you. I didn't really understand what I felt for you two months ago. But I do now. I love you, Penelope."

Her bottom lip quivered, smiting him where he stood. "You cannot know how much it hurts to say this, but I don't believe you."

His heart seemed to crack. "You cannot know how much it hurts to hear that."

"It's not love but responsibility you feel. I'm a duty and an obligation—things I never wanted to be to anyone. Especially not my husband."

Damn it, that hurt. He raked his hands through his hair. "Is it so difficult to believe I've fallen in love with you?"

"Under the circumstances, given your feelings regarding Edward's death, yes, I'm afraid so." A bitter sound escaped her, then she muttered something that sounded like *and it's only going to get worse,* but before he could ask, she began walking toward the door.

An acute sense of loss invaded his entire body. "Where are you going?"

"I must think. There is much for me to consider. And I wish to do so alone."

He caught up with her in three long strides and grasped her arm. "Look at me."

She turned her head and his heart sank at the complete lack of warmth in her eyes. "Let me go, Alec. Please."

Letting her go in any manner was the exact opposite of what he wanted to do. But clearly his cause wouldn't be helped by detaining her. "Very well. But I want you to know, to understand this: regardless of how our marriage came about or began, the fact is that I love you. My heart is yours. Not because I feel obligated to give it to you, not because you're a duty to be borne, but because I'm helpless *not* to give it to you. Because you've owned it since the first time you smiled at me. And while I understand that you're angry and hurt and upset right now, I shall remember the words of Alexander Pope that hope springs eternal, and I'll hope that you'll believe me."

Silence swelled between them for several seconds. Finally she inclined her head, then without a word, quit the room.

Chapter Eleven

*S*ilence echoed in the library. Alec stared at the doorway through which Penelope had just departed. A shudder ran through him and he sank down on the settee then dropped his head into his hands. Jesus, he felt gutted. By her hurt. By the fact that she didn't believe he loved her. By her unexpected anger over something he'd never expected would anger her. But mostly by the understanding and compassion she'd shown when he'd confessed his role in Edward's death. It had never occurred to him that she wouldn't blame him. Would insist he not blame himself. That she'd still consider him heroic.

He blew out a sound of disbelief. Penelope had surprised him from the moment he met her, and she continued to do so. Yet, he supposed he shouldn't have been surprised by her kindness. It was one of the many things he loved about her.

I don't believe you. Bloody hell, those words had stabbed him in the heart. How could he change her mind? Make her realize that she was everything he'd always wanted? Everything he needed? That she was—

Everything.

He raised his head and his gaze fell on his desk. An idea formed in his mind and he nodded as it took shape. He rose and quickly crossed the room. Sat at his desk and pulled open the top drawer. Withdrew a sheet of vellum and began to plan.

She was everything. And before this day was over, by God she was damn well going to know it.

When he finally put down his quill, he glanced at the mantel clock and was shocked to note that more than four hours had past. But they were four hours well spent. He folded the sheets of vellum that were the results of his labors and tucked them in his waistcoat pocket.

It was time to find his wife. And pray that the last four hours would convince her how much she was loved.

As he rose, thunder rumbled in the distance. Perfect timing to seek out Penelope, for one of the many things he'd learned about his wife was that she disliked thunderstorms.

He exited the library and began looking for Penelope. He first searched all her favorite spots in the cottage but one by one found them unoccupied. It wasn't until he found their bedchamber empty that he began to worry and started calling her name. Another few minutes of calling and searching revealed that she wasn't in the house at all.

Damn it, how long had she been gone? It hadn't occurred to him she'd leave the cottage without telling him—she'd never done so before. Panic cramped his entire body. Bloody hell. Was it possible . . . had she left him? No, surely not. She must be in the garden. Or the barn where Apollo was stalled. Yet if she'd been in either place surely she would have returned to the house immediately upon hearing the thunder.

He strode to the foyer and jerked open the front door. Fat raindrops pelted him, falling from a slate gray sky. He ran to the rear of the cottage, calling her name. The sky seemed to open, dropping a veritable sheet of water that quickly soaked him through to his skin. After a quick search of the garden revealed she wasn't there, he dashed toward the barn. A flash of lightning illuminated the gloom, followed by a deafening crack of thunder. He burst inside the barn, shouting her name, but was greeted only with a soft nicker from Apollo.

Alec quickly saddled the gelding, then headed toward the path leading into the thick woods that eventually ended at the edge of the village. Penelope loved walking there and his best guess was that's what she'd done. He hoped she was currently dry and safe inside one of the village establishments rather than caught outside in this storm, but he knew either way she'd be frightened.

As if to confirm the thought, another blaze of lightning streaked across the sky. Thunder boomed, and it required all Alec's strength and agility to keep Apollo from rearing in fright.

After regaining control of the horse, they raced along the path. Alec's unease and worry and fear for Penelope increased with each passing second. They rounded a sharp curve and he pulled up when a wet, bedraggled Penelope came into view. She clutched her drenched shawl around her hunched shoulders, her face downcast as she concentrated on the wet, uneven ground.

Relief walloped him. He shouted her name and she looked up, squinting through the sheet of rain. He pressed his heels to Apollo's flanks, and they started forward, his entire being focused on reaching her, getting her home and dry. They were nearly upon her when lightning rent the sky. Blinding light lit the woods, followed by a clap of thunder that made his ears ring. A deafening crack sounded, splitting a tree directly in front of him. He saw the heavy branch swinging toward him a split second before it connected with his head. White-hot pain jolted through him and he felt himself falling. More jarring pain as he crashed to the ground, knocking the air from his lungs. Blackness swallowed him and he felt no more.

Chapter Twelve

"Alec, wake up . . . dear God, *please* wake up!"

Kneeling next to him, heedless of the rocks digging into her knees, Penelope frantically patted his pale cheek, her gaze alternating between his closed eyes and the terrifying bruise blooming on his temple. Rain cascaded over them and she prayed the wetness would help revive him.

"Alec, please . . . you must open your eyes." She brushed his wet hair from his forehead and continued to lightly tap his face. Her gaze flicked to the branch that had felled him and her stomach turned over. Dear God, she'd never forget the horrifying crack of it smacking against him. The dreadful sight of him falling. Hitting the ground. Then lying so still. So very frighteningly still. Her fault. All her fault. He had to be all right. *Had* to be.

Just then he groaned, the sound piercing relief into her frantically beating heart. She grabbed his hand and lifted it to her mouth. Pressed her lips against his wet fingers. "Alec . . . can you hear me? Please open your eyes."

Another moan, and then his eyelids slowly blinked open. Unfocused dark blue eyes looked up at her, the most welcome sight she'd ever seen. "I'm right here, Alec. Can you hear me? Please say something."

His eyes drifted closed again. "Hurt."

She swallowed the panic threatening to overwhelm her and gently ran her hands over him, praying no bones were broken. "I know. Where does it hurt?"

"Not me. You." He opened his eyes and this time they focused on her much more clearly. "Are *you* hurt?"

Her heart stumbled. Dear God, he was delirious. "I'm fine. *I* am not the one who was just knocked senseless."

He made a move to sit up, sucked in a quick breath, and his eyes slammed shut. "Bloody hell."

"Stay still," she ordered, gently pressing a hand to his chest. "I want to determine if anything is broken. Tell me if anything I do hurts."

She ran her hands over him, gently testing the movement of his arms and legs. "Nothing appears broken," she reported with relief, once again taking his hand. "Nor are you bleeding anywhere, although you're sporting an egg-sized lump on your temple. How does your head feel?"

"Like a battalion of bloody demons are banging on it with hammers." He opened his eyes and scanned her face. "You're all wet."

"It's been raining. So are you."

"I don't mind. You don't like storms."

"It's almost over. The rain has nearly stopped."

Once again he tried to sit up, and this time, with her assistance, he succeeded. He sat immobile for a moment, with his eyes closed, taking several deep breaths, then slowly nodded. "Better." He opened his eyes and her heart turned over with relief that their blue depths were now perfectly clear. And seemed to bore into her soul.

"I tried to find you. You were gone." He reached out a hand she noted wasn't completely steady and brushed his fingers across her cheek. His throat moved with a hard swallow. "I have to know. Did you leave me?"

There was no mistaking the anguish in that quiet question and Penelope mentally flogged herself for causing him both injury and distress. "No. I merely walked to the village. I was on my way home when the storm broke." She pressed his hand to her face, then turned to kiss his palm. "I'm so sorry you were hurt. And so relieved you're all right." She turned back to him. "I did a great deal of thinking during my walk, and realized many things . . . things I'd planned to tell you as soon as I returned to the house, but regardless of the fact that we're both wet and sitting in the mud, I cannot wait another second. I love you, Alec."

He went perfectly still. "Are you only saying that because you feel a sense of responsibility over the lump on my head?"

Penelope's cheeks heated. "Based on what happened this morning I cannot blame you for thinking so, but no. I didn't only just realize I love you—I've known for weeks. It's one of the things I'd planned to tell you in the library this morning. During my walk I realized that it doesn't matter why you married me nor does it matter if you're in love with me. What matters is that you've been incredibly kind to me. I know you care, and that's enough. I should have told you this morning how grateful I am to you for your kindness toward me. The reason I didn't stemmed from my disappointment of feeling like an obligation. I suppose I always dreamed of romance . . . and well, as you know, hope springs eternal. But I am truly grateful."

"I don't want your gratitude. I want your love."

"You have that. All of it. Always."

"And I want you to accept mine. I don't simply *care* for you, Penelope. I meant every word I said to you in the library. I love you. Perhaps this will show you how much." He reached into his waistcoat pocket, withdrew several folded pieces of vellum and held them out to her.

"What is this?" she asked, taking the damp papers.

"Open them."

She carefully unfolded the sheets and looked at the top one. "These are room plans," she whispered, her heartbeat giving a hard kick. Her gaze lingered on the words he'd written across the bottom of the drawing. "For an art studio."

"Yes. Do you like it?"

"I . . . it's perfect." She touched her finger to the date written in the corner: July 1, 1816. "Why that date? Today is June eighteenth."

"I'm planning that construction will begin on July first."

Tears swam into Penelope's eyes. Dear God, what a fool she'd been. She'd allowed her hurt to blind her to what was so clearly obvious. Alec loved her. It was there, in his eyes. And in this beautiful gesture. "Alec, I . . . I don't know what to say."

He brushed a damp curl from her cheek. "Does it please you?"

"More than I can say."

"Then I hope the rest of it pleases you as well."

He nodded toward the papers she held and she realized she'd only looked at the top sheet. She slipped it behind the bottom one and stared. At a copy of the wish list she kept in her sketch pad, written in Alec's precise, neat hand. Each wish was numbered—all fifty-three of them, and next to each was a date.

"I've had the list since the night of our first kiss," he said.

"In the gallery. I dropped my sketch pad."

"Yes. I copied down your list before returning the pad. It is my intention to make certain every one of those wishes comes true by the date I've noted."

She noted the date beside "Get a Hugo" was only a few weeks away. This time there was no stopping the tears that rushed into Penelope's eyes. "Alec, this is too much."

"No. It's not nearly enough." He framed her face in his

hands and all the love and desire she'd ever dreamed of seeing glowed in his eyes. "I want to do this because I love you. Do you believe me?"

"Yes. God, yes. I'm so sorry I ever doubted you. The fact that you love me . . . that alone fulfills every wish I've ever had. And I love you, too. So much." She leaned forward and touched her lips to his. "So very much."

"Thank God." He tugged her onto his lap, pulled off her soggy bonnet and kissed her until her head spun. When he lifted his head, she said, "There's one small problem with wish number twenty-three."

"Oh?" He took the list from her and frowned. "You don't wish to travel to the Continent next spring?"

"It might be too soon."

"Too soon?"

"After the baby is born."

She felt him go perfectly still. "Baby?"

She nodded. "While I was in the village I visited Doctor Williams. He confirmed I'm with child."

A slow smile creased Alec's face, stealing her breath with its beauty. His arms tightened around her and he gently kissed her. "Have I told you how much I love you?"

"Yes. But I'd certainly not be averse to hearing it again."

"I love you." He rested his hand against her abdomen and splayed his fingers. "Thank you."

Emotion clogged her throat. "I hope it's a boy."

"I don't care. Boy, girl, it doesn't matter. I will humbly accept and adore any child you give me." He dropped a quick kiss on her lips. "And now it's time to get you home and out of these wet clothes."

She raked her fingers through his wet, silky hair. "I thought you'd never ask."

A strangled laugh escaped him. "That's not what I meant. Although now that you mention it . . ." He nuzzled her neck, shooting tingles of pleasure down her spine.

"You did promise we'd make love every day. Several times. At least."

"Then we'd best get home, Mrs. Trentwell. We're behind schedule."

They rose and with Alec holding Apollo's reins, they walked arm in arm back to their cottage, where every wish Penelope had ever hoped for had come true.

Epilogue

April 1817

"I believe I'm going to start charging you a fee for my modeling services, Penelope."

Penelope looked over the top of her easel in her new art studio at her very naked, very aroused husband. "Oh?"

"Yes. Whoever heard of a painting taking an entire year to complete? At this rate you won't be finished until Colin and Andrew are grown men."

She inwardly smiled at the mention of their twin sons, currently napping, then pursed her lips and shot his erection a pointed look. "Perhaps. Yet if that is a complaint, it is somehow not ringing true." She heaved an exaggerated sigh. "Very well, sir. What is your price?"

"You. Now."

She cocked a brow. "I see. A flesh payment. You realize that's an outrageous sum."

Eyes glittering with unmistakable intent, he abandoned his position and slowly approached her. Her breath caught at the sheer beauty of him and a heated shiver rippled through her in anticipation of his touch.

When he reached her, he simply scooped her up in his arms and without missing so much as a step headed toward their bedchamber.

"Your portrait isn't finished, Alec," she said, wrapping her arms around his neck and leaning in to lightly graze his neck with her teeth.

"My darling Penelope, that is hardly news. I still expect you to pay your debt."

"Very well. I shall endeavor to meet your exorbitant price."

"I was hoping you'd say that. And as you know . . ."

She smiled into his beautiful eyes, and in unison they said, "Hope springs eternal."

Fate Strikes a Bargain

Candice Hern

Philippa
Reynolds

Nathan
Beckwith

Chapter One

London
April 1816

"It is a good hiding place, is it not?"

Nathaniel Beckwith gave a start at the soft voice, and turned to find a young woman seated on the other side of the potted tree he stood behind—the lush orange tree with dark leaves that allowed him to see the ballroom below without himself being seen. Or so he had hoped.

"What makes you think I am hiding?" He stepped away from the plant and straightened his coat with an air of nonchalance.

"Standing behind a tree was the first clue."

Nat heard the smile in the woman's voice and stopped fussing with his coat to look at her. The small balcony alcove was bathed in shadow, with only the diffused light from the chandeliers in the room below and one single candle sconce on the wall behind, but he could see her clearly enough. She was young, but no fresh-faced schoolgirl. Probably no more than two-and-twenty at best guess. Dark hair. Brownish, with flashes of auburn picked out by the candlelight. It was pulled away from her face in a simple arrangement twisted and pinned at the back of her head, with a few flowers woven in. She did not have the ubiquitous girlish curls spiraling down from her forehead and at the nape of her neck. Neither did she sport one of those elaborate styles he saw on other women, the ones made up of jeweled combs or braided fabric or strands of pearls or diamond ornaments tucked among complicated plaits and coils. The only jewelry she wore was a simple heart-shaped locket on a gold chain.

Was she a poor relation who could not afford fripperies? Or did she simply not care about the latest fashions?

His other first impressions were of large dark-colored eyes, lovely arched brows, a bow-shaped mouth with the upper lip slightly fuller than the lower, a longish nose, a well-defined jaw and slender neck. She wore a pink lace-trimmed dress that gave no hint of what curves might be underneath.

She seemed a pretty enough girl. Not beautiful, but nice-looking. Considering his current objective, he decided she was worth a closer look.

He stepped around the tree and stood beside the little bench where she sat. "Perhaps I was merely studying the tree. I ask you: who puts a full-sized orange tree inside the house? An army of servants must have been employed to haul the deuced thing up from a conservatory. I have spent time in Spain and Portugal, where orange groves are plentiful. I've never seen one indoors. I was intrigued."

She shook her head and smiled. "No, you were hiding. You clearly used the foliage to shield yourself as you peered through it. Plus, you have that look."

"What look?"

"The one that says you are reluctant to enter the ballroom. I know the look well. I wear it often myself. I am hiding, too, you see."

He arched an eyebrow. "Are you indeed? From whom?"

"My mother. What about you? Who are you hiding from?"

"No one. I told you, I am not hiding. I am merely doing a bit of reconnaissance, getting a lay of the land before joining the fray."

"Ah. I will hazard a guess that you are a military man, sir."

"I was until this morning." He'd sold out today, given up his commission and the life he'd loved for so many years. "Captain Nathaniel Beckwith, retired, at your service, ma'am." He sketched a bow and she nodded in acknowledgement. "I beg your pardon. I am not supposed to introduce myself, am I? I keep forgetting all the rules." Ignoring them, more like. He did not mind rules. He'd lived by them for years in the army. But there, it was to instill discipline, which was essential to an effective fighting force. Here, in a ballroom? Rules just seemed so much foolishness.

"It is quite all right, sir, I shall not chastise you for impertinence as I was the one to speak first. And as we appear to be kindred spirits in hiding, it seems right that we introduce ourselves. I am Miss Reynolds. Philippa Reynolds. If anyone should ask, we will invent someone who made the introductions. An elderly dowager, I think. Yes, the dowager Lady Kumquat, who sadly fell into a fit of the vapors and had to leave, the poor dear."

"Lady Kumquat, eh?" It was an effort not to smile. "I am indebted to the phantom dowager for the introduction, Miss Reynolds. Now that we are acquainted, tell me why you are hiding from your mother."

She shook her head. "It's a dull tale, Captain. I'd much rather hear why you are hiding. Is it because you feel awkward and unnatural not to be in uniform?"

"Something like that, though I have not worn my uniform in almost a year."

"A year? But you only sold your commission today."

"I have been rusticating on half-pay since the wars ended."

"Ah. And what prompted you to sell out now, if I may ask?"

"Family obligations. I am to be married, you see."

"Well, then, you have my sincerest congratulations, sir. My I ask the name of your betrothed? I have been out in society several years. Perhaps I am acquainted with her."

"I do not yet know her name, Miss Reynolds."

"I beg your pardon?"

"I haven't met her yet." He looked at her more closely. "At least, I do not think I have. I have been given orders to find a bride and to set up my nursery at once."

Her eyes flashed with amusement. "Indeed? Is it your mother or your father who has issued the command?"

"My elder brother, actually. He is Lord Dearne, and as he has only managed to sire daughters, I am his heir. His countess has been told she cannot endure another pregnancy and—Damn, that is too indelicate to mention, is it not? I fear, Miss Reynolds, that I am hopelessly gauche. Anyway, my blackguard of a brother is convinced he cannot live in peace until he knows the earldom is secure and our loathsome cousin Leonard will never inherit. And so I am ordered into familial duty."

Duty. Nat had always put duty first in all things. Along with honor, of course. But his adult life—nine years in the army—had been defined by duty.

Nat had loved the army, though. He'd found purpose in life with the 52nd Foot, and had loved every aspect of that life. Training companies of soldiers, leading them into battle with solid strategy and planning. The nervous excitement before a battle. The steadfast confidence of command. The thrill of outfoxing the French.

Every moment of his military service was cherished, both the victories and the defeats. Some of the defeats had been horrific. Hell, even some of the victories had been horrific. But he'd begun and ended every battle with confidence and pride, had thrived on battlefield strategy and action. He missed it. Desperately missed it. Deep in his heart, he wished he'd never been talked into selling out, wished there was some new conflict he could join. But he'd always followed the orders of his commanding officers, and Dearne was the commanding officer of the family. Nat had no choice but to do his duty.

And so here he was at his first Society ball in almost a decade, lurking in the shadows with a very intriguing young woman.

She tilted her head to one side and a sudden brilliant glint of copper shone in the candlelight. Her hair was more auburn than he'd originally thought.

"You were speaking truthfully, then," she said, "about getting a lay of the land from up here, were you not? You were looking to see what sort of girls you would find among this year's crop of beauties who might be prime candidates for your bride."

He shrugged. "Yes, that's it exactly." The moment he'd entered the ballroom, after waiting about a hundred hours in the interminable receiving line, he'd spied the little balcony alcoves above the room, and had made a dash for the stairs before one of the hopeful mothers giving him the fish-eye could run him to ground. He wasn't ready. His heart had been racing and his throat was dry. He ought never to have allowed himself to be talked into coming, though he knew he would have to make an appearance among the *ton* sooner or later.

"I still say you were hiding." She gave him a charming, completely uninhibited grin, so unlike the forced smiles of many of the young ladies he'd seen in the ballroom. "You might just as easily have searched from down there."

"The view from up here is better."

She clicked her tongue in mock disapproval. "Such cowardice from a soldier."

He flinched at her words. His jaw was clenched tight so he spoke through his teeth. "I. Am. No. Coward."

Her face paled and he realized he had snapped at her, probably even frightened her. Dear God, he knew this would not work. He was not ready for society.

Nat had come to London last summer after Waterloo. He had not wanted to follow the 52nd into France as he had no stomach for the tedium of peacekeeping. In London, he was expected to participate in all the celebrations of victory, to be wined and dined as a hero, but he'd hated it all and bolted to the estate his father had left him in Oxfordshire. He'd felt somewhat worn out, though he would never have admitted such a thing to anyone, and had believed that time back home would revitalize him, so he'd gone on temporary leave at half pay.

But it had not, after all, been revitalizing. It had been quite the opposite. Nat had grown increasingly melancholy as he realized that the fighting at Waterloo had left him more than physically worn out. He simply was not himself. Something had changed inside him, and he sometimes thought he might be a little insane. He hated the nightmares and flashbacks of the battle. They'd been victorious, for God's sake, and the 52nd had been integral to that victory. He ought to have been basking in glory, knowing that he and his men had done well. Instead, his damnable brain insisted on reliving the worst parts, the most frightening parts of the battle. Nat had never considered himself a weak man, but this last battle had somehow weakened him, and he felt nothing but shame for it.

To hear Miss Reynolds suggest he was a coward, even in jest, brought it all back to him. It was what he feared most about himself, in the darkest, most secret recesses of his heart, but he'd never dared to allow that word even to form itself in his head. This young woman did not know that, however, and he had no right to lash out at her for a bit of innocent teasing.

"Forgive me, Miss Reynolds. I've spent too many years in rough company. I'm afraid I've forgotten how to converse with a gentlewoman. I no longer know how to behave properly. And, to be frank, I do not much care to do so. This whole social Season business makes my flesh crawl. That's why I was hiding. Yes, you were right, dammit, I was hiding. Or at least putting off the inevitable. I will never fit in, you see, and having to pretend I do is abhorrent to me."

Her expression softened and her eyes became very bright. Good Lord, he hoped she was not about to cry. Bloody frigging hell. His first foray into society again, and already it was a complete cock-up. The first woman he'd spoken to at his first ball of the Season, and he'd made her cry. Dammit all, he should never be allowed out of the house.

He was going to kill Dearne for making him go through this.

Philippa's heart ached for the poor man. He really was quite terrified of entering the ballroom, though he would never admit it. She could have cut out her tongue when she saw his reaction to her mention of cowardice. She ought to have had better sense than to say such a thing to a soldier. How mortifying.

"I know exactly how you feel, sir."

His eyes narrowed. "Do you?"

"I do not fit in, either, Captain. That's why I'm hiding."

"A pretty girl like you? How can you not fit in?"

"I have a limp."

"A limp?"

"Yes. Some people try to ignore it, others can't stop staring in horror. Either way, it makes people uncomfortable, which means *I* make them uncomfortable, which means I don't fit in. "

"Good God. Are you serious? Is the bloody—forgive me—*ton* that narrow-minded over a little bit of a limp?"

"It's not so little, Captain."

"Bah. I have seen fellow officers who've lost an arm or leg in battle mingle perfectly easily in society. How can a minor limp cause such a fuss?"

"In the first place, I did not lose a limb in a battle to save our country from that dreadful Corsican. A wounded hero is still a hero. A girl born with a displaced hip is not. In the second place, it is not a minor limp. It is rather severe."

"Show me."

"What?"

"Stand up and show me. I want to see you walk."

Goodness, what a request. Philippa did not believe he mocked her, though, or had a morbid curiosity. She got the impression he simply wanted to see for himself whether or not she exaggerated her condition. Well, then, let him be the judge.

"All right." She rose from the bench and stood facing him. Her skirts disguised the fact that she did not stand quite straight, that she had to keep one knee bent so that she did not tilt to one side. It was a posture that was second nature to her, but she was excessively conscious of it at the moment, as she stood before the handsome Captain Beckwith with his straight-backed military bearing. "Stand aside and let me pass."

He did, and she lurched past him, her crooked hip forcing her to lift her right leg awkwardly and high at each step in order to maintain balance, then place it carefully and drag the left forward quickly. Because she could not put much weight on the right hip, her steps were uneven—one short, one long, one high, one low. Philippa had lived with her disability her whole life and was well accustomed to it. But having to demonstrate its effects to a man who looked to be as perfectly formed as one of those Greek statues at the British Museum was unnerving at best.

She turned around and walked back toward him. He frowned as he watched her, his eyes on her feet and legs, and stood back so she could take her seat on the bench again. She arranged her skirts nervously, then looked up at him.

"You're right," he said. "That's a hell of a limp."

He said it without sympathy or pity, just as a statement of fact. Philippa could not help herself. She burst into laughter.

He first looked stunned, then rolled his eyes. "Damn, I've done it again, haven't I? I must make a better effort to guard my tongue. I am more accustomed to being around other military men and not mincing words. My apologies, Miss Reynolds. That was a harsh thing to say."

Philippa wiped her eyes and grinned at him. Heavens, he

was adorable. Could one say that about a man who stood at least a foot taller than her and outweighed her by four or five stone? "No, Captain, it was not harsh, it was honest. It *is* a hell of a limp, but no one has ever before had the courage to say so to my face."

"I'm so sor—"

"Do not apologize, sir, I beg you. I far prefer blunt honesty to lies and euphemisms. It is irksome to have people always watching what they say to me, thinking they might offend if they dare to notice that my hip is twisted and bent. I hate dissimulation, even when kindness is behind it. I would rather hear plain speaking any day."

"Then I am your man, Miss Reynolds."

Her heart skittered for an instant. Perhaps he was.

"I am more than plainspoken," he continued. "I fear I am too often gruff and tactless. Vulgar, too, I suppose. I have forgotten the art of guarding one's tongue in polite conversation. You may not credit it, because I have certainly given you no reason to do so, but I was actually taught how to behave as I ought. My mother was a stickler for proper behavior, and she did her best. I was never good at fitting in, though, and tact never came easily to me. It's one of the reasons why I went into the army. I thought I might fit in better with other rough customers. My father gave his enthusiastic support, as he knew I would likely disgrace him one day. And it was his fondest hope that the military might make a man of me. It did."

He let out a disdainful huff, and his next words were muttered so low Philippa had to strain to hear. "Not the sort of man he would have expected, though." He raised his eyes to hers and his voice to a more natural timbre. "I am sorry, Miss Reynolds, that you were forced into the company of such an uncivilized lout without an ounce of charm."

"Ah, but sir, there are many types of charm. Most are based on guile and flattery, which I find tiresome at best. In fact, I find I much prefer your brand of charm, Captain. Charm based on honesty."

He uttered a snort of disbelief. "Most would say there is no charm in honesty, ma'am. No, I think nine years in the military leeched any hint of my mother's teachings clean out of me. But tell me," he said and leaned back against the balcony balustrade to face her, "what the devil—damn, I beg your pardon—are you doing at a ball if you cannot dance?"

She shook her head and gave a hollow, mirthless laugh. "Silly, isn't it? It is Mamma's hope that I will meet some compassionate soul who will take pity on me, or her, and marry me."

"At a ball? Where your impediment is most exposed because you cannot dance?"

Goodness, he really was plainspoken. This was surely the most refreshing conversation she'd ever had.

"What a beastly thing to do to you," he said.

"Not at all. It was my doing as much as hers. I *wanted* to go to balls like other girls. In my first Season, I did not mind sitting out as I loved to watch the dancers. But the more I watch, the more I wish I could join in. That's why I was hiding up here. I sometimes tire of watching others do what I cannot."

"I do not doubt it. You've a great deal of forbearance, Miss Reynolds. I suppose no compassionate gentlemen have yet come to your rescue?"

"The occasional gentleman will kindly sit out a dance with me, or take me in to supper. I have two brothers, and they often send their friends to keep me company. But this is my third Season, and I have grown tired of pretending to be part of the marriage mart when it is clear that no one will ever marry me."

"Do you wish to be married?"

"Of course. Doesn't every woman? But I do not bother to dream of what will never be."

"But your mother does?"

"Yes. I am her only daughter and she wants me to have everything in life that she has had. It pains me that I cannot be the sort of daughter she wants. Oh, do not misunderstand. She loves me and understands my disability better than anyone. But she still thinks I can be like other girls, when it just isn't true."

"No wonder you were hiding."

She could not help staring at him. Not because he was handsome, though there was that, but because she had never met anyone who spoke to her so candidly about subjects others found unpleasant or awkward to mention. Someone who did not treat her with kid gloves because of her lameness. It was both exhilarating and touching.

"So," he said, "this is to be your last Season?"

"Yes, I think so. I enjoy many of the social events, but I tire of being patronized as though I were an invalid."

"What will you do after this Season is over?"

"How will I spend the rest of my life?"

The captain shrugged. "I almost said exactly that, but thought better of it. I suppose I am not entirely lost to good manners. But yes, since we are being honest, that is what I meant."

"I will stay on at Harcott Manor in Wiltshire with Mamma. It is where I grew up and is now my elder brother's estate. Sir William Reynolds. He inherited it from Papa and allows Mamma and me to live there. I will act as companion to her while she lives, and then will likely do the same for William's daughters. And I have my music and my needlework to give me pleasure, and some charity work from time to time, when Mamma allows it. In truth, it is a very comfortable life and the grounds are lovely. I am more than fortunate, and have nothing to complain of."

"Except the lack of a husband and family of your own."

She lifted her shoulders in a little shrug. "As I said, I no longer dream of what will never be. But I will admit, since we are being honest," she said, smiling as she threw his words back at him, "that I regret having to be so dependent on others. It is the lot of women in general, of course, but my disability makes me even more dependent. My mother and brothers feel responsible for me and always will. I will forever be a burden to them, and I dislike that very much."

Nat sympathized completely. In the last year, since Waterloo, he had been so off balance that he had hidden himself away in the country rather than impose himself and his bad moods on anyone else. He'd suffered since that last battle in ways that still surprised and disturbed him. After nine years of hard-fought battles in Copenhagen and Spain and Portugal, he thought he'd been inured to the hardships of war, both physical and mental. For reasons he did not understand, he had not yet been able to shake off that final stand at Waterloo. Nat found that sort of weakness intolerable. He hated what he'd become, and it made him constantly angry and frustrated and irritable. He'd tried to convince his brother that he was not fit to enter society again, but Dearne would not be dissuaded and insisted that Nat come to Town and find a bride.

So Nat had some understanding of Miss Reynolds's frustrations. Neither of them wished to inflict themselves and their weaknesses upon their well-meaning families.

He suddenly realized he'd been speaking with her for at least a half hour without the usual tight knot in his chest that kept him on edge in polite society. He was almost entirely at ease with a perfect stranger. A female stranger at that. How extraordinary.

As he looked down at her—an attractive young woman with a charming personality who would surely have been snapped up by some young swain by now if she did not have the limp—an idea burst upon his brain full-blown, like a kind of epiphany. The perfect solution to both their problems.

He was reminded of those turning points in a battle, when a breech unexpectedly opened or the enemy faltered and he had to make a decision instantly to take advantage. Even a moment of hesitation would have meant a missed opportunity, or worse. And so, before he could convince himself it was not an absolutely brilliant idea, before he could second-guess himself, he blurted it out to her.

"I think we should marry, Miss Reynolds."

Her mouth dropped open as she glared at him wide-eyed, then, in a thin voice she said, "I beg your pardon?"

"Forgive me. I ought not to have come out with it so baldly like that, but hear me out, please. You wish to marry but have no hope of doing so. I need to marry and have no desire to go through the bother of finding a bride who will have me. You have no wish to sit out another Season without hope of finding a husband. I have no wish to endure a Season where I have to pretend to be someone I am not in order to find a bride. We could save ourselves a great deal of fuss and bother by becoming betrothed."

"But we've only just met, sir."

"Yes, but consider our conversation. We have each been frank about our situations. There has been no pretense or artifice between us. I suspect we already know each other better in half an hour than many betrothed couples do in half a Season. I have enjoyed our conversation, and believe me, I do not enjoy the company of very many people these days. I think we would rub along nicely together, don't you agree? I already know I like you, Miss Reynolds, which is more than I was expecting to find in a bride."

She looked flustered and confused, a bit embarrassed. Damn, he had not done this well. Naturally. But he still thought it a grand idea and hoped she would consider it. "Miss Reynolds? Have I put my foot in it too far this time? You must think me a complete idiot and wish to fling me over this railing to land crashing on the dancers below. But I assure you, I am quite serious. Will you consider it? Marrying me, I mean, not sending me over the railing."

Philippa was glad she was seated, else she would surely have collapsed from astonishment. Could this truly be happening? Her very first marriage proposal after an acquaintance of half an hour? It was incredible.

More incredible was the fact that she was actually thinking of accepting.

Could she? Should she?

It would certainly be the answer to all her prayers. She could finally relieve her family of the burden of looking after her, and have a home and family of her own. It was what she had always wanted and never dared hope would happen. And her husband would be this tall, handsome soldier who did not patronize her. Yes, he was a bit rough around the edges, but that was part of his charm. Others might not see any appeal in the stern expression he wore, in the severe lines of his face, in the way he never smiled, or in his unpolished way of speaking. But through years of watching people in society while not herself participating, Philippa had learned to read a person's character rather well, through his face, his movements, his speech, his behavior. There was much more to Captain Beckwith than met the eye. She sensed something troubling or painful beneath his austere demeanor, a vulnerability about him that touched her, though he would not want to hear her say that. It intrigued her, though, and made her want to know him better.

What better way to get to know him than to marry him?

Heavens, had she lost her mind?

"It is an interesting idea, Captain."

"Ah. I am encouraged that you have not rejected it outright."

"No, I have not. Quite foolishly, sir, I am considering it. Seriously considering it."

His eyes brightened, though he did not smile. "As you should. It is an excellent idea. And quite logical. People enter into marriages of convenience all the time. And think of all those arranged marriages among people in our class, marriages made solely to expand rank or fortune. Those are marriages of convenience, too—convenient for the families. Why should we not be able to do the same? Would it not be exceedingly convenient for us to marry? You would like to be married, and I need to be married. Quid pro quo, Miss

Reynolds. Plus, not to put too fine a point on it, but it is likely that neither of us will ever find anyone else who will have us. You because of your limp, and me because of my roughness and moodiness. We are both misfits, in our own ways. Why not join forces?"

"Well, that is certainly plain speaking, sir."

He looked chagrined and was about to speak again—no doubt to apologize for his bluntness—when she held up a hand to stop him. "Do not apologize, Captain. Plain speaking is most definitely in order in such a situation. And so, let me be plain with you, if I may."

When he nodded, she continued.

"I have said that I dislike being patronized for my lameness. One of the reasons I am willing to consider your offer is that you have not done so. You have been straightforward and honest with me. If we were to marry, I would expect that sort of honesty to continue. If I wanted indulgence, condescension, and well-meant cosseting, I could remain with my family."

"I think you can rely on me not to cosset, Miss Reynolds."

"Good. But you are a soldier, sir, and no doubt protective both by nature and training. Which is a good thing, for the most part, but I have no wish to be overly protected, packed in cotton wool like a fragile doll. Nor do I wish to have everything done *for* me. I am lame, not an invalid. I would not want my disability to encourage coddling. I would hate that from you, above all things. If we marry, you must promise not to coddle me."

He placed his hand over his heart. "No coddling, I promise. I further promise not to treat you like an invalid. If I thought you were the sort of woman who wanted such treatment, I would never have suggested an alliance because, believe me, I am not the sort to coddle. It pleases me that you want to do more for yourself. In fact, it rather irritates me that you have apparently not been allowed to do so. However, if you should happen to trip and fall flat on your face, or if you are thrown from a horse, am I to be allowed to help you up? Or must I leave you to your own devices, sprawled on the ground with your skirts around your ears?"

Philippa laughed. Oh, she really did like him. "I will ask for help when I need it, sir, I promise."

"All right, then. Do you have any other concerns we should discuss?"

She had a thousand of them, and would likely have a thousand more when she took time to think about it. But none of them could be answered with any certainty, so what was the point of airing them? "The promises you have made are sufficient for me at the moment."

"Very well." He frowned and began to pace the short length of the balcony. After a long, silent moment, he spoke again, keeping his head down, his gaze on the floor, as though embarrassed. "There is more you should know about me, ma'am. I'm a bad bargain, to be sure. I have no social skills, as you have seen, and don't really care if I ever develop them. I fear I will never fit in, and quite frankly I don't care much about that, either. I prefer my own company to anyone else's, which is why I have spent the last year alone. I am battle hardened and battle scarred, in both body and . . . and mind."

He stopped pacing and ran a hand through his longish, dark blond hair. His mouth was a grim line set in the harsh planes of his face. Philippa suspected it was difficult and painful for him to admit to any aftereffects of war, especially those of the mind. She did not entirely understand what that meant, but she knew that had she been thrown into battle to kill or be killed, then she would not have been able to shake off the effects either. She had often wondered how men returned from war and fell back into ordinary lives so easily, after all they'd been through. Maybe it wasn't always so easy.

"Look here, Miss Reynolds," he said. "You need to know that I am frequently cross and irritable for no reason. I can be dreadfully impatient. I am accustomed to command others, and tend to order people about. I don't sleep well and often wander the house at night. And I sometimes drink too much." He shook his head. "There. I've sunk myself, haven't I? You'll want nothing to do with me now."

"I can be cross and impatient, too, when people fuss over me or treat me as if my crooked hip somehow affected my brain. Do you know there are people who raise their voices when they speak to me, as though I were hard of hearing? Why would they think that because I limp I must therefore have a whole host of other problems as well? No, Captain, you have not sunk yourself. Indeed you have risen in my esteem once again through honesty. We both have our crosses to bear. Perhaps we can ease each other's burden."

"Yes, perhaps we can." His silvery blue eyes, clear and steady, were fixed intently on hers. "Shall we try?"

"First, I want you to be honest with yourself as well as with me," she said. "Are you absolutely certain my lameness does not bother you? That you will not be embarrassed to be seen with a wife who cannot walk properly?" She probably ought not to have given him the opportunity to reply to such a question, but it needed asking. No matter how much she wanted to fall into this impetuous scheme, she could not go through with it if she had any suspicion that he might, in time, be sorry he married a cripple.

"I've known countless good men," he said, "whose limbs were blown clean off by French artillery, or savagely amputated by a camp surgeon." She winced and he added, "I'm sorry. That was too vivid, was it not? You see how unfit I am for polite company? In any case, each of them was still a good man, even when missing an arm or leg. You merely have a limp, Miss Reynolds. A serious one, to be sure, but just a limp. You still have all your important bits, as far as I can tell, and your brain is obviously in fine working order. My gut tells me you are a good person inside." He tapped his chest. "Where it matters."

All her life Philippa's family had said that her character was more important than her crooked body. But for the first time, this man, this stranger, actually made her believe it.

Made her believe that *he* believed it. She almost fell in love with him on the spot.

By God, she was going to do it. This rough-edged, plain-speaking soldier just might be worth taking a chance on.

"All right, Captain. I think we have a bargain."

She reached out her hand to him, but he did not take it. Instead, he looked her squarely in the eye, as though measuring the sincerity of her commitment.

"Before we agree to anything, Miss Reynolds, I must warn you one more time that I am no prize. You might want to think twice or three times or ten times before aligning yourself with me. You see, I have certain . . . demons I contend with. "

"Indeed, sir, I can see that. One is tempted to describe you as dark and brooding. But you are almost blond and your eyes are blue . . . no, more gray than blue. Could one describe you, then, as light and brooding?"

His lips gave the tiniest twitch, as though they wanted to smile but he would not allow it.

"No," she said, "that doesn't sound right at all, does it? Fair and brooding? No, I think not. We shall have to devise another description for you. Reserved? Stern? Perhaps we shall just wait until those demons disappear, and then we may describe you as that handsome gentleman who is always smiling."

This time he did smile, and it transformed his face from severe to almost boyish. Dear heaven, he was gorgeous.

"Ah. See? I knew you would be very handsome when you smiled. You must do it more often."

"Perhaps with you, Miss Reynolds, I will have more reason to."

He took her proffered hand, and instead of shaking it, as she'd expected, he brought it to his lips.

"Miss Philippa Reynolds, will you do me the very great honor of becoming my wife?"

"I do believe I will, sir."

And so, it was done.

Chapter Two

I cannot say I am entirely happy about this."

Philippa's mother had that concerned look she so often wore, brows furrowed, lips pursed. It was not surprising, considering what she'd just learned. Philippa had hoped, though, that she and William might be just a little bit pleased for her. But Captain Beckwith stood very stiff before all their questioning, giving no hint of warmth or humor. Despite keeping his unruly tongue surprisingly in order—not a single curse or indelicate comment had passed his lips—he was not making a favorable impression.

"I know, Mamma," Philippa said. "This must come as a tremendous surprise."

"That is putting it mildly," her brother William said. He had behaved with as much severity as the Captain, and with considerable less civility. "I would never have expected so rash a decision from you, Pip. It smacks of . . . desperation."

Philippa flinched. Was it truly the desperate act of a hopeless, helpless female, to align herself with a perfect stranger? Who was she kidding? Of course it was.

But she did not believe she would have agreed to it with just any gentleman. She had never met another gentleman who was so open and honest with her, who did not make her feel like a poor, pitiful lame girl. So, it was a serendipitous moment of desperation joined with opportunity. And by God, she was not going to let this opportunity pass her by.

"It may seem a desperate action, William, but I assure you it is not entirely so. The captain and I believe it will be a good arrangement for each of us. Captain Beckwith is a fine man, William, a soldier who fought bravely for our country. I would be honored to be his wife."

"And, of course, you would be a countess one day," William said. "We must consider that, Mother. I suppose it could be a good match for our Pip."

"I trust it will be a very long time, sir, if ever, before I inherit the earldom with your sister as my countess." A muscle twitched in the captain's jaw. It was the only indication that his back teeth must be clenched fair to cracking, that he was making a prodigious effort to keep his temper in check. "My brother is barely forty and healthy as a horse. In the meantime, you should have no concerns for Miss Reynolds's welfare or security. I have a profitable estate in Oxfordshire, a generous settlement from my father's estate, and a handsome annuity from my maternal grandmother. I am happy to have my man of affairs lay out the particulars for you, at your convenience."

"I will take you up on that offer, Captain," William said. He turned to Mamma and said, "I am willing to accede to Pip's wishes in this matter. What do you say, Mother?"

She turned to the captain, who had remained standing throughout, his hands clasped behind his back. "You must understand, sir, that our Philippa has lived her whole life among people who know her limitations, and anticipate the requirements of her condition. She is not an ordinary girl, sir. She needs looking after. I'm afraid it is hard to imagine her getting along without us."

"You speak as though you never intended for her to leave you, ma'am," the captain said. "And yet I believe this to be the third Season when you have brought her out, in hopes, one assumes, of finding a husband. Well, she has found one. Though perhaps not one to your liking."

Philippa's mother had the good sense to flush at his words. "I just want my only daughter to be happy, sir. Yes, I have long hoped she would be fortunate enough to marry, but in the end, it is difficult to let her go, to give her into the care of someone else. Anyone else. I do not know you well enough, Captain, to have any objections to you personally. It is merely the way this has come about. This . . . this arrangement you have made after a single meeting. It is hard to imagine that you fully comprehend her special needs."

Philippa hated being discussed as though she were not right there in the room, sitting no more than a foot away from her mother on the sofa. But Mamma meant well. She always did, even if Philippa sometimes felt suffocated by all those good intentions.

The captain caught her eye, and a look of understanding passed between them.

"I have known Miss Reynolds only a very short time, ma'am," he said, "and yet I believe I comprehend precisely what she needs. I would make it my life's work to ensure her happiness."

Would he? Or was he instinctively falling back on the good manners his mother taught him? Philippa studied his face for a moment. His gaze had not left hers, even though he'd addressed Mamma. No, this was not artful dissembling to placate her mother. He meant it. He really would try to make her happy.

He was already doing so.

Her mother heaved a deep sigh. "All right, then. I will agree to this impetuous marriage of convenience. But do not think for a moment that I will allow a rushed-up hole-in-the-corner wedding. I will not have people thinking a quick marriage is necessary. There will be a proper courtship,

Captain Beckwith. In public." She turned to Philippa. "You must be seen together at social events. And I want you to spend more time getting to know each other. At the end of the Season, if you still feel that you want to go through with this, my dear, I will not stand in your way."

Philippa leaned over, wrapped an arm around her mother's shoulders, and gave a squeeze. "Thank you, Mamma."

A short time later, she walked with Captain Beckwith downstairs and to the entry hall. Her mother granted them these few moments alone, and there was so much to be said. Philippa could not contain herself, and the words came spilling out.

"I think it went well, do you not, sir? I so admired how you stood up to my family throughout their ruthless questioning. It was not completely without a rough spot or two, but overall you gave the impression of a serious gentleman who will take good care of me, which is, of course, their primary concern. They will not think I have made a frivolous choice. Impetuous, yes. Frivolous, no."

"I do not imagine anyone thinking me frivolous."

"Indeed, no. You are the most somber of gentlemen, who's probably never experienced a moment of frivolity in his life. Ah, there's that smile again. I do wish you had shown it to Mamma. You could have won her over completely with that smile."

"I doubt it. Your mother is a fearsome woman. I do believe I'd rather endure a dressing-down by Wellington himself than to stand again before Lady Reynolds's fierce interrogation."

"She only wants what's best for me, Captain. Do not begrudge her, or William, the right to be protective of me. Oh, but sir, when William asked who had introduced us, and you looked over to me with one eyebrow cocked, I had to bite the inside of my cheek to keep from laughing. I was sure you were going to mention Lady Kumquat!"

He grinned. "I was tempted, just to see your reaction. But neither your brother nor your mother would have bought that tall tale. I'm not certain they bought my excuse of not re-membering the woman's name, but then you jumped into the breach, changing the subject before either of them could pursue the matter. To be honest, I suspect they both know full well that we had no formal introduction, but there is no point in worrying about that now."

"One thing I am sorry for, Captain. I know that the whole idea of our bargain was for each of us to bypass the Season and the marriage mart. However, Mamma will not be gain-said on this. She will insist on a full Season. If that is com-pletely unacceptable to you, I will understand if you wish to back out. There will be no dishonor in doing so, I assure you."

He stopped walking and touched her elbow to turn her toward him. "I will not back out, Miss Reynolds. I gave you my promise, and I have no intention of breaking it. Yes, the idea of a full Season of society events makes my belly ache, but I will gladly go through with it if you agree that, in the end, we will wed."

"That was our plan, sir. I see no reason to change it."

"Good. It will make it easier for me to endure the infer-nal Season if I know from the beginning that you and I are promised to each other. I won't be forced to dance atten-dance on insipid girls with little wit and no conversation."

"But you may be forced to *dance*, sir. You cannot sit out every set with me. Only two sets with one partner, whether dancing or sitting out, is considered proper."

"Is that another one of those abominable Rules? Who makes up these idiotic restrictions?"

"I do not know, but Mamma will not allow us to ignore them completely. Again, sir, if you wish to back out—"

"Nonsense. We will get through this, Philippa. May I call you Philippa? We are practically betrothed, after all."

"Of course."

"Unless you'd prefer Pip." One corner of his mouth twitched, and his silvery gray eyes sparkled with amuse-ment. "I thought it a rather charming sobriquet."

"Don't you dare call me Pip. Only my brothers ever use that name and I've always hated it. It makes me sound even smaller than I am."

"It does not suit you, in any case. Philippa does. My given name is Nathaniel, but hardly anyone uses that mouthful. I am called Nat by my friends."

"Then I should be pleased to call you Nat. In private, of course."

"Of course. The confounded Rules."

He touched her elbow again to indicate they could resume walking. He did not take her arm, as most men—and women—were generally quick to do, assuming she could not walk without assistance. She liked him all the more for allowing her to hobble along on her own. She might look ungainly, but she was not helpless.

"I know we spoke of making a marriage of convenience," he said. "Two social misfits joining forces and all that. But let me be clear, Philippa. Ours would not be a marriage in name only. I never meant that we would have anything but a true marriage. I have no desire to embark on a cold, bloodless alliance, typical of so many arranged aristocratic marriages. We already like each other, do we not? Over time, we will no doubt develop affection for one another. And we *will* share a marriage bed. In case you wondered."

She felt her cheeks warm and Philippa knew she'd broken out in bright pink blotches. She silently cursed all her redheaded ancestors for that unwelcome inheritance. "Let me be frank as well, then," she said, hoping her firm, even tone counteracted the flushed cheeks. "I never wanted a bloodless alliance either. But neither do I want a sophisticated marriage in which we each turn our heads at the other's indiscretions. I do not believe I have the stomach for it. I want a true marriage, too, Captain."

"Good. We are in agreement, then. Now, let us get on with this damnable courtship your mother has insisted upon."

* * *

Nat led his horse down South Audley Street and onto Curzon Street. He had no wish to face his brother yet, to tell him of the proposed courtship with Philippa. So, instead of returning to Dearne House on St. James's Square, he headed toward Kensington, where there was a cozy little tavern he frequented. He never met anyone he knew there, and was left in peace to nurse a pint or two.

Or maybe three, after the trying morning he'd had.

When Philippa had introduced him to her mother last night at the ball, he'd known he was in for a controlled battle. Lady Reynolds was a formidable hen, fiercely protective of her disabled chick. Though he had not yet spoken to her of marriage—he still had enough wits about him to know a ball was not the place to request her daughter's hand—she was not stupid and knew something was afoot, and clearly was not happy about it.

Nat had girded his loins for battle when he'd called on her this morning.

He had not been surprised to find Philippa's brother, Sir William, in attendance as well. It had been an awkward meeting at best. Nat tried to be on his best behavior, calling on remembrances of days longs past, before he'd gone to war, and when his mother had tried to teach him fine manners. It was difficult to be amiable when both mother and brother probed and prodded to discover if there was some ulterior motive to his offer. As though it was impossible that any man could seriously want to marry Philippa.

No wonder the girl was so quick to accept his offer. She must be anxious to escape a family who thought so little of her. No, that was unfair. They loved her, that much was clear. But they saw her as a cripple first, and a young woman second. They wanted happiness for her, but more than that they wanted her to be protected.

Nat had every intention of protecting Philippa, but even after a short acquaintance—not even twenty-fours hours—it was evident to Nat that she did not need the kind of protection her family intended. Yes, he would keep her safe from harm, from unhappiness (as best he could), and from financial want. More than that, however, he would protect her from being smothered to death by her well-meaning family. Nat had promised not to coddle her, and he would keep that promise.

He had a notion that she just might blossom into something quite extraordinary, if she was allowed a bit more freedom.

He was pleased that his talk of a true marriage had not shocked her. She had blushed rather prettily, but had spoken with equal candor regarding her own expectations. One of the things he liked best about her was that he did not need to guard his words with her. Philippa actually seemed to enjoy his unpolished ways.

He was glad she had not spoken of love. How could she, on such brief acquaintance? But ladies liked that sort of thing, he knew, liked to talk of love and happily-ever-afters. Nat had never been able to do that, had never been one to offer Spanish coin. He hadn't given it much thought until Dearne had extracted that accursed promise from him, but it was very likely he was incapable of love. Yes, there had been affairs over the years, some of which had burned hot on a physical level, but never for longer than a few months. In the end, one woman was much the same as the next, which was why he'd agreed to Dearne's request to find a bride. He did not much care whom he married, so long as she was not a complete shrew.

He did not pick up any hint of shrewishness from Philippa. Quite the opposite, in fact. She was not one of those brightly polished society jewels who'd had all the interesting bits smoothed down and any sign of true character buffed clean out of her. Perhaps her family had not thought her worth the effort of a high polish when she was deemed imperfect due to her lameness. Dashed unfair, to be sure, but there it was and he was glad of it, for it made her all the more available to him. He *liked* her, which was more than he could say about other young woman of the *ton* he'd met who were indistinguishable, one from another, each modeled from the same tiresome pattern card.

Philippa seemed so much more open and guileless than other young women, more genuine. Everything that was unique and interesting about her seemed to spring from a single source: the limp. Since there was no disguising it, and since it apparently made her unacceptable to most men, perhaps she saw no reason for artifice. Whatever the reason, he liked her. He knew that he could appear aloof and even cold and that young women were often uncomfortable in his presence. And yet Philippa was not at all intimidated by him. He did not want a woman who would be cowed by him, though he had not realized that until he'd met one who wasn't. He had decided on the spot that she would do for him.

Yes, her mother had insisted on a public courtship, which meant he would have to attend more balls and parties, would likely have to dance with a girl or two, God help him. But at least he would not have to consider them seriously as potential brides. He'd found his bride, and he was content with her.

Even more content than he'd been last evening. As he watched her with her family, he was witness to a level of kindness and compassion he'd rarely encountered. Not from Sir William or Lady Reynolds, but from Philippa herself. She accepted their over-protective fussing and cosseting with grace, even when he suspected she hated it—all because they did it with love. She would not toss that love back in their faces through ingratitude. That took a strength of character Nat could only admire.

He'd learned something else about her today that pleased him. She was much more attractive in the daylight than he'd expected. He would have married her regardless, because he truly liked her and thought they would suit each other. But discovering she was pretty was an added bonus. No, pretty did not describe her accurately. She was not the typical fair-haired, blue-eyed English rose pretty. Her appearance was much more striking than that.

Her hair was extraordinary. Thick and shiny, it was one of the loveliest shades of red he'd ever seen—somewhere between bright coppery red and darkest auburn. He'd had a horse for several years in Spain—a chestnut with a dark red coat that gleamed bright and shiny in the sun. Philippa's hair was almost exactly that color, or maybe even a shade darker. He suspected it was quite long hair, judging by the thickness of the various twists and knots at the back of her head. How far down her back did it hang, he wondered? And would it feel as satiny in his hands as it looked?

Her eyebrows were, quite naturally, the same dark red, and were delicately arched over large eyes. Most fascinating of all was that her eyes were also the same brownish red color. Or perhaps a touch lighter. The color of Spanish sherry, a good amontillado.

All that sameness of color ought to have been dull and uninteresting, but against the pale, fine-textured skin, it was actually quite stunning. Beautiful, even. And that skin. Lord, he'd wanted to touch it from the moment he first saw her. He'd often heard beautiful skin compared to porcelain, but had always thought it so much poetic exaggeration. Yet Philippa's skin did indeed bring to mind fine porcelain. Clear, white, smooth, translucent. She was one of those rare redheads who was not freckled. At least on her face and neck. He wondered about the rest of her, and realized he would enjoy finding out.

All in all, he was quite pleased with the arrangement with Philippa Reynolds. Though clearly he was getting the better end of the bargain. She deserved more than a sullen, broken-down soldier who could barely open his mouth without putting his foot in it.

"Do you not find him a bit austere, my dear?" Philippa's mother was still struggling with this new situation. It had been hours since the Captain had left them, and between discussions of balls and parties and dressmakers, she continued to drop in these little probing questions. "Austere, and even somewhat cold? And I am not quite sure his manners are all they should be. He seems a bit unpolished for the son of an earl."

"I don't mind his lack of polish, Mamma. In fact, I find it rather refreshing. As for his austerity, remember that he is a military man, one who has spent many years in battle." She remembered his mention of having demons, of being scarred in both body and mind. A lesser man would never have confessed as much, and she was pleased that he had trusted her enough to do so. "He has probably seen and done things during wartime that would harden any man. I suspect he is more sensitive than he lets on, and those experiences affected him deeply. I believe that is why he is so uncomfortable in society. He hasn't yet shaken off the horrors of war, and is finding it difficult to adjust."

Mamma's eyebrows lifted in question. "You learned all this about him in one short evening?"

Philippa shrugged. "Just intuition."

"Well, you've always been a good judge of people. But I can't shake the impression that he might be an ill-tempered man. Are you certain you will be safe with him?"

"Physically safe? I have no doubt of it. Remember, he is a soldier at heart. He will go out of his way to protect me, to keep me safe."

"I hope you are right."

"I know I am." And she did. She trusted him, was ready, in fact, to trust him with her future happiness. It was possible, of course, that she was the biggest fool ever born and that once married, Captain Beckwith would treat her like so much dirt beneath his feet. But she knew he would not. Philippa was willing to bet her life on it.

It was time to change tactics. "And just think, Mamma. I might even be a countess one day. Won't that make you proud, to introduce your daughter as Lady Dearne?"

"Yes, I suppose so."

"And everyone will know that you were right to trot me out each Season just like any other girl. That you knew someone would finally make me an offer."

"That is precisely what I am hoping, my dear, and why I have insisted on a public courtship. I would not want for anyone to know the truth of how this marriage actually came about. A harebrained scheme concocted after half an hour's conversation. Really, Philippa, I am beyond astonished at you. I would never have dreamed—"

"But do you not think him handsome, Mamma? The lame girl with no marital hopes will be seen on the arm of an incredibly attractive man. I will be the envy of every other girl this Season."

"Hmm. I daresay it will do you some good to be seen to have a suitor at last. And I suppose Captain Beckwith might be handsome if he did not insist on fixing a scowl on his face at all times."

"You and William made him nervous, that's all. You're a formidable pair, you know. I can assure you that he does not always scowl. When he smiles, it is actually quite dazzling."

Her mother arched an eyebrow. "Are you dazzled, Philippa? Is that what this is all about? An attractive man notices you and you lose all common sense?"

"No, that is not what happened. He won me over with honor and honesty. His good looks only sweetened the bargain."

Her mother grabbed her hand and squeezed. "Oh, I do hope you know what you are doing, Philippa. It is not like you to be so impetuous."

"I know. But I want this, Mamma. And something tells me it will be all right."

"Your intuition again?"

"Perhaps. Please trust me. I know it will work out. I just know it."

The open courtship of Captain Nathaniel Beckwith for Miss Philippa Reynolds became fodder for *ton* gossips. It was a most unusual pairing to be sure. Until a few weeks ago, the former army captain had been an infamous recluse for reasons unknown and widely speculated about. He was a somewhat dour man, but the heir to an earldom was still a prime catch. Why was he so interested in the poor lame girl whose mother had been hopelessly thrusting her into the marriage mart for three Seasons, when his rank and fortune could win him any number of more suitable young women?

In was generally believed that there was more to this odd courtship than met the eye. They were invited everywhere, as each hostess hoped that her ball or party would be the scene of some new and interesting development.

Philippa found the increased attention given her to be by turns embarrassing and amusing. Most times, she tried to ignore it and focused on Captain Beckwith.

In public, he wore an air of command that marked him as a military officer. It also put a distance between him and everyone else, as though he might snap the head off anyone who spoke to him. Philippa had come to understand that his manner was meant to discourage hopeful mothers, matchmakers, and anyone else who might want something of him. She did not know why he did it, why he felt so uncomfortable in the world to which he was born. But she was perversely glad that he appeared so formidable and unapproachable. It meant she got to keep him all to herself.

At the Easton Ball, her friend Lillian Faulkner sat out a set with her and chatted about the new bonnet she had purchased that afternoon. Philippa barely listened as she watched Nat partner Clementina Easton in a country dance.

"I do believe you are infatuated with the captain," Lillian said.

"Not infatuated. But very intrigued."

"Are you sure it is not more than that? You've been stealing glances at him all evening. I'm not the only one to notice, you know. Tongues are wagging, Philippa."

"Let them wag. I am enjoying myself for once, after two awkward Seasons."

There were no doubt many who believed she was besotted and could not take her eyes from him. There was some truth in that, she had to admit. But only to herself. She was not yet ready to openly confess her most private feelings, even to Lillian. The real reason she watched Nat, though, was to see how he fared in such close company. He maintained a stiff-backed, soldierly composure, but she saw signs of uneasiness and knew he held himself under tight control. Phlippa wondered if he would ever lose that enforced restraint and feel comfortable in his own skin again.

Sometimes she watched him simply because he was glorious to look at. His complexion was sun glazed, setting off the golden lights in his tawny hair, and acting as a bold and attractive contrast to the crisp white of his linen. His gray eyes were a striking silver against the dark skin. He stood with the straight-backed bearing of a military man, his shoulders broad, his waist narrow, his legs long and well muscled. Nat looked handsome in his blue coat and gold breeches, but oh, how she would love to have seen him in full regimentals. How grand he must have looked.

She really did try not to stare at him too obviously. She did not wish to appear a lovesick fool: the poor, pitiful cripple with a hopeless infatuation. Philippa knew the *ton* was fascinated with the lame girl who'd never had a suitor and the glorious golden god who might have had any woman but openly courted her. She wished that at least some of them were happy for her good fortune, but she suspected most of them expected Nat eventually to abandon her and were anxiously watching to see what she would do.

In fact, she was quite confident he would not abandon her. They had made a bargain and he would honor it. Besides, Philippa did not believe he was interested in breaking their bargain, even if he could honorably do so. He showed no partiality for any other woman, even the ones who blatantly threw themselves in his path. He was polite, but spoke very little. Nat still had a tendency to speak a bit too bluntly, and she believed he often remained silent so as not to embarrass himself or others with one of his unvarnished truths. Philippa adored his bold tongue, and was delighted that he did not feel the need to curb it in her presence. She had the impression he said things to her that he was not comfortable saying to others, shared things with her that he hadn't shared with anyone else. He was at ease with her.

Now and then, though, her confidence waned, especially when she saw him with a beautiful woman who moved with grace and elegance. Like Clementina Easton, who was smiling brightly as they danced together. She never doubted Nat, but sometimes she could not help but worry that he would ultimately realize that he'd got the worse end of their bargain. He deserved more than an unremarkable redhead with a crooked body.

Nat watched the dancers from the edge of the room. So many pretty young ladies, with their fresh faces, charming smiles, and graceful movements.

They all looked the same to him.

His eyes sought out Philippa's brilliant hair, and found it easily, shimmering like garnets in the candlelight. She was the only one he wanted to see. He honestly did not know how he would have survived the damnable social whirl without her. It would have probably come to the point where he would simply have asked Dearne to pick a bride for him. How could he have chosen for himself from among so many? Especially when he couldn't bring himself to care.

He thanked his lucky stars that he'd met Philippa on that fateful evening a few weeks ago. He'd been reprieved of having to throw himself into the marriage mart, and had been allowed to squire around a young woman he genuinely liked. Everything was going his way, so he ought to have been happy.

But he was still too often tense, his nerves stretched tight as a drum. Overly crowded rooms could send him into a sweat, bringing images to mind of those packed squares of infantrymen battered by French artillery. Sharp noises

sometimes took on the sounds of that incessant French cannonade. At such times, it was all he could do not to turn
tail and bolt. But he was determined not to give in to those
wretched moments of weakness. He fought them, closing his
eyes and taking deep breaths until he came back to himself. Many times when he opened his eyes he found Philippa
looking up at him with quiet understanding, though she
never said a word. Then she would smile, sometimes touching his hand, and he forgot all about the war. If she continued to smile at him like that, surely the damnable episodes
would eventually cease.

Nat had danced once this evening with the daughter
of the hostess, who'd given him no choice but to ask her,
but had not allowed himself to be persuaded to dance
with anyone else. He disappeared into the card room for
a while, then wandered about the room, chatting briefly
with a fellow officer or two, but primarily he waited, impatiently, for the next set promised to Philippa. Sitting with
her for half an hour was the only part of a ball he enjoyed,
the only time he was truly at ease. They spoke of random
topics, of family and friends, of books and music. She was
better read and more cultured than Nat, but she somehow
drew him into conversation without any hint of condescension on her part, or boredom on his. Even the sound of
Philippa's voice, and especially her laughter, had become
a balm to his soul.

The instant the previous set ended, Nat was at her side.
He acknowledged Lady Reynolds with a nod, then gave
Philippa his arm and led her away.

"I have done some reconnaissance," he said. "There is a
small terrace off one of the anterooms that no one seems to
have discovered. We can be private there."

"You know, sir, that people have noticed how you and I
disappear together for at least one set at every ball."

"It seems foolish to simply sit and watch. I much prefer
to take you someplace where we can actually have a private
conversation."

"It might be thought that I am trying to encourage a compromising situation."

"Bah. Only your mother thinks that, admit it."

Philippa smiled. "She has mentioned it. Not about my engineering a compromising situation. She knows that is not necessary when you and I already have an agreement. But she worries that other people may get that impression."

"She worries too much about what other people think. Here we are. See, there is a door to the terrace." He guided her through the empty room and out the door. "There is no bench, I'm afraid. But I thought you might appreciate the cool night air for a few minutes."

"I do, thank you."

"I have come to a decision, Philippa. About balls."

"You hate them."

"So do you. I see you watching the other dancers with longing. I do not understand why your mother insists you attend them." Because Philippa could not participate, more attention was drawn to her disability. It seemed incredibly cruel to Nat.

"They are important social events," Philippa said. "She wants us to be seen together."

"We have been seen together often enough. I believe it is obvious that I am courting you. I spoke to an army colleague this evening, and he mentioned it. I think we are doing quite enough to ensure that we are seen together. I intend to tell your mother that there are to be no more balls."

"Oh."

The look in her eyes made him reconsider. "Damn. Am I coddling?"

She smiled. "No, you are being kind."

"That is often the same thing, is it not? I am accustomed to issuing orders. I should have asked about your feelings on the matter. Do you enjoy balls?"

"Now and then. I love the music. I like to watch the dancers, but I do sometimes get a bit wistful that I cannot join in. I watched you and Clementina Easton. You dance very well, as I knew you would, and I found myself wishing it could have been me. But those are fleeting regrets that I do not dwell on."

"Ah, Philippa." He took her hand. "I would rather sit out ten sets with you than dance one set with Miss Easton."

"Thank you for saying so. But you mustn't worry about me. I've had a lifetime of not dancing, so I am well accustomed to sitting out. I do tire of always being with the dowagers and chaperones, though. These stolen sets with you are what I most look forward to."

"Suppose we limit them. Balls, I mean, not stolen sets. I have no wish to give up those. I rather enjoy finding hiding places. One never knows what interesting people one may encounter while hiding."

She threw back her head and laughed. "Or what interesting circumstances may result."

His laughter joined hers, and then he brought her gloved hand to his lips. "I am quite pleased with our interesting circumstance, ma'am."

She flushed a lovely shade of pink and lowered her eyes. "As am I, sir."

"What would you say to no more than one ball per week?"

"I would say that is more than reasonable."

"Good. Consider it done."

Three weeks into his "courtship" he escorted Philippa to a rout party given by Lord and Lady Craig. It was the sort of event he most hated, where one stood in long lines to get in, then stood shoulder to shoulder with a throng of people one didn't know, or did know and disliked, and then one turned around and made the slow progress to get the hell out. He would never understand the appeal of such a gathering. Nothing ever happened. One simply milled about in over-warm, over-crowded rooms with other over-dressed people and engaged in over-long meaningless conversations. If one was lucky, one might be served a glass of wine, if one could get near a footman with a tray of full glasses. But there was never food or cards or dancing to offer a moment's distraction.

Sometimes there were several such parties in an evening, but Nat refused to squire Philippa to more than one. He'd established that rule shortly after the one-ball-per-week rule, much to Lady Reynolds's chagrin. He had stood his ground against her protests, though, and she had no choice but to capitulate. Despite what she might have thought, he did not establish these rules purely for selfish motives. Besides his own aversion to crowds and noise and pointless socializing, he did not like to see Philippa forced to stand for such a long period without hope of a chair to give her hip a rest. She never complained, and probably never would as she wanted so badly to seem normal—for his sake, he thought, rather than for her own—but he had become aware of tiny signs of fatigue that signaled to him it was time to leave. A tightness around her mouth. A more frequent shifting of weight. A slight tilting of her body away from the bad hip. The limp a bit more pronounced.

After noticing one or two of those signs at the Craig rout, he'd begun to steer her toward the exit, when they became stalled behind a group of loud, swaggering young men whose conversation turned to Waterloo and the rousting of Napoleon. A year later, the famous battle was still being rehashed, primarily by those who were not there. Armchair generals who would not know a line from a column made Nat want to spit.

He was in no mood to listen to such prattle right now, and tried to elbow his way past them, when one of the men said, "Thank God for the Prussians. Wellington's 'scum of the earth' troops would have fallen without them."

Nat saw red. He'd commanded some of those troops, and they had performed bravely and well at Waterloo. Hell, if not for the 52nd Foot, there might not have been an Allied victory at all, or at least not that day. Yes, many of the men had come up from the lowest levels of society, some even from the criminal ranks, but with good training and army discipline, they had become a proud fighting force. Nat would have trusted any one of them with his life. These prosing fools with their pomaded hair and high shirt-points could not be trusted with the time of day.

"You should be damned grateful for those 'scum of the earth' soldiers." He ought to have kept his tongue between his teeth, but when did he ever?

The dandified pup who'd spoken turned and glared at Nat through a quizzing glass that hung from his neck on a black ribbon. He might have been examining a particularly nasty insect. "I beg your pardon. Were you speaking to us, sir?"

"I was indeed, you insolent cur. You have no idea what happened on that battlefield, and what the Prussians did or did not do. You do not even have the right to an opinion."

"And *you* do?"

"I was there. You were not. I advise you not to make a fool of yourself by pretending to know what happened. And by the way, that lot of scum you talk about was responsible for routing the last of the Imperial Guard and bringing an end to the battle. Those scum soldiers saved your prissy, indulgent way of life, sir. I'll thank you to remember that next time you dare to criticize them."

He took Philippa's arm and led her away from the gaping young man.

"I'm sorry, Philippa. That was badly done. I should have kept my mouth shut."

"I'm glad you did not."

"You are?"

"Yes. I have often noticed that you get angry or irritable when there is talk of Waterloo. You usually become silent and morose. I am glad you spoke up this time. I know it must be difficult to leave the horrors of war behind, and you should not. It made you the man you are. I also believe it is a good thing to air your opinions now and then, to vent a bit of steam, so to speak."

"It will take more than a bit of steam, Philippa." He kept her close as he led her through the crowd, speaking almost directly into her ear so that she could hear him above the din of voices, but not loud enough to be overheard. These were not words he wanted others to hear. "You cannot know what I have seen and done, how many men I have killed, how many of my own men I've seen killed. Not so much at Waterloo, where we suffered few losses. We fared much worse as breach assault teams at Ciudad Rodrigo and Badajoz." In fact those sieges had been gruesome, with his company among the party known as the Forlorn Hope at Badajoz. He still treasured his "Valiant Stormer" arm badge earned by 52nd survivors of those campaigns. He had suffered no mental weakness afterward, though both sieges had been ten times worse than Waterloo. He still did not understand it. Perhaps it was because there was always another battle and therefore no time to reflect on the last one. Waterloo had been his final battle. Since then, he'd had nothing but time to replay in his mind that last stand and the horrific, ceaseless pounding of French cannonade.

"I will never know what you have lived through," Philippa said, "but I suspect the faces of your fallen men, and even those of the enemy fallen, will stay with you forever."

How could she know that? Did she know that his dreams were filled with those faces still, long after battle?

"I know you cannot leave it all behind," she said. "I believe it would be impossible for the most heartless of men to do so. And you are far from heartless. You are a man of fierce honor and duty and loyalty. I cannot make you forget, and would not presume to try. The best I can do is to help you cope with the past, and try to make the rest of your life peaceful."

"Peaceful? I don't know . . ."

"Well, perhaps a minor skirmish now and then." She smiled, almost coquettishly. "But no battles, if you please."

By God, she was flirting with him. Nat bit back a grin. "I knew from the first that I would like you. Let's get the hell out of here."

Chapter Three

Nat entered the club with some trepidation. It was an exclusively military club, for infantry and cavalry officers only. He was a member but almost never showed up. However, when his close friend and fellow officer of the 52nd, Reginald Kenning, had asked Nat to join him for a bottle and a bird, Nat hadn't the heart to refuse.

It was bad enough being among London's social elite and trying to hide his particular anxieties. To be among other soldiers could be disastrous. What if they guessed? What would they think of him?

Lord, he could not wait to get back to the solitude of his Oxfordshire home.

His "troubles" manifested themselves more frequently in Town, probably because of the incessant noise and crowds. He sometimes felt smothered, closed in, stifled. He had more nightmares, longer bouts of melancholy, and was easily startled. He had little patience for London social life and found nothing purposeful in the way most so-called gentlemen spent their time. Some days he wanted to scream with frustration. He hated what had become of him, this prickly, tentative existence, a life only half lived. It had been a year since he'd seen battle. A stronger man, a better soldier, would have shaken off the effects by now. If not for his commitment to Philippa, he'd have bolted long ago.

Nat was hailed by several acquaintances as he entered the club's coffee room, where he was to meet Kenning. It was a boisterous, jovial gathering, and he was welcomed warmly. He relaxed only slightly as he studied the men around him. They were good men, most of them, and he liked them. Part of him was pleased to be among friends and colleagues again; another part remained guarded and watchful.

None of the others seemed to exhibit the same tension and stressfulness he had felt during the last year. He did not see wariness in their eyes or tension in their shoulders. He saw only laughter and hail-fellow-well-met camaraderie. No one spoke of battle at such gatherings. Lost friends were mentioned and lauded, but specifics of battle were never discussed. Nat would like to have known if any of his fellow Light Bobs had been affected by the extraordinary cannonade the infantry squares had endured on that northern ridge. He'd never seen the like in nine years in Copenhagen, Spain, or Portugal, and had been shaken to his core, literally and figuratively. That deafening, ceaseless pounding of French artillery still haunted him, keeping him constantly on edge.

But none of his fellow officers seemed fazed. Not even Kenning, who'd commanded a square under the same bombardment.

Nine years of battle had, of course, taken its toll on his body. He'd been shot, slashed with sabers, and bayoneted. He'd been thrown from horses and struck by artillery debris. He'd been treated by surgeons so exhausted or drunk or inexperienced that it was a miracle he survived. But he *had* survived, and returned to battle time and time again with no more ill effects than a few scars. Never, ever had war affected his mind. Until now.

He was determined, though, to overcome whatever it was that ailed him. He would not give in to weakness, whether of the body or of the mind. He. Would. Not.

"Ah, there you are, Beckwith." Kenning waved him over to a leather chair next to his own, then signaled for a waiter to pour a second glass of wine. "Glad you were able to tear yourself away from Miss Reynolds for an evening."

"The devil you say." Nat took a seat and the proffered glass of wine, which he downed in a single swallow. He felt the need of a bit of Dutch courage to survive an evening at the club.

"Or did you have to get Lady Reynolds's permission for a night off from squiring her daughter around?"

"Bugger off, Kenning. It is not like that."

"Isn't it?"

Nat groaned. "God, is that how it looks?"

"It looks as though the young lady has captured your attention. She is an interesting choice, Nat."

"Because she is lame?"

"Well . . . yes."

"What the bloody hell does that matter? She is a charming girl, with a razor wit and a kind heart. Handsome, too, by God. I'll not have you speaking ill of her."

Kenning held up a palm. "Fall back, old boy. Didn't mean anything by it, I assure you. No need to bite my head off."

"Sorry. I am just so damned tired of being the latest *on dit*. Why can't people mind their own damned business and leave us the hell alone?"

"Because society thrives on gossip and innuendo. Yours is an unusual courtship, so people will talk. I've met Miss Reynolds once or twice, you know, and quite liked her."

"So do I. But what the deuce is so unusual about a limp?"

"It's not so much the limp, old boy. It's you."

"Me?"

"You've been least in sight for a good year. Then you suddenly show up courting Miss Reynolds. Naturally, everyone is curious. Was there some sort of family arrangement over the winter?"

"Not exactly." Nat held out his empty glass to a passing waiter, who refilled it with the club's best claret. When he'd gone, Nat lowered his voice and said, "If I tell you how it came about, do you promise to keep your trap closed?"

Kenning promised, and so Nat gave him the whole tale about two misfits hiding behind a tree in a ballroom and joining forces. By the end of it, Kenning was wiping tears of laughter from his eyes, and drawing far too much attention with his guffaws.

"Quiet, you bonehead," Nat said, unable to keep back his own smile. "I don't want every Nosey Nellie in here to come over and ask what is so funny. You are *not* to repeat this, Reggie. I swear, if I hear one word—"

"Enough! I have promised to keep my lips sealed, and I shall. Even though it is by far the best story I've heard all Season. Lord, what a time the printmakers would have with it. I can see it now: scandalous prints with the two of you hiding behind a potted plant, sealing the deal with a kiss."

"It was a tree, I tell you. *A frigging orange tree.* But if I happen to see any such print making the rounds, Reggie, I shall be forced to call you out. And you know I am the better shot."

"I do, indeed. Reason enough to keep this entertaining tidbit to myself. It's a shame, really. I could dine out on that tale for months. But seriously, Nat, regardless of the unorthodox way it came about, I think you have chosen wisely. An impetuous choice, but a good one."

"I am glad you think so." Nat could not keep the sarcasm from his voice. He did not need anyone's approval of his choice of bride, not even Kenning's.

"I like her, Nat, and think she is just the right woman for you. You are alike in many ways, I think."

"How the devil are we alike? I'm a rough-spoken soldier with no social skills and a sullen nature. She is a lady, born and bred. Gentle and sweet. About as different from me as she could be."

"She puts herself at a sort of distance from the rest of the world. Because of the limp, no doubt. But you do the same, especially since Waterloo. I don't know how much she knows about that battle, or what it did to you—hell, I'm not sure I know, and I was there. But I think she understands what it is to have to shield oneself from the world, to guard against showing too much vulnerability. She understands you. And I'm guessing you have a better understanding of her difficulties than many others do. It's a good match, Nat."

They did not speak of Philippa again that evening, but Nat never forgot his friend's words. Was he right about Philippa understanding him because of her lameness? Kenning hadn't said it outright, but it was clear that he meant they understood each other because each was crippled. One crippled in body, one in mind. Was he right?

He had certainly felt drawn to her enough to hint of his troubles. He could not have, in good conscience, allowed her to agree to a marriage of convenience without knowing something of the truth. And she was smart enough from the beginning to realize his troubles related to Waterloo. She already knew almost as much as Kenning, though she had never asked for details and he'd never offered any. Nat did not want his weakness, his shame, to touch her in any way. He wanted to keep it apart from her.

Yet she did not want to be protected like that. She had been overly protected and patronized her whole life, and did not want that from him. She had said from the first that the reason she was willing to form this alliance with him was because he'd spoken honestly to her, and she hoped their marriage would be based on honesty. If he was to maintain a level of honesty with her, she would soon discover the depth of his pain and his shame. Strangely, that did not bother him as much as he'd expected. He hated for anyone else to know of his weakness, but he did not seem to mind that she would know.

Perhaps because she would understand? Cripple to cripple? No, he would not accept that word. She wasn't crippled. She merely had a limp. And he . . . well, he may be experiencing moments of confusion or weakness, but his mind was not crippled. He still had most of his wits about him, most of the time. Philippa would not give in to her disability, and neither would he, by God. He might not be ready to bare his soul completely to her, but he could learn from her. He could, and would, try to be a better man for her. A man worthy of her.

They entered the park a bit earlier than the fashionable hour to take advantage of the fragile sunshine, the first to be seen after a week of gloomy days. Philippa enjoyed having the parklands to themselves for a short time. She was admiring his profile as he expertly handled the team when he said, "Do you ever drive, Philippa? Are you allowed?"

"There is a groom at Harcott Manor who allows me to drive from time to time, when he can be sure no one will see and report us. William and Mamma have strict orders about such things, as you can imagine. They fear that I will injure myself."

"What about riding? Do you ride?"

"Oh, I love to ride. When I am atop a horse I feel like a whole person. His legs become mine, and I see the world from a grand height. It is thrilling to me. I am allowed an occasional ride at Harcott, but only on the slowest, gentlest mare, and only with an army of grooms and family members with me. It is all very sedate. Too sedate for the very smart habit I had made last year. Green velvet with lots of gold braiding. And a jaunty little hat with a feather that curves around my face. I look quite dashing in it, I'll have you know."

He smiled, and said, "More than merely dashing, I'd guess." He slid her a glance that raked her up and down in a most disconcerting manner. A tingly sort of heat trickled down her spine like warm honey. "And now you are going to tell me that same groom sometimes sneaks you out alone on a more spirited horse."

Philippa laughed. "He does indeed. Not often, for fear of losing his job. But I can coax him into allowing me a good ride from time to time."

"I should like to see you ride. When we are married, I will buy you a proper horse and we will ride about the estate together. I might even challenge you to a race or two. And you shall have as many dashing habits as you please."

All at once, there was a lump in her throat so high and hard she couldn't swallow, could barely even breathe. He was promising a level of freedom she'd never been allowed. Did he know how much that meant to her?

What a gift he was.

She ought to have known she would fall in love with him. He grabbed a small corner of her heart the moment he'd said she had a hell of a limp, and said it without any sympathy at all, merely as a statement of fact. Other women might have preferred words of love and devotion. Philippa much preferred a man who treated her like an ordinary woman with no disability, and no man had ever done so. Until Nat Beckwith. To him, it seemed her displaced hip was nothing more than a minor inconvenience. She had always treated it that way. She knew her limitations, but otherwise went about day-to-day living just as everyone else did. As best she could anyway, with well-meaning people constantly behaving as though she were an invalid and could do nothing for herself. When a man finally came along who refused to treat her with kid gloves, she was bound to fall in love with him. And, of course, she had done so. She was now thoroughly, irrevocably, head over heels in love with him.

"And in the meantime," he said, "I see no reason why you shouldn't have the pleasure of driving now and then. Would you like to take the ribbons now?"

"You are a wicked man, sir, tempting me with all my favorite things."

He held out the reins to her and she took them. He kept

a loose hold for a moment, until he saw that she knew how to manage the team, then allowed her full control. Philippa thought her face might crack from smiling. To have the power of such a fine team in her own hands was exhilarating, and more fun than she'd had in an age.

Life with Captain Beckwith was going to be breathtaking.

She would like to have given the horses their heads for a time, but the park had begun to fill up with the usual afternoon crowd. It was to be a dignified drive. This time.

Several people passed by in carriages or on horseback and nodded in their direction. Some even stopped to exchange a few words. The whole time, Nat allowed her to keep the reins, and showed no discomfort at being driven by a woman. When an officer in uniform rode up, introduced as Captain Baird, he joked about Nat relinquishing control to a female.

"I am in very capable hands, Baird," he said, "as you see. Miss Reynolds could have managed a supply wagon with ease."

"I do not doubt it. We could have used you in Spain, ma'am. It was good to see you at the club last night, Beckwith. You have been too long absent." After a few more pleasantries, he bowed to Philippa and rode on.

She handed the reins back to him. "I have had too much fun for one day. You will spoil me, sir."

He gave her a look that said he understood her true motive. "Silly woman. You can drive whenever you want. You need only ask."

"I know. Thank you, Nat.

He gave a mock bow. "Your servant, ma'am."

"I did not know you were part of a military club," she said. "It must have been nice to be among your fellow officers once again. Men who've been through the war with you."

He did not answer, but merely lifted one shoulder in a noncommittal acknowledgement of the question. She watched him closely, but he kept his eyes straight ahead, his lips in a tight line.

"You did not enjoy it at all, did you?"

He shook his head. "You know I dislike social situations, especially loud and boisterous ones."

It was more than that, she knew, but did not press him. She sat quietly at his side on the carriage seat. After long, silent moments, he said, "I don't fit in."

She looked at him, pleased that he said anything at all, hoping he would say more.

"I can't abide all the back-slapping," he said, "the singing, the toasts, and the are-we-not-magnificent-heroes attitudes. No one wants to actually speak of the war. Of the particulars of battle, I mean. They only want to speak of the glory of victory, not the costs. No one else . . ."

He clamped his lips together and shook his head as though he had no more to say on the subject, perhaps even thinking he'd said too much. But Philippa did not want to let the moment pass. She wanted him to know he could confide in her.

"No one else suffers as you do?"

He turned sharply and glared at her beneath deeply furrowed brows. "What do you know of my so-called suffering?"

"Very little, to be sure. But I know you struggle with demons of some kind. You told me so yourself. And since you spent most of your adult life soldiering, it is logical that your demons are war demons."

He nodded, but said nothing.

"I do not know what you may have experienced," she continued, "but it is clear to me that whatever it was affected you deeply. And you think because your fellow officers do not speak of it, that they were not similarly affected. You are wrong, though. You are not alone in your pain."

His frown deepened. "How do you know? How can you possibly know?"

"Because anyone who lived through the carnage of a fierce battle and came out unmoved would not be human. He would be an unfeeling automaton, without heart or soul. I doubt you would describe your friends in that way."

"No, of course not. They are all good, honorable men."

"Then they, too, have been affected by the wars. They just hide it better, that's all. And are too proud to speak of it. Men can be foolish creatures at times."

He did not respond, and returned his gaze to the path ahead. His brow remained furrowed, but not so much in anger. Instead he looked pensive. Philippa hoped he was considering her words.

"Please do not think you are alone in this, Nat. We are all human and fraught with frailties. Some are permanent, like my bent hip. Others are temporary and ultimately overcome. You will overcome yours. One day you will wake up and realize those demons are gone. Then, you can stop fighting them and live in peace again."

He turned toward her once more and said, "I hope you are right, Philippa, though I fear any such peace will be a long time coming."

"Then we shall wait for it together, and rejoice together when it comes."

He gazed at her intently, a slight frown on his face, then said, "If we were not on a public road in a crowded park, I would kiss you right now."

"And I would let you."

He smiled. "Later, then."

Oh, she hoped so.

The next evening, Nat escorted Philippa and her mother to a musical evening at the home of his sister Eugenia, Lady Thorpe. At his insistence, Genie had agreed not to patronize Philippa or her lameness, and she had been as good as her word. She'd been all that was kind and gracious, and Philippa had in turn charmed her. Within five minutes, they seemed to be fast friends.

"I like her, Nat," Genie whispered when Philippa was engaged in conversation with her friend Lillian Faulkner. "One is tempted to condescend to her lameness, but she does not encourage it, does she? She is no shrinking violet. And she makes me laugh."

"Me, too."

"Does she? Oh, I am so pleased to hear it. You have been too somber for too long. I do hope this is a serious courtship, Nat. You really should marry her. She will do you a world of good, I think."

"I intend to marry her," Nat said. "But her mother insists that we endure an entire godforsaken Season before we may do so. Lady Reynolds is a slave to appearances and Rules."

"So are most of us, my dear. But I am very pleased at your plans. You must allow me to hold a betrothal ball when you are ready to announce. Dearne House is much too stuffy, as is our brother. Our ballroom is much more comfortable. Oh, but wait. Perhaps a ball is inappropriate when the betrothed couple cannot lead the dancing. Should I arrange a large dinner party instead?"

"That is dashed good of you to offer, Genie. Go ahead and plan a ball. Philippa and I met at a ball. It is fitting that we should celebrate our engagement at one. Talk to Lady Reynolds about it. She will want to help with the planning."

When Philippa joined him again and he told her of Genie's ball, she beamed with pleasure. "How very kind of her. What a lovely family you have, Nat."

"You haven't met them all yet. Genie's the best of the lot. One or two of the others are downright harridans. Did I mention I have seven sisters?"

Philippa chuckled. "No, you did not."

"Worse, I am the youngest. A battalion of girls between Dearne and me. Damnation. Speak of the devil. Here comes Dearne himself, looking very lordly and imposing. That's his wife, Adelaide, beside him. Buck up, my girl, you are about to be introduced."

As his brother approached, people milling about waiting for the concert to begin stepped out of his path as though he were the Regent himself. Dearne had that way about him, an air of importance that sat comfortably upon his shoulders.

He'd been trained from boyhood to assume the earldom, and it showed.

Nat sketched a bow. "Dearne. Adelaide. Good to see you both. Allow me to present Miss Reynolds." Turning to Philippa, he added, "This is my brother, Lord Dearne, and his wife, Lady Dearne."

Philippa made a creditable curtsy. She must have been made to practice for years. One would hardly know she was lame. The fact that she favored her right hip was barely noticeable.

"Lord Dearne, Lady Dearne. I am pleased to meet more members of Captain Beckwith's family."

"And we are delighted to meet you," Adelaide said, offering a warm smile. "What a pretty dress. That shade of blue is the perfect complement to your lovely hair." She took Philippa's arm and steered her toward the music room. "Come, you must tell me the name of your modiste. I am most envious of the set of your sleeves."

And the two of them disappeared into the next room.

"Why do I get the feeling," Nat said, "that Philippa has been ushered out for your benefit? Did you ask Adelaide to sweep her away?"

"I would hardly call it a sweep," Dearne said, his brow furrowed into a deep frown. "That would require speed and grace, which your Miss Reynolds is sadly unable to accomplish."

"Careful, Frederick. You're a tick away from being out of line."

"I only meant to express regret that the poor girl's disability makes it difficult for her to move quickly."

"And your point?"

Dearne shrugged. "I simply mention it to remind you that many other unattached young ladies possess graces that Miss Reynolds will never be able to achieve. I trust you will give your attention to some of them."

"You told me to look about for a bride," Nat said. "I looked, and found Miss Reynolds. I intend to look no further."

Dearne's face grew red with rage. He disliked being defied, though in fact, Nat had not defied him. He'd done precisely as asked.

"Have you deliberately set out to thwart me, Nathaniel?"

"Quite the opposite, old boy. I am thwarting my own desires to address yours. I did not come to London willingly, did I? Ah, the musicians are tuning up. Let us find the ladies and hope that the soprano does not screech like camp trull."

Dearne mumbled something about coarse language that Nat chose to ignore as they entered the music room. He sought out Philippa's distinctive hair, and found her seated with her mother and Adelaide.

After introductions were made, Lady Reynolds, who was positively beaming, turned to Dearne and said, "My lord, I am beyond thrilled. Your countess has done us the very great honor of inviting Philippa and me to spend a few days at your villa in Richmond."

Dearne glowered at his wife. "Has she indeed?"

"Yes," Adelaide said, "I thought it would provide an opportunity for us all to become better acquainted. It is not our primary residence, Lady Reynolds, which is, of course, the earl's seat in Wiltshire. Nunbridge Park was built in the last century when it was fashionable to have a country home within easy reach of Town, so it is close enough that we will not lose too many days of the Season. Three or fours days at most, I should think. We shall invite your sons, Sir William and Mr. Edgar Reynolds, as well as whichever of Dearne's sisters is available. And Nathaniel, of course. It will be a cozy gathering, nothing formal. Please call on me tomorrow and we shall discuss the schedule and guest list."

Dearne uttered an exasperated huff. "It appears a *fait accompli*, my dear. You seem to have matters well in hand."

"Naturally. Come and sit down, Dearne. The music is about to begin. Nathaniel, you will wish to sit beside Miss Reynolds."

He did so, and when the music started, Philippa leaned

close and whispered, "Lady Dearne is very kind to invite us, don't you think? Mamma is in raptures."

"Adelaide is an excellent hostess, as I recall. I confess that I welcome a respite from the curst social whirl of London. It's a pretty little estate. You will like it, I think."

"I know I will." She surreptitiously slipped her hand into his. He entwined his fingers with hers and smiled.

Before the end of the evening, Nat had been dragged about by Eugenia, who wanted everyone to meet her brother the War Hero, a role he was loathe to play. Philippa, too, was introduced around, and though everyone was polite, several were cruelly, if unintentionally, condescending. She said nothing, but he knew she felt their patronizing deference deeply.

Nat managed to convince Lady Reynolds to allow him to escort Philippa home in his carriage while she attended another rout party with Adelaide. Lady Reynolds seemed so pleased with his solicitousness, not to mention the chance to spend more time with a countess, that she agreed without even bringing up the issue of propriety.

After Nat had settled Philippa on the carriage bench and climbed in beside her, he asked if she minded very much missing the rout party.

"Not at all. I find I am a bit tired."

"I thought as much. I wanted to slap some of those old biddies who didn't seem to think you could put one foot in front of the other without their help. Some people never quite know how to treat you, do they?"

"A great many people either smother me with unnecessary concern or keep their distance as though my lameness were somehow contagious."

"Idiots."

"Well-meaning ones, though."

"A friend recently told me that you and I are very much alike in the way we keep distance between ourselves and the rest of the world. Yours is not always self-imposed, though, is it? Idiots and fools impose that distance. It is their loss. They never get to see the warm, beautiful woman behind the limp. But I do. If we marry, Philippa, I will try never to deliberately put up walls between us. You may have to deal with me in my worst moments—my bouts of melancholy, my lack of patience, my damnable temper—and wish that I had indeed built a wall to hide behind. The first time we met, both of us were hiding from the world. I suspect there will be times when we will still want to do that. But let's never hide from each other."

"I will never hide from you, Captain. I have no wish to do so. I have never been more perfectly at ease with a gentleman."

After a few moments of comfortable silence, he said, "I do not know how you bear it here, Philippa. Town life is unsettling to me."

"How is it better in Oxfordshire?"

It was not, in fact. It was simply quieter there, with fewer opportunities to run into people he had no wish to see, and to whom he was forced to be polite. All things considered, however, living outside the military world was no easier in the country than in Town. He could find no joy in country life, no meaning, certainly no excitement. No life-or-death decisions, only decisions regarding which field to plow or how high to build a fence. He found the mundane nature of it stifling, even demoralizing.

"There is always something to keep me busy there. Digging drainage ditches, building new fences, repairing tenant roofs. It is not important work, by any means, but it keeps my mind and body occupied."

"Why is it not important?"

"I am accustomed to soldiering, where every day can be a life-or-death struggle. I cannot find purpose in ordinary work."

"You would rather be on the battlefield again?" Her big sherry-colored eyes were filled with incredulity tinged with sadness. "Putting your life, and the lives of your men, at risk?"

"God help me, I would." There. He'd said it. He'd finally confessed aloud to her, and himself, that he'd rather be back on a battlefield. And he was apparently about to confess more. "I would love nothing more than to put my life on the line once again, to rush headlong into battle, knowing I might not make it out alive."

"But why?" Her voice was tremulous, as though she were on the edge of tears. "Why would you want to risk your life like that?"

"To prove that I can. To prove that I still have the courage to do so."

"But *of course* you have the courage. Did you not prove it over and over again in your career, risking your life for your men and your country? Heavens, Nat, even I know of the bravery of the 52nd Foot. Some say 52nd turned the course of the battle, paving the path to final victory. And you led them, Nat. Not only at Waterloo but at countless battles in Spain and Portugal. I don't believe I have ever met anyone so courageous in all my life. There is surely no need to prove it. Certainly not to me." She paused and looked directly into his eyes. "Please tell me you have no need to prove it to yourself."

Oh, but he did. More than anything, he did. His inexplicable reaction to that final unprecedented French bombardment smacked of cowardice, and it had been tearing him apart inside.

He shook his head, as though denying her statement without actually doing so in words. "It's hard to explain," he said, "to those who have not experienced war. It sounds silly, I suppose, but life feels flat without that rush, that surge of energy that fills your blood and propels you into battle. I can find nothing here in England that gives me that same thrill. Dammit, Philippa. Am I insane, do you think?"

"No." She smiled and an expression of relief gathered in her eyes, as though she had in fact momentarily considered that he might indeed be mad. "No, you are not ready for Bedlam yet, Captain. I am sure it is simply a matter of learning to live a different kind of life. You need to find a new perspective. To find joy in things that do not threaten your existence. Learn to appreciate peacefulness."

Peace. He shook his head. Peace was killing him. "I wish I could be like you, Philippa. Content. Happy. I truly do. Sometimes I feel as if I might fly apart at the seams. I wish I could forget the wars and get on with my life."

"No, you should not forget. It is important to remember what happened, no matter how horrific. You will never forget the lives lost and ruined, but neither will you forget what you fought for, and how those sacrifices made our country safe. Don't try to forget. Try instead to remember well, and fight in other ways to make sure it never happens again."

"How did you get to be so wise?"

"I learned long ago that sometimes the best way to overcome pain is by staring it straight in the face."

He almost said that such things were easier said than done—dismissing that old adage about adversity building character—but realized how insulting that would be to her. She had certainly faced her own infirmities head on, and he was quite sure she was a better person for it. She was not pitiful or pathetic or needy. Quite the opposite, in fact. Could he learn from her example, or was he too damaged?

"Soldiers are not the only ones impacted by wars," she said. "May I take you somewhere tomorrow? I'd like to show you one of the ways I have found to give purpose to my life."

The curricle's bonnet was up against the threat of more rain when Nat drove them to their destination the following afternoon.

"I know you are feeling somewhat lost without the life-and-death struggle of war." Philippa waited for Nat to come around to her side of the curricle and help her down. After he did so, she said, "But there are more ways to find one's life threatened than at the end of a bayonet or rifle. There are daily battles to stay alive right here in London. This is Marlowe House."

"What is it? Looks like an old almshouse."

"It once was, I believe. But it has been greatly expanded and is now a facility for the widows of soldiers and their children."

Nat blinked owlishly. "Soldiers' widows?"

"The soldier husband and father was the sole source of support for many families," Philippa said as they walked toward the entrance. "When they lost him, they also lost his desperately needed income, no matter how meager it might have been. Some of the widows are able to find work—brutal unskilled labor with long hours and little pay. But others are forced into the lowest levels of existence—thievery, prostitution, and worse. The children fall under the thumbs of petty criminals, pimps, or ruthless chimney sweeps. It's a life of wretchedness, filled with despair, illness, hunger, and early death. Yet their husbands and fathers sacrificed their lives for us."

"Many a time I wrote letters for soldiers, to be enclosed with a portion of their pay and sent home to wives and mothers. I remember times when the pay was late—months late, sometimes—and those men would be frantic with worry. We tried to send back pay to the families of those killed, but were not always successful in locating them. And even if we did, there was always another battle to distract us, so the widows of the dead were, I am ashamed to admit, sometimes forgotten."

"They were forgotten by everyone, including the government. But a group of wealthy widows determined to do something for their less fortunate sisters. The Benevolent Widows' Fund has raised enormous amounts to support war widows and orphans. They took over and expanded this old almshouse and made it into a sort of halfway house where the families can stay until they can find honest work and a safe place to live. Marlowe House provides training for the women, to provide them with skills to find decent employment, and schools for the children. No one leaves Marlowe House, mother or child, without being able to read and write.

"I have been a volunteer here for two years, when Mamma allows it. I help out in the schoolrooms. It has been the most rewarding thing I have ever done. Would you like to come inside and see what we do?"

"I would indeed."

They toured the schoolrooms and kitchens, the various workshops where women were trained in sewing and house-keeping and gardening and more. They observed a class in session where women were being taught basic arithmetic. Philippa could see that Nat was impressed. It made her proud to know she had a small role in keeping this humanitarian project alive. She hoped Nat would understand and be proud of her, too.

After the tour, as they were thanking the supervisor for her time, a woman shyly approached and bobbed a curtsy. "Beggin' yer pardon, sir, but I 'eard as 'ow you was called Cap'n Beckwith. That right?"

"Yes, I am Beckwith. I was once a captain, though I have sold my commission. Is there something I may do for you, ma'am?"

"Oh, sir. It's right pleased I am t'make yer acquaintance. Name's Daisy Garth. My Alfie spoke real well o' yer, sir, in 'is letters from Spain. Didn't write 'em 'isself, o' course, but told whoever took down 'is words what t'say. An' 'e always 'ad summink nice ter say 'bout 'is Cap'n Beckwith. Right proud, 'e was, ter be under yer command, sir. Right proud."

Nat smiled at the woman. "Alfie Garth. Sandy hair, notch in his left ear, forever whistling through that big gap between his front teeth?"

Daisy Garth grinned, showing a similar gap. "That's 'im, all right. Gar, yer 'member 'im. Outa all them soldiers, yer 'member my Alfie."

"Of course I do. Who could forget that smile? He was a good soldier, ma'am. Worked hard and never complained.

He fought bravely and well. I was proud to have him in my regiment. He fell at . . . Orthez, wasn't it?"

"Yes, sir, so I were told. It mean a lot t'me, sir, that yer 'member 'im and 'as such kind words fer 'im. 'E'da been right pleased."

"And I am pleased to have met you, Mrs, Garth. I am glad you were able to find such a fine place as Marlowe House."

"I'da been dead fer sure wifout it, mos' like, an' me little uns, too. This place be a godsend fer all us living 'ere, an' no mistake."

"Orthez was over two years ago. Have you been here all that time?"

"Gor, no. I din't even know 'bout this place 'til six months ago or there'bouts."

"Then where did you—" He stopped as Philippa caught his eye and shook her head. It would not be wise for him to ask such questions of the women here. He would likely be appalled at the answers. And outraged.

Daisy Grath shrugged and dropped her eyes. "I managed. 'Ad to feed me babies, din't I? But now I'm learnin' fancy needlework an' 'ow to make patterns for clothes and such. They tell me I might be able to get me a position in a fine 'ouse with a gentry family, 'elping out with linens an' darnin' and maybe even makin' new clothes fer the children. Ain't that summink? Who'da thunk it?"

When they left Marlowe House, Nat wondered aloud if he might be able to find her a position at Dearne's estate, or maybe even his own.

Philippa smiled. Sometimes it took the pain of others to make one forget one's own difficulties.

Chapter Four

The next day, Nat was invited to join a party of Lady Reynolds's friends at Vauxhall. He hadn't been to the famous pleasure gardens since he was a young pup and had heard it was no longer as fashionable. He was, though, counting on all the dark walks still being there. He planned to lead Philippa down the darkest path he could find and finally kiss her. He was going to kiss her senseless, by God.

At every recent party or other social event he'd been dragged to, there had been no opportunity to sneak away and steal a kiss. Even that evening of Eugenia's musicale, when he'd escorted Philippa home in his carriage, or when they'd visited Marlowe House, it had not seemed the right time. The conversation had been too serious, too uncomfortable. A kiss would have been awkward at best.

He'd been wanting to kiss her for some time now. It fact, it was rather startling how much he looked forward to it. And to more than kisses.

When they'd made their bargain, he'd assumed their eventual physical intimacy would be comfortable and pleasant, but not heated. He had believed it would be a true marriage of convenience, with a solid core of friendship. But no passion. No fire. No rapture. He no longer believed that. His attraction to her had increased tenfold. And he was fairly certain she was not indifferent to him, in that way.

She was so sweet and innocent, though, having been kept in cotton wool like a china doll most of her life. And even though she clearly was not as fragile as everyone believed, Nat had no wish to frighten her with his own heated desire. It was time, though, to start getting her accustomed to his touch and his kisses. Vauxhall was the perfect venue for a first kiss.

After a cold meal of chicken, cheeses, custards, and the obligatory paper-thin ham, several members of the party left their supper box in the Grove to join in the dancing near the orchestra pavilion.

Nat approached Lady Reynolds. "If you have no objections, ma'am, I should like to take Philippa on a walk through the gardens."

Philippa beamed. "Oh, I should enjoy it above all things, Mamma."

"Do you really think you ought, my dear?" Lady Reynolds said. "You do not want to become overtired. You did a good bit of walking on Bond Street today."

"That was shopping, Mamma. There was hardly any walking at all. In fact, the only exertion involved was the trying on of a dozen bonnets." She turned to Nat. "I purchased the most fetching chip straw confection you ever saw. I plan to wear it to Lady Dearne's house party."

"I look forward to seeing it on you," Nat said.

Lady Reynolds frowned. "But Philippa, the gardens are vast here and the paths are long. If you tire your hip, you'll be in bed for a day or more recovering."

Nat had to stop himself from rolling his eyes. Devil take it, but that woman was insufferably imperious. It never ceased to amaze him that Philippa had somehow managed to maintain not only a cheerful disposition but a keen sense of humor while under her mother's domination.

"I believe," Philippa said, "that there are many benches and small pavilions throughout the gardens. I promise you I will stop and rest if I get too tired."

"And I promise to make her do so," Nat said. "She will come to no harm under my watch."

"I sometimes wonder, Captain," Sir William Reynolds interjected in a voice dripping with scorn, "if you fully appreciate our Pip's limitations. She cannot be always dashing about like other girls."

"I do indeed appreciate her limitations, sir," Nat replied with equal scorn. "But I also appreciate her strengths. I believe she can accomplish more than you give her credit for."

"Really, sir," the baronet said, "you have only known her for a short time. We have watched over her for her entire life. You must trust that we know what is best for her."

"When we marry, it will become my responsibility to watch over her, as you put it, and you must trust me to do so. A short walk along the garden paths will do her no harm. I promise to bring her back in one piece."

He did not wait for a response, but took Philippa by the elbow and led her out of the box.

"That was masterfully done, Captain."

Philippa could not stop smiling as they strolled along the wide public paths crowded with other groups and couples. She had heard tales of darker, more private paths deeper in the gardens, and hoped that was where they were headed. She was determined to be kissed tonight.

"I sometimes wonder that they ever let you out of the house," Nat said. "God's teeth, Philippa, how do you bare it?"

"I am used to it. It is the only life I've known. And all that over-protectiveness is based on love. They care for me."

"So do I, but I hope I never smother you with so much concern. When we are married, I should like to better understand your physical condition. I do not wish to make assumptions regarding your stamina that may not be true."

"You understand my condition very well, Captain. Do you know that I feel more steady on my pins with you than with almost anyone else? But I will certainly arrange for you to meet with my physician."

Philippa felt steady with him because Nat always compensated for her limp by adjusting his weight and the angle of her arm in a way that made her feel that she was walking almost normally, with less of a lurch. It was almost a natural adjustment that he seemed to do without conscious thought. Or perhaps it was a very conscious thing, a more subtle, less obvious solicitude. Longer walks did sometimes cause her hip to ache and her limp to become more pronounced, but Nat always seemed to be aware of the slightest sign of fatigue, and stopped when he noticed it. Best of all, he showed no shame in being seen walking with a woman with so jerky a step. Her limp did not appear to embarrass him at all. Instead, he seemed pleased to have her on his arm. Even as some curious glances followed them as they strolled down the Grand Walk, he was unmoved by the attention.

Soon, after many turns through the grid of pathways, the pretty lanterns hanging from trees had become more sparse, and the paths darker as a result. Philippa experienced an odd fluttering in her stomach, and lower. She was almost certain she was going to be kissed for the first time in her life.

Nat turned down a dark path to the left. There were no other people on this particular path, as far as she could see. And no more lanterns. They were quite alone and in the dark.

"Should I be worried, sir, that we seem to have lost our way in the darkness?" She sent him a smile that told him she was not in the least worried.

He stopped and leaned back against a tree, tugging her

close up against him. "I promised your family that I would bring you back uninjured. I did not, however, mention other sorts of dangers that may lurk in the darkness. I—"

A sudden explosion rent the air and brilliant light filled the sky.

And Philippa was thrown to the ground.

Breathless and more than a little stunned, Philippa found herself crushed beneath Nat's formidable weight. At the sound of exploding fireworks directly overhead, he had moved instinctively to cover her, to shelter her with his own body. When he lifted his head and looked down at her, his eyes shone with the ferocity of a soldier on alert. At the next explosion, he shifted to cover her head with his shoulders.

His breath came in shallow gasps and his body trembled. He had not yet shaken off the sense of danger. His focus was elsewhere, someplace beyond her, beyond now.

She had not been wrong in the assessment of his character that she had given her mother on that first day: he would indeed protect her at all costs, even when the threat to her was unrealized, and he most definitely had not yet shaken off the horrors of war. Ah, Nat. And now, no doubt he would be embarrassed at his overreaction to the noise, at the uncharacteristic display of vulnerability.

Philippa was almost overcome with tenderness for him. She wanted nothing more than to comfort Nat, to show him that she was pleased at how quick he was to protect her, and that there was no actual danger. "Nat." She spoke against his shoulder. "It's only fireworks, nothing more." She reached up and touched the back of his head, threading her fingers through the soft hair at his nape. "Nat. Nat."

The sound of his name seemed to bring him back to earth. He raised his head and shoulders and gazed down at her with a bewildered expression, followed almost instantly by a look of sheer horror. He quickly rolled off her. "Good God." He rose to his knees beside her and his assessing gaze swept up and down her body. "Are you all right? Have I hurt you? Is your hip injured?"

She looked up at him, her eyes filled with concern. "I am fine. Perhaps a grass stain or two, but nothing more."

"Damnation. What have I done?" He was mortified, and more than a little frightened. He'd heard what his weakened brain had believed to be artillery fire and had reacted without conscious thought. It did not occur to him that he was in the middle of London a year after the French defeat. All he'd known was that there was someone he had to protect. Someone precious. His soldier's reflexes had taken over, throwing his body into action. For the merest instant—at least he hoped to God it was only an instant—he was no longer at Vauxhall but was on another battlefield, reaching for the sword that should have been at his side but was not.

He'd had similar episodes in the past, but had never before put a woman in danger. A lame woman. He'd pushed a defenseless lame woman to the ground, for God's sake. Over a bloody fireworks display.

He ought to be shot.

He grabbed her hand and pulled her up to a sitting position. He'd never been more mortified in his life. "I am so sorry, Philippa. I didn't mean to hurt you."

"I know. And you didn't. Truly, I am fine."

"It was an unconscionable thing to do. Do you really have grass stains on your dress? Dammit all, your mother will kill me. And I will deserve it."

Philippa examined her skirts. "I do not think there are any stains. Just a few leaves."

He helped her to brush them off. She gave a little squeak of alarm and Nat thought he'd hurt her, but saw her eyes fixed on a rather large spider that crawled up her skirts. He flicked it off along with the leaves, and she uttered a sigh of relief. How odd that she seemed more afraid of a spider than the brute who'd just thrown her to the ground.

"If we'd been seen," he said. "I could have been arrested for assault. Thank heaven we were not on a more public path."

She looked up and smiled. She actually smiled at him

after he'd just knocked her down. "I've always heard the dark paths at Vauxhall can be quite dangerous."

"I don't believe being knocked to the ground by a maniac is the sort of danger normally encountered here. God, Philippa. What must you think of me?"

She reached out and placed her fingers against his cheek in a gesture so tender it was enough to make a hardened man weep. "I think you are a good man born to protect those around him. Your reaction was perfectly logical for a soldier accustomed to taking cover at the sound of gunfire. I ought to have warned you about the fireworks, but I assumed you knew. You are not to be faulted for trying to protect me. In fact, if we are to be married, I will depend upon it."

"Ha. You cannot still want to marry me now that you have seen firsthand that I might not be entirely sane."

"Of course you are sane. Just a bit battle worn. And yes, I do still want to marry you."

"But what if this happens again and I really do hurt you? I don't know if you should feel safe around me. You ought to be afraid."

"I'm not afraid of you, Nat. How could I be? You would never hurt me."

"Not deliberately."

"Not at all."

He took her hand away from his face, turned it, and kissed the palm. "I do not deserve you, Philippa."

"No, you deserve much more."

He pulled her to her feet, a bit awkwardly due to her bad hip, then leaned back against the tree he'd used earlier when he was about to kiss her. After making such a fool of himself, he had no right to kiss her now. But he still wanted it. He wanted her.

He needed her.

He gathered her close and put his lips to hers.

Philippa's heart raced. It was all that she'd expected, and more. His lips were surprisingly soft and supple. And constantly moving, as he seemed to explore her mouth, first from one direction, then another. She had not expected that. She'd assumed a kiss was two mouths latching onto each other in a firm, possessive hold. This gentle exploration was more sensuous than she could ever have imagined. He reached around her waist, holding her close and steady, so she would not sink bonelessly to the ground, as she feared she might.

Her fingers threaded through his beautiful golden hair, relishing the silky softness of it. He deepened the kiss, pulling her closer, moving one arm down, down, over the curve of her bottom and below, finally lifting her slightly so she was pressed tightly against him, against the hardness that both shocked and excited her.

His lips slid away from hers and trailed down her jaw and throat, finding sensitive spots she'd never known she had. Boldly, she arched her neck to give him better access.

Philippa breathed deeply as his mouth worked miracles, taking in the masculine scent of him: hints of bay rum, leather, horse, linen starch, and something warm and musky and uniquely Nat. She would be able to close her eyes and know him anywhere.

Finally, he pulled back slightly and looked down into her eyes. "I am sorry, Philippa. After such an ignominious display, I ought not to have done that. But I have wanted to kiss you so badly for so long. After . . . what happened, I couldn't stop myself."

"Please do not apologize, Nat. I wanted it, too. I have never been kissed before, you know."

"No, I did not know." He ran the backs of his fingers along her cheek. "But now that the first kiss is over, all the next ones should be easier, less frightening."

"I was not frightened. I wanted you to kiss me, Nat, and I enjoyed it. In fact, if you would like to do it again, I would not object."

He grinned boyishly, and her heart turned over in her chest. "Let's see if the second kiss is better than the first."

And it was. So was the third, and the fourth, and the fifth.

* * *

Lord Dearne's villa in Richmond was in fact a rather grand estate, at least to Philippa's eyes. Nat told her it was a Palladian villa in the Roman style, built by a former earl who'd been inspired by his Grand Tour in Italy. She could not imagine what the earl's country seat must be like, if it was considered to be even more grand. Her own family was not without a degree of wealth, but she suspected it could not compare to the fortunes of an earl.

She was glad to be marrying a younger son, which was much less intimidating. But then she remembered that Nat was the earl's heir. Philippa might one day be a countess. And this estate, and others, might be hers. It was a heady notion, but one she would not dwell on. As Nat had told her brother, the earl was young and in good health. There would be no inheritance for many, many years. Which was perfectly agreeable to Philippa. She was not ready to be a countess.

The gathering was not quite as cozy as she'd expected. Besides her own family—Mamma, William and his wife, and her younger brother Edgar—there were several of Nat's sisters. Lady Thorpe, Lady Sutcliffe, Lady Hilliard, and their husbands. Other friends of the family had also been invited. Lord and Lady Marchdon and their daughter, Lady Camilla. Lord and Lady Randolph and their daughter, Lady Serena. And, much to Philippa's delight, Lillian Faulkner and her parents had been invited. Lady Dearne said she wanted Philippa to have at least one friend among the guests, and hoped she would enjoy the company of the other young ladies as well. She was, as Nat said, an excellent hostess.

Despite her efforts to make the party perfect, Lady Dearne could not control the weather. They had all hoped the sun would come out after so many weeks of chilly gloom and rain, but they were not to be so fortunate. The skies darkened and the heavens opened up during the first afternoon of the party. Lady Dearne despaired of having to cancel picnics and riverside breakfasts, but Philippa did not mind. It was pleasant just to spend time with Nat, away from the bustle of Town, in a setting more comfortable for him.

Over the last few weeks, Philippa had seen his forbidding demeanor begin to soften, ever so slightly. He still, she knew, disliked *ton* events with their endless insipid conversations and false flattery and forced gaiety, for he commented on it privately to her often enough, and would say as much, bluntly, to anyone who happened to ask him. But he was also somewhat less stiff and uncomfortable than he'd been when she first met him. Nat would probably never enjoy being out in society, which he found frivolous and artificial, but he was apparently becoming more accustomed to it. As long as she was at his side. He seemed to treat her like an anchor, never wanting to be too far from her. Others no doubt thought he was overly protective of her because of her lameness. But Philippa knew he wanted her nearby for his own sake, not hers.

"You ground me," he'd said to her after a particularly tedious party. "Without you by my side, or at least nearby, I would lose my temper a thousand times at one of these curst events."

She did not understand how she provided him with that security, or why he needed it, but she was glad she was able to help him make his way back into the world.

In spite of the incessant gloom, she and Nat took long walks along the river and through the estate gardens. Philippa's family fussed and complained that he was overtiring her, or that the damp air would cause her hip to ache. Even Lady Dearne and Lady Sutcliffe joined in the general concern for her health. It was only Lady Thorpe who seemed to understand, as Nat did, that she did not need or want to be so cosseted.

On the third day in Richmond, when it appeared there would be only more gloom but no rain, Nat invited Philippa to go for a walk along the riverside. As usual, her mother objected.

"I am sorry, Captain, but I cannot agree to it. You are forcing our Philippa into too much exercise and exertion. You forget, I think, that she is lame."

Dear God, but Philippa was tired of this same conversation every time Nat wanted to do anything outdoors with her. He repeated his usual assurances, but Mamma was relentless in her objection. It might rain. She might slip and fall. She might catch a chill. The damp might cause her hip to seize up. She might overtire herself and be forced to take to her bed.

Philippa could not take it anymore.

"Really, Mamma, I am not an invalid." The anger in her voice surprised her, but she had been pushed too far. "I know what I can and cannot do. So does the captain. He does not overtire me. In fact, I have never enjoyed myself so much as I have this Season since meeting him. Please do not ruin it for me." It was unlike her to speak up like this, to question her mother's solicitude. But she felt she had to take a stand. "I am sorry, Mamma, but you must trust me not only to know my limitations, but also to know what I *can* do. I am not stupid. I have no wish to cause myself harm. If any of those things you worry about does happen to me, it will be my fault and I will suffer the consequences. But the risk is worth it, Mamma. Please, let me decide."

Her mother was apparently struck dumb. She stared at Philippa as if she did not recognize her. Finally, with a parting glower at Nat, she said, "Do as you wish, then."

And so they set out along the river. "Well done," Nat said.

But Philippa was secretly ashamed. Her mother loved her and only wanted to protect her. "No, it was not well done. I should not have lashed out at her like that, especially in front of Lady Dearne and the other guests. I will apologize to her when we return."

"You are kindhearted, Philippa, but do not be sorry for standing up for yourself. When we are married, I will expect you to stand up to me. I will probably try to dominate you because I am so accustomed to command. But you must never fear to put me in my place. If I ever become overbearing, I expect you to tell me so."

Philippa offered a smart salute. "Yes sir, Captain, sir."

During the course of their river walk, they came across a fallen tree that provided a comfortable bench, and they sat and watched the river traffic. Conversation turned to the various party guests, and Nat expressed pleasure that she had her friend Lillian at hand. "She does not patronize you like everyone else does," he said. "That is no doubt why she is your close friend."

"That's exactly right. We've been friends since we were schoolgirls. I can be open and frank with her. She knows how I feel about having my lameness be the center of attention. She knows that I am more than a girl with a limp. As you do."

"You are much more than that," he said. "You are a beautiful woman, Philippa. A beautiful, desirable woman."

He took her in his arms and kissed her.

It was not like the other kisses, gentle and exploring. This time, it was urgent and ruthless and heated. He coaxed her lips open and set up a dance with her tongue that sent her mind reeling with shock. It was a ravishment of her mouth, inside and out. Dear heaven, she'd never imagined a kiss could be like this. She gave herself up to his mastery, submitting to this new intimacy, allowing him to plunder her depths as she sank into a sea of sensation.

After long moments, he rested his forehead against hers. "God, Philippa, you do not know what you do to me. I had no idea I was entering into a bargain with a firebrand when we met behind that absurd orange tree."

"I hope you are not disappointed, sir."

He smiled and nipped her ear. "Silly girl. I could not be more pleased with you. And to think, I found you after only thirty minutes into my first ball. I must have been born under a lucky star after all."

And he kissed her again.

* * *

"He is certainly an attractive man."

Philippa pulled her gaze away from Nat—heavens, she really must try to stop staring so obviously—and turned to Lillian, who sat beside her on the terrace while they watched the gentlemen play a game of cricket on the lawn. She could not watch him now without recalling his lips and his hands and how he made her feel. Unable to suppress a delighted grin, she said, "He is gorgeous, isn't he?"

And he was hers. This golden god with the silvery eyes had pledged himself to her. He displayed strength and grace on the makeshift playing field, put together at a moment's notice when the sun deigned to peek through the clouds for a moment. Watching all that masculine vigor and health made Philippa wonder if it was fair that he should be saddled with a small women with a bent hip. He really ought to have someone as strong and healthy as he was.

These tiny doubts had begun to niggle at her conscience during the stay in Richmond. There were so many pretty young women here to remind her of how unworthy she was to have a man like Nat.

But then there were his kisses, which had become like a potent drug to her. A man would not kiss a girl like that if he felt her unworthy, would he?

"Yes, he is handsome," Lillian said. "But is he not a bit too . . . aloof? Even stern? Mamma says he has been in seclusion in the country this past year and there are rumors that he might have suffered some sort of . . . injury at Waterloo."

"No need to worry, Lillian. He was not injured. His regiment was important to the final victory but suffered few casualties. All his parts are intact, I assure you." At least she assumed they were. She had no reason to believe otherwise.

"But there are other sorts of injuries," Lillian said. "I understand that head injuries, for example, can cause more than physical harm."

"You think he might have been struck on the head and lost

his senses?" When Lillian blushed, Philippa felt a surge of anger. Is this what people thought of him? That he was no longer completely sane? "And I suppose being seen to court a cripple further encourages the idea that he is not quite right in the head?"

"Oh no, Philippa, I did not mean—"

"Dear God, Lillian, I hope you will put any such notion right out of your mind. It's rubbish, I tell you. He is as sane as you or I. Captain Reynolds fought in one of the worst battles ever, and many more before that one. Can you even begin to imagine what he saw and did? Having to kill or be killed. Watching his men blown to bits, and friends fall under enemy fire. Did you hear they ran out of carts to carry away the dead? That bodies lay on the field for days before they could all be recovered? How would you feel if you'd had to live through that? None of us would be quite the same, would we?"

"I . . . I hadn't thought of that. It's just that most other soldiers—"

"—strut about like cocks of the walk, inviting glory and adulation. To be honest, Lillian, I suspect all of them are changed from the war, deep inside themselves. They would have to be, wouldn't they? Most of them cover it up well, at least in public. I think Captain Reynolds finds it more difficult than others to ignore the change in himself. Or perhaps he saw worse carnage than most, I don't know. But just because he is more obviously changed than other soldiers does not mean he is insane. You must not judge him for having strong feelings."

Lillian placed her hand over Philippa's. "Oh, my dear friend. You are in love with him, aren't you?"

Philippa felt her cheeks flame, and looked away. "I am very fond of him, Lillian, and I admire him a great deal. Best of all, he never treats me as an invalid."

"Ah." Lillian smiled. "Then of course you are in love with him."

Philippa squeezed her friend's hand. "I think, Lillian, that meeting Captain Reynolds quite by chance behind a potted orange tree may be the best thing that has ever happened to me."

Lillian gave her a fond smile, tinged with the merest hint of trepidation. "I hope you are proved right, my dear. And I swear, if he makes you unhappy, soldier or no soldier, he will have me to deal with."

Chapter Five

"Damn. Your mother was right."

Nat looked at the dark clouds gathering overhead. When he'd announced he was taking Philippa for another walk—because it was the only way they seemed to be able to spend time alone together—Lady Reynolds had muttered something about rain, but she had stopped fighting him. He suspected she would be happy if Philippa caught a chill or was injured simply so she could say, "I told you so." But she had been right this time. It was most definitely going to rain. And very soon.

"We'll be drenched when we return," he said, "and your mother will gloat."

"She probably will. Oh dear, I felt a few drops already. We'd better hurry."

Nat took her firmly by the arm. He didn't mind if they got wet, but the last thing he wanted was for Philippa to lose her balance on the wet path.

"It is times like this," she said in an amused voice, "that I wish I could run. Is there perhaps a large tree we could take shelter under?"

"There is something better than that. We could reach the folly on the east garden if we hurry. I know a short cut."

"Let's go!"

She set a faster pace than he would have liked, but he kept her as steady as possible. Damn, she was amazing. No, she was not graceful, but she certainly had more strength and energy than many believed. Such a woman should never be coddled like an invalid.

The next turn in the path brought the domed and pillared folly into view. It was a circular Palladian building known as the Temple of the Muses. Corinthian columns supported a gadrooned roof from which the dome rose in bronze splendor. On the outer wall of the structure was a series of nine niches, each filled with a life-sized statue of one of the Muses.

Nat guided Philippa up the short stairway into the entrance, set between the niches of Melpomene and Polyhymnia. Once inside, they shook out their coats and hats and laughed at the folly that had brought them to a folly.

"Oh, it is lovely," Philippa said as she looked around the circular room.

The walls and floors were set in patterns of varied colors of marble. Cushioned benches lined the walls, and glass roundels were set above them to bring in light, when there was sunshine. There was none today.

"This little folly has often been used for small parties," Nat said. "Our mother used to set out tables around the central pit, and have dinner served in here."

Philippa pointed to the circular pit in the center of the room, lined with darkened brick. "This is a fire pit?"

"Yes. And see." He pointed upward. "There is a chimney opening in the center of the dome. My grandfather, the old earl, thought the place was too cold and had the pit built.

There is a storage closet over here. Let me see if the gardeners still keep dry wood inside. Ah, well done. A good supply. Shall I build us a fire to keep warm?"

"Yes, thank you. Whoever thought we would need a fire in June?"

Nat built up a roaring good fire and they warmed their hands on it. He found some of his mother's collapsible chairs in another closet, and set them near the fire. He shrugged out of his jacket and draped it over a chair.

"Give me your pelisse, Philippa. I'll hang it here to dry."

He helped her out of the coat and hung it beside his own. When he turned back toward her, he saw that the thin white muslin of her dress was damp from the rain and clinging to her every curve. His groin sprang to life at the sight.

Philippa was small in stature and her frame, though more slender than plump, was nicely rounded. In all the right places. How on earth was he to resist her?

And was there any reason why he should? They were to be married, after all.

"Your dress is wet," he said. "Should we take it off and let it dry before the fire?"

She looked down at her dress and must have realized what was revealed, because her face and neck flushed pink. "You want me to take it off?" Her voice trembled.

"Only if you want to."

"I think I do, but I'm a bit frightened. I know what will happen."

"Do you?"

"I think so. Not from any firsthand experience, of course."

Nat smiled at her attempt to cover her anxiety with humor. "Philippa, my dear girl, nothing will ever happen between us that you do not want. I promise you. Will you let me kiss you?"

She opened her arms, and he stepped into them. He did not kiss her right away, but just held her close, his chin resting atop her head. Philippa's nose pressed against his waistcoat, and she breathed in the familiar scent of him. His arms banished the chill, and she thought she could have stayed here, with him holding her like this, forever. After a moment, he lifted her chin with a finger, and touched his lips to hers.

He kissed her sweetly and tenderly, and she almost wept with love for him. He had implied there could be more between them if she wanted, but he was gentle with her, not pressing for anything she wasn't willing to give.

But she *was* willing. God help her, she was. She loved him and wanted to be as close to him as possible. Although it shocked her to realize it, she was ready for him to do anything and everything to her. But he would not, unless and until she let him know that she wanted it.

She wrapped her arms more tightly around his neck, and teased his lips with her tongue, seeking entrance. He obliged her, and the kiss deepened, and quickly became lush and heated.

When he pulled away, panting, she tried to pull him back, but he stepped away to strip off his waistcoat and neckcloth. She could see the golden brown skin of his throat through the open neck of his shirt, and she wanted to kiss him there, to taste his skin. Where had such an idea come from? She giggled softly to imagine how brazen she'd become. In the next moment, he pulled off his shirt, and she was spellbound at the sight.

He was beautiful. Broad-shouldered, slim-waisted, well-muscled, with skin bronzed from the sun, and a light dusting of golden hair on his chest. Dear Lord, he was perfect.

And she was not.

How could she bare herself to this perfect man?

He stepped close to her and turned her around so she was facing away from him. He fingered the tapes at the back of her bodice and said, "Shall I?"

And all at once a great sob escaped from her. She covered her mouth with her hand and walked away from him. Oh God, she hadn't meant to cry. How mortifying. She blinked furiously, trying to stop the tears, but a few managed to run down her cheeks. She was ruining everything.

Nat came up behind her and touched her shoulder. "What is it, my dear. Did I frighten you?"

"No. No, of course not. It is just . . ."

"Just what, sweetheart?"

"I am bent, you know. Crooked. My hip . . ."

He turned her around and took her in his arms. "I've lost count of the number of scars I have," he said. "Saber wounds. Gun shots. Got in the way of a French bayonet at Bussaco. That one almost killed me. A supply wagon mule once bit me in the leg."

He felt her chuckle and knew the storm had passed. "I'm not perfect, either, Philippa. But I am ready to give myself to you completely, scars and all, if you will have me."

She looked up at him, her eyes still bright. "You know I will."

He kissed her again and the heat flared between them almost instantly. She wanted this, he knew, but she was an innocent, and insecure about her body. He would try to take it slow, but at the moment, he was on fire for her. Crooked hip and all.

Once she was almost limp in his arms, he set her gently aside and pulled several of the bench cushions onto the floor beside the fire. He looked at her and raised an eyebrow in question. She bit her lip and nodded.

He helped her out of her dress, and she stood before him in her chemise and stays, looking diminutive and lovely and very innocent. He unlaced her stays from behind, and as the corset fell to the floor, he caught her breasts in his hands. They were soft and round and perfect. He teased them with his fingers while he kissed her neck and shoulders, and her soft moans of pleasure were almost his undoing.

He turned her in his arms and kissed her deeply, while his hands slipped the straps of her chemise over her shoulders and down her arms. She gave a little cry of alarm when it slid to the floor. She was naked now, except for her stockings and garters.

Nat stepped back so he could gaze at her, but she instinctively covered herself. He took her hands and held them out. "Don't hide from me, Philippa. You are very beautiful."

And she was. Yes, her pelvis was tilted and one thigh was more muscled than the other, but her curves were quite luscious, her breasts high and round with dark nipples, and her skin was snowy white and flawless. The triangle of hair covering her sex was dark red and thick. She was perfectly, deliciously lovely.

"I think we will leave your stockings on," he said, thinking how erotic she looked wearing nothing else. "But there is one thing more I want to see. Can we let your hair down?"

Thankfully she did not wear a complicated arrangement today. It was the matter of removing a few pins and uncoiling a long plait, and the beautiful red tresses fell almost to her waist. He lifted them in his hands, wrapped them around his arms, and buried his nose in their depths.

It was too much. He could wait no longer.

In a matter of seconds, he'd stripped off his boots and pantaloons and small clothes. Her eyes widened, and he allowed her to study him, to accustom herself to his nakedness. And his erection. "I am all yours, Miss Reynolds."

"And I am yours, sir. All yours."

Nat lifted her into his arms and laid her gently on the cushions. He stretched out beside her and began to slowly stroke her breasts while he kissed her neck and shoulders. Soon, his mouth had replaced a hand and he teased her cold, puckered nipple with the warmth of his tongue. Philippa had never felt anything like it. Her whole body trembled and tingled, from her toenails to the roots of her hair. Her breath caught. Her head fell back. Her body arched. She was almost delirious with pleasure. When one hand snaked down her belly, she moaned. When his fingers found her most secret, private place, she gave an involuntary jerk of astonishment. She knew in that instant that she had been waiting all her life for such sweet astonishment, and from a man who was not only beautiful, but gentle and patient with her innocence. She was ready, though, to give up her innocence. She leaned into him to see what other delicious surprises he had in store.

He did not disappoint. His hands and mouth stirred up almost unbearable sparks of sensation, no quarter given. He gave attention to every part of her body. Her hair, which he seemed to adore, her neck, her shoulders, her breasts. His hands skimmed her thighs and hips and belly in ways that made her forget that she was not perfect. He made her feel perfect.

And she touched him, too. Shyly at first, but more boldly as he encouraged her to explore.

Finally, he lay over her and nudged her knees apart. "Are you afraid?" he asked.

"No." Anxious, excited, but not afraid. She would never be afraid with Nat.

"It will probably hurt this first time. I will try to be gentle."

He took her mouth first in another lush, languorous kiss in which his tongue moved in and out in a way that sent heat rushing through her veins. All the while he gently urged her knees apart and she felt his erection hot and hard against her. When his fingers reached down again to her sex and began to circle a tiny bud of pleasure, her body arched off the floor and she cried out in surprise. This touch, this new touch, stimulated her in a way she could not have imagined. Tension built and swelled until she was mindless with pleasure and practically thrashing against his hand. And finally the tension uncoiled and reached a peak of explosive sensation she had not known to expect.

"Oh, Nat." Her breath came in pants so she could barely speak. "I had no idea."

"There's more to come, darling."

He kissed her again, and before the kiss ended, he had entered her and made her his own. There was a brief instant of pain, the sense of stretching, a still moment while he allowed her to adjust to him, but as soon as he began to move in her, it was all pleasure and more new sensations, and a profound intimacy she had never imagined.

As his rhythm increased, she felt waves of hot sensation overtake her again, and soon another explosion had her arching and bucking against his thrusts, and crying out his name. He uttered his own cry soon afterward as he reached his own peak of pleasure.

They lay entwined and panting for several long, languorous minutes. Finally, he moved to his side and pulled her up against him. The feeling of his firm chest against her soft breast was still a fresh miracle. She would be happy if they never moved again, if they lay here together for all eternity.

"Are you all right?" he asked.

"More than all right. I am . . . dazzled."

"And your hip?"

"Is fine. You made me forget all about it."

He ran his fingers along the edge of her hip, then over her breast. "I will be happy to make you forget as often as you like, ma'am. And on a proper bed. Without the wind sweeping down on us."

"The wind. Oh, Nat. It has stopped raining. We must go. I want to stay, but we must go."

Nat sighed and sat up. "I know. Soon."

He kissed her again, slowly and deeply. She was delicious, his Philippa. And he was mad for her. He wanted her again, and was pleasantly startled to realize that he was ready. But it was her first time and she would be sore, perhaps. And Lady Reynolds would soon be sending out a search party.

"I suppose now I have to figure out how to get you put back together so you don't look as though you've been tumbled in a folly."

Before he could stand, she stopped him with a hand on his arm. "Thank you, Nat. I never thought I could have this. Not that I actually knew what it was. But I never dreamed I would know this kind of pleasure."

"Neither did I, Philippa. Who would have thought that

two misfits given to hiding behind trees could find so much pleasure together?"

"It was fate."

"And the sweetest bargain ever struck."

He stood alone on the terrace after dinner the next evening, enjoying a cheroot, and musing on the changes in his life.

Everything about his life was changing. Everything he'd hated about himself and what he'd become since Waterloo was changing, slowly but irrevocably. It had all started when he'd first met Philippa while hiding in that damned ballroom. From the moment she'd spoken to him, nothing had been the same. Or ever would be.

Nat had allowed himself to wallow in self-loathing and doubt for a year. Now, he wanted more from life. Philippa made him want more. She'd found the empty place in his heart, the one he kept carefully hidden, the one filled with disappointments and fears and impossible dreams. She'd swept all that clean and taken up residence with her hope and cheer and fierce courage, her endless possibilities. He did not know if he could ever again be the man he once was, but he could certainly improve on the morose creature he'd become since Waterloo. With Philippa by his side, he believed he might ultimately be able to grow beyond the aftereffects of battle and become a new, stronger person he could be proud of.

When they'd made their bargain, he had thought she was a safe choice. Not insipid or giggly. Not clingy or possessive or needy. Not dramatic or complicated. And despite a physical flaw, she did not wallow in self-pity. A perfectly ordinary woman with whom he could share a comfortable life. A safe choice.

Instead, he'd fallen alarmingly in love with her, and that changed everything.

He found himself smiling at that heady realization when he heard the terrace doors open. His brother came to stand beside him.

"Wretched weather," Dearne said as he looked over the gardens below. "Dashed cool for this time of year. Haven't had a full day of sunshine for months. Heard some crops are already suffering. It's an odd thing, isn't it?"

"Very odd."

"Almost as odd as this damned foolish courtship of yours."

"There is nothing at all odd about it. Philippa is a perfectly fine young woman and I am lucky to have her."

"Balderdash," Dearne said, his lips curling into a sneer. "I know about the ramshackle way this courtship came about. Eugenia told me—"

"Damn her, she was not supposed to—"

"—and I must say it is a very odd business indeed. What the devil were you thinking, Nat? Oh, I know you hated the idea of diving into the Season and the marriage mart, but I thought you understood why it was necessary."

"Of course I understood. You told me often enough."

"I can only assume that you did not, in fact, understand. I must say I am not entirely surprised that you cooked up a convenient bargain with a perfect stranger in order to avoid the marriage mart. But she is a cripple, Nat! How could you have been so stupid? Did you not know she was a cripple? Did she somehow hide it from you until an agreement was made, and then you felt obliged to go along with it?"

"God's teeth, Frederick, you can be such an ass. Of course I knew about her lameness. It doesn't matter to me. What the hell does it matter to you? Are you ashamed to think of a woman with a limp one day being the Countess of Dearne? If that is all that worries you, then I don't see the problem. If she becomes the countess, it means that you, dear brother, will have passed on to your heavenly reward. So I don't see that it should make any difference to you whether or not the new Lady Dearne walks with a limp. You won't be around to be offended by it."

"Now who is being an ass? You know very well it is more than that."

"I do not know. Perhaps you had better explain it to me. I'm only an ignorant soldier without any social skills or ready repartee. There must be something in your meaning that is too subtle for the likes of me."

"Don't be patronizing. You know precisely what I mean. My request was that you marry and *set up your nursery*. It is all about an heir, as you well know."

"And? I still see no problem."

"By God, you really are thick, aren't you? Or do you deliberately misunderstand? We need an heir. You need a wife who can give us one. Miss Reynolds is a cripple. Her mother says she has been disabled since birth with a displaced hip. Her pelvis is bent. Do you really think a woman in her condition could bear a child?"

"I have no idea." Nat had not even given it a thought. Dearne might be right, for all he knew. But he didn't care. And the fact that his brother would even broach the subject made him seethe. Anger roiled in his belly so that he could hardly breathe.

"No, and that is the point, isn't it?" Dearne said. "We don't know, but the possibility that she cannot conceive or deliver a child must be considered. It is best, Nat, for you to turn your attentions elsewhere. There has been no formal betrothal, as I understand. Sever the connection now before it is too late. You must find another, more suitable bride. That is why the other young ladies were invited here. I thought one of them might pique your interest. Either Lady Camilla or Lady Serena would be a far better choice than a cripple."

Philippa pressed a hand to her mouth and turned away from the terrace doors before they could see her. Her heart plummeted to her toes. All the joy she had been feeling today drained out of her. She stood with her back against the wall adjacent to the doors, empty and bereft.

She moved slowly away, skirting the large drawing room where most of the other guests were gathered. As she made her way up the stairs to her bedchamber, Lillian was coming down. She stopped and her eyes widened with anxiety.

"What is it, Philippa? Are you unwell? May I help you to your room?"

"No, I am fine, Lillian. A bit tired, that is all. Will you do me a favor, though? Will you find Sophie and send her to me?"

"Yes, of course. Shall I ask her to bring something? Tea, or a posset?"

"No, thank you. I just want to go to bed early and would like her help."

"All right. I'll have her sent right up. You are sure nothing is wrong?"

"Quite sure, thank you. Good night, my friend."

When Philippa reached her bedchamber, she sat on the bed and tried to bring her racing thoughts in order. What Lord Dearne said might be true. She did not know if she could conceive—no woman knew that for sure—but her bent pelvis might indeed be an impediment to conception or delivery. And she had been wrong not to consider it.

When she first met Nat, he said he had to marry and sire an heir because Lady Dearne was no longer able to have children. It was the one and only reason he had set out to find a bride. Her own ability to have children ought to have been a foremost concern. She ought to have denied his offer on those grounds alone. But she hadn't thought to do so.

She hadn't thought.

She'd been captivated by a handsome soldier who treated her as she'd always wished to be treated. Nothing else had mattered.

How unutterably selfish.

Lord Dearne was right. It was not too late to back out of their bargain. Nat was too honorable to do the right thing. It was up to Philippa to make this right.

The bedchamber door opened and her maid, Sophie, stepped in. She bobbed a curtsy and said, "Can I help you get ready for bed, Miss?"

"Not just yet, Sophie. First, I'd like to get my things together so that we can leave in the morning."

"Tomorrow? But the party is to last another two days."

"I know. But I find I must leave early. Will you help me to pack?"

Nat stood over his brother, who was sprawled on the hard terrace floor with blood streaming from a nostril. "If you say one more word against Philippa, I will plant you another facer. And another and another until you are a bleeding pulp."

"Good God, man." Dearne rubbed his nose with the back of his hand, apparently stunned to find blood on it. "I think you have broken it. Have you gone mad?"

"No, I am sane enough to know that you have insulted the woman I intend to marry, and I will not have it, do you hear me? You will not speak of her like that ever again if you value your life. I learned how to fight in the army, not only with swords and guns but with my fists. And I have ten years on you, old man, so there is no hope you could best me. But if you persist in this nonsense about Philippa and an heir, I *will* fight you."

"Egad, Nat, be reasonable. It's important that we have an heir. You know that."

"We have an heir. Let odious Cousin Leonard have the damned title. I no longer care."

Dearne awkwardly got to his feet, still a bit unsteady. "You do not mean it. The girl has bewitched you somehow."

"She has done more than that. She has given me reason to live for the first time in a very long time. I will marry her, Frederick. You cannot stop me. If we are able to have children, fine. If not, I really don't care."

Dearne glared at him, rubbing his nose. "My God, you are in love with her."

Nat smiled. "Yes, I am, much to my surprise. I thought I had no love in me, but she proved me wrong."

"Hmph. I guess there is nothing more to be said."

"Nothing at all." And Nat walked through the terrace doors to find Philippa.

"Shall I put the blue sarsnet carriage dress out for tomorrow?"

"Yes, thank you, Sophie. And don't forget—"

"May I come in?"

The familiar voice sent a flush of anxiety to Philippa's cheeks. She was not ready to see him yet, but this meeting would have to happen sooner or later. "Of course, Captain, come in."

He stepped inside, looked around at the clothes strewn about and the open bandboxes, and scowled. Looking to Sophie, he said, "Would you excuse us, please?"

The young maid looked to Philippa for direction, and upon receiving her nod, left the room, leaving the door conspicuously ajar. Nat reached behind him and shut it.

"I understand you are leaving," he said, his gray eyes hard and flat as flint.

Philippa nodded, unable to form the right words yet.

"Were you going to say anything to me first," he asked, "or did you plan to sneak away and leave me wondering what the hell happened?"

"I was going to speak with you after we were finished packing." She could not control the trembling in her voice.

"Speak to me now. Why are you leaving, Philippa? I thought after yesterday that things were settled between us."

"No, we are not yet formally betrothed, and I think it best that we not be." The words felt like shards in her throat.

Nat's eyes darkened with anger. "The devil you say. Have you forgotten how you melted in my arms during that rainstorm?"

"No." She would never forget it.

"Well, if that doesn't matter to you," his sharp tone sliced through the air like a blade, "you might consider that you could be carrying my child."

"But I might not," she said, pleading with her eyes for him to understand. "And that is the point. You need someone who can give you an heir and I do not know if I can."

Nat let out a string of curses that made her ears burn. "Has my brother said something to you? Is that what this is all about?"

"I overheard what he said to you. And he is right. What if I cannot conceive? Or if I can, what if my body will not allow me to deliver a child? My pelvis is crooked, after all."

"To hell with your damnable crooked pelvis. I don't care if you are able to give me a child or not. I want you regardless. *You*, Philippa."

"But wasn't that the point of this marriage of convenience we set out to do? To produce an heir to the earldom that Lady Dearne was not able to do?"

"Yes, dammit, that was the point, initially, but it no longer matters to me."

"Why? You still need an heir."

"I have one. Our cousin Leonard will inherit the earldom after me, and he is welcome to it."

"I thought you both hated him."

"We do. He is a nitwit of the first order and an embarrassment to the family. Yes, I hate him, but I love you more."

"What?" Had she heard right? Oh, God, she hoped so. Her heart swelled in her chest.

He came and took her in his arms. "I love you, Philippa. You have brought joy back into my life. You have helped me to cope with what happened at Waterloo, to learn to accept that I was affected, but not to let it rule my life. My nightmares are less frequent, and will likely disappear eventually. I still jump at loud noises, but that will get better, too, I suspect. And it's all because of you, Philippa. I need you. I love you. I want to marry you whether or not you can provide an heir. My brother can go to hell, and so I told him. After I bloodied his nose."

"You hit him?"

"Of course I did. He insulted the woman I love. Will you still have me, Philippa, bad bargain that I am? Will you marry me?"

"You are an excellent bargain, Captain. The best I ever made. I shall be honored to marry you. I love you."

"Then let us be properly betrothed. And dance at our engagement ball."

"Dance? Me? You must be in love, you foolish man, if you think I can do that."

"You can do anything you set your mind to, my love."

"At the moment, I have a mind to kiss you."

"Then do it, girl."

She reached up and pulled his head down to hers, and kissed him with all the passion and desire and joy of a woman in love.

An invitation to the Reynolds-Beckwith betrothal ball was one of the most coveted of the Season. Half the ton was in attendance, still fascinated by one of the Season's oddest matches. Lady Thorpe had done a splendid job decorating the ballroom. At the future bridegroom's request, there was a full-sized orange tree in a Versailles box placed in each corner, and their sweet fragrance filled the air. The trees seemed to have some special meaning to the betrothed couple, as they laughed each time they happened to glance at one of them.

Miss Reynolds looked lovely in a gown of pink tissue gauze over white satin, while the groom looked handsome in a blue velvet tailcoat and frilled shirt. Most startling of all was the uncharacteristic broad smile the groom wore, so unlike his usual dour demeanor. Those scandalmongers among the guests were forced to admit that there would not, after all, be a sad scene, where the couple parted ways. They had been wrong about this curious pair. The happiness in their faces could not be denied.

The happy couple left the receiving line before the first dance began. Nat pulled Philippa behind one of the orange trees where a small bench had been hidden just for them. "I have a betrothal present for you," he said. "However, I am afraid it did not seem quite the thing to bring her into the ballroom tonight."

"Her?"

"A pretty little chestnut mare. She is a beauty, my love, almost the same color as your hair. And she is spirited enough to give you a good ride without tossing you arse over ears."

"Oh, Nat, how wonderful. My own horse! What is her name?"

"She is called Thalia. And you will look splendid on her, in one of your jaunty habits. We shall ride like the wind together, side by side. And you shall have that lovely pink glow you get whenever you exert yourself." His heated gaze hinted at other exertions. She felt her cheeks warm, and his smile widened.

"Shall we try her out with a ride in the park tomorrow morning?" he asked.

"I think not. My mornings have become a bit difficult this past week or so."

Nat grabbed her arm. "Why is that?" Anxiety gathered in his eyes. "Are you ill? Have I pushed you too far?"

Philippa shook her head and smiled. "I did not want to say anything until I was more certain, but I think, Captain, that we have proven your brother wrong."

He looked confused, and then his eyes grew large as her meaning apparently became clear to him. "Philippa? My love? Are you saying what I think you are saying?"

"We have made a child, Nat. The mad soldier and the lame lady have made a child together. Is it not wonderful?"

He gathered her in his arms and kissed her, oblivious to who might see them. "I am the most fortunate of men. Whatever did I do to deserve such happiness? I will take care of you, my love. I want no risks with your health. Or the child's."

"Not too much cotton wool, I beg you. But a bit of coddling for *this* reason would be lovely."

He rose and lifted her to her feet. "Come, my dear," Nat said as he offered Philippa his arm. "The opening set is about to begin, and we have much to celebrate."

She smiled, perfectly happy to watch others dance in celebration of their betrothal.

"I have requested a waltz," he said.

She raised her brows in question. "A waltz? But a line dance or march usually opens a ball. Certainly not a waltz."

"Now that we have completed this infernal Season and are officially engaged, I no longer feel compelled to follow the confounded Rules. I want a waltz, and we shall have it."

Philippa grinned. "All right, then, my captain. It shall be as you command."

But Nat did not lead her to a chair along the edge of the room where they might watch the dancers. Instead, he led her to the center of the dance floor.

A knot of pure panic coiled in Philippa's stomach. "What are you doing?"

"I am going to dance with my betrothed and the mother of my child at our ball."

"Oh, Nat. I don't know if I can."

"Of course you can. I want to dance with you, Philippa. And I want you to have this dance. Just follow my lead. We can do it."

Her heart melted with love for him. She did not care how clumsy she would look. She was going to dance with Nat, and it would be wonderful.

"Oh, but Nat. I do not have permission to waltz."

"You have my permission. That is all you need."

She squeezed his arm and laughed with pure glee. "And to hell with the Rules!"

"To hell with the Rules. That, my love, shall be the guiding principle of our life together."

Other couples stepped back when they saw the betrothed couple take the floor. Silence fell as everyone watched, agog that the lame girl was going to dance. The scandalmongers fizzed with excitement. There might yet be a frightful scene to report.

The couple smiled at each other as the music began. Miss Reynolds positively glowed as Captain Beckwith skillfully compensated for her limp, dipping and bending his body to accommodate her awkward movements, holding her tightly aloft on one foot as he twirled her across the floor. They were not the most elegant or graceful couple ever seen on a dance floor, but they were certainly the happiest.

The sound of applause and cheers filled the room as they danced.

Epilogue

*H*er eyes are so blue." Philippa held their tiny daughter on her lap, still in awe of her perfection. There had been no mishap during the birth, like the one that had displaced Philippa's hip. Little Charlotte Beckwith had all her fingers and toes, hair so blond it was almost white, and the bluest eyes her mother had ever seen. "I wonder if they will lighten over time and become more gray, like yours."

"I like them just the way they are," Nat said, gazing fondly at his wife and daughter. "She is a beauty, isn't she? Lord, how will I bear it when she grows up and worthless young swains lie in smitten heaps on the entry steps? How will I ever be able to let her go?"

"With the reluctance of any doting father. But that won't be for a long, long time, long enough for you to become accustomed to the idea. Oh, Nat, I still find it so hard to believe. I spent my whole life believing I could never have any of this. A husband I adore, and a family of my own. It's a miracle."

"No, it was fate. It was no miracle that brought us together behind that ridiculous orange tree. We were fated to meet, and that's a fact. And now I am fated to have a beautiful daughter to spoil and worry over."

"And what about the heir?"

"*He* is most definitely a miracle." Nat reached into the second of two cribs and lifted his son to his shoulder. "When your mother brought out Charlotte and placed her in my arms, I thought there could be no greater happiness. I did not care that she was not a son. It was love at first sight. Then my damned fool brother, who'd come solely to welcome the Dearne heir, began stomping about the room and grumbling about the curse of girls on our family."

"He does have five daughters, Nat."

"And my mother had seven."

"It is no wonder he thought there was a curse."

"No healthy child is a curse. If I hadn't had the babe in my arms, I'd have broken his nose again. But then the miracle happened. The doctor came out with a second bundle, and told me I had a son. Andrew." He held out a finger and the baby grabbed it and held tight. "My clever Philippa had given us twins."

"At least I made your brother happy."

"To hell with Dearne. You made *me* ecstatic. And always will."

At that moment, his son made a face and Nat realized his arm was damp. Never good in these situations, he called for the nurse, who gently took baby Andrew from his arms and laid him in his crib. "Best give me the other little mite too," she said. "She'll likely need a bit of cleanup as well."

Once Philippa was satisfied that both babies were in good hands, she and Nat strolled out onto the terrace. The sun was just going down, and the spring air was crisp. Nat wrapped an arm around his wife to keep her warm as they looked out over the brilliant green meadows and clay vales of Oxfordshire, crisscrossed with hedgerows and streams.

After long moments of contented silence, Nat said, "Thank you, my love."

"For what?"

"For everything. You. The twins. Peace. You changed my life, Philippa. Not by giving me children, but by giving me back myself."

She leaned her head on his shoulder. "Quid pro quo, Captain. Although you have given me a self I'd never known, one who could dance and ride like the wind. And have babies."

"We were fated to be together, it seems, to change each other's lives."

"Fate again? Or a miracle?"

"A bit of both, I think." He turned her in his arms and smiled. "And I have a surprise for you, my love. For the christening party."

"Allowing the party is surprise enough, considering your aversion to social gatherings. What else have you planned?"

"It is a wonderful thing, is it not, that two misfits produced two such beautiful children? I have decided we need something special to celebrate this miraculous, fateful event."

"And what is that?"

"I have ordered a fireworks display."

Philippa stared at him in astonishment. One more demon laid to rest. She threw back her head and laughed with pure joy.

At Avon Books, we know your passion for romance—once you finish one of our novels, you find yourself wanting more.

May we tempt you with . . .

- **Excerpts** from our upcoming releases.

- Entertaining **extras**, including authors' personal photo albums and book lists.

- Behind-the-scenes **scoop** on your favorite characters and series.

- **Sweepstakes** for the chance to win free books, romantic getaways, and other fun prizes.

- Writing **tips** from our authors and editors.

- **Blog** with our authors and find out why they love to write romance.

- **Exclusive content** that's not contained within the pages of our novels.

Join us at
www.avonbooks.com

AVON

An Imprint of HarperCollins*Publishers*
www.avonromance.com